Pride Publishing books by Simone Anderson

Single Books
Finding Love
Roping His Man
At All Costs

Smuggler's Cove
Knight of Pleasure

Bound Hearts
To Love Again

Heart of a Hero
Uniform Desires

Collections
Yuletide Yearnings: A Christmas to Remember

I0662038

AT ALL COSTS

SIMONE ANDERSON

At All Costs
ISBN # 978-1-83943-926-1
©Copyright Simone Anderson 2020
Cover Art by Louisa Maggio ©Copyright November 2020
Interior text design by Claire Siemaszkiewicz
Pride Publishing

This is a work of fiction. All characters, places and events are from the author's imagination and should not be confused with fact. Any resemblance to persons, living or dead, events or places is purely coincidental.

All rights reserved. No part of this publication may be reproduced in any material form, whether by printing, photocopying, scanning or otherwise without the written permission of the publisher, Pride Publishing.

Applications should be addressed in the first instance, in writing, to Pride Publishing. Unauthorised or restricted acts in relation to this publication may result in civil proceedings and/or criminal prosecution.

The author and illustrator have asserted their respective rights under the Copyright Designs and Patents Acts 1988 (as amended) to be identified as the author of this book and illustrator of the artwork.

Published in 2020 by Pride Publishing, United Kingdom.

No part of this book may be reproduced, scanned, or distributed in any printed or electronic form without permission. Please do not participate in or encourage piracy of copyrighted materials in violation of the authors' rights. Purchase only authorised copies.

Pride Publishing is an imprint of Totally Entwined Group Limited.

If you purchased this book without a cover you should be aware that this book is stolen property. It was reported as "unsold and destroyed" to the publisher and neither the author nor the publisher has received any payment for this "stripped book".

AT ALL COSTS

Dedication

To Ryker, Jeremy, Kai, Tala, Naomi, and Kenzie —
for showing courage and true belief in yourself
beyond your years.

Chapter One

Riley Hamilton, RJ to his friends, smiled at the pretty brunette behind the bar and slapped his credit card down on the counter. Any other night and he would have tried to sweet talk his way into the cute little bartender's bed. She was his favorite type—petite and slender with a larger-than-average bust size, accentuated by a tight black V-neck T-shirt. He'd never had trouble bedding any woman he wanted. He never lied about his intentions. There was no need. There were more than enough women who would rather have a night of fun over anything long term, especially in New Orleans. The Big Easy was simply crawling with groups of women. Sex hadn't been a problem. Life hadn't been a problem.

"Macallan M, double, straight up. And a beer. Whatever's dark and on tap."

"We don't have that."

Riley scowled. "Well, do you at least have Johnnie Walker Blue? That's drinkable."

The woman nodded and poured him the drink.

Riley paid for his drinks and slammed back the whiskey. He picked up the plastic cup of beer and pushed his way out of the crowded bar and onto Bourbon Street. He mumbled an apology to the group of men he bumped into. This week was supposed to be one last final hurrah with his friends before he started working for his father. He was being groomed to take over the family business. One he had no interest in at all. He hadn't been asked. He'd been told.

Riley blew out a breath and jammed a hand through his hair. He'd managed to stay out of his father's business for nearly five months after graduation under the guise of applying for a job. He had. He just didn't have any experience outside of school. No real marketable experience was what he'd been told more than once. He didn't care. Charles did.

"Hey, handsome, something on your mind?" a pretty blond asked, tracing a long-painted fingernail up and down his arm.

"Ah no," Riley answered, shrugging off the contact. It was a blatant lie. "Not interested, sorry." The phone call from Charles in the early afternoon had effectively killed his mood. Two hours later his day went from bad to worse after an unexpected run-in with a moron who wanted to fit into a world that he didn't belong in. He tossed the empty cup into a nearby trash can then ducked into the nearest bar and made his way to the counter. Unsure why it bothered him still, Riley ordered another shot of whiskey and a beer. Paying for both, he left a generous tip. Riley slammed back the shot and carried the beer with him back outside.

A commotion farther down the street drew his attention before he turned back toward his hotel.

Strong arms grabbed him on either side. Beer spilled all over him as the cup tumbled to the pavement. Forced away from the gathering crowd, Riley fought his attackers, struggling to get away. Turning his head from one side to the other, he tried to catch the details.

"You're coming with us, pretty boy," the man on his right said in a thick Southern accent.

Both men had similar builds, slightly taller than himself with muscular bodies and dark hair. The rest of their features were masked by matching New Orleans Saints ball caps.

"Don't think so." Riley's words slurred together even as he pulled and kicked. His stomach rolled and the hair on the back of his neck stood on end. He was overmatched. He knew it without a doubt. Maybe if he threw up on them, they'd let him go. It was a good thought, except he'd been drinking long before he'd been legal and could hold his liquor. There was no way he'd had enough to drink for that.

Riley stumbled and fell to his knees. Shaking his head, he tried to orientate himself. The man who'd been on his right lay several feet away, face down on the street. A man in a black leather jacket kicked the other man, sending him flying backward. Riley pushed himself to his feet. He swayed and stumbled. The newcomer caught him before he fell.

"Let's go." The voice was commanding, the vise-like grip insistent.

"Who are you?" Riley tried to wrench his arm away from the other man. "Like hell! I'm not going anywhere with you. Or them."

People around them started to stop and stare. The newcomer swore and maneuvered him through the crowd and down the next block.

"Come with me if you want to live." The man pulled him down the street.

Riley yanked his arm free. "Okay, seriously, that is the cheesiest pick-up line ever. And completely wasted." Riley shook his head. "I'm not gay."

"First, it's not a pick-up line. Second, gay, straight, in the closet or not, I don't care. You need to come with me if you want to live," the man said, peering over Riley's shoulder.

"The only place I'm going is back to my hotel room to sleep." Riley rolled his shirt sleeves up.

"Riley James Hamilton, we have absolutely no time to stand here and debate this. Your hotel room, your entire life, in fact, has been compromised."

Riley stopped and stared at the man. The buzz he'd been working on disappeared. It was the same man he'd had the run-in at the hotel with earlier in the day. A soldier with the military's Purple Heart patch sewn on his jacket. Riley groaned. He hadn't exchanged names with the other man. There was no way the man should know who he was.

"You're the guy from the hotel. Who are you? How do you know who I am?" he asked, leaning against the wall.

The man pulled him down the block to the next intersection and up the street. "Right now, probably one of the few people who doesn't want you to end up in the morgue. And the only one who can keep you out of it."

"Okay, enough with the cryptic espionage bullshit, James Bond. Not only am I not going anywhere with you, I don't have any idea who you are, and no one wants me dead. If anything, I'm better alive to use as ransom. However, that would mean Charles would have to actually give a shit about me, which he doesn't." Riley stopped outside a small grocery store.

"Shit!" The man grabbed Riley's arm. He pushed and pulled Riley farther down the street.

Riley forced himself to focus on where they were and where he needed to be. They turned onto Bourbon Street. Riley tried to pull away. His hotel was down the street a few blocks. If he could get there, he could shower, change, and sleep off this nightmare.

"In here." They ducked into a bar just as one of the men who had tried to abduct him rushed by them.

Riley's stomach rolled. Several minutes passed before they stepped outside. Still holding his arm, the soldier took a step before he turned and pushed Riley up against the wall. "Play along, or you'll get us both killed," the man whispered harshly. His attacker and another man stopped five feet from them.

Riley resisted the urge to fight the man holding him. Some doors were never allowed to be opened. Not without drastic consequences. He may not like where he was, but the idea of losing everything wasn't worth it. Praying he wasn't making a mistake, he swallowed the forming lump and put his hands on the man's arms before moving them to his waist. He needed to survive long enough to get back to his hotel room.

"That's it." The soldier bent and captured his mouth.

The man shifted positions and Riley's hand bumped something hard. A gun. Riley's head began to spin. The man reportedly trying to save him had a gun. He was beyond screwed. He was a college graduate with a trust fund and a father whose company manufactured and sold perfume and colognes. There was nothing in his life that warranted the current position in which he found himself.

"Hand me your phone!" the soldier demanded.

"My what? No, I'm not giving you my phone." Riley shook his head, trying to push away from the stranger again.

Keeping him pinned to the wall, the man ran his hands over Riley's body. Riley fought the hold, not caring who noticed. The man pulled his phone out of the back pocket of his jeans.

"Enjoying yourself?" Riley bit out.

"Yes, babysitting a trust fund brat in the middle of New Orleans is always how I want to spend my nights," the man retorted. He pulled apart the phone and removed the battery before handing the pieces back to Riley. "Don't put it back together."

"What the—"

"Welcome to the twenty-first-century equivalent of a homing device," the man said. "You can get a cheap burner phone tomorrow."

Riley shook his head, tried to follow the man's train of thought and failed. "A what?"

"A burner phone. You know, a nearly untraceable by-the-minute phone." the man sneered. "You have seriously got to stop drinking."

Riley scoffed. That was not likely to happen. Alcohol made life bearable.

"Look, the French Quarter is packed with people. It's *always* packed with people. Tourists, locals, businesspeople, law enforcement. There are dozens of streets, shops, restaurants, and bars jammed into a relatively small area. There is no way they should have found us that quickly," the man replied, drawing his attention to the swarms of people around them. "Or really at all."

"Great."

"Let's go." The man pulled him back onto the street.

"Who are they? Who are you? What in the hell is going on?" Riley demanded.

"Let's get off the street and we'll talk."

"Do you have a name or will James Bond work?" Riley asked. "I swear this type of shit only happens in freaking Hollywood."

"Yes, but only in Hollywood can the bad guys miss the broad side of a barn from ten feet away with an unlimited supply of ammunition. In the real world, not only is ammunition limited for everybody, both sides have snipers."

"Thanks, *James*, that makes my night so much better. Now, if you don't mind, I'll stop being the heroine in your little melodrama and go back to my hotel. Next time pick a chick to co-star with," Riley bit out, needing to regain control of his life.

"Name's Kaden. Chicks don't do it for me. And you're stuck with me."

Riley groaned. "Great, a gay James Bond. Because that's *so* much better." He blew out a breath and surveyed his surroundings. He recognized some of the bars, but he wasn't completely sure if they were heading back to his hotel or not. The man, Kaden, had checked into the same hotel he was staying at earlier in the day. The streets were filled with people, far from Mardi Gras packed, but enough, Riley admitted to himself, that they shouldn't have been found as quickly as they had. "Who's after me? Why? How many people?" Riley shoved a hand through his hair, Kaden never denied being a spy.

"So you do have a modicum of a survival instinct. Not nearly as dumb as you want people to believe."

Riley repressed the urge to scream and shrugged. "I seriously couldn't care less about what anyone thinks."

"I noticed."

They rounded another corner and their hotel came into view. Relief flooded Riley. He wanted a hot shower and clean clothes. The Royal Sonesta hotel was in the heart of the French Quarter, its elegant and modern interior in turns at odds with and complementing the century-old building and surrounding three hundred years of history. He'd liked it from the beginning and hoped that their return to it meant that either the danger had passed or it was all a big joke meant to humiliate him or blackmail him into doing something he wouldn't normally do.

"I thought you said my hotel room and life were compromised. So, why are we back here?"

"They are. Do you have everything of importance out of your room?"

Riley shook his head. "What does that have to do with anything?"

"Get only what you need. Since I wasn't expecting to have to change hotels so soon, I have to get something from my room."

"I need to change and take a shower."

"You can—"

"I am covered in beer," Riley fumed. "I have what I need in my room."

Kaden sighed and shoved a hand through his hair. "Fine. But, be quick and quiet. You're going to change, then we're going back out to have a night on the town," Kaden ordered.

Riley nodded as the valet opened the door for them. He kept his face carefully neutral. Knowing the hotel would have cameras everywhere was truly only going to help him if they found him dead in the hotel. Kaden bustled him into the lift and punched the number for Riley's floor.

"How do you know —"

"Later."

"My friends are going to know something is wrong. If I don't show up, they'll go to the police."

Kaden nodded. "Probably, but it will take about forty-eight hours. They'll assume you found someone to screw tonight and will wake up late in the day and probably have sex with said partner again. They'll go out, and when you're still not back, they'll think they crossed paths with you. It'll be late afternoon or early evening the day after that before they'll start to get worried and call the police, who will say you're an adult and this *is* New Orleans."

Riley's stomach sank as he digested Kaden's words. "I'm screwed."

"Not yet, but you almost were," Kaden answered.

"I didn't mean that literally."

"You can be screwed in more ways than sex. And I don't do the unwilling." The doors opened and Kaden led the way through the hall to the suite that Riley shared with his friends. Kaden stepped aside to let Riley open the door. Once inside, Riley went to his room, while Kaden searched the suite.

"It doesn't look like anyone has been here," Kaden said, walking in on him. "So much for survival instinct."

"Says the guy with the gun." Riley stripped out of his wet shirt and tossed it into the corner. "Do you mind?"

"Not at all." Kaden smiled.

"Creepy." Riley pulled a pair of clean slacks out of his suitcase.

"Jeans."

"What?" Riley turned to face his unwelcomed visitor. "Can't you wait on the other side of the door?"

"No. For the foreseeable future, I'm not taking my eyes off you."

"Seriously? That's completely unnecessary. This is a hotel. There is no other exit except through that door." Riley pointed behind the other man. "Maybe whatever second-rate rat-infested hotel *you're* used to staying in has multiple exits and adjoining rooms, this is not one of them. I pay too much money to be that close to others."

"Windows. Balconies. Wear jeans."

Riley scowled. "Great. Just great. Now, I'm getting fashion advice from a James Bond wannabe who dresses in holey jeans and a beat-up leather jacket instead of a suit."

"Hollywood. Reality. Two totally different things. Jeans are more durable than dress pants."

Riley shoved the hanger back in the closet and spun around. "Okay, enough. I'm absolutely not going anywhere until you tell me in the hell is going on. No more cute answers. I don't know you. I've never seen you before this morning. But yet, you seem to know everything there is to know about me."

"Afternoon, not morning."

"Morning to me and you're avoiding the question." Riley crossed his arms over his chest.

"I'll tell you what I can. My name is Kaden Tennison and I've been instructed to keep you alive and safe at all costs. As to the men who grabbed you, they're probably nothing more than hired goons. Who hired them and why is the real question. And one I don't have an answer for."

"Alive or dead?"

"Honestly, I don't know." Kaden shook his head. "I suspect alive, at least until you're of no further use."

"Why?"

"Again, I don't know. I was given very little information to go on."

"How is this even possible?" Riley sat down on the edge of the bed. "Why would anybody want me? Seriously? I don't own a business. And kidnapping me isn't going to have an effect on my family. It's not like the family business is guns, medicine, or politics. We make perfume and cologne."

"Which you don't wear."

Riley shrugged. He wasn't going into personal details with a stranger.

"Riley, we need to move. Staying here isn't an option. You post your entire life online."

"And disappearing isn't going to raise suspicions at all," Riley replied sarcastically.

"Phone batteries die all of the time." Kaden smiled. "Get dressed. The sooner we move, the sooner we can figure out who's behind this."

Riley shoved his hands through his hair and stared at the floor. "It still doesn't make any sense. Who hired you? Can you tell me that?"

"An interested party."

"That makes a whole lot of sense. A complete stranger wanting to keep me alive and another complete stranger wanting me dead. How do I know I can trust you?"

"You don't. You just don't have a choice."

"Because you have a gun?" Riley quipped.

"I do, several of them in fact, but in this case it's because right now, I'm the only one who has a chance of keeping of you alive."

"I can take care of myself!" Riley shouted, jumping to his feet.

"I didn't say that. But, have you ever shot a gun before?" Kaden demanded. "Have you evaded capture before? Were you aware that you were being followed since you left the hotel?"

Riley opened his mouth and closed it.

"Now, get dressed. Pack a couple changes of clothes if you want, but we're leaving. Both of us."

"I need to take a shower. I stink and I'm sticky," Riley protested.

"We don't have time. They know where you're staying."

"So what? They know what hotel I'm staying at. It's not a huge secret."

"They know your room number."

"Seriously? You know that how? Nothing in here is missing. Nothing's been missing."

"Nothing's been moved? You and your roommates haven't misplaced anything?"

Riley shrugged and dug out the only pair of jeans he'd brought with him. "We're on vacation, James, and there is maid service." Riley took off his pants, tossing them in the corner with the soiled shirt.

"Silk boxers? A little outdated for you, aren't they?"

"Some of us have taste and style and can afford to wear good clothes." Riley grabbed his jeans and a clean pair of boxers and headed for the bathroom.

"Where are you going?"

"Shower. I cannot stand the way I smell or feel."

"We don't have time."

"Just because you say it's so, doesn't mean it is. I don't know you. I don't trust you. I don't even like you."

"Riley—"

"Man, enough. Joke's over. You've had your fun. You need to leave." Riley tossed his clothes on the edge of the desk.

"I'm not joking."

"Joking. Lying. Same thing."

The room's phone rang, startling him. Riley answered it before the other man crossed the room. "Hello."

He heard only heavy breathing on the other end of the phone.

Riley rolled his eyes. "Dramatic. Very Hollywood of you."

Kaden pulled the receiver away from Riley's ear. "Who is this?"

"That's effective." Riley smirked.

"Your bodyguard isn't going to be able to save you." The voice was robotic.

Riley stilled.

"You should put some clothes on before we get there."

Kaden slammed the phone down. "Now do you fucking believe me? We need to leave."

Riley nodded and stepped into the jeans, pausing for a moment. He hated tight clothes and jeans, even as loose as these were, and it always took him a minute to get used to them. Grabbing a clean shirt, he finished dressing and grabbed his backpack that had doubled as his carry-on. He checked the contents before adding clean underwear, socks, and a couple of changes of clothes. He'd started to throw in his shaving kit and deodorant when Kaden stopped him.

"Leave them."

"But—"

"The toiletries, like your tablet, and power cords need to stay."

"Why?"

"We need the time. If those things are missing your friends will call the police sooner rather than later."

"Isn't that what we want?" Riley asked, tossing the items onto the bed. "Why aren't we going to the police now? Surely, they can handle something like this."

Kaden shook his head, putting the kit and deodorant back from where Riley had grabbed them. "This is out of their—" Kaden paused for a moment. "Jurisdiction."

"Fantastic. So, what, you're a part of a secret group dedicated to saving the world and random people when you're asked to?"

"Something like that."

"Cryptic asshole," Riley said, zipping up the backpack.

"Do you have a jacket?"

"It's New Orleans, there's no need for one." Riley shouldered his bag. "Are all secret agent superheroes assholes or are you just special?"

"Job requirement." Kaden smiled.

Riley scowled as Kaden led them down the hall and around the corner to his room. Kaden entered the room first, pulling Riley in after him. Ordering Riley to wait by the door, Kaden searched the room before grabbing a black duffel bag off the center of the king-size bed.

"So, did you ask for a room on the same floor?"

"Didn't have to."

"You didn't unpack?" Riley asked. "You get to take all your stuff?"

Kaden nodded and checked the contents of his bag. "Unlike you, I don't have roommates, friends, or anyone else who will be looking for me."

"What about surveillance video? I mean, if they start looking for me, they'll see us on the video together. Arriving and leaving together."

"Probably." Kaden slung the bag over his shoulder. "Let's go."

"Where to? Some one-star dump in the warehouse district, I assume," Riley said, adjusting his backpack.

"That's an option."

"Asshole," Riley muttered and followed Kaden out of the room and back outside. Once outside, Kaden handed him a plain ball cap and ordered him to put it on. Despite the crowds of tourists, street performers and musicians filling the streets of the French Quarter, Kaden led them through a dozen bars and restaurants, slipping out of back doors and down alleyways, across Jackson Square, by the St. Louis Cathedral, and through another maze of streets until they ended up at another hotel. Riley raised an eyebrow. The new hotel, the Bourbon Orleans, was four blocks down from their old hotel and two blocks from the gay bar they'd stopped in while evading his attackers.

"Try not to draw attention to us," Kaden bit out, leading them into the hotel.

Riley stayed silent as Kaden led them through the lobby, down a hall to an elevator that took them to the second floor. Their room sat halfway down the hallway. Kaden entered the room first, with a curt order for Riley to stay where he was. Riley heaved a sigh and followed him into the room.

"Well, at least there are two beds." Riley tossed his bag onto the bed closest to the door.

"Do you ever listen?"

"Why? It's a hotel room. It comes standard with beds, bathroom, closet, TV, and a minibar. The good ones have balconies. There is no reason to be cautious." Riley flopped down in a chair.

"There are still plenty of places to hide or booby-trap."

"God, you're paranoid." Riley shook his head. "Your boyfriend must be either super impressed or nuts."

"No time for a boyfriend. Tonight, I'm babysitting," Kaden snapped. "The shower is yours if you want."

"I take it this means we're in for the night?"

"Yes. Go take your shower."

"Seriously? It's not even midnight. I haven't had a curfew in years. And we're in New Orleans, one of America's best playgrounds. I don't think curfews are legal here." Riley pushed himself up out of the chair. To be honest, he'd never paid attention to curfews.

"Maybe you'll get lucky and you'll only have to be inconvenienced for a couple of days, then you can go back to your life of privilege and overindulgence, rich boy."

"You don't like me, do you?" Riley asked, stopping and turning around. There was a bitterness in Kaden's voice that couldn't be missed.

"What I like and don't like isn't important. My job is to keep you alive. Somebody thinks you're worth saving." Kaden turned his back on Riley, set his bag down on the other bed and began digging through it.

Riley picked up his bag and stalked into the bathroom, slamming the door behind him.

* * * *

Kaden shoved a hand through his hair and walked to the window. He'd asked for a room with a balcony, knowing that if they needed to, they could jump to the street below. The thugs who had tried to grab Riley earlier in the evening hadn't been common street criminals, nor had they been trying to pick someone up for a quick grand. They had been too determined for that. It didn't narrow down who they worked for, though. That part still bothered him. No one, not his boss, Russell Lawrence, or the mysterious original informant, had had any idea of who wanted the boy dead or why. Kaden still wasn't convinced that threat was as big a deal as Lawrence claimed, but the man was his boss and if he wanted to give him a blank check to babysit the son of a perfume manufacturer, he'd do it. Hell, he'd even had a couple of days while he was scouting the French Quarter and surrounding city to enjoy the local food and music.

Riley Hamilton was proving to be as superficial as the initial reports suggested. And he was apparently so far in the closet he wouldn't even admit to himself that he was gay. Or at least bi. Kaden's gaydar hadn't been wrong since he'd figured out what it was and why it led him to some men but not others.

Waiting until the water turned on, Kaden picked up the phone and dialled his boss's number.

"Anything new?" Russell Lawrence demanded.

"Yeah, a pair of goons almost succeeded in kidnapping him tonight." Kaden peered out of the window to the street below.

"How almost?"

"They were almost to their vehicle with him."

"Any clues to who?"

"No. Find out who wants him."

"My hands —"

"Bullshit, Lawrence. Figure it out. There are clues. You need to get them. I'm shooting blind and he isn't the type to stay put just because someone said so," Kaden bit out. "The kid has no fucking sense of self-preservation."

Kaden looked back at the bathroom. His gut told him that they were wading into a shitstorm with no way out. He had a safe house that he could take the kid to, but making him disappear could alert whoever was after him that they were onto them. Although, if the goons tonight were regular employees of whoever hired them, they already knew. "What a clusterfuck. I shouldn't even be assigned to this mess."

"You're the best I have."

"What you need is a babysitter, someone who knows how to say and do all of the right things. You didn't need me," Kaden said. He wasn't the type of person usually chosen for high-profile jobs, mostly because he tended to be blunt with supervisors and leadership instead of pandering and sugarcoating things for them in a way that soothed their egos. "Who is this kid? Why is he so special? And why in the fucking hell do I have a nearly unlimited budget to keep his stupid ass safe?"

"It's your job."

"Yeah, that doesn't answer the question, though, Russ. He's a spoiled rich boy who's never had to work a day in his life and outside of whatever he learned in those private schools of his."

"I gave you everything you need to know."

"No, you didn't. Not this time." Kaden hung up and turned away from the window. Shoving the phone in his pocket, he grabbed his bag and pulled out a handgun and checked the magazine before returning it to his bag. He pulled out a small black box and double-checked the handful of magazines locked inside. Tomorrow he would need to see if he could locate the men who had tried to kidnap Riley earlier and find out who they worked for.

"Are you any closer to finding out who wants me dead?" Riley asked, walking back into the room.

Kaden turned and swallowed. Young men in their twenties should look ridiculous in silk and soft cotton. "No," he said flatly. "And you have no idea who would be after you or your family?" Kaden zipped and locked the bag before setting it down on the floor next to his bed.

"I told you before no. The company makes perfume, cologne, and some body sprays. Nothing worth killing or kidnapping over. I mean, some singer, Angel something or other, did just sign a deal to produce a couple of fragrances, but that's not public knowledge." Riley sat down on the edge of the bed.

"What else did you take from your hotel? I didn't see you stick those pyjamas in your bag." Kaden crossed the room to where Riley sat.

"I didn't. I always keep a pair in my bag when I travel." Riley shrugged.

"What about a personal vendetta? Maybe someone out to get your father?"

Riley laughed, the sound hollow and bitter. "They would have better luck with one of Charles' floozies."

Leaning against the dresser holding the television, Kaden cocked his head and rubbed the back of his neck. "Who would know that, though?"

"Ah, probably everyone," Riley answered, running his fingers through his hair. "It's no secret. I was shipped off to boarding school as soon as it could be arranged. Charles doesn't keep the same woman around for too long, usually only three or four months."

There had to be something the kid had that no one else did. No one wasted time, money, and resources on someone or something that didn't truly matter. "Did you come into any money or property recently?"

"No. My grandfather died when I was twelve."

"Did you buy or acquire anything of value lately?"

"Not unless someone is after my clothes. But none of those are custom made. Well, the tux is. But I got that last year. And the tailor is open to everyone. If you can afford her."

Kaden's phone beeped. "I doubt it's your clothes or your tailor." He looked down at the phone. "Stay put."

Kaden pushed off from the heavy wood furniture and walked out onto the balcony, hoping the combined glass from the doors and crowds below would muffle his call. He dialed the number that had popped up in a text message.

"Took you long enough," Kaden growled.

"Hello to you too, asshole. I'm great, by the way, thanks for asking," the lilting voice replied.

"Fine. Hello, Ace. How are you?" Kaden blew out a breath. "Small talk and formalities aside—"

"Goddess, you're a bitch when you don't get laid enough."

Kaden mentally swore. Ace was a genius, the best researcher and computer geek he knew. Unique from the DNA out, Ace was genderfluid, open to loving everyone and, more often than not, looked like a rainbow threw up all over them. The last time he'd seen Ace, the researcher had been sporting a waist-length mohawk in blue and purple with flecks of silver, in homage to the Milky way, they'd said.

He'd met Ace outside a bar when the researcher was getting beat up by three large men. Kaden had only been on his permanent duty station a couple of weeks and had been exploring his attraction to men. At the time he'd thought it was something he'd only needed to get out of his system, so he could go back to his normal life. Coming to Ace's rescue and saving their life, Kaden had inadvertently also met a friend for life and the first person so completely out there and blunt that had been willing to help him sort out fact from fiction where his own sexuality was concerned. Kaden was sure there were other people who would have helped him had he asked. He hadn't, though. He'd hadn't even asked Ace. Ace had told him. Brilliant and far too observant for Kaden's comfort, the pair had formed an unlikely friendship.

"I'm babysitting, I don't get to get laid when I'm working," Kaden said, shaking his head. "Not everyone gets to work from home."

"You should find another line of work. Yours sucks," Ace answered. "Or rather, doesn't suck enough."

"Gee thanks for the brilliant observation." Kaden laughed. "Are you sure you're a genius."

"I'm beyond genius level."

"Whatever. What did you find out?"

"I hear jazz music in the background. You're still in New Orleans. You absolutely have to go to Lafitte In Exile." Ace ignored his question. "Take the closet case with you. Show him some love."

"Ace..." Kaden clenched his jaw.

"Lafitte's. Trust me."

Kaden turned. The hotel room door slammed closed. "Damn it! Damn it all too fucking hell! Ace—"

"Kid ran?"

"Yes. He's going to get his fool head blown off." Kaden stormed back into the room.

"Go save the day." The line went dead and Kaden shoved the phone into his pocket. He stopped long enough to grab a spare clip before racing out of the door.

Chapter Two

Kaden took a deep breath and forced himself to appear normal. He walked through the glass double doors of Royal Sonesta, smiling and waving in response to the young woman standing behind the desk. She had been working when he'd first arrived at the hotel. Riley had been overly angry at something relatively minor and had been taking it out on her. Kaden had come to her defense before the manager could placate the younger man. Riley had dismissed Kaden, but he'd seen Riley flinch in response to something he'd said. Kaden shook his head, pushing the memory of their first encounter out of his mind.

He crossed the lobby to the elevator bank, waiting impatiently for the elevator to take him to Riley's floor. Kaden swore under his breath. It was a hunch more than concrete fact that Riley would return to his hotel room. From there, he couldn't be sure where the younger man would go—if he would find his friends or a bar to get drunk at, both of which seemed to be more plausible than returning home to his family for not only answers but relative safety.

Kaden approached the suite of rooms Riley had been sharing with his friends. The door stood open about an inch. The hair on the back of Kaden's neck stood. Silently, he withdrew his gun and paused to listen before slowly pushing the door open. Systematically clearing the suite, he holstered his weapon and returned to Riley's room. He couldn't be sure if the younger man had returned to the hotel or not. Unlike the other three bedrooms, the room was in complete disarray. Clothes were everywhere, the toiletry kit had been upended in the center of the bed, the laptop and iPad had been moved, drawers sat cockeyed in the dresser, and the linings of the suitcases had been cut open. Kaden scrubbed a hand over his face. The damage was localized to this room — evidence that whoever it was knew at least what room Riley was staying in and didn't care if someone knew the room had been searched or not. Kaden surveyed the suite again. There were a set of double doors leading out to a balcony. If Riley had stepped outside, his location would have been known to anybody watching the hotel. Whoever had broken in had been looking for something specific. Expensive electronics and watches had been left sitting out in each of the bedrooms including Riley's, along with a couple hundred dollars in cash, none of which had been removed. It also told Kaden that whoever was doing the looking either had steady, reliable income or wasn't smart enough to make it look like a robbery.

Walking into the bathroom, he saw signs of a struggle. Tossed in the corner, under the counter and behind the trashcan, was Riley's backpack. Carefully, he searched for anything that shouldn't be there, before pulling out the bag. The soft blue and green plaid sleep pants and blue T-shirt Riley had worn earlier lay crumpled up on the floor. Kaden picked them up along with the bag and looked around the room one last time. He had no idea if anything else was missing. Grabbing the pajamas and the bag, he ducked out of the room and made his way down the hall to his room.

Once there, he tossed everything onto the bed. Relief rushed through him. The jeans and shirt Riley had changed into earlier in the night were missing. Kaden emptied the rest of the bag item by item. He pulled out a small camera, an iPod, small containers of fragrance-free soap, shampoo and conditioner from some company called Earth Science in a clear plastic bag, a set of keys, a travel toothbrush, and a small tube of toothpaste. Hidden in pockets that snapped were an antique pocket watch and a small leather business card holder with two faded photos instead of business cards. The same woman was in both photos, but in one she held a newborn baby. Kaden replaced the bag's contents and pulled out his phone and opened an app on his phone.

He'd shoved a small tracking device that looked like a thumb-drive into the pocket of Riley's jeans while they had made their way through the crowded streets of New Orleans. If his luck held out, he would be able to find Riley's location. He didn't relish the thought of telling his boss that he'd lost the kid on the first night. Even if it was the kid's fault. It was Kaden's job to keep Riley safe. He should have known Riley would try to run and should have planned for it. A map of New Orleans appeared with a pulsing green dot on the edge of the French Quarter.

The tracking device was in one place, in the city, and still working. It couldn't tell him if Riley was still alive or if he was still in the same place as the device, but it was a start. Cautiously optimistic, he called down to the front desk to request his motorcycle be brought around. Kaden shouldered the bag and left the hotel room. He drove through the crowded streets and around the drunken masses as he zigzagged through the French Quarter toward St. Louis Cemetery. The signal indicated a spot just beyond the cemetery.

Kaden parked the bike between several cars and trucks next to a construction site. Tracking the signal down the street, he ducked between cars and down small alleyways connecting dilapidated warehouse buildings. The dot was in a building just ahead. Among the layers of graffiti and shuttered doors and windows was a faded supermarket sign painted on the brick, the owner's name chipped away by time.

Weeds and the debris of city life pushed at the foundation. Chain-link fencing surrounded the gravel-packed parking lot of the abandoned building. The driveway was blocked by a simple length of chain with a sign reading 'keep out' dangling from the center. Kaden made his way around the perimeter. The signal never moved. Riley, or at least the tracking device, was inside. Kaden shook his head and swore. Why couldn't bad guys ever hide in places that didn't stink like a rancid combination of bar and outhouse? The area was festooned with detritus of better times and home to more rodents than Kaden wanted to think about. He pried open one of the doors and stepped inside. Seconds slipped into eons as he waited for his eyes to adjust to the dark. Metal racks of shelves stood like drunken sailors among scattered boxes, cans, and paper. A thick layer of grime covered everything.

Kaden withdrew his weapon and flicked the safety off. He pulled out a small flashlight equipped with a night filter and turned it on. Crossing his wrists so the gun and light pointed the same way, Kaden swept the red light around the large room. Turning to his right, he searched the room, ensuring he was alone. Methodically he looked in rooms and behind doors, making his way deeper into the building.

"What are we doing here?" The gruff male voice carried annoyance and anger on a Brooklyn accent throughout the corridor. "We should get him out of the city while we can."

Kaden stopped and listened.

"To where? We're surrounded by swamp. Can't fly him anywhere." The response came from a man with a New Orleans accent.

"Move him out of the city to one of the smaller airports. We can get a private plane in and out easily enough," Brooklyn suggested.

"Boss doesn't want him in DC, New York or anywhere on the East Coast," a third man said. There was no discernible accent, leading Kaden to place him from somewhere in the Midwest.

"Feed him to the alligators," Brooklyn sneered.

Kaden heard a thud followed by a muffled cry. He flipped his flashlight off and crept closer. Riley was bound and gagged on the floor and covered in dirt. The four men were all similar in height, weight, and build. They had a handful of black, cylindrical camping lamps positioned around the room. A table where two of the men sat appeared to be original to the building. The third man sat on an upended wooden crate, while a fourth man kicked Riley in the back before turning to the others.

"Not until he tells the boss what he wants. Seriously, though, Drake, why here? You have to know better places than this."

"None that *he* can go to. We have an hour, two tops, before everyone finds out he's missing," New Orleans, Drake, responded.

Kaden shifted positions slightly to get a better look at the group. He recognized the group as the men who had almost succeed in kidnapping Riley earlier. The mixture of accents told him little in the way of who was after the kid.

"I doubt it. His friends will be three sheets to the wind before they return to the hotel," Brooklyn sneered.

"Where is the key, boy?" Drake asked, pushing up from the table to stand over Riley.

"I-I don't know." Riley cried out as Drake kicked him in the stomach.

"Did you search all of his stuff?" Drake asked, turning back to the other two men.

"Everything he had here," the fourth man, also with a thick New Orleans accent, answered. "Maybe the fucker left it at home."

"Find it!" Midwest demanded.

"I ain't getting paid enough to leave the city, Ike." Drake gestured at Riley. "You two is from the north, you go find the key and take pretty boy with you." There was a slight nervous undertone in Drake's voice that Kaden hadn't heard before. He'd put money on Drake not trusting Ike or Ike's companion. The group seemed split with Ike and Brooklyn on one side and the men from Louisiana on the other. Kaden blew out a breath, hoping that might work in his favor.

Brooklyn looked over at Ike and shrugged. Kaden watched as Ike withdrew his weapon and shot Drake first then aimed it at the other man from New Orleans. Drake fell to the ground, blood pooling around him. The second man jumped up, gun drawn.

"What'd you do that for?"

"Loose ends." Ike pulled the trigger.

The second man fell forward on to the table with a crash, and one of the legs gave out. The whole thing lay at an odd angle. Blood smeared along the chipped Formica as the body slid down to the floor. Riley had curled up in a ball, wincing at each of the shots fired.

Withdrawing a knife from his boot, Kaden took aim and threw the blade. Midwest, the man called Ike, gasped, dropped his gun, and fell, landing next to Riley. Brooklyn withdrew his gun from his waistband, spun around with the weapon aimed and fired. Kaden ducked as the bullets embedded themselves into the wall. Stepping out of the shadows, he squeezed the trigger. The bullet hit right between Brooklyn's eyes.

"God, I hope these are the stupid brand of criminal," Kaden said, retrieving the knife and wiping his blade off on the man's shirt.

Riley struggled against his bonds. "Kaden! Help me!"

"Just a minute, kid!" Kaden sidestepped Riley and searched the room and the adjacent areas before returning to the younger man. Kneeling, Kaden cut the tape holding Riley's wrists and ankles together and helped him sit up. "Stay here," Kaden ordered, pulling a pair of rubber gloves from his coat pocket.

Donning a pair of rubber gloves, he walked over to where Ike lay. Kaden searched the body and retrieved the man's wallet and phone before picking up his gun. Next, he made his way to Brooklyn. A quick search revealed a second wallet and phone set, which he pocketed before digging the bullet out of the dead man's head. Standing several feet away, Kaden shot Brooklyn with Ike's gun before placing it back where the man had dropped it. The bullet followed the same path as the original bullet, and would hopefully cause just enough confusion or misdirection. Kaden searched the bodies of the two men from New Orleans. They each had phones and a handful of bills on them, but neither one possessed any form of identification.

Kaden pocketed everything before helping Riley to his feet.

"Who are you?" Riley asked, holding his stomach. "What are you? What did you do? How did you find me? Why did they kidnap me?"

"Let me see. Stomach or ribs?"

"Both." Riley grimaced.

Kaden felt along Riley's ribcage. Nothing felt obviously out of place. "Can you walk?"

Riley nodded. "I think so."

"We have to get out of here," Kaden said. "A safehouse might just be the best idea for you."

"I'm not going anywhere with you. Not until I have answers." Riley shook his head.

"You aren't going to get them here. Let's get back to the room and get you patched up," Kaden said flatly.

"The tape, it has to come off." There was a crack in the arrogance.

"It will wait." Kaden grabbed Riley's hand and started to pull him through the abandoned super-market.

"Kaden, stop!" Riley stumbled and fell.

Swearing, Kaden helped Riley to his feet, wrapping an arm around him for support. They slowly picked their way across the debris field and out of the building. Kaden half-carried Riley to where he'd stashed his motorcycle.

Riley hissed in pain. Kaden looked up. Riley had squeezed his eyes shut. His jaws were clamped firmly together. Riley pulled the tape off bit by bit. Red welts rose everywhere the tape had been. Riley continued to cry out in pain. Kaden's patience eroded with each noise.

"It's tape, it's not that fucking big of a deal," Kaden snapped. "You don't have tons of hair being ripped out. Get a fucking grip."

"Fuck you," Riley said. Clutching an arm to his stomach, he pushed Kaden away, sidestepping him.

"Get back here. You won't make it very far in your condition." Kaden grabbed Riley's arm.

"You killed the guys who kidnapped me. I'll be fine."

"Those were hired thugs. The guys who paid them, they're still after you," Kaden said, pulling Riley back to the bike. "When they don't report as scheduled someone else will come looking for them and for you."

Riley chewed his lip and removed the tape from his other wrist, tossing the second piece onto the ground with the first.

"Spoiled and a low pain tolerance," Kaden muttered, scooping up the discarded tape and shoving it into his pocket. "You need to go home and hire a fucking bodyguard."

"Think whatever you want, *James,*" Riley bit out.

"Are you allergic to it?" Kaden asked, seizing both wrists. The markings were virtually identical.

"Just cursed."

Kaden nodded and released Riley, ordering him back onto the bike. He headed back to the hotel. They would need to move. Soon. There were benefits to staying where they were, but the challenges of trying to keep Riley safe coupled with the fact that the kid's whereabouts were already known made leaving a better option. Riley was quiet and sullen the short ride back to the hotel and up to their room.

"We need to leave. Before dawn."

"I can't. I need—I need to get my backpack."

"I have it. Your hotel room was trashed. Hard to know if anything was taken or not."

"Probably not. They kept asking about a key. And it. Whatever 'it' is." Riley sat down on the edge of the bed. "Do we have to leave tonight?"

"In a couple of hours, yes." Kaden sat down across from Riley, looking the man over. "Why cursed?"

"What?"

"Earlier, you said you weren't allergic, you were cursed. What did you mean?"

"Just that. Cursed. It's not that I have a low pain tolerance, or am a wimp, or whatever else you want to call it."

"What is it?"

"Hypersensitivity."

"To what?"

"Everything. Touch, sound, sight, taste, and smell, which is probably the worse."

"And drinking like a fish is a good thing then?"

Riley nodded. "Alcohol is a depressant. It makes life tolerable."

Kaden raised an eyebrow. "Tolerable."

"I'm sure you've undergone some sort of sensory deprivation training, or at least experienced it." Riley shrugged. "When you lose your sight, everything else becomes sharper, and when you get it back it hurts to see. And eventually, your senses return to normal."

"Yes."

"Mine are stuck in the hypersensitive mode. Permanently."

"I've never heard of that."

"Yeah, I'm special."

"Who knows?"

"My doctor."

Kaden shook his head. "That's it?"

"Ah, yeah, James. Because nobody else cares. And that kind of knowledge is dangerous in the wrong hands." Riley stood, grabbed his backpack, and disappeared into the bathroom. He returned moments later dressed in his pajamas and sat down on the edge of the bed. His movements were slow and measured. "Why did you shoot that one guy twice? I saw you remove a bullet."

"Countermeasure. If the locals get to him first, it'll stall them."

"First? Who else— Wait, like the clean-up people that spies and bad guys always seem to have in the movies?" Riley asked, pain and fear littered his voice.

"Rats. Mice. Scavengers of any variety." Kaden shrugged.

"Wake me when it's time to go."

"What made you decide to tell me?" Kaden asked.

"You saved my life." Riley rolled over and faced the wall, pulling the covers up to his chin.

Chapter Three

"Wake up!"

Riley opened his eyes and slammed them shut again. Whatever time it was it was way too early to be up. The lights flipped on. Riley groaned and pulled the covers over his head. He started to roll over and stopped. His body protested the movement. Pain rushed through him. The horror of the last twenty-four hours crashed over him. The realization that he'd also told his biggest secret to a perfect stranger exacerbated his horror. Riley's stomach pitched and rolled. He was going to be sick. Pushing himself up, he hissed in pain and prayed he didn't throw up in front of the other man. One who probably already thought he was a nutcase.

"Easy there. You took quite a beating last night." Kaden crossed over to him. "How are you feeling? Does anything feel broken or out of place?"

"Everything," Riley snarled. His whole body hurt. At least most of the welts on his wrists had disappeared.

"Is this normal for you?" Kaden asked, snagging his wrist and examining it.

Riley cringed inwardly. Kaden's touch was lighter than it had been last night, as though he were afraid Riley would break. It was one of the reasons he'd never told anybody. He hated being treated like he was too weak to do anything, wasn't man enough.

"I actually need to know the answer," Kaden said, jerking his hand slightly.

Riley growled, trying to pull his hand away. "I'm fine."

"That's a bullshit answer if I've ever heard one. They weren't holding back."

"Look—"

"You've never been kidnapped and beaten like that."

"I've been in fights before." Riley shrugged. He'd fought more times than he could count.

"Admitting you're hurt or need help isn't weak. It takes more gut to admit something like that than to keep it in and pretend to be okay. Shit like that gets people killed. Good people." Kaden's voice softened at the last words.

"Easy for you to say. You have a Purple Heart and an Army patch," Riley grumbled. Kaden didn't have to prove he was man enough or good enough.

Kaden's eyes narrowed. He grabbed Riley's shirt and drew him closer. "It was one of the hardest fucking lessons I had to learn," Kaden ground out. There was a haunted look to the other man's eyes that Riley hadn't noticed before.

Riley swallowed and nodded. "They're usually gone in a few hours, although they've lasted a couple of days before."

"Can you ride?" Kaden released his grip and walked over to the chair where his duffel bag sat.

"Ride?"

"Yes. We need to leave the city. Head someplace safe, someplace without other potential hostages or victims."

Riley moved slightly, his body protesting. He wasn't sure he was up to more than lying in bed all day. Riding on the back of a motorcycle seemed like a particularly bad idea. "Isn't that counterproductive, though? I mean, crowds mean a lot more attention. Wouldn't they want to avoid that?"

"You were in the middle of a crowd when they attacked the first time. And in your hotel room when they succeeded," Kaden replied. "They aren't worried about crowds. But I can't keep you safe in the middle of an unpredictable mob of partying drunks."

"I didn't know or believe you before. I wasn't looking or paying attention." Riley rolled his shoulders. "That has to count for something."

"Maybe, maybe not. It's easier to protect you when I can control the surroundings."

"I can't ride today and I can't just disappear. My friends are going to call the police as soon as they discover the room was ransacked. We can show up there, collect my stuff, and show them I'm okay. Buy some time."

"And say what? That you were kidnapped. That—" Kaden tossed the bag onto the end of his bed. He stopped stalked across the room to Riley. "You were you already in the room when they attacked you, weren't you?"

Riley nodded. "I was in the bathroom."

"Did you hear them come in?"

"What? No, I was—"

"You said your senses are in overdrive, all of the time. Hearing is a sense. Did you hear the door open? Did it sound like someone was trying to break in? Was there any pounding on the door? Any of them?"

Riley started to shake his head and stopped, replaying the events in his mind. He'd changed out of his pajamas before leaving Kaden's hotel room. He hadn't thrown the security latch, but he'd closed the bedroom door on the way through. He'd gone straight into the bathroom when he'd arrived back at his own hotel room, intent on taking a shower. Riley shoved a hand through his hair. He hadn't heard the men come in. "No. I was in the bathroom. I heard something in the bedroom, opened the door, and there they were. I hadn't even turned the water on yet."

"All four of them?"

Riley looked down at the floor then back to Kaden. "Sort of. The one called Drake was in the living room. The other one with the New Orleans accent, um, Charlie, I think, was outside of the hotel room door."

"So, it was Ike and the guy from Brooklyn who attacked you in the bathroom?" Kaden ran a hand through his hair and sat down on the bed.

Riley nodded. "I hadn't thought about it until you asked. How did they get in without making any noise?"

"Key card would be my guess. Either a master key from one of the hotel staff or from either you or your roommates. Any of you lose a key?"

"Dakota did. Second day we were here. Not sure if it was by the pool or when we went out to eat. He didn't realize it until later that night. Girl at the desk gave him a new one." Riley pushed himself up from the bed, biting his lip as pain lanced his body. His body might not want to move, but his bladder wasn't going to give him any choice.

"How long have you known the guys you're traveling with?"

"Years." Riley stood, walked in and slammed the bathroom door shut behind him. He was pretty sure he knew where Kaden was going with his questions. Would his friends turn him over to kidnappers? No way. They might be a little on the shallow and flaky side, but something like that, he couldn't see them doing. He paused in front of the mirror after relieving his bladder and carefully lifted his shirt up. His torso was covered in a variety of colors where his captors had kicked and beat him. Riley swore silently and lowered his shirt. He cleaned up, inhaled, and let it out slowly before opening the door. He wasn't in the mood to argue today. He wanted to sleep and get back to his life. What there was of it.

Kaden sat at the small table where he'd set up his laptop. "Can they be bought?" he asked as soon as Riley walked back out of the bathroom.

"For the right amount, maybe." Riley shrugged and slowly climbed back into bed. "But someone who isn't paid enough to leave New Orleans doesn't begin to have the money it would take. Portfolio and trust funds in the millions. Each."

"Maybe to impress someone?"

"People are impressed by money."

"Ambition?"

"Seriously, dude? Their ambition is to bed as many hot chicks as possible. Although, pretty sure Dakota likes men too, so probably bed as many hot *people* as possible. And drink. Who in the hell wants to spend the best years of their life working?" Riley hissed as he lay down.

"Most people have to," Kaden admonished. "Let me see."

"I'm fine. I'll be fine."

"So, you keep saying. Take your shirt off."

Fresh waves of pain coursed through him as he obeyed. Riley stared at Kaden as the other man swore before closing the distance between them.

"There is no way this isn't going to hurt more."

Riley knew that. Even if he had a normal body, it would hurt. He clenched and unclenched his fists, biting his cheek as Kaden felt his way around the bruising. The soft touch was clinical and left Riley confused over his reaction.

"Nothing feels broken. My best guess would be a couple of cracked ribs on top of bruising."

"Your best guess?" Riley asked, incredulous, looking down at Kaden kneeling in front of him. "You don't know?"

"First, we're in a hotel room, not a hospital. Second, what I know about medicine amounts to advanced first aid. At no point was I a doctor. Nor do I have X-ray vision," Kaden snapped. "Since leaving today is not going to happen, I'm going to go scrounge up pain meds for you. And food."

"What about my friends? If we need to buy time, won't making an appearance be advantageous? Show them I'm fine, before leaving. They'll be less likely to call the police that way."

"Maybe," Kaden conceded. "If you can move without revealing how much pain you're in this afternoon."

Riley allowed Kaden to help him put his shirt on and slide back under the covers. He heard Kaden moving around the room before the lights flipped off.

* * * *

Riley grimaced and opened his eyes. The room was blissfully dark and silent. Threads of sunlight seeped in around the edges of the curtain. The flicker of light from a laptop was the only other light in the room.

"What time is it?"

"A little after three in the afternoon. There's Tylenol and a glass of water next to you on the nightstand." Kaden closed the lid to his laptop.

"Thanks, I didn't mean to sleep all day."

"You obviously needed it." Kaden stretched his legs out in front of him and crossed his arms over his chest.

Riley pushed himself up and swallowed the pain relievers. "Can we get my stuff from my hotel room?" Riley set the empty glass back down.

"And tell your friends what? What would they believe?"

"You're a hired bodyguard?"

Kaden shook his head. "First, they generally wear suits and second, there would need to be a valid reason. How likely is it that your father would hire a bodyguard for you? Has he ever in the past?"

"Point. Got it!" Riley pushed the blankets back. He needed to get a change of clothes, something that wasn't going to aggravate his nerves. "My vacation is being cut short and you're a security guard who works for Charles, who also cut your vacation short to escort me home."

"No one would believe that."

Riley stiffened, pursing his lips together in a tight smile. "Actually, Charles would do something like that and they know it." Riley shoved a hand through his hair and stood up, hissing as a fresh wave of pain coursed through him. "If you have a pair of dark sunglasses and a more nondescript jacket, you'll be less recognizable." He grabbed his bag and headed into the bathroom.

Kaden watched Riley disappear into the other room and wondered at the layers of pain he was beginning to see. He'd taken the time while Riley was asleep to dig into the Hamiltons. He hadn't been able to do the exhaustive research he preferred before acting on his assignment. The scarcity of information had bothered him, but he trusted his boss. It hadn't been the first time he'd been handed so little information on a subject. But it was the first time he remembered being handed so little, with so much available. Kaden had used every resource at his disposal and had even researched Café Lafitte in Exile, which claimed to be the oldest continuously operational gay bar in the country. He'd learned that while Charles Hamilton was a widower, he'd been married once before, and that relationship had ended up in a quiet divorce with a woman who had simply disappeared. Charles had a long history of womanizing, he traveled extensively, and he was always seen with beautiful women, but never with his son.

Kaden rolled the information around in his head, fitting it into the empty spaces. He hadn't been able to find any information about Riley's family prior to the foundation of the Hamilton Perfume Company in the 1950s. The company was one of the most profitable perfume companies in the country, only entering the international market in the 1980s. The family, however, stayed out of the press and tabloids. Even Riley was rarely seen, although the dossier said that he had a penchant for trouble.

Pulling out his phone, Kaden dialed Ace's number.

"Ace's Stab and Slab," Ace said, answering the phone.

"The information." Kaden shoved a hand through his hair.

"Did you take the boy to Lafitte's?"

"No, I'm not taking him to Lafitte's or anywhere else. He's not in any shape for drinks at a bar."

"Not just any bar but the oldest continually operating gay bar in the US."

"Not a vacation Ace," Kaden ground out. "I need—"

"You need a different job and a real vacation."

"Ace—"

"I sent you a couple of pictures you'll be interested in. Finish your ghost ride after this."

The line disconnected. Kaden toyed with the idea of calling Ace back and demanding a straight answer, but past experience reminded him that it wouldn't help. Very rarely did the researcher alter a course of action.

"How are you feeling?" Kaden asked, shoving his phone in his pocket as Riley stepped out of the bathroom.

"It hurts to breathe and move, but other than that fucking peachy." Riley dropped his bag next to his bed.

"Ready to see your friends?"

"No, but it's not like I have a choice or other clothes to wear."

Kaden nodded and led the way through the hotel and out onto the crowded streets.

"Is it safe?" Riley asked, looking around. "I never realized how crowded the streets were or how much could be hidden."

"Don't worry, you'll be fine," Kaden replied.

"I don't remember that place before."

Kaden followed Riley's gaze. "Lafitte in Exile, the oldest continually run gay bar in the US, according to Ace."

"And Ace knows this how?" Riley quizzed.

"The internet probably. I think they know all of the queer businesses in the country. Probably Canada too."

Riley shook his head. "I'm not supposed to like that, you know?"

"Like what?"

"Kissing men."

Kaden led the way through the maze of streets, past quaint shops, restaurants, bars, and street musicians, back to Riley's hotel. He hoped the younger man's friends would be there so they wouldn't have to wait for them or chase them down.

"I take it your father doesn't know that either."

"What Charles doesn't know about me could fill a library," Riley said quietly. "Were you talking to your friend Ace earlier?"

"Yes, I was hoping they had information that can tell me who is after you and why. What do you know about your family?" Kaden asked as they walked into Royal Sonesta.

"Not a lot." Riley winced as he took a deep breath.

"No big movements. Let me lift anything that's needed." Kaden put on a pair of sunglasses.

Chapter Four

Riley nodded and stepped into the elevator. The ride up was quiet, tension mounting as they neared their destination. Riley couldn't remember a time when he'd flat-out lied before. He'd told plenty of half-truths and lies by omission, but this was different. He was purposely misleading his friends and probably the authorities. People he should be turning to for help. Riley rolled his shoulders and blew out a breath. He had to admit, if it hadn't been for Kaden, he'd probably be dead. Or wished he was.

"Let me do the talking?" Riley asked, quietly inserting his key card into the door.

"Of course."

Riley pushed open the door and stepped inside.

"Hey, look what the cat dragged in!" Brock Kingston called out. "You forget how to text?"

"RJ!" Dakota Ellsworth shouted. "You hook up with a chic?"

"She worth it?" dark-haired Joey Collingwood asked, walking into the living room.

Riley flinched at the barrage of questions. Brock Kingston, his oldest friend, sat back in a chair, resting his left ankle on his right knee, crossing his fingers behind his neck. Riley recognized the pose and the look on Brock's face. It was the one that said he knew there was more to the story than anyone else knew or believed and he was simply waiting to be proven right. Riley used his right thumb to crack each of the fingers on that hand. He seriously doubted that his friends could fathom the nightmarish reality of his life.

"That ain't no chick," Dakota said pointedly, glaring at Kaden.

"Where you been?" Joey asked, grabbing a beer from the wet bar before sitting down. "Heard about a new club we want to check out tonight."

"Long story," Riley snarled before turning and glaring at Kaden. He hoped the other man understood enough to play along. "Was with a pair of twins, they were fantastic."

"Tried to call you. Your room is trashed." Brock unlaced his hands, his brown eyes flashing.

"Phone is dead. There were twins." Riley flopped down in the nearest chair, hoping his friends would buy his story. Pain shot through his body. Riley prayed he didn't give anything away. Kaden's presence would be easily believed even if they didn't believe that Riley trashed his own room. He'd forgotten to ask Kaden how bad the damage had been.

"Then who's the goon?" Joey asked, pointing his beer at Kaden.

"Works for Charles." Riley shrugged. Tension rolled through him and settled in every part of his body.

"Doing what? Bodyguard?" Joey asked, taking a drink from the bottle.

"Yeah, like Charles would hire a bodyguard for anybody but himself," Brock scoffed.

"Point there." Dakota nodded. "You're not going to get laid with a babysitter."

"Not going to get laid anyway. He's not a babysitter or a bodyguard. Charles sent him to drag me home."

"Dressed like that?" Dakota asked incredulously.

"He was on vacation. Ruin two vacations with one stone."

"Again? What a prick." Brock pushed himself up out of the chair and walked over to the wet bar.

Riley nodded. "Pretty much. I'll pay for the room, well, Charles will, but I've got a plane to catch."

"Asshole." Joey shook his head.

"Somebody needs to put your father in his place." Dakota downed the contents of his glass.

"Yeah, but he'd have to have a heart and give a fuck first." Riley grunted and pushed up out of the chair. He turned to Kaden and pointed at him. "And if you say anything to Charles about what was said—"

"I'm not getting paid to report what I may or may not have heard," Kaden answered. "As far as I'm concerned you came along peacefully."

Riley crossed over to his room and quickly packed his belongings in his carry-on, making room for his electronics. Kaden followed him silently, playing the part of the pissed-off employee sent to retrieve him perfectly. Waves of anger and disgust rolling off of him. Riley blew out a breath. He was glad his friends were drinking and preoccupied. They would be less likely to notice the bulge under Kaden's jacket where the man's gun was secured. Kaden hadn't removed the shoulder holster or weapon when they'd returned to the room yesterday. It had still been on when Riley had woken up. It was worn with a comfort level that suggested years of wear. He wasn't sure what was more unsettling, the weapon or Kaden's ease and confidence with it.

"Charles is actually dragging you back home?" Brock asked, pushing his way into Riley's room, beer in hand. "He didn't mention that yesterday when you talked to him."

"He is. And no, he didn't." Riley shoved his shaving kit into his suitcase. "Probably had a problem with me pointing out the fact that he was beginning his two-week business trip to Asia with a week in the Bahamas that he was also writing off as a business expense."

"Did he say why?" Brock dropped onto his bed.

Riley laughed dryly. "Same as last time."

"What an ass. His girlfriend leave him?"

"Probably." Riley shrugged. "She probably wanted to be his wife and have his kids. They usually do."

"Not all women are like that," Kaden quipped from behind them.

"Nope, but the ones after Charles generally are. Mostly, they want his money. He's too much of a cold-hearted prick for anyone to actually love," Riley argued.

"Your father's taste in women is sketchy anyway." Brock took a drink from the bottle.

"True, but at least I don't have to worry about half-siblings showing up, demanding their portion of this or that."

Brock nodded and pointed his beer at Riley. "Point."

Kaden raised an eyebrow.

Brock laughed. "Charles Hamilton had a vasectomy years ago. After one of his girlfriends turned up pregnant."

"Yep." Riley zipped up the suitcase and snapped a lock on it. "Wasn't his kid. She was seeing someone else, a junior partner at some law firm. She'd told him she was on birth control, but had stopped taking it. She was hoping to use the pregnancy to become his wife."

The banter between him and Brock wasn't unusual, nor was his friend's opinion of Charles Hamilton, but Riley's stomach churned. He could have easily been killed and his father wouldn't have cared. His grandmother might have, or at least at one point in time she would have. He wasn't so sure anymore. He wasn't even sure what his friends would think if he'd been killed. The kidnappers had had ample opportunity to kill him, but they kept asking about a key or it. He wasn't sure if the 'it' they referred to was the key or not. Either way, he didn't have anything like that. Pain rippled through him every time he moved or breathed. Riding a motorcycle was probably still far from a good idea. Maybe he could convince Kaden to stay in New Orleans one more day. Being hotel bound wasn't his idea of fun either, but it still sounded better than getting on the back of a motorcycle.

"Thanks for the room, man." Brock smirked.

"Thank Charles." Riley shrugged. Schooling his features, he braced for the onslaught of pain as he lifted the carry-on off his bed. "Let's go," he groused. Leading the way out of the room, Riley didn't relax until the elevator doors closed behind them.

"Give that to me," Kaden demanded, yanking the suitcase from him. "As much as I don't want to stay another night here, there is no way you can ride tonight."

"Thank you." Riley's voice cracked. "I have to stop by the front desk."

"You're actually charging the room to your father?"

Riley nodded. "Yes, when he pulls stupid shit like this, absolutely. He won't actually notice."

"But he's not behind this."

"No, but they don't know that. They do know that he has done shit like this before. And he wouldn't have sent me a bodyguard. I may not know who sent you or why, but it wasn't him, you being here has screwed up my life, and anyway it's probably because of him. Or at least my relationship to him."

"You honestly don't think your father would have hired protection for you?" Kaden asked as the elevator descended.

Riley shook his head. "Not unless it was in his best interest. And right now, I'm not useful to him. Another few years, maybe. He'll pawn me off to the right woman with the right business or money connections. Preferably both."

"Those kinds of marriages don't generally happen anymore."

Riley laughed, the hollow sound echoing off the walls. "They do in Charles' world."

The elevator doors opened and Riley led the way past a middle-aged couple back to the counter where he'd first encountered Kaden. Kaden walked over to a large, opulent sitting area and sat down with the case at his feet and pull out his phone.

"Yes, sir, may I help you?" the young woman behind the counter asked him, drawing his attention away from Kaden.

Riley winced internally at the memories pushing forward. He had been an ass to her the other day and Kaden had called him out on it. "I need to change the payment for my room. I'm paying for the room by myself." Pulling out his wallet, he handed her a credit card.

"Yes, sir."

"Is there computer check-out available? We have an early flight out, but I'm generally not human until three and only after several pots of coffee."

"Yes, sir. Just log in and click the self-checkout link."

"Thanks."

Riley replaced the card and his wallet away before heading toward the sitting area. Kaden nodded toward the double doors. Riley continued on through the doors and outside. He stopped near the valet station to flirt with a young woman. She blushed and shook her head. Riley continued across the street, looking at a rack of Mardi Gras beads in a souvenir shop. He didn't have any interest in the woman, but he wanted to buy time for Kaden to join him. He couldn't shake the feeling he was being watched. The person behind the kidnapping hadn't been identified, which meant people were still after him. He still had no idea why.

"Damn it, you were supposed to let me do the lifting," Kaden said, catching up to him outside of the tourist shop full of T-shirts, Mardi Gras-style beads, and hot sauces.

"That would have been too suspicious. Brock may or may not buy it as it is." Riley replaced the string of beads. "He wouldn't have bought someone who had their vacation ruined willingly carrying my bag. Not unless you were one of the house staff, which you aren't."

"Do you always call your father by his first name?"

"Since I was seven or eight."

"Mind if I ask why?"

Riley shrugged. It wasn't that he hadn't been asked before, but he couldn't remember a time if someone asked if it was *okay* if they asked. "It was winter break, Christmas Eve, and he was taking off with some floozy for the Caribbean. He and my grandmother got into a fight over it in his home office. He said he didn't understand what the big deal was, he hadn't wanted 'the little brat' anyway, and it was too bad that my mom died when she did because now he was saddled with me. They didn't realize I was there and heard everything," Riley answered quietly as they slowly made their way back to the hotel. "I ran and hid, cried my eyes out. About an hour later I was called down to say goodbye. I said 'goodbye, Charles', instead of 'Dad'. Didn't bother asking when or if he was coming back or if he could stay."

"Any attention is better than no attention?" Kaden asked as they stopped to listen to a group of street musicians.

Riley allowed the music to wash over and through him, taking the bulk of the uncomfortable memory away with it. He had to admit that New Orleans jazz had grown on him and some of the street musicians were the best he'd ever heard. "Sort of. More, I wanted to see how he would react. He just shrugged and said he'd see me later. He came back from his vacation after I went back to school. Christmas morning there were mounds of gifts under the tree, supposedly from Charles. I knew better."

Kaden's hand wrapped around Riley's waist and squeezed gently. "Come on."

Riley permitted Kaden to guide him through the crowd and back to their hotel room, accepting Kaden's help undressing before crawling back into bed. His entire body ached. Closing his eyes, he willed his body to get better.

* * * *

Kaden turned on the nearby light, looked over at the sleeping figure, shoved a hand through his hair and sat down at the small table with his laptop and a cup of coffee. The callous attitude Riley had for his father had taken him by surprise and prompted Kaden to look deeper into Charles Hamilton's personal life instead of reviewing the information Ace had provided. It had taken considerably longer than it should have to uncover Charles Hamilton's travel history. The man traveled exclusively for business, even to traditional vacation destinations. Pinching the bridge of his nose, Kaden wondered if the IRS thought that it was as suspicious as he did.

Kaden scanned the data on the screen. "Strange." For a man vocally determined that Riley would inherit the company from him, he had never once taken his son with him. Instead, he'd always taken a young female companion. He never dated a woman more than a year, ones who both of Kaden's grandmothers would describe with more than a little disdain as floozies. Kaden had to agree with Riley's friend Brock — Hamilton's taste in women was sketchy. They appeared to be little more than high-priced hookers, although the women he knew in those occupations had more class and better taste in bed companions than the women Charles was frequently seen with. Kaden made a mental note to see if any of the women he knew had any information about Riley or his father.

Jealousy was a powerful motivator. The courts and jails were full of people jealous of someone else for any number of reasons. Kaden finished the cup of coffee and shifted in the seat. There were more than a few women who had reason to hate Riley, if they saw him as competition. Kaden scrubbed a hand over his face. Crazy was crazy. He would probably have to ask Ace for help. Again. Kaden logged into his email and downloaded the photos that Ace had sent. The first one was of an old fashion paddle wheel boat and the other was of artists surrounding Jackson Square. He ran the photos through an encryption program and began sorting through the information Ace had sent. He needed a better understanding of the Hamilton family so he could piece together who was after Riley.

"Fuck!" Kaden swore and re-read the notes, flipping between images of handwritten immigration records, passenger manifests, a marriage certificate, and a death certificate. There were differences that couldn't be explained and possible signs of forgery. Kaden powered down the laptop. He'd hoped to be able to let Riley have the rest he needed. "Riley, up. We have to leave. Now."

"Ow. What? Why?" Riley asked, sleep crawling through his voice.

"Sorry, man, we have to leave now."

"I can't ride yet."

"No choice." Kaden stowed his laptop in his duffel bag, tossing clothes and toiletries in alongside it.

"Shit, how are you even dressed?"

"I've been up since six. Shower and change. Jeans are better for riding in. We'll have to get you a leather jacket, though."

"And a helmet." Riley pushed himself up.

Kaden shook his head. "I have the nutshell you can use again."

"That thing was uncomfortable. I'm already in pain, so, I'd like a real helmet, if you please."

"Fine, but we'll need to get it before we leave New Orleans."

"Why?"

"So your whereabouts are harder to trace."

"Why? What happened?" Riley pulled himself to his feet, hissing in pain. "Damn it, Kaden, tell me what the fuck is going on!" Riley dug his fingers into Kaden's arm.

Kaden stopped and turned to face his charge. "Are you aware that your family has no history? Your grandmother first appeared on immigration records out of Canada in 1947." Kaden stared into the forest-green eyes. He needed to know if Riley knew or suspected anything about his family. "And your grandfather's family doesn't exist anywhere prior to processing through Ellis Island in 1940."

"No. I don't know. How am I supposed to know?" Riley scoffed. "Why does it matter where they came from? Not only that, I seriously doubt that mine is the only family to spring up from nowhere. Pretty sure some people wanted to pretend they were from someplace nice or from something better than they were. The whole America-is-the-land-of-milk-and-honey shit."

"No one ever told you stories about your grandparents or great-grandparents?" Kaden demanded, yanking his arm out of Riley's grip.

"Are you serious?" Riley snapped, anger edging his voice. "I wouldn't know my mother's name except for the fact that it's on my fucking birth certificate! We didn't have family dinners with stories about how bad things were. I know my great-grandfather started the

Hamilton Perfume Company along with his oldest son. My grandfather was a chemist and businessman who met my grandmother at a holiday party while she was working for the company. That's all I know. I have no idea about anything else. And I only know that because one of the maids thought it was romantic how my grandparents met and it's on all of the company information crap."

Kaden winced internally at the flash of pain quickly covered by anger. Dropping his hands, Kaden rubbed the back of his neck. "Look, I'm sorry you don't know more about your family, but I have to know everything you know. Because if what I've found is correct, the people looking for you have extremely deep pockets and everything to lose."

"I told you what I know."

Kaden watched as the calm, carefree façade slid back into place. The words were quiet and flat. Kaden nodded. "Get dressed, we need to leave." Shoving a hand through his hair, he waited until Riley had disappeared into the bathroom before digging a second mobile out of the bottom his bag. He put the phone together, praying it still had a charge. Dialing a phone number, he shoved the rest of his belongings into his bag.

"Hello?" a gruff male voice asked on the third ring.

Kaden took a deep breath and let it out again. "I need a favor."

"Nice to talk to you too. I'm fine by the way, thanks for asking."

"Shit, sorry, man."

"Giving you a hard time. What do you need?"

Kaden outlined what he wanted from his friend, refusing to go into details.

"When will you be here?"

"I'm about five hours away, but it'll take about seven."

"Sunset it is."

The line went dead and Kaden turned the phone off and pulled it apart, hiding it in his bag. Riley came out of the bathroom dressed in jeans and a T-shirt. "We need to mail your carry-on back to you. There's no room on the bike."

"I figured as much. I have what I need in my backpack," Riley answered. "I need to know what you found."

"It's what I *suspect*."

"Same thing." Riley shrugged. "You still know more about my family than I do."

"No one springs up from nowhere. Especially people with careers in engineering or chemistry."

"So? What's your point?"

"Given the sketchy details and the time frame your grandparents and their families immigrated to the US, my guess is they are, or were, spies. From one of the Eastern Bloc countries. Most likely Russia, given the politics of the time."

Riley laughed. "You do know James Bond is a fictional character? That kind of thing doesn't actually happen."

"Spying in some form or another has been happening for centuries. Hell, your father has corporate spies on his payroll, I can almost guarantee it."

"That's absurd."

"That's basically what you said when I told you people were after you," Kaden replied.

Chapter Five

Riley rubbed the back of his neck, trying to process what Kaden was telling him. The idea that anyone in his family was a spy was completely ridiculous. They checked out of the hotel and ate breakfast before mailing his suitcase home. It would sit at the post office until he was able to pick it up. Kaden had offered him his jacket, but it was too big and too uncomfortable. It meant another stop, something that wasn't sitting well with Kaden. Riley had bought one he liked and fit him before they found a place to get a better helmet. Kaden had grown more uneasy every time he swiped his credit card. They were walking back to the motorcycle when Riley detoured across the parking lot to the bank next door's ATM and withdrew several hundred dollars. Not being able to track his movements meant cash, and he wanted his own. Kaden gave him half a smile—the same one he'd given when he'd complimented Riley on his survival instincts before.

The small bit of praise simultaneously had him letting go of some of the worry and tension that had surrounded him since he first met Kaden, and made his heart flutter. Riley wanted to crush the feeling, while reveling in it. It shouldn't matter. It did. Just as Kaden's words when they first met had affected him in ways that shouldn't have mattered. He'd been called spoiled brat, and rich boy before. More times than Riley wanted to think about.

Initially, Riley had looked down on Kaden, taking in the torn jeans and tattered leather jacket and dismissing him immediately as unimportant. The idea now turned his stomach, but at the time it didn't. It was normal for him. Kaden hadn't been about to be dismissed, though. He'd called Riley out on his behavior then and there, not caring who heard. Shame flooded Riley at the memory. It had seemed as though everyone in the hotel had been watching and listening. If he looked back at it, it was probably fewer than he'd imagined. He couldn't recall the scene without being flooded with embarrassment.

The tattered leather jacket had brightly colored patches sewn on it. They declared the wearer an Army veteran who had served in both Iraq and Afghanistan, who had probably lost one or more friends in the war, and had earned a Purple Heart. That had stopped Riley cold. This was a man who had probably seen the worst that humanity could dole out. Riley had simply nodded and walked out of the hotel. It hadn't been his intent. He'd spent the better part of the afternoon wandering the French Quarter ending up on a bench in Jefferson Square listening to street musicians and watching the tourists crowd around the psychics and artists. He had been halfway through his fourth beer when his friends had found him a handful of hours later. He'd waved them away, intent on getting drunk alone.

Hours later, Kaden had found him again. This time on the streets, saving his life. And changing it. Riley might be spoiled and rich and everything Kaden accused him of, but Riley considered himself an optimist-leaning-realist. He looked for the good, believed happiness happened, but only for those who sought it out and fought for it. His father ignoring him meant he could do what he wanted without a whole lot of repercussions and he didn't have to fake something he didn't feel.

"So, where are we heading?" Riley asked, buckling on his helmet. He took several deep breaths and tried to get used to the confines and weight of the plain black helmet. Riley wasn't sure if Kaden would answer him or not, but he refused to bury his head in the sand. He might not be a hero, but he wasn't a coward.

"The other side of Houston." Kaden shrugged into his jacket.

"That safe house you mentioned?"

Kaden shook his head and secured his helmet. "Army buddy."

"How is that a good idea? Shouldn't we head someplace safe?"

"His place is safe. It's also temporary." Kaden climbed on the bike and started it.

Riley swore and waited until Kaden had backed the bike out of the parking spot and had it turned around before climbing onto the back. This time was no less awkward or painful than last time he'd had to get on and off the bike. He grabbed onto Kaden's waist as the motorcycle lurched forward.

The wind pushed into him, the face shield and sunglasses protecting his face. Stomach clenched, heart thumping with the roar of the bike, Riley smiled. He'd heard bikers speak of the freedom of the open road. He hadn't believed the stories before. It was an incomparable feeling. He would definitely be getting his own motorcycle as soon as he could. Providing he survived the nightmare he currently found himself in. Riley leaned with Kaden as they took the on-ramp to the freeway. As long as Kaden did his job, which he seemed at least capable at, Riley would live through this. He hoped.

* * * *

Riley's entire body ached. His ass hurt from spending the entire day on the back of the bike, and his torso and ribs hurt from holding himself up. Kaden had stopped every couple of hours so Riley could stretch, but he wasn't sure it had helped at all. They had stopped at a small out-of-the-way biker bar for dinner on the east side of Houston. Despite Kaden's assurances that the food was good, Riley had settled for a burger and homemade French fries, convinced they wouldn't be able to cook a steak properly. He'd been surprised by the burger — it was easily one of the best he'd ever eaten.

The sky turned various shades of pinks and purples as Kaden turned down a dirt road. They had left the main road a while back. Riley was certain they passed a sign that said Backwater-ville, although they may have left the town's boundaries by now. Kaden slowed the bike down further and turned down an overgrown two-track that appeared to be doubling as a driveway. Riley looked around. There was nothing for miles. A 'no trespassing' sign was nailed to the tree — it was the only sign of human life he could see besides the trail they were on. They rounded the corner and a large, well-kept house and an assortment of outbuildings appeared.

"What the hell?" Riley muttered to himself. He'd expected an ancient, weathered shack held together with luck more than anything else, maybe a booby trap or two. That was always what was at the end of overgrown, barely used roads or driveways. They were never two-story suburban-styled homes with wraparound porches, satellite dishes, running water, and electricity. The driveway continued past the house to a large dark brown pole barn with the door standing partially open.

Riley was stunned by how inviting the house appeared. Kaden rode the bike straight into the barn and parked alongside a sleek black Harley Road King. Riley swung his leg over and got off the bike, looking around. A Humvee and a full-size pickup truck, both in black, were also parked in the barn. A black tarp covered a third vehicle. Riley guessed it was some sort of sports car from its shape.

He'd just removed his helmet when he heard the audible click of a gun being cocked. Riley's heart stopped. Had Kaden led them into a trap? Knowingly? Unknowingly? Kaden grabbed Riley's arm, pushing and pulling him until he was between Kaden and the motorcycle and sitting on the ground. Kaden's weapon was out and pointed up toward the ceiling. He crouched next to Riley.

"I'll kill him," Kaden threatened.

Riley nodded. The underlying, illogical fear that Kaden was either using him or taking him to the people who wanted him eased. Kaden actually seemed to want to keep him alive and safe.

"Have you ever shot a weapon before?" Kaden held out a matte-black gun.

Riley stared at the gun then at Kaden and shook his head. "No. Where did you get that?"

"Saddlebag," Kaden replied. "Quick lesson, then. This is the safety. The 's' is for safety and the 'f' is for fire. Lever up is safe. This is the slide. Pull it back and a round will chamber. Flip the safety down and it's ready to shoot. This is the trigger. Squeeze it. The gun won't fire unless you pull the trigger. This end goes towards the bad guy."

"No shit, James, I'm not stupid."

Kaden released the slide and handed him the weapon. "Hold it parallel to the ground when shooting. Don't try any Hollywood-style shit. And try not to shoot me." He withdrew a second weapon from the inside of his jacket.

"Where the hell are you going?"

"To take care of business. Run to the truck. Trust nothing and no one. And assume everything is loaded or hiding something that will kill you."

"Fantastic."

Heart racing, Riley braced himself to race to the truck. Waiting until Kaden nodded, he ran as fast he could, sliding between a stack of hard plastic bins and the pickup. He maneuvered so he could see Kaden. Riley pulled the slide back, surprised at the weight. The other man squeezed a round off at the ceiling and something metallic clattered to the ground. Turning, he shot again. Riley followed Kaden's line of sightto cameras mounted in the corners. One by one, Kaden put a bullet through the lens of each Then he holstered the weapon, ran from the bike to the Humvee, climbed to the top, jumped, and hoisted himself up to the rafters. Riley lost sight of Kaden but heard him moving across the beams. Riley cocked his head to trace the movements based on sound. However, he was careful not to track them with his body.

An eternity passed before he heard a deep male voice shout, "Jesus, Ten, relax. I wasn't planning on killing you or the boy."

"Down." The order came from Kaden, but his voiced possessed a quality Riley had never heard before.

"I had to be sure."

The two men came fully into view. Kaden grunted. "It's safe."

Riley pushed himself up from where he'd been hiding, his body protesting the movement now that the adrenaline was seeping back out of his body. "Who is this?" Riley asked, faking confidence he didn't feel. "Ten? As in the number?"

"Cute," the newcomer said, smirking. "Not your usual type, though."

"Funny." Kaden reached for the gun he'd loaned Riley.

"Usual type?" Riley asked, handing over the weapon, unsure if he wanted to know the answer.

"Ten likes his men big, ripped, and experienced. Preferably, ones that can take a poundin'." The man chuckled. "You're a baby he'd rip in half in a heartbeat."

"I seem to remember you had no preference, Preacher. Male. Female. Furry," Kaden snapped.

The newcomer, Preacher, snarled and slung his rifle over his shoulder.

"Fucking awesome. Why are we here?" Riley demanded, shoving a hand through his hair. "It can't be to trade dick stories."

"Someone's mama didn't teach him any manners. Obviously, you're not a Southern boy," Preacher stalked across the pole barn to a side door. "A Yank, Ten? Never pictured you'd find a Yank of all things."

Riley clenched and unclenched his fist, his anger rising. Of course, his mother hadn't taught him anything, his mother was dead. She'd died from complications from childbirth. Anger rising fast, Riley stepped forward.

Kaden blocked his progress, grabbing his shoulder. "Don't. He's not worth it. He's a stupid Southern boy who doesn't know anything and whose mama really didn't teach him any manners."

"He — I — "

"I know. Let it go," Kaden demanded, the pressure on his shoulder increasing. "Food, showers, and sleep, Preacher." Kaden continued to stare at Riley.

"My — "

"I'm aware," Kaden said, his voice calm and soothing. "Let's get you a shower and food if you're up for it. We still have a long way to go tomorrow."

Riley nodded, the anger ebbing slightly. He grabbed his bag and followed Kaden and Preacher from the building across the yard to the house. He'd briefly dated a professional chef, and she had taken him along when she went house hunting. He'd gotten bored and had ended the relationship before she'd bought a house. Riley shook his head, trying to make sense of what he was seeing. The kitchen was top of the line. Riley recognized some features like stone countertops and stainless-steel appliances, but it was the large professional-grade gas stove that dominated the room. There was nothing that hinted that a woman lived there or was even a regular visitor, but the house was clean and modern.

"Impressed, Ten?" Preacher asked, interrupting his thoughts.

"Not bad."

"You did this?" Riley asked, looking around again.

Preacher smiled. "I'm a respectable civilian contractor."

Riley cocked his head at the phrase. There was something off about the statement, but he wasn't sure what.

"Respectable my ass!" Kaden laughed. "Shower, man. Need to wash the road dirt off."

"You've been covered in worse for longer. You'll live."

Riley stopped and turned to look at Kaden. He'd known the man had been in the military — the obvious signs were on his jacket, and it was also in the way Kaden carried himself — but Riley hadn't given thought to what that meant before. He wanted to know more, but Kaden's playful had attitude disappeared. He was stiff, his eyes dark and haunted.

Kaden crossed his arms. "I know. Shower for him. He's a civilian."

"Sure thing, man. Upstairs," Preacher said, leading the way to the second story. "Only one room is finished. You two will have to figure that part out yourselves."

Riley wasn't sure he wanted to share a room with Kaden. He needed quiet and sleep after the ride over today. Preacher led them past a room painted an obscene shade of pink covered in white patches with the floor only partway finished, pointing out the bathroom. They were led to a second room. This one was in muted shades of blue and gray.

"Clean up and come on down. We'll spill a couple."

Kaden dropped his bag on the floor by the dresser. "Go ahead and go first."

"I'm not going to touch your boy, you know," Preacher insisted.

"I'm not worried," Kaden replied. "As you said, I've been covered in worse for longer." Kaden crossed his arms. "And I'd kill you if you tried."

Riley debated briefly on arguing with Kaden, before taking his bag into the bathroom. Preacher pointed out where everything was kept and left, shutting the door behind him. Riley rolled his head along the back of his shoulders, trying to relieve some of the tension. Pulling out his own soap, shampoo, and conditioner, he turned the shower on to the right temperature before stepping in.

Water ran over him, getting rid of some of the tension away along with the road dirt. Displaced anger bubbled forward. Why did Preacher keep referring to him as Kaden's boyfriend? Why hadn't Kaden corrected him? He wasn't Kaden's anything. Well, he was Kaden's job, or client at least, he supposed, but he certainly wasn't dating the other man, even if he did find him mildly attractive, which was infuriating by itself. The whole situation sounded like something straight out of a James Bond movie. Except he'd never found Bond attractive.

Riley swore. There was no room in his life for a male lover. He'd considered taking a boyfriend briefly, expressly because it would piss Charles off, but it wasn't worth the price he'd pay. Riley had been caught kissing another boy from school by a servant who had told both of them that their families not only disapproved, but would disown them instantly if they found out. The older woman had never told and Riley had made sure she got an all-expense-paid trip every year to wherever she wanted. The other boy, Christian Howard, had graduated from college two years before Riley and had come out to his parents the day after he'd received his diploma. True to the woman's words, he'd been kicked out and disowned. Riley had run into him at a New Year's Eve party. Christian worked for one of his father's competitors and was engaged to a man named Michael.

Forcing his thoughts away from his father, and everything Charles wanted and expected, left Riley to focus on Kaden. He found himself wanting to know what Kaden had seen, what he had experienced. He knew what a Purple Heart meant—it meant that Kaden had been wounded in combat. Obviously, it hadn't been bad enough to keep him from being a bodyguard and all-around badass, if the scene back in New Orleans was any indication. Reluctantly, he finished his shower, dried off, and changed into clean clothes. He dropped his bag in the room Preacher had shown them, half expecting to see Kaden waiting there. Instead, he followed the sound of the voices downstairs and out to a screened-in back porch.

"You never told him?"

Riley stopped outside the door and listened.

"Nah, there was never a good time. I mean, our lives? Come on. Happy shit only happens in stories."

"A good time would've been anytime you told him. It would've made him happy," Kaden countered.

"Yeah, until the brass learned, then there would have been a whole mess of shit to deal with. Including getting separated. Or jail," Preacher said.

"Still—"

"Then it didn't matter." The words were quiet and final, holding a wealth of emotion and information.

Riley tried to swallow around the lump in his throat. Had Preacher lost someone in the war? Riley thought back to Kaden's comment about Preacher not being particular.

"He could still be out there."

"Five years, man. Do you think that if there was even a half of a fucking rumor, I would be here? On the wrong damn continent? That I would've gotten out in the first place?"

"I'm sorry, man."

There was a long pause before Preacher spoke again. "So, what have you told him?"

"Somewhere between more than I should have and not nearly enough. All of which is hampered by what I don't know."

Riley took a deep breath and stepped through the door. "What don't I know?"

"You clean up real well, boy," Preacher said, holding out a beer. "Have a seat."

"Thanks." Riley sat in the chair closest to Kaden, facing the two men.

"Listen, sorry for being an ass earlier." Preacher downed the last of his beer.

Riley looked up. "Which time?"

Kaden burst out laughing.

"Ha ha, very funny." Preacher smirked. "The comment about your mom. Kaden informed me of my mistake. I hadn't realized she had died, nor that long ago."

Riley shrugged. "What don't I know? What aren't you telling me?"

"I'm pretty sure I know why your family sprung from the middle of nowhere."

"How nowhere?" Preacher asked.

"No records, no past, nothing that logically makes sense." Kaden tipped his bottle back and drank.

"I don't understand." Riley shook his head. There had to be records. His father owned one of the largest and most profitable perfume businesses in the country. There was simply no way that there was no record, no paper trail of his family. His grandmother had worked for the company for years. Now she sat on the board, as well as countless other boards around the community and country. Most of them were for charities or nonprofits, but not all of them.

"Your family has no records, no past, because it doesn't exist," Kaden answered.

"I'm sorry. Are you fucking stupid?" Riley jumped to his feet. His body protested the jarring movement. "My family runs a multi-billion-dollar international company. My family actually does exist!" Riley shouted, aware that both Kaden and Preacher were also standing.

The beer bottle was pulled out of his hand. Kaden closed the gap between them. "Not legally."

Chapter Six

"How can we not exist legally? That makes no fucking sense!" Riley demanded, unable to wrap his mind around what Kaden was saying. There was no way they could have legal documents saying they existed and not be legal at the same time.

"There are three general reasons people spring up from the middle of nowhere." Kaden paced the porch as music poured out through unseen speakers. "They're either illegal immigrants trying to cover their tracks, they are given new identities by the government, in which case they are instructed to keep a low profile, or they're spies."

"There is a fourth possibility—legal immigrants or refugees who want to hide their identities." Preacher handed Riley back his beer.

"Illegal immigrants, criminals, or spies? That is where you're saying my family came from. We travel internationally. You did get that part, right? Any of what you're saying makes what my family does on a regular fucking basis impossible. Hello — Homeland Security anyone?"

"Your family has been here since before Homeland Security. They've probably been here since World War II. You told me you don't know anything about your family."

"What does what I know matter? I can't think of anyone who knows their family history and extended family?" Riley shouted, raising his arms. "Why does it matter? Who cares?"

"Someone wants you dead, so right now everything matters!" Kaden yelled. "Something about you or your family is either important enough or dangerous enough or both to someone with money and resources to follow you. And for some time."

"Nobody was following me!" Riley shoved a hand through his hair.

"They were following you in New Orleans. In order to find you there, that meant they were at Yale with you."

"Why do you say that?" Preacher asked.

"Was the trip to New Orleans planned?" Kaden asked.

Riley shrugged and shook his head. "No, not really. We were at the bar and someone said we should take one last trip to party before settling down."

"Who?"

"Who suggested the trip?" Riley asked, grabbing his beer from the nearby table.

Kaden nodded.

"Brock did."

"And whose idea was it to go to New Orleans?"

Riley tipped back the bottle and drained the contents. "Mine."

"And how long was it between deciding on the trip and leaving?"

"Dinner on Monday to lunch on Thursday." Riley tossed the bottle in the recycling bin.

"Did you tell anyone where you were going?" Kaden demanded.

"Our roommates."

"Roommates?" Kaden raised an eyebrow.

"The four of us share a house near school with two other guys. We invited them along, but one had plans with his girlfriend and the other is leaving for Europe in two weeks."

"So, essentially, you each dropped several thousand dollars to fly down to New Orleans on a whim and stay in one of the most exclusive hotels in the French Quarter with little or no notice to anyone. That means they've been watching you and they can pull at some of the same types of resources you can."

"How long have they been watching me? Why? And that still doesn't answer the question of who *they* are!"

"I think I can answer that one." Preacher grabbed the tablet from the table. "Recognize this man?"

"No. Should I?" Riley shook his head.

"What about him?" Preacher slid his finger across the screen, changing the picture.

"No, wait, maybe. He kind of looks like the guy from the warehouse. The one with the New York accent," Riley replied. "Who is he?"

"Mikail Ivanovich, youngest son of Russian immigrants by the name of Sergei Ivanovich and Oksana Ivanova Petrova."

"Russian mob?" Kaden asked.

"No mob connections as far as anyone knows of, however, Sergei's older brother was Russian

Intelligence and one of his cousins married one of the Russian political elite."

Riley grabbed another bottle of beer and began to pace the small space. "Why would Russians be interested in my family?"

"That would be the million-dollar question."

Riley stopped and turned to Kaden. "You're saying my family is spying for the Russians."

"It's a possibility."

"Bullshit! No way!" Riley resumed pacing. "Jesus, this is like some crappy B-rated spy film." Pain shot through his body. "Exactly what do you think we're going to tell them? The chemical breakdown of perfumes? The different scents each one has in it? Perfume and cologne are luxury items, and there isn't a major top fifty perfume or cologne out of Russia. France dominates followed by the US and Great Britain. Italy and Spain are starting to produce some decent scents, but most countries aren't up there. We've had one or two make the top fifty international every year for the last thirty years. Not to mention the extensive benefits military and veterans receive as employees." He didn't add that it was something that his grandmother had insisted on. It was the one thing his father couldn't change, no matter much he complained.

Riley turned and came face to face with Kaden.

"Sit down before you hurt yourself more," the taller man ordered.

"I'm fine." Riley gritted his teeth. He had ignored pain before. He might not have had his ribs broken before, but he'd been in plenty of fights, and fallen out of more than one tree and window growing up.

"Sit. Down."

Riley stuck his middle finger up at Kaden and sat down, leaning against the back of the chair.

"What's hurt? How did it happen?" Preacher demanded.

"Ribs, back, and stomach. Kidnappers," Riley replied.

"And you rode all the way here on a damn motorcycle? Are you fucking new, Ten?" Preacher pushed up from the chair. "Into the living room, kid."

"Because staying in America's playground with dead bad guys and cops crawling around is a smarter idea," Kaden growled. "Not leaving the bike."

"From the beginning, and don't skip the details," Preacher demanded. "Riley, living room couch. Now."

"You're a pain in the ass," Kaden snarled.

"You're asking a lot."

Kaden nodded. Riley pushed himself up from the chair and did as he was told, wondering about the relationship between Kaden and Preacher. He wasn't sure if they argued more like siblings or lovers. He was equally sure their level of knowledge and idea of what was normal outstripped the average person. If he had to guess, he'd put both of them in military Special Forces. Or Intelligence. Maybe both. Either way, he was pretty sure that life as he knew it was done.

"Generally, I know the name of people before they go touching my body." Riley sat on a dark-green easy chair and raised an eyebrow when Preacher returned with a large red duffel bag.

"Seriously? Where did you dig this kid up, Ten?" Preacher pulled on a pair of rubber gloves.

"French Quarter." Riley shrugged. "So, did your mama name you Preacher?"

"Great. Just great. Name's Jake Shannon. Everyone calls me Preacher. Now, can we get on with it?"

Riley smiled and nodded.

Preacher poked and prodded, checking Riley from head to toe while Kaden explained the events that had led them there. Riley had noticed that Kaden hadn't told his friend some of the details, but Riley wasn't sure why. Kaden obviously seemed to trust the man. When the exam was complete, Preacher stated he'd broken two ribs and probably fractured several more along with a variety of bruises and muscle strains. Anything conclusive would need X-rays and a visit to a hospital. Pain meds and time to rest were the best things for it.

"Since I know this is a pass-through, where are you heading?" Preacher tossed a pill bottle at Riley. "Two pills as needed every six hours."

"What are they?"

"Tylenol with codeine."

"How the hell do you get these?"

Preacher shrugged and sat down in a matching easy chair on the other side of the room.

"Someplace safe." Kaden gave his friend the same answer he'd given Riley every time he'd asked.

"Not on the bike. He can't ride."

"Hence our visit," Kaden explained. "Need to store the bike and get a truck."

Riley shoved a hand through his hair. That was why Kaden had chosen to come here. He couldn't blame him. There was no way Riley would leave a vehicle in a place he had no ties to with little way of knowing when or if he'd be back. Especially one that couldn't be secured.

"You can borrow Bubba," Preacher said. "Betty Sue is too conspicuous. And no one drives Mary Jane but me."

"Bubba, Betty Sue, and Mary Jane?" Riley furrowed his eyebrows.

"Preacher names his vehicles." Kaden chuckled. "All of them."

"Hey, they have personalities too," Preacher said in mock offense. "Besides, they always brought us home safe."

"That sounds like a story." Riley rested his left ankle on his right knee.

"Damn near every vehicle we rode in had to have a name, including the 747 we took back stateside. Wouldn't get in the bloody thing until it had a name."

"We got home safe, though," Preacher huffed.

Riley cocked his head. There seemed to be more to the story than either man was willing to tell. Briefly, he wondered if it had anything to do with the friends they'd lost. The ones he'd overheard them talking about. Superstitions in war zones were probably common. "Isn't Mary Jane another name for marijuana?" Riley asked. Preacher being into marijuana didn't surprise him.

Preacher nodded. "Not why she's called Mary Jane, though. She's fast and sweet and just as heavenly as the girl she's named after." The change in topic lifting his mood and the tension that had descended.

"You'll store the bike?"

Preacher rubbed his chin. "I'll keep it safe for you. Won't guarantee it'll be the same nameless void of metal when you come to reclaim it, though."

"Fair enough."

Riley shook took two pills out of the bottle and downed them with the last of his beer, then sat back and listened to Preacher and Kaden tell stories and raise a toast to lost friends. It was both sobering and awkward, like observing a secret ritual or ceremony he had no business watching and could never hope to either understand or be part of. The sun had set long before they headed up to bed, Kaden reminding them they needed to be up and moving early the next morning.

"We both have to sleep in the same bed?" Riley asked after the bedroom door closed behind them. It wasn't that he'd never shared a bed with anyone. He had. All night in fact, but he'd never shared a bed with another man.

"No other real choice. Yes, there is a couch, a chair, and a floor, but none of those are as comfortable as a bed. None are options for you, and we have a long day ahead of us tomorrow. I would rather do it awake than falling asleep."

"I've never —"

"I have." Kaden shrugged. "We're going to sleep. Nothing else."

"I don't know —"

"No other option."

* * * *

Kaden pushed against the steering wheel and looked over at his sleeping passenger. It had been a long, slightly awkward, night. Despite his assurances to Riley, he hadn't slept sound. Kaden had known he wouldn't. He was glad for the help from Preacher, but he couldn't help but wonder what he'd gotten himself into taking on this assignment, and hoped he hadn't put his friend in danger. He needed to keep Riley safe, but in order to do that, it looked like they were going to have to dig up a past nobody wanted revealed. There was more to the story—he knew it in his gut. He had the growing suspicion that someone was after whatever was buried in the past. Kaden shoved a hand through his hair and scrubbed it over his face. A life built on lies rarely had a chance of succeeding, and it was always the innocent who paid the biggest price.

Russian spies. Kaden swore. The end of World War II had seen the disintegration of the relationship between Allied Forces and Russia. The geopolitical history of the forties and fifties had provided the foundation of the Cold War and a nuclear arms race between the United States and Russia. Every country had wanted to know what its enemies were doing. Active agents, as well as sleeper agents, made sense. Kaden stretched. A family of spies wasn't unheard of, but he had to admit that Riley was right—perfume and cologne weren't national security secrets. It wasn't even an industry that would have granted them access to the kind of information the Russian government would have been after. Even before the Cold War. Security had been too high. He had to take a deeper look at Riley's extended family.

Riley yawned and stretched, hissing in pain. "Where are we?"

"About an hour or so outside of Nashville," Kaden supplied. "Sleep well?"

"No," Riley ground out. "I'm stiff on top of the pain. Are we stopping soon?"

Kaden flexed his fingers and nodded. "Next exit." Kaden stiffened and clenched his jaw.

"You don't want to?"

"To stop? No. Too many loose ends, too many unknowns. I want you someplace safe," Kaden answered. "Do I understand the need to? Yes."

"Where are you taking me anyway?"

"Someplace safe."

"Great, thanks, James. That was really helpful," Riley said, sarcasm dripping from his voice. "How about an honest answer this time?"

Kaden smirked. "I was honest. Someplace safe. And no, I'm not going to tell you any more than that."

Kaden shoved a hand through his hair and prayed that he was doing the right thing, heading to the right place. He didn't think Lawrence would double-cross him, but something about this whole case felt shady — and about a step and a half from the biggest mistake of his life.

"Who am I going to tell?" Riley pushed himself upright.

"How long before you will actually be missed?" Kaden asked, ignoring Riley's question.

"A week, maybe two," Riley answered, stretching.

"How maybe?" Kaden pressed. He needed to know how much time he had to work with.

"Charles is expecting me to be at work on the twenty-eighth. Since I don't have the best track record of actually showing up on when I'm supposed to, I might be able to squeeze more time. Except, I just lied to my friends. There's a chance they'll tell Charles what happened in New Orleans. Or rather, complain about it to someone who will tell Charles."

Kaden nodded.

"Exactly how long am I going to be kept hidden in your spy lair?" Riley demanded. He shifted and hissed in pain.

Kaden shrugged and followed the exit signs pointing the way toward the nearest hotel.

"You don't know?" Riley asked incredulously.

"My job is to keep you safe. No, I don't know how long that's going to take."

"I can't stay away forever. Charles isn't going to let me simply disappear. Somehow I doubt him plastering my picture everywhere will be helpful."

Kaden shoved a hand through his hair. No, Charles looking for his son would definitely not help keep Riley safe. There was no way that the people who were after Riley didn't know who he was, so it wouldn't come as a surprise, but a plea for help for the missing heir could push up whatever timeline they may have. It would also make traveling harder.

Riley raised an eyebrow when Kaden pulled into the first motel they came to. "Um, isn't there someplace else?"

"Like what?"

"Clean," Riley suggested hesitantly.

"It's clean. It's safe."

"How safe?"

"Safe enough that I don't have to worry about you showing up on surveillance cameras," Kaden answered flatly, pulling into a parking spot in front of the office.

"There isn't security here?"

"Yes, there is most certainly a camera in the lobby. Maybe one more in the parking lot, but realistically, security is probably the owners with guns and locking doors to the office." Kaden pocketed the truck keys and climbed out of the truck. "Stay here."

"Where in the hell am I going to go? Civilization is still an hour away."

"Careful, your brat is showing." Kaden slammed the door closed.

Riley crossed his arms over his chest and leaned back against the window.

Kaden smiled and shook his head. From the beginning, Riley's reactions had surprised him. Their first interaction hadn't been planned, it had been a spur-of-the-moment comment aimed at someone so wrapped up in their own privilege who saw everyone else beneath them. The comment had been out before he'd been able to censor the thought. He had intended to follow the kid from a safe distance before approaching him.

Kaden didn't believe that he wasn't the first person to insult Riley. He'd expected a dismissive comeback aimed at cutting him mercilessly without a care for the damage inflicted. He'd seen the beginning of a retort form, before it had withered and died and Riley had simply walked out of the hotel. What Kaden couldn't figure out, then or now, was why.

Shoving a hand through his hair, he made his way through the glass door and into a small lobby. The walls were painted an off-white color that always looked dirty and reminded him of military buildings. A pair of worn, brown-vinyl-covered chairs sat pushed against one wall of a small alcove. A large rack overflowing with tourist brochures was tucked between a large picture window and a small coffee station. The black plastic coffee maker looked like it had seen better days, along with the requisite containers of cream and sugar. A flat-screen TV was mounted on the wall in the corner where it could be viewed by both the attendants at the desk and the waiting area. Two large, round mirrors hung across from the desk near the ceiling, giving a view of the entire area.

The woman behind the desk looked like she was in her mid-thirties, was plump with curly red hair and a pretty face. She looked up at him from what appeared to a large science textbook and smiled.

"That looks intimidating."

"Genetics. Nothing like going back to school when you're an adult."

"Better late than never," Kaden replied. "I need a quiet room in the back. Someplace out of the way."

"True. I have a queen that should work. End room. Nobody above or to the side."

"Perfect."

"Light sleeper?"

"That and people. I prefer to be farther away from people."

"I have a brother like that. Two tours in Afghanistan."

"Is he getting help?"

The woman shook her head. "Pretty sure he thinks it'll make him less of a man or some such bullshit. Ah, sorry, crap."

"I was in the Army. No need to apologize to me. I've heard and said worse."

"How long will you need the room?"

"Just tonight. Passing through."

"Eighty-seven twenty."

Kaden paid for the room and scribbled a note on the back of hotel stationery. "Thank you. Give this to your brother. Get him to the VA. They help guys like us."

"I will." She handed him the key card. "Thank you for your service."

Kaden gave her a partial smile. "Just doing my job, ma'am. Good luck. To both of you." Kaden turned and left the office. Riley was in the same position as when he'd left the younger man.

"Were there any problems?" Riley asked, opening his eyes as Kaden climbed into the truck.

"We're all set. A room in the back, away from traffic and prying eyes."

"What about a credit card trail?"

"Paid cash," Kaden responded. "And if I had used a credit card, the moment any sort of trace was run on it, I'd be alerted, along with several other people."

"I'm not sure if that's a comforting thought or not."

"Pretty much."

"Dinner before we have to go sit in a room all night?" Riley asked. "There has to be a restaurant nearby."

"It won't be fancy," Kaden warned, putting the vehicle into reverse.

"Yeah, kind of figured that when you pulled in here."

"There are advantages to things being a little less glamorous."

"A step or two from rundown is not a little anything," Riley muttered. "And what kind of advantages?"

"The big one for you is that they operate entirely out of the public eye." Kaden pulled out of the parking lot and headed toward the cluster of restaurants.

"And here I thought you were going to say something cheesy like loyalty, honesty, or that they couldn't be bought."

Kaden laughed. "For the right person, those are very real traits. Ones you want in your friends and family.

For strangers like me and you, not so much. And they can easily justify their actions as someone who takes several million dollars."

* * * *

Kaden glanced over at his passenger. Riley had been silent most of the time they'd been out. He hadn't been impressed by the restaurant. Kaden had figured that part out easily enough. Riley hadn't said anything against it, though. He'd eaten what he'd ordered as though he weren't sure when he'd be eating again. Riley's questions had been limited to why a chain restaurant and not a local place and their destination. Kaden had kept his answers as vague and noncommittal as possible.

"Separate beds. Thank God," Riley exclaimed as they walked into the room.

Kaden pushed past him and searched the small room. There were two beds with matching sheets and blankets that looked clean and comfortable. A small table and two matching padded armchairs sat in front of the window. A medium-size flat-screen TV sat atop a dresser. The drawers were empty except a small binder of information pertaining to the surrounding area, a pen, and a notepad with the hotel's name, logo, and address printed on it. A telephone and an alarm clock sat on the nightstand separating the two beds. There was a small closet next to a decent-size bathroom.

"Decorating tips from the seventies?" Riley quipped.

"Cheap motel, cheap linens, cheap furniture. At least everything is clean." Kaden shrugged, holstering his weapon.

"You don't actually have to search every room we enter." Riley dropped his bag on the bed closest to the bathroom.

"It only takes one time."

"Whatever, James. I'm going to shower and sleep."

"How's the pain?"

"On the one-to-ten scale? About an eight and a half. Preacher's pills help. Are they legal to take? Safe?"

"Yes, you'll be fine. Go take a shower."

Kaden waited until he heard the water running before he called his boss.

"What the fuck have you gotten me into, Lawrence?" Kaden demanded as soon as his boss picked up the phone.

"Language."

"Don't 'language' me," Kaden argued. "You've given me far less than you know or I needed to know in order to keep this kid safe from the beginning. Russians. Russian spies. What else do you know?"

"Russians?" Lawrence repeated.

"Don't play with me, Lawrence. I need to know everything you know. Now."

"I don't—"

"Find it. I need to know who's on the field, who's calling the shots, and how long this has been going on."

"Mafia?"

"Doesn't appear to be."

"How do you know it's Russians?" Lawrence pressed.

"Connections you don't have. And aren't going to have. Now, get me what I need to know. This kid may have no choice but to disappear."

"Your job is—"

"My job is to keep him safe. At *any* cost, that is what you said. You handed me a blank check and a nearly empty dossier. I need information. Everything that's available."

"Take him to the safe house," Lawrence said after pausing a moment.

"I need everything you have, Lawrence. If you don't have it, find it. I'll take care of him."

The water turned off and Kaden ended the call. Pulling out his laptop, he plugged in his hotspot and scrambler and began going back over everything he had on Riley and his family. If the Russians were involved, he needed to not only know who was involved, but how and why — and what were they after.

Chapter Seven

Riley stretched, wincing as his body protested. They'd been on the road for three days. They'd been through Nashville, Knoxville, the Smoky Mountains, parts of Virginia, Maryland, and Pennsylvania. Last night they'd left another small motel just outside Hershey, Pennsylvania, at one in the morning. They'd driven until they'd reached someplace in Ohio, where Riley had finally convinced Kaden to pull over and sleep. They'd found another motel and slept for a handful of hours before they'd left, heading northwest through Ohio and into Michigan. No matter how many times he'd asked, Kaden refused to tell him what had spooked him in Pennsylvania.

"Where are we headed?" Riley asked, looking over at Kaden. "I know it's not where you were originally headed, wherever that was."

"Someplace for you to rest."

Riley twisted in the seat. "Can we stop someplace where I can stretch?"

"There aren't any rest stops along this stretch of road. Not until after we cross the bridge."

"Fine, I could use a drink too. And pee."

"Ball cap and jacket."

"Not stupid, *James*. I actually don't have a death wish."

Kaden muttered under his breath as he pulled into the next gas station they came across.

Riley pulled the ball cap down over his head and shrugged into the motorcycle jacket he'd bought in New Orleans. His helmet had been left with Kaden's bike in Preacher's barn. He waited until Kaden turned the truck off before opening the door and into the building. Riley put his bottle of water and a pair of apples he grabbed from a basket of fruit near the checkout counter next to Kaden's protein bar and energy drink.

"This plus forty on pump three." Kaden pulled out his wallet and indicated the black pickup truck.

"Thanks," Riley muttered. He hated it when Kaden bought anything for him. Riley had noticed that Kaden had stopped using his credit card after they left Pennsylvania.

"No problem. Bridge open?"

The woman behind the counter smiled and nodded. "Yep. A bit windy, but not enough to close the bridge."

"Wait, the bridge closes because of wind?" Riley asked in disbelief. Bridges closing because of events and construction he understood, but just because of wind was something he'd never heard of before.

"Yep, and snow and ice. It's the longest suspension bridge in the US and the third-longest in the world," the woman explained, and pointed to a pair of photos on the wall. A black-and-white one of a bridge and one in color showing the same bridge largely encased in ice and snow. "It's not as popular as the Golden Gate Bridge, probably because that's in California."

"We're driving over *that*?" Riley asked. It was fall—there was no snow or ice anywhere. It didn't change the fear that had dropped into his stomach.

Kaden chuckled. "It's safe, don't worry. Come on."

Riley shook his head and followed Kaden out to the truck.

"How many times have you crossed the bridges in New York City and Boston?"

"They never looked like that!" Riley answered, pointing back to the store.

"Most of the time, neither does this one. It will close for snow, ice, and strong winds, but that doesn't happen often."

"Not sure that helps." Riley dropped his stuff in the passenger side of the vehicle before closing the door. "Be right back. Restroom."

Kaden nodded and turned his attention to the pump. Riley saw Kaden pull his phone from his pocket and as he walked back into the building.

Riley wondered how close to James Bond's life Kaden's was. He'd never thought about it before. Everyone knew agencies like the CIA, NSA, and FBI existed, but they were usually seen as just another government agency hoarding secrets and fueling conspiracy theories until they crossed your path. He couldn't be certain that Kaden worked for either agency, but it seemed only slightly more plausible than some super-secret group of rich people hiring other people to save the world and forming their own version of the Justice League. Either way, it was unsettling and didn't give him any answers to Kaden's theory that his family — or at least someone in his family — was a spy.

Kaden was sitting in the truck waiting for him when he climbed back in. Kaden cocked his head to the side. "Everything all right? You're not worried about crossing the bridge, are you?"

Riley shrugged. "I'm still not convinced that you're right about my family."

"It's not just me who thinks there is something off about your family's history."

Riley rubbed the back of his neck. "I know, but you and Preacher are or were probably some sort of black ops guys, who probably saw more than most people would believe."

"What's that supposed to mean?" Kaden asked, pulling out of the gas station.

"It means that maybe you're looking for something that isn't there? You know, maybe it has nothing to do with spying, for the Russians or anywhere else. Maybe whoever first came to America..." Riley paused. The idea that he was descended from immigrants was still weird. "Maybe they weren't spies. Maybe they were running from a crime they committed, or a bad debt, or maybe it was simply because they married someone they weren't supposed to. Hell, it could be because they were the wrong religion."

"That's a lot of maybes."

"It makes way more sense than spies. Why would they still be here? Why not head back home? Wherever home is," Riley asked as they passed a large metal sign warning drivers that it was the last chance to get off the road before they got to the other side of the bridge. "Okay, that's different. They're really serious about this whole bridge thing, aren't they?"

"It's a five-mile long suspension bridge. It's not like you can just turn around or stop."

"Great. Fantastic. So, what else makes you suspect spies instead of something more commonplace? I mean, running away to another country and lying about who you are has to happen way more than spying does. And it explains why we're still here."

"Maybe." Kaden's response was flat and unconvincing as he dug out a five-dollar bill.

Riley pulled his ball cap farther down and huddled into the corner of the cab, burying his face in his jacket. He didn't want to take any chances that a camera would pick up his face. He'd watched enough cop dramas to know that places like toll booths had cameras. He doubted traffic cams happened too much outside of major cities. They were expensive. Kaden paid before pulling out onto the road. Riley held his breath as the vehicle climbed the incline to the bridge.

"So, um, how did you find me?" Riley asked, breaking the silence. If Kaden wasn't willing to talk about his family or why they'd bolted from Pennsylvania, maybe he would answer the question that had been bothering Riley almost since Kaden rescued him from the warehouse.

"What do you mean?"

"How did you find me?"

"Which time?"

"Um, ah, both. Actually."

"Finding you in New Orleans was easy. And would have been easy even if I hadn't been given your location. You post everything on social media. Your hotel. Bars. Restaurants. Checking in everywhere makes you an easy target to find. It also lets everyone know when you won't be home, so they know when it's safe to rob you. You should probably re-think that idea."

"So, I'm learning," Riley bit out. He could feel the wind whip around the truck. Glancing over at Kaden, he swallowed. Kaden's grip on the steering wheel tightened. "This is safe?" He turned his attention to the view of the lake.

"It's—"

"Holy shit! There are holes in the road!" Riley exclaimed, pushing back against the seat. "Why are there holes? That can't be right."

Kaden chuckled. "Relax, they're supposed to be there."

"Why? Why are they there?" Riley demanded, swallowing the welling panic. "You can see the water under us!"

"I'm not an engineer, but my guess is that it's so the bridge moves with the wind. This is the only thing that connects the Lower Peninsula with the Upper Peninsula. Well, unless you want to drive all the way around Lake Michigan through Wisconsin."

"Uh-huh. So, um, so how did you find me in that warehouse?"

"Tracking device."

"I thought you broke my phone so nobody would be able to track me."

"I did. That's not what I was tracking. I planted a tracking device in your jeans at the bar."

"What? How? I didn't feel anything."

"Flash-drive size, you weren't supposed to. But now that you know, keep it on you unless I say otherwise."

"So, you can find me?"

"Yep. Hopefully, it'll only be a few days' inconvenience for you."

"Anything more than that and I'm going to have a lot of explaining to do." Riley shoved a hand through his hair. "I will anyway."

"So does someone in your family. Maybe your grandmother knows something. What do you know about her? What about your grandfather?"

Riley shrugged. "Only what I told you before, that she met my grandfather when she worked for him."

"As a secretary?"

"No." Riley chuckled. "Although, you would think so. No, she was a perfumer."

"A what?" Kaden asked.

"She dealt with scents in perfumes. Was able to travel the world doing it."

"I didn't think you knew anything about your family."

"I don't. Again, female servants and romantic notions. And, I'm not sure what's true and what's not. I do know that one of the labs is named after her. But it's a family company, so that doesn't mean anything," Riley answered.

"And your grandfather?"

"He started the company with his father. They were both chemists. My grandfather was also a businessman. Rumor has it that there was some sort of split between them after my grandfather met my grandmother. Again, according to stories the servants have told and retold."

"How would they know?"

"Some biography that was written about my grandmother for something she was speaking at over Christmas one year. Don't remember which one, and don't care to try and remember. I'd say go ask the household staff about my family, but there's a fair chance they won't say anything."

"Loyalty?"

Riley laughed. "No, confidentiality clause in their contracts. Fired immediately. Loss of any pay and benefits owed or accumulated. And blacklisted."

"Is that even legal?"

"Yep. Commonplace. But Charles' lawyers would win the argument."

"Or bankrupt them if they tried to sue."

Riley shrugged. "We pay well for their services and our privacy." He hated Kaden for disrupting his life, for turning his world with its balance of black and white on its head. Not only was he contending with people who wanted to kidnap him for some unknown reason, but it also forced him to see things he'd never seen before. To question what had always been. Crossing his arms overs his chest, Riley stared out of the window of the truck as they crossed the bridge and blew out a breath. What if Kaden was right? Where did that leave him? If his family was here illegally, did that mean he wasn't an American? What did that make him? The thought of having to live in Russia or really anywhere else turned his stomach. How was he supposed to live in a country where he didn't know the customs, laws, or even the language? Was his trust fund secure or would it be confiscated? Could the government take everything? Riley scrubbed a hand over his face and resettled his ball cap. He didn't see this blowing over quietly. Charles was a brash businessman who used whoever he wanted for whatever he wanted. The company was a success, but Riley knew it had less to do with Charles and more to do with his grandmother's influence. And if he were honest, more to do with how things were running at the ground level. "Jesus, does this thing never end?"

He needed out of the truck. And a few minutes to himself away from Kaden. He doubted Kaden would be willing to let him go anywhere himself, but maybe he could stay about fifty feet away from him, so he at least had the illusion of being alone.

"It's five miles long. Don't worry, we're almost to the other side."

"Great. Tell me we're stopping soon."

"As much as I don't want to, yes."

"Why not stop back there? You know *before* we started over this—this thing. It looks fairly small and inconspicuous. Hardly the place you'd expect someone to hide out in."

Kaden shook his head. "The city we just went through, Mackinaw, the big island over on the right with the huge white building on it, is Mackinac Island, and combined with Fort Michimilimack, Fort Mackinac, and St. Ignace on the other side, it makes up probably the biggest tourist destination in the state. They filmed the movie *Somewhere in Time* on the island."

"Really?" Riley asked, raising his eyebrows.

"Yeah. Best fudge in the state, hell, the best I've ever had, comes from a shop on that island." Kaden grinned.

"Seriously? You don't look like the type."

"What type would that be?"

"You know, the kind that likes sweets or good food."

"There's a lot about me that you don't know."

"I already figured that part out, James, thanks for the reminder," Riley snapped. He turned back to the window and stared at the passing scenery. "Look, I'm sorry. I'm tired. I need to stretch my legs and get out of this fucking car for more than fifteen minutes. Or even eight hours."

Riley looked down as Kaden squeezed his knee. "One more day of traveling, then we'll be at our destination."

"Where? There doesn't look like there's anything up here."

"Not a whole lot, which is the point."

"Great, just great."

"Listen, hotshot, the whole point of this expedition is to keep your ass alive. Not only is it hard for anyone to find you in the middle of nowhere, there are no cameras to catch you, and most importantly, there are way fewer innocent people who could get hurt if it comes down to a shoot-out."

"I get that," Riley shouted. "Running around the country, jumping out of airplanes, or zigzagging through traffic on a motorcycle while chasing bad guys may be your idea of fun, but it's not mine. I didn't ask for this. I'm not a spy or superhero or anything else. I'm tired of being in a car. Tired of being cooped up. Of being in pain. Of not being able to do even a little bit of what I want. And I'm really fucking tired of not knowing who wants me dead and who wants me alive. It's a bit much to take in, especially when you're telling me that I might be related to people who want to spy on the US and that I might be an illegal alien with ties to a country that has a history of killing anyone it doesn't like. What if I lose everything?"

Kaden let out a deep breath. "What if you do lose everything?"

"That's your answer? That's what you have to say? Turn somebody's entire world upside and ask so what?"

"I didn't say 'so what', I said 'what if you do lose everything'," Kaden reiterated as they left the bridge, following signs to downtown St. Ignace. "As in, okay, if the worst happens and you lose everything you have right now, what do you do next? I think it's fairly safe to say that you're an American citizen."

"How can you be sure?"

"Even if your father or one or both of your grandparents or great-grandparents were here illegally, your mother was most likely an American and you were born here in the States. Do you know anything about your mother's side? Her family?" Kaden asked as they pulled into a motel with its vacancy sign lit.

Riley shook his head. "I know her name from my birth certificate. But I've never really looked for them."

"Why not?"

"And get rejected by another family? Yeah, no thanks."

"I'll be right back. Fantasy is better than potential reality?" Kaden parked the truck between a bright-red Porsche and a battered black Chevy Impala and slid out of the cab before Riley could form the right response. It wasn't a question he actually wanted to explore, so he was grateful for Kaden's sudden departure.

Riley took a deep breath and let it out slowly. After motels with little to nothing surrounding them, the small town was different. There were hotels, motels, restaurants, dozens of shops, signs for ferries to the island, and hundreds of people everywhere. Several minutes passed before Kaden reappeared.

"Bless Ace's scrawny ass." Kaden climbed back into the truck.

"Who's Ace and why would you bless him?" Riley asked, turning to look at Kaden. "And why are we staying here and not someplace else? You know, rundown and out of the way. I'm sure there are those types of places here."

Kaden nodded. "Yep, there are. But, I'm exhausted and driving any farther is beyond stupid at the moment. Besides, Bubba here will be nondescript and unassuming next to Cadillacs, Lincolns, and Porsches."

"This place is really that special?"

"It's not exotic, and it doesn't have the appeal of New Orleans or Key West, but it works for some. They shot a movie on the island a few years back." Kaden pulled the keys out of the ignition. "Get your stuff."

"We're parking here? Surrounded by all of these people? After parking in empty lots behind shady motels. Is that smart?"

Kaden shook his head. "No choice. Parking lot is full." Kaden shrugged. "Tourists. Again, it won't stand out. And neither will we."

"So, who's Ace?"

"Just someone I know."

"And why are we blessing them?"

Kaden handed him a key card. "We're in room one twenty-eight. Go ahead and take a shower first then we'll go get something to eat."

Riley nodded, grabbed his bag and slammed the door behind him. He beat Kaden to the room and went straight into the bathroom. He had to admit, this motel was the least offensive of all the ones they'd stayed at so far. It didn't smell like an ashtray or like some sort of orgy had just taken place. He hadn't said anything to Kaden about the rooms—he never did. He knew he smelled things others didn't. There was something to be said for the hotels he usually stayed at. They almost always smelled clean and their linens were the least irritating to his body.

Standing under the water, Riley allowed it to relax his sore body. He was going to have to ask Kaden for a favor. One he knew wasn't going to sit well with the other man. Riley still wasn't sure how hiding out in the woods was going to help them solve who was trying to kill him, even if did keep him safe. He would have to ask Kaden about it. Again. Tension rolled back into his body. Riley finished his shower, dressed, and joined Kaden in the room. Dropping his bag on the free bed, Riley sat down and looked over at the other man, his weapon on the table next to him.

Two queen beds were separated by a nightstand. There was a small combination fridge and microwave next to a large dark wooden armoire that housed a television. The furniture looked like it had been purchased in the last ten years rather than sometime in the seventies. There were lights and an abundance of outlets and a sign proclaiming free Wi-Fi for guests to accompany the plethora of electronics people always seemed to have with them.

"Feel human again?" Kaden asked.

Riley shook his head. "No, but I don't feel like a used tire, so that's an improvement." Riley shrugged and ran his hands through his hair. "So, this Ace person, he's a genius, right?"

"They."

"I thought you said he was one person."

"They are. It's they, not he."

"They?" Riley cocked his head, waiting for something about Kaden's statement to make any amount of sense.

"They. As in not he or she. As in non-binary."

"Oh? That's a real thing?"

"You don't think so?" Kaden asked. Riley could hear tension rising in the soldier's voice.

"No, it's not that." Riley shrugged. "It's just not something I've come across before. Well, not in real life. And everyone knows half of what's on the Internet is bullshit and the other half is highly suspect."

Kaden nodded slightly. "So, what about Ace?"

"They're a genius, right? Since I'm pretty sure you aren't going to let me order anything online, I'm hoping you'll let him, them, I mean. Sorry."

"No, you can't. What do you need?"

"Soap, shampoo, and conditioner."

"What, that's all? There's a grocery store or drug store we can stop at before we get to our destination where we can pick something up for you."

"The stuff I use doesn't have a whole lot of smell to it. It's easier on my senses and it's not available in most stores," Riley admitted. "If it matters, they could create some sort of bill of lading and send it to my house or to Charles to pay."

"Ace is *not* a personal assistant. Mine or anyone else's."

"You said food. Can we eat? Someplace where we can sit down like human beings. Someplace not connected to a gas station."

"Riley—"

"Save the speech, James. Not interested. You made your point. I want to eat, walk along the beach with the illusion that I am actually free and alone, then I want to sleep." Riley held up his hand. "Next time you decide to save someone, find out if they want to be saved." Riley left the motel room without waiting for Kaden to respond.

Chapter Eight

Kaden shoved a hand through his hair. Riley had barely said more than a handful of words to him since dinner last night. He'd spoken more to the waitress at dinner than he had to Kaden all night. Even when they'd gone down to the beach along Lake Huron, Riley had stayed twenty-five feet from him. The younger man had checked to see where Kaden was several times, and spoken to no one except a pair of older women who wanted their photo taken. Kaden had to give Riley props for wearing his ball cap and jacket and keeping a low profile. Some of the questions Riley'd had, Kaden didn't have a good answer for, if any, and other questions were not ones he was comfortable answering.

They had stopped at a grocery store and picked up groceries for a week along with the toiletries that Riley needed. An inordinate amount of time was spent looking through all of the available brands, smelling several before Riley settled on what he wanted. Kaden had started to say something, but stopped, remembering what the younger man was dealing with. Kaden had raised an eyebrow at the earplugs and sleeping mask, but Riley had merely shrugged. The younger man had stood aside and let Kaden pay for everything himself. The extent of his explanation had amounted to, "Not my choice, not my responsibility."

Kaden pulled to a stop on the side of a dirt road. "I assume you can drive."

Riley nodded. "And?"

"Slide over. I'm going to open the gate. When I do, I want you to drive through."

He climbed down from the truck and Riley slid over. Ten minutes later they pulled into the barn behind a small cabin.

"This is it?" Riley asked, disbelief lacing his voice.

"Two bedrooms, kitchen, living room, and bathroom on fifteen acres."

"Fantastic. Does it actually have running water and electricity?" Riley snapped, grabbing his backpack and a bag of groceries.

"Amazingly enough, it does."

Kaden unlocked the door to the cabin and led the way in. He searched the building room by room while Riley set the bag of groceries down on the kitchen counter. "Let me give you the tour."

"I don't get the impression you live here."

"I don't." Kaden shook his head.

"Then how is this not cobweb central?"

"I have a service come in bi-weekly to clean and make sure nothing is damaged or broken," Kaden explained. He showed Riley the cabin and pointed out his room before they finished unloading groceries.

* * * *

An hour later, Kaden found Riley sitting on the back deck.

"There you are."

Riley jumped to his feet. "Seriously? We're a thousand miles from anyone. There are trees all the way around. You can't see the house from the road and even if you could, you can't see the back deck." Riley yanked the ball cap off and threw it on the ground. "If you were just going to keep me in a cell like a prisoner, then you could've done that in the city. Taken me to whoever wants me safe and left me there. Or left me where you found me. Because right now, whoever wants me alive is no different than whoever wants me dead. And you, you're the same as they are. A hired thug meant to keep me under lock and key."

"That's not—"

Riley stomped into the house and into his room, slamming doors behind him.

* * * *

Three days passed in uneasy silence. Kaden made dinner at night, leaving Riley's on the counter. He left the younger man to his own devices for lunch and breakfast. As far as roommates went, Riley wasn't bad. He was quiet, kept to himself, always ate standing at the counter, washed his dishes, and never used all the hot water. That was the extent of the interaction Kaden had had with the other man since the day they arrived. He hadn't even had a chance to explain what he'd meant.

Kaden was just finishing his dinner when Riley walked into the kitchen. Kaden swallowed as Riley stood at the counter with his back to him. The other man hadn't worn more than a pair of silk boxers since they arrived. A lean, athletic body had been hidden under the baggy clothes. Riley was not the type of man that Kaden usually found himself attracted to. He was reasonably sure he could chalk the attraction up to close quarters, or the fact that Riley was practically nude all of the time, but there was no way to explain the spark of attraction Kaden had felt the first time he'd seen Riley's photograph, before Kaden had left for New Orleans.

"You can sit at the table to eat, you know. I don't bite," Kaden said, trying to make it sound like an invitation.

Riley turned around, his plate in his hand. "Isn't it customary for prisoners to eat by themselves?" Riley snapped. Every trace of vulnerability Kaden had seen before had disappeared. He leaned against the counter and started to eat.

"Oh, for heaven's sake, you're not a prisoner!" Kaden slammed his silverware onto the table.

"Really? I can't go where I want. I can't see who I want. I can't have the things that make my life a bit easier. I certainly can't *do* what I want. So, that actually makes me a prisoner," Riley spat.

"Brat," Kaden muttered under his breath.

"What was that?" Riley demanded.

Kaden swore. He'd forgotten about Riley's superior hearing. "You heard me."

"Yeah, so have the balls to say it to my face instead of under your breath," Riley shouted, tossing his plate and fork on the counter.

"You're acting like a brat." Kaden pushed his chair back and jumped to his feet.

"Yep, absolutely." Riley stepped forward. "Because I'm demanding unreasonable information like who wants me dead. Who claims to want me alive. Who you actually are. Who you work for. Why anyone believes my family, whose company had benefits for military and veterans in place before it was popular, by the way, are spies or were spies. I'm absolutely a brat because I want to know where I am. How long I have to be here. Why hiding out in the woods, where I can't even go outside, is going to get any of the answers needed. Yes, that absolutely makes me a brat."

Kaden held up a hand.

"You want to take a swing at me. Go ahead, James," Riley spat. "Like I care. You're a thug for hire. A cage is a cage is a cage. I have a life to get back to. Playing hide and seek in the woods is your idea of fun, not mine. I want nothing to do with this crap."

"You prefer a gold-gilded palace?" Kaden shot.

"Yeah, gaudy isn't my grandmother's taste. Too ostentatious."

Kaden grabbed Riley's arm to keep him from leaving. Riley turned and stepped forward, closing the distance between them. Twisting his arm, he broke Kaden's hold. Riley's other hand shot forward, his thumb pressed against Kaden's windpipe. The self-defense move was unexpected. Kaden didn't move. He wanted to see what Riley would do.

"Do. Not. Touch. Me," Riley seethed. His green eyes flashed. Kaden saw everything the man was trying to hide. The sanity he was hanging onto by a thread. Pain commingled with confusion. "I'm your assignment, not a boyfriend or lover. Your hands do not ever belong on me."

Riley loosened his grip, turned and walked away, disappearing down the hall. Kaden stood where he was until he trusted himself enough to move. He was angry with both himself and Riley. He wasn't sure who he was angrier at. In the end, it didn't matter because Riley had raised questions that he didn't have the answers to. Ones he'd begun to ask himself.

After taking several deep breaths, Kaden made himself move, distracting himself from the torrent of his thoughts with cleaning up from dinner. Looking over at the chair he'd occupied most of the day since their arrival, and the laptop with everything Ace had discovered, Kaden swore and headed down to the guest bedroom he'd given Riley. He knocked on the bedroom door several times and warred with himself before he decided to walk into the room.

Kaden stopped and swallowed. Riley lay in the middle of the bed, completely naked. Kaden's cock hardened slightly. He cleared his throat. If he was honest it was only partly to get Riley's attention. Mostly it was to keep from sounding like he was still going through puberty. When Riley didn't respond, Kaden crept forward until he saw Riley's earplugs and the sleep mask he wore.

Kaden swore again and tried to figure out the best way to approach Riley. Kaden didn't want to scare him, but he was equally certain there was no choice. In the end, he lightly touched the top of Riley's knee before jumping backward.

Riley scrambled back, ripping off the mask and taking out the earplugs. "What the hell? Don't you knock?"

"I did. Plus tried to get your attention when I walked in," Kaden countered. "Why are you naked?"

Riley shrugged and looked at the small pieces of plastic and foam. "These work great. I'm going to have to get more of these."

"Um," Kaden cleared his throat, "put something on and come into the living room when you get a chance."

* * * *

Kaden was sitting in the easy chair when Riley walked out of the bedroom, this time in his sleep pants and a T-shirt. "Sit. Please."

Riley nodded and sat on the far end of the couch.

"I'm going to answer what I can, but there are going to be some things I can't answer because it could get me fired or killed. Hell, even telling you what I'm going to could get me fired." Kaden rubbed the back of his neck. "But first, tell me what's going on."

"Nothing I can't handle."

"I didn't ask that. I asked what's going on. Why the nudity?"

"I stay in my room. I'm not allowed to do what I want in there?"

Kaden took a deep breath and let it out slowly. "I don't care what you do in your room. I don't care if you sit out in the living room or on the back deck. Part of the reason for coming this far north is that no one knows this place is here. At least no one I don't want to know. That means you can walk outside if you want. Now, if there is a reason for being nude other than you want to, I need to know."

"My senses are overwhelmed by everything," Riley said finally. "I'm trying to keep the irritation down as much as possible."

"Is this common?"

"Sort of." Riley shrugged. "Stress makes things worse. Little things add up. I'll be fine."

"And the self-defense moves? You didn't use those on your attackers."

"I was drunk, well, buzzed. Nicely buzzed and on my way to drunk. And they surprised me."

Kaden nodded, willing to take Riley at his word. "Okay, some of what I'm going to tell you may or may not be new. I'm not going to tell you who I work for. What I will tell you is that I was assigned to keep you alive at all costs with a blank check, which rarely happens. I already told you that I suspect that your family or someone in your family is spying for another government, or was. And most likely the Russians."

"Why Russians?" Riley asked. "Doesn't the US have a lot of enemies?"

"Enough, yes. You have to look when your family would have come over and what the political climate was at the time, not just here in America, but around the world. Our biggest enemy at the time was Russia. Both countries were racing to build atomic weapons. None of our other enemies were as close at that point. World War II had decimated most of Europe and the South Pacific, including Japan."

"So, why spies? Why not anything else?"

"Now, I hadn't gotten this far into your family's history when we left New Orleans," Kaden said, shoving a hand through his hair. He wanted to give Riley the Hollywood ending that he wanted to the story, but he couldn't. There was no way. "This was buried pretty deep, but it looks like your grandmother's father was a chemical engineer of some sort. He was working on one of the government's top-secret projects. One of his sons was a nuclear physicist working for the government, and the other was a chemist who worked for the government before working for a pharmaceutical company. If they were hiding their identities because of religion or possible criminal behavior, they wouldn't have been able to produce the needed degrees or pass the background checks required to work in those programs."

"My grandmother has brothers?" Riley asked in disbelief. "Why doesn't she ever talk about them?"

"I take it you didn't know about them then?"

Riley shook his head.

"There is more. Your grandfather's older brother also worked on the atomic bomb, as did his father after he left the company he founded. A sister worked in an administrative capacity for the program." Kaden took a drink of water from his water bottle, giving Riley a moment to digest what he was saying. "Are there any photographs of your grandparents when they were younger with people you don't know?"

Riley laughed. "Maybe. I've never seen any, though. I mean, we're not exactly a normal family. There are no walls of pictures of families or family portraits. Charles has a portrait he had painted of himself hanging in his home office. There are portraits of my grandparents and Charles that hang in the lobby at the company headquarters. Other than that, I don't know. I don't generally go into my grandmother's or Charles' offices, and never into their bedrooms if I can help it." Riley drew up a knee. "Do any of their siblings have kids?"

Kaden nodded. "Yes. Children and grandchildren."

"I don't get it. Why wouldn't they talk about them? I mean, I guess I can see why my grandmother wouldn't talk about my grandfather's family, he passed away years ago. But nothing was ever said about other family members." Riley picked at the hem of his sleep pants. "You know, when I was younger, maybe five or so, I remember asking her why I didn't have any cousins like my friends did. I think I remember one of the kids I was friends with at the time had like twenty or so. I was jealous. He had this huge extended family and it was only ever me."

"What did she say?" Kaden asked, closing the laptop and leaning forward.

"That neither she nor my grandfather were lucky enough to have siblings," Riley replied. "At least, I think that's what she said. I think I asked her what 'sibling' meant and couldn't pronounce it correctly, and she changed the subject. I want to say she was sort of sad when she said that. But I don't remember. Hell, I don't know why I'm remembering it now. I didn't before."

Kaden shrugged. "Memory is a strange thing. The brain is still one of the greatest mysteries of all."

"The assholes who kidnapped me before, what do they think I have?" Riley asked, getting up and pouring himself a glass of water. "I don't have any sort of key."

"That part I don't know. The notes I have say there's a lot more information that's considered classified."

"What the hell does that mean?"

"It means I have to go meet my boss."

"Wait, we're leaving here?"

Kaden shook his head. There was no way he was ready to produce Riley yet. "I'm going. Alone."

"Isn't that dangerous?"

"The most important part is you not leaving this property until I come back."

"How long do you plan on being gone and why wouldn't you bring me? Especially to talk to your boss."

"Three days."

"So why can't I go?"

Kaden raised an eyebrow, wondering if Riley would figure it out on his own.

"You don't trust them, do you?"

"Bingo. Besides if you show up, all leverage to finding out the truth is gone."

"So, I'm still a pawn."

Kaden nodded. "Until this is over. The only difference is who controls your moves and why." He felt bad for the kid, but he didn't see any other options and he didn't want Riley anywhere nearby when he confronted Lawrence about everything he and Ace had found. With Riley's whereabouts unknown, it also gave Kaden a slight edge to walking out of the encounter alive. While there had never been a reason to doubt Lawrence, there was almost no possibility of long-term spies staying in the United States for any length of time without help. Especially a family as public as the Hamiltons were. There was still the unanswered question of who had handed the case to Lawrence, not to mention exactly why Kaden had been chosen.

"So what's the plan?" Riley asked, taking a deep breath. "You do have a plan, don't you?"

"There's a plan and a back-up plan, but it still may come down to me making it up as I go along," Kaden explained. "I'll drive down across the bridge and fly into Chicago for a connecting flight, then what should be a short meeting and a flight back."

"So why three days then?"

"I plan on getting in early and leaving later, and traveling back in a roundabout manner."

"What happens if you don't make it back? I can't stay here. I can't stay here permanently anyway, but seriously, what if everything goes sideways?" Riley asked, walking over to the window.

"Ace will know how to find you."

"And Ace will protect me?"

Kaden laughed and shook his head. "They would try, but no. They would arrange to get you back to your family. And hire a bodyguard."

"Not someone like Preacher, I hope."

"While that actually would be something Ace would do in order to try and push a button or three of mine, they wouldn't under those kinds of circumstances."

Riley nodded, but Kaden could tell he wasn't convinced.

"I leave in the morning." Kaden stood, placed a hand on Riley's shoulder, and gently squeezed. "For what it's worth, I'm sorry your world has been turned upside down."

"Um, thanks. You don't think this is going to end well, do you?"

"I think that there is no way that you will be the same person at the end of this — or that your family will be the same. Whether we succeed or not."

"Not succeeding means I'm dead, so let's skip that part." Riley turned from the window.

"Keeping you alive is only one part of the equation. The rest depends on who wants you dead. Keeping you alive and out of danger will depend on exposing them and taking appropriate action," Kaden answered. "I'm not going to lie to you, a bodyguard, or even two, may become a very real necessity at all times."

"For how long? How high can this go? And what is 'appropriate action'?" Riley asked, nerves straining his voice.

"Possibly for the rest of your life." Kaden squeezed Riley's shoulder again and walked into the kitchen.

Kaden was looking through their supplies when Riley went out of the back door. He didn't like the idea of leaving Riley at the cabin on his own. He wanted the other man where he could see him, where he could protect him. Riley in the same city was what Lawrence would be expecting. He would want to have proof that Riley was still alive. Kaden walked into his bedroom and packed his duffel bag. Picking up a holstered HK45 and the pieces of a phone, he checked the magazine, grabbed a second one, and joined Riley on the back deck.

"Do you know how to use a gun?" Kaden asked, handing the firearm to the other man.

Riley shrugged and straightened up. "Point and shoot."

"Cute." Kaden sat the phone on the table between two of the chairs. He pointed out the magazine release button, magazine, trigger, safety, and the sights before showing Riley how to use the sites to aim the gun. "You need to chamber a round before you shoot. This is the slide, grip it like this and pull back." Kaden showed Riley how to grip the slide and pull it back. "Aim for the torso. Hold the gun straight up and down, don't try anything like you see on TV or in the movies. There will be a recoil. Shoot. Reset yourself, shoot again." Handing the gun to Riley, he had the younger man repeat what he'd shown him.

"Why are you telling me all of this? Which, by the way, is more instruction than what you gave me at Preacher's."

"Preacher's was more heat of battle. This is different. Keep it with you always. I never have any visitors. I'm not working with anyone. And anyone that Ace sends will say that Ace sent them."

"Do you think someone will find us up here? There's literally nothing for miles."

"Sparsely populated is still populated. No one knows I own this place. No one should know who Ace is and my connection to them. Should and could are two different things and I don't want to take any chances."

"Great, just great."

"Let's practice a bit. That way you can get a feel for how the gun handles." Kaden grabbed two boxes of earplugs out of a drawer and led the way to a small range. "Put these in. Aim for the bullseye, pretend it's center mass."

Riley rolled his eyes and fit ear plugs into his ears. He aimed and squeezed the trigger. A small hole appeared in the upper left-hand corner of the paper target.

"Nice." Kaden smiled and showed him how to aim using the sights. Riley shot again. This time the shot was in the outside circle. He shot both magazines with Kaden helping him correct his aim. Riley was proud of his accomplishments. Most of the shots from the last magazine were in the middle. Not bullseyes, but it was close enough.

"Now, straight back off the corner of the house, at forty-five degrees, there's a small shack. You can hide there if you need to." Kaden pointed to a building nearly hidden in the trees.

"Wouldn't it be better if I came with you? Someplace where I'm not stranded and you're not a day of traveling away?"

Kaden rubbed the back of his neck. "This is the best option."

"That is not inspiring hope for success, Kaden," Riley quipped, walking back into the house.

"I'll be back in three days, then we'll decide what to do from there."

"So what is the phone for?"

"Put it together only if you need to, and at nine in the morning the day after tomorrow. At noon or after I call, take it apart."

"Is it traceable?"

"No."

"Then why take it apart?"

"Safety."

Riley shook his head. "No, see if I need it in an emergency, it's going to take extra time for me to put it together. And if I panic, I'm really not going to be able to put it together."

"I don't foresee anything happening or you panicking."

Riley shrugged. "It could happen."

"Aliens landing could also happen."

Riley laughed. "I think they already did. Area 51. You have heard of that, haven't you?"

Kaden chuckled.

"Wait, why from nine to noon?" Riley asked, all traces of humor gone. "To prove I'm alive, right?"

Kaden nodded.

"Don't they trust you?"

"They do. But, I'm not ready to hand you over to anyone without knowing exactly who's behind this."

"Do you think they aren't who they say they are or someone else isn't?"

"I think that any family with questionable origins can't stay hidden in the United States for decades without help. And, no, I'm not ruling out a double agent."

"More spy shit. Why am I even involved in this? I am not a spy. Charles is not a spy. My grandmother is not a spy."

"Are you sure?"

"About Charles and my grandmother?" Riley stood and walked to the edge of the deck. "Yes. Charles runs the business. He can do that. Get into and out of countries or places without attracting attention, yeah, that never happens. He likes attention. My grandmother travels in style and isn't going gallivanting all over Europe or the Middle East. Certainly not in khakis, boots, and covered in a layer of dirt."

"Do either of them hunt or shoot?"

"My grandmother thinks guns are uncouth and barbaric. Charles golfs, but I don't think he's ever shot a gun. As far as I know, we don't have any at the house."

"Not even trap shooting?

"No. You can't seriously suspect Charles or my grandmother of being spies?"

"I think there is a lot more that is unknown than is known at the moment."

* * * *

"Coffee?" Kaden asked, walking into the kitchen the next morning. "I didn't know you —"

"I can microwave food and I know how to work a coffee machine, antiquated as it is. A man cannot live on beer alone." Riley sat at the kitchen table, sipping coffee. "I make no promises about taste or quality. I still prefer to buy mine from the coffee shop near campus. Good coffee and the best pastries."

"Peace gesture?" Kaden grabbed a mug from the cabinet and filled it halfway.

Riley shrugged. "Do not forget me."

Kaden took a tentative sip. "Hmm. Not bad. Better than military coffee, so you're good."

"I'm not sure that's a compliment. I've heard that stuff walks around on its own."

"Damn near." Kaden filled his cup the rest of the way.

"Seriously. Do not forget me here. Stranded and left to die a thousand miles from anywhere is not the future I want."

"I won't," Kaden promised. "Have you thought—"

"I still think you're nuts. No way anyone in my family is a spy. Maybe one of them is descendent from that one Tsar, Romanov. You know, an illegitimate kid."

Kaden quirked an eyebrow. "An illegitimate prince or princess?"

"Sure, why not? It's a well-known fact that male leaders are rarely faithful to their wives. How many affairs and illegitimate kids did the kings of France and England have? Maybe Romanov had an affair with some staff woman, then once the Romanovs were killed, she ran. Made for Germany or Poland or something. Maybe she was Jewish. Acquired new identities, maybe found a man who just lost a wife and had a kid or two of his own. Made a business deal.

Immigrated as a happy family. No one is the wiser. Especially if you pay the right people the right amount." Riley stood and refilled his mug.

"Maybe."

"It's a possibility. How did you come up with that?"

Riley shrugged. "When are you leaving?"

Kaden looked at his watch. "Fifteen minutes."

"Don't forget about me or I will spend the rest of my life doing everything I can to screw yours up in every possible way." Riley turned and walked out of the back door.

Chapter Nine

Kaden grabbed his hands behind his back and raised them, trying unsuccessfully to release the growing tension. Riley had been awake when Kaden had walked out of his bedroom yesterday morning and coffee waiting. He'd been surprised by the gesture. There were layers to Riley, more than anyone thought or had cared to discover. Some carefully constructed, others haphazardly thrown together. Sarcasm, humor, and distraction were tools the younger man used to keep people where he wanted them, allowing them to see only what he choose. Riley had ordered Kaden to not forget him, or he would find multiple ways to screw him over for decades to come. Kaden had nodded at the demand, not bothering to remind his charge that if he didn't return, there was little chance of revenge being necessary. There was no way to screw up a dead man's life.

* * * *

Taking a drink from a water bottle, Kaden watched a black SUV back into the only open parking spot in the parking deck. A handful of minutes later, a middle-aged white man with a shock of dark-brown hair and dressed in jeans, work boots, and a flannel shirt, exited the vehicle and made his way out of the garage. With a quick check for traffic, he crossed the street and ducked into a small coffee shop. Just as Kaden was about to move, a pair of police cars parked across the street.

"Damn it."

Kaden shifted his weight, silently wishing he'd been able to bring his gun. In general, he didn't believe in coincidences, nor did he completely trust the man he was about to meet. He took another drink of water and watched the officers walk into a nearby Greek Restaurant. Blowing out a breath, he tossed the half-full bottle into the nearby trash can before moving quickly across the busy street. He'd scoped out the entire area before contacting Lawrence, choosing the popular coffee shop, knowing it would be busy. He spotted his target before opening the doors and stepped in line.

Dropping change into the tip jar, he took his latte and breakfast sandwich over to the table where the driver of the SUV sat. "Morning." Kaden sat down in the empty chair.

"You look like a bum. Jesus, Tennison," Russell Lawrence said, the slight lift in his voice giving away his surprise. "You're early."

"So are you." Kaden smiled and sipped the chocolate and coffee concoction.

"Why here? Like this? Where's the kid?" Lawrence demanded.

"Kid is safe."

"I need proof."

Kaden set the cup down and leaned back. "I need answers. All of them."

"I told you everything I know."

"No, you told me what you wanted me to know. Two different things. Proof is the fact that you're sitting in front of me and not in your office."

"That's—"

Kaden held up a hand. "Save it. I'm not interested. Who is this kid? Because whoever is after him has some very deep pockets."

"How deep?"

"Deep enough to hire a tail that could fly from the house he shares with some friends near Yale down to New Orleans with almost no notice. The price to buy a ticket for a flight with less than a few hours' notice is astronomical and not an option for most people. As in, bought while sitting at the airport. And to hire two local thugs who know how to grab someone and hide them while waiting for instructions."

"He's the son of an important businessman."

"No, he's not," Kaden replied. "Charles Hamilton is a wealthy businessman, but not one the Company or the government would actually care about. They make and sell perfume and cologne. Not weapons, pharmaceuticals, or anything that is actually of use to anyone outside of attracting someone for sex or romance or some such bullshit."

"Did they catch him?" Lawrence asked, concern resonating in his voice.

"I barely got there in time." Kaden nodded. "Whatever you know I need to know. Starting with why there is no real history to either side of this family. His mother is dead and he has no interaction with her family. He's never even met them." Kaden leaned across the table. "What do you know?"

"I have no idea what you're talking about."

"This kid is going to die because you can't figure out what is more important, giving me the information I need to actually do my job or covering your ass!" Kaden spat.

"Watch yourself. You're operating outside your scope." Lawrence threatened.

Kaden smiled, leaned back in the chair, and nodded. He had suspected as much.

"I need proof he's alive," Lawrence demanded.

"I need more information."

"Proof."

Kaden hesitated a long moment before he pulled out a phone and dialed a number. "Riley?" Kaden asked when Riley finally answered.

"James, so nice of you to call. I—"

"There's someone here who needs to speak to you." Kaden interrupted the younger man, hoping Riley wouldn't give anything away. Kaden pushed the speaker button.

"RJ?" Lawrence asked, reaching for the phone.

Kaden pulled the phone back. "It's on speaker. Go ahead."

"Is this RJ?"

"Who are you?"

"That's non of your concern," Lawrence replied.

"It's *my* life." Riley demanded, anger punctuated every word "If you're so interested in keeping me alive, why don't you show yourself? I have broken ribs because of something you know and someone else thinks I know."

"Are you safe?" Lawrence asked.

"Did you miss the part about the broken ribs, asshole? I'm pissed. I'm tired of whatever game you're playing."

"It's not a game, son—"

"I. Am. Not. Your. Son," Riley seethed. "Obviously, someone thinks it's a game, otherwise I would have spent my trip with a bevy of hot, horny women and not double-oh-asshole. Are we done yet?"

"RJ—"

"Dude, seriously, if you're not going to tell me what I need to know, I have no use for you. Figure out why someone wants me dead and either kill them or arrest them. I don't care which. Later."

The line went dead. Kaden turned the phone off and shoved it in his pocket.

"Well, isn't he delightful?" Lawrence asked, sipping his coffee.

Kaden leaned back in the chair. "Why did you call him RJ?"

"That's his name." Lawrence shrugged.

"It's a nickname. One his friends call him. Not one I used," Kaden stated. Lawrence shifted uncomfortably. "Don't move. Keep your hands where I can see them," Kaden ordered.

"You can't believe—"

"I think there are more unanswered questions than there are answers. And you're not *willing* to divulge any of them. You obviously spoke to someone with first-hand information, as his nickname isn't in the file. So, let me give you a hint. I will use whatever means I have to in order to keep this kid alive. Not only do these people have some seriously deep pockets, they will buy or kill whoever is needed in order to get what they want. They think he has something. I need to know his importance. And who he's important to. Who has those kinds of resources? Who wants this kid dead?"

"Any number of people."

"Quit being obtuse, Lawrence. An individual or business isn't going to try to kill some rich kid who spends most of his time drunk. That leaves government, organized crime, or another country," Kaden replied. "I'm betting on the latter."

"Why would another country be after one of our citizens who, like you said, spends most of his time drunk?"

"Go ask your source. You have a week. Possibly less. Even drunk kids don't voluntarily walk away from vacations." Kaden slid a folded piece of paper across the table to Lawrence.

"What is this?"

"Find out who these men are. Isaac Richardson is from the Midwest and Carmine Russo is from Brooklyn. These are the men, along with a man named Drake and another man, also from New Orleans, who kidnapped Riley. See if there is any connection to a Mikail Ivanovich."

"Did you even try to interview them?"

Kaden shrugged. "Isaac, aka Ike, killed the men from New Orleans."

"That's sloppy."

"Take it up with them." Kaden shrugged again. "Drug deal gone bad." Kaden stood. "A week. Less. I'll be in touch." Kaden turned and left the coffee shop. He had no intention of telling Lawrence that the phones and wallets had been sent to Ace to see what they could make of them before they were to be sent to Lawrence for further processing.

Turning left, he walked past several stores before ducking into a Subway. Pushing his way through the line of people, he walked down the short hallway and out of the back door, removing the grubby black-and-gray hooded sweatshirt as he did. Kaden tossed the sweatshirt behind some bushes and ran down the alley to the main street. He made it in time to see Lawrence cross the road and head back to the parking deck. The man was on the phone and looked angry. Kaden swore silently. He'd give anything to listen in on the older man's conversation. Blowing out a breath, Kaden watched until Lawrence pulled out of the parking deck then headed in the opposite direction.

Kaden took a circuitous route back to his hotel. He searched his room, ensuring it hadn't been entered and nothing had been tampered with or stolen. He'd taken the extra precaution of booking and checking into two hotels with the credit card his boss knew about, and staying in a third that he'd paid with a pre-paid Visa gift card. Grabbing his gear, he left the room, stopping at the main desk long enough to check out. He had a two-and-a-half-hour drive to the airport in order to catch his flight into Traverse City. From there he would drive back to the cabin. He didn't foresee any problems. He hadn't seen a tail and he'd been looking. He hoped to get in and out of the city without anyone noticing.

Kaden left the hotel and made his way across the parking lot. It was mid-afternoon on a weekday and the area was deserted. It didn't surprise him, but something was off. Opening the back door of the SUV, he tossed his duffel bag onto the backseat, hoping to catch a glimpse of whoever else may be in the parking lot.

The crunch of boots coming from his right caught Kaden's attention. He saw the barrel of the gun out of the corner of his eye. Turning, he reached for the gun and pulled. The weapon flew from the man's hand, skittered across the top of a gold sedan and down the other side. Twisting as he pulled, Kaden felt the bones in the man's wrist pop. The man howled and stumbled into view and into the side of the car. He was dressed in baggy blue jeans, a black T-shirt, and black boots. The man turned and swung, catching Kaden across the jaw.

Kaden took a step back and shifted his weight to his right leg. He balled his fists, jumped, and kicked, connecting with the attacker's solar plexus. The move sent the man stumbling backward into the middle of the parking lot. Kaden followed the attacker, intent on getting the information he desperately needed. The man shook his head and rushed forward. Kaden jumped, spun, and kicked the man in the head, sending him backward into a work truck, his head bouncing off the metal objects before he slid to the ground. Creeping forward, Kaden hoped to find some form of identification, something that would give him an idea of who he was up against.

A bottle clinked against a concrete parking block. Kaden stopped and turned toward the sound. He watched a second man approach. There was a large detailed tattoo of a knife with a cross as the hilt, piercing the skin inked all in black with the exception of a spot of red indicating blood dripping from the bottom of the blade on the forearm of the attacker. Kaden waited for the other man to make the first move. It allowed him to study his opponent, to decide if he was angry on behalf of his friend or if they were following someone else's orders. The man drew a knife, lining it up along his forearm. The move was one Kaden knew well. It meant the other man had training. Those who didn't usually attacked with the blade pointed out, using wide motions that were easy to block and disarm. The pair circled each other. Kaden waited for the man to make a move or a mistake.

The man feinted right then left before he lunged forward. Kaden moved to block the attack. The blade cut into his arm. Kaden sprang forward, kicked the man in the stomach and jumped back. The blade came at him again. Kaden used the man's motion against him, capturing the man's wrist and turning it the opposite way, causing his attacker to release the blade. Kaden released his grip and kicked the man's ribs, sending him stumbling across the parking lot.

The man found his footing and rushed forward. Kaden blocked swing after swing, taking a shot to the gut before he made contact with the attacker's jaw. The two men traded blows until Kaden's attacker finally staggered back and fell to the ground. When the man didn't move, Kaden knelt and dug through the man's pockets. Rocking back onto the balls of his feet, he'd just opened a familiar black wallet when a gun barrel entered his line of sight. The gunman motioned for him to back away with the barrel. Kaden shifted his weight, balancing on his right foot. His left leg kicked out, sweeping the other man off his feet. Kaden jumped to his feet, putting distance between them. He found himself back between his truck and the gold sedan.

The gunman swore and scrambled to his feet. "Fuck this." He leveled his weapon and opened fire. Pain exploded in Kaden's chest and head.

Chapter Ten

Gravel cut into Kaden's cheek. He opened his eyes. His head throbbed. His whole body ached. Darkness had fallen. Kaden swore silently. He strained to hear anything that might let him know if anyone was nearby. Carefully, he maneuvered out from under the vehicle, taking careful inventory of his body. Aside from the pain in his head, his ribs and chest hurt. The knife wound was caked with blood and dirt, but had dried at some point.

He checked his pockets and the rented SUV and swore. His disposable phone was missing. The keys to the SUV were under the car still parked in the next space. The duffel bag had been rifled through. Kaden searched the spare tire and retrieved his phone and wallet with the fake credit cards, family pictures, and identification. He stripped off the extra layers of flannel and sweatshirts before removing the bulletproof vest and shoving it into his bag. He put the phone together and called Riley, praying the man answered.

Kaden started the truck and swore again when he got voicemail. "Run! Hide! Don't trust anyone. I'm coming," Kaden yelled into the phone before throwing the truck in reverse and speeding out of the parking lot. He'd missed his flight, but hopefully he could catch the next one and make it back to Traverse City tonight.

Sitting at a stoplight, Kaden dialed Lawrence's phone number, swearing impatiently.

"Tennison, I didn't expect to hear from you so soon," Lawrence said politely.

"Tell me you had people following me. That they have orders to get Riley back at all costs."

"Thought about it, but no. Unlike you, I trust you."

Kaden guffawed. "No, you knew I'd make them as soon as I saw them."

"So, what happened?"

"We could be screwed seven ways from Sunday." Kaden stomped on the gas, zigzagging through traffic. Lawrence's hesitation in having someone tailing him was less about trust and more about his current assignment. He wondered if his mission was even sanctioned.

"Why?"

"I was jumped. Two, possibly three. They have the phone I called Riley on earlier and they left me under my own truck. Since I wasn't tied up and I'm obviously not dead, they were probably interrupted."

"What?"

"Yeah. Also, one of them was carrying an FBI badge."

"Are you sure?"

"Saw it right before a gun was shoved in my face." Kaden swore and changed lanes.

"Get a name? Description?"

"The one with the badge was white, about five-foot ten inches, one hundred and eighty-five pounds, brown hair, green eyes. Has a large, mostly black tattoo of a cross piercing the skin on the forearm with blood dripping down. The other guy looked Asian, black hair and eyes, hair little more than stubble, six-foot, two hundred and twenty pounds or so. Never actually saw a third guy, but the Asian bounced his head off the concrete, so it's possible – unlikely, but possible – he recovered."

"Was he there when you woke up?"

"No, and I'm not surprised."

"You do know what you're saying, don't you?" Lawrence asked.

"I'm saying that I was jumped by someone possessing what looked like an FBI badge. I didn't get a chance to find out if the badge was stolen, faked, or authentic."

"Did it look fake?"

Kaden shoved his hand through his hair as he pulled into the airport car rental spot. "No, it didn't. It looked real. Keep me posted on what you find. See if you can figure out how they know about me. I'm not buying some sort of mistaken identity bullshit."

Kaden turned the rental car in then argued with the airline agent for twenty minutes, barely making the last flight into O'Hare. There were no more flights into the Cherry Capital Airport until tomorrow morning, nothing more could be done tonight. Anger and frustration fought for dominance as he strode through the airport. Kaden swore at the long line of people waiting to clear security. He chose the last line on the right and hoisted his duffel onto the belt. Stepping out of his shoes, he placed them next to the bag, certain that the vest would set the sensors off. Kaden shoved a hand through his hair. There was nothing that could be done. He didn't dare leave it where local law enforcement could find it. That would be nearly as bad as bringing Riley to this meeting would have been. There wasn't enough time to mail it or dispose of it. Rolling his shoulders, Kaden turned his thoughts to his attackers. He hadn't been followed. So, either Lawrence had had him followed or someone was either tracking Lawrence's movements or intercepting his phone calls. Or both.

The machine beeped. Kaden and the bag were ushered over to the side. Kaden grabbed his shoes and followed the TSA agent, prepared to argue if needed.

"You should use more care when traveling with souvenirs." Dez rifled through the duffel bag.

Kaden raised an eyebrow and dropped his gaze to Dez's name tag. The name read Tyrone Johnson. "New job?"

Dez shrugged, his voice low. "Keeps me busy and out of trouble. Caught Anne cheating with Cornwell and Kennedy. At the same time."

"Holy shit!" Kaden shook his head. He hadn't spoken with either man in years. Kennedy had been dishonorably discharged for dealing and using cocaine. "I'm sorry to hear that, man."

"Yeah, well, she turned out to be a piece of work. Do you remember that miscarriage she had while we were deployed?"

Kaden nodded. He remembered. The news had devasted the other man to the point where they had all been worried for his sanity and safety, afraid he might try something stupid or permanent. Or both.

"Never happened."

"What? You can't be serious?"

Dez nodded. "She lied about being pregnant."

"What the fuck, man?" Kaden clenched and unclenched his fists. Anne had gotten Preacher and a couple of the wives to help her surprise Dez with the news. "That is seriously fucked up."

"Yep. All came out when she asked for alimony and half of my retirement. One of the wives she'd asked to help her with the announcement found out it was a lie and confronted her. She recorded the whole thing. She got nothing."

"Holy shit, man. I'm sorry to hear that." Kaden stared at the other man in disbelief.

Dez shrugged. "You know, I didn't know."

Kaden cocked his head, trying to follow Dez's train of thought. "What?"

"I didn't know."

Kaden clenched his jaw. "You suspected."

"Not until it was too late. I wasn't the only one who suspected. Others knew."

"Not the point. You knew and Kennedy took the fall."

"He saved my life. Literally."

"But how many have paid the price for that?"

"Kennedy wasn't innocent." Dez zipped up the duffel. "Have a safe flight, Mr. Smith."

Kaden slung his bag over his shoulder. He made it to the gate as it was boarding. He checked in at the counter before standing off to the side. Pulling out his phone, he made a reservation for a small sedan to be waiting when he landed at O'Hare. He wasn't looking forward to the six-hour drive to the airport and another four to five hours to the cabin.

The flight into Chicago was blessedly quiet and uneventful. The rental agent was tired and anxious to go home, mentioning their long day more than once while he checked the vehicle out to Kaden. He pulled out of the parking lot, spying several police cars. He balled his fists and pounded on the steering wheel. Unable to push the vehicle's speed without risking a ticket, he did his best to cut his drive time weaving in and out of traffic. At one point he caught himself drifting across the highway, waking as the car hit the rumble strip. Just inside the Michigan border, he'd grudgingly pulled into a rest stop, pushed the seat back as far as it would go and slept.

Caught between traffic and construction, the four-hour drive took him nearly six hours to reach the Cherry Capital airport. He returned the car and hailed the lone cab sitting outside the small building, ordering it to take him to Meijer, the large grocery store where he'd left Bubba. The store was less secure than a storage unit, but he didn't have to worry about producing any form of identification, credit card, or bank account information. After paying cash for the ride, Kaden waited until the cab was out of sight before he turned from the store entrance and headed across the parking lot. He retrieved the ignition key and his weapon from their hiding spots in the wheel well before he climbed into the truck and sped out of the parking lot.

The two-hour drive to the bridge spanned an eternity as he tried several times to get a hold of Riley. The wind picked up as fat drops of rain bounced against the windows. As he neared the Mackinaw Bridge, the weather worsened. Passing a blue sign advising travelers to listen for current bridge conditions, Kaden turned his radio on to the AM station and swore. The bridge was closed due to high winds. There was no way to cross the straits and into the Upper Peninsula tonight. Not until the bridge opened.

Kaden pulled into a gas station just off the last exit before the bridge and turned on his phone. The radar showed storms until late in the night. Throwing the truck into gear, he turned right out of the station and drove to the end of the block, pulling into the parking lot of the first hotel he came to. A couple standing in line in front of him had booked the last room. The woman had informed him that between the tourists and the storm, finding a room was going to be nearly impossible.

Irritated and angry, Kaden returned to the gas station and pulled into a spot in the back. He wasn't sure what was worst, that he'd been followed and ambushed, that possible FBI agents were involved, or that he couldn't get back over the bridge to Riley. The weather was out of his control. He replayed the events over the last couple of days, trying to figure out how he had been discovered. He'd snuck into the city early to avoid being discovered. Tension dug in as he tried to force himself to relax.

If his boss hadn't ordered the attack, someone who had access to either his or Lawrence's files or travel itinerary might have given the information to whoever wanted Riley. It was possible that Lawrence might have been tailed to their meeting. That meant someone knew or suspected they were involved with guarding Riley. Kaden swore again. He would have to be extra cautious from now on.

He would need to change vehicles and find a new place to stow Riley — something he knew the younger man was not going to like. Rifling through his duffel bag, he grabbed a small bag from the bottom. He took apart one phone then put together another and called Preacher. He was going to owe his friend if he made it through this assignment alive. Kaden pinched the bridge of his nose and rubbed his forehead. When it came to work, he'd never asked his friends for help. He'd never involved them in anything or even talked about his job. He'd been in similar situations before, where trusting the wrong person could get him killed. But operating on American soil—that was new. He didn't operate on American soil. His skills were better served elsewhere.

"I take it you need something," Preacher said, answering the phone.

"Hello to you too." Kaden chuckled.

"Turnabout and all that," Preacher scoffed. "What's up, brother? Didn't expect to hear from you so soon. Did you hurt Bubba? Having relationship troubles with the kid? Fine ass he has."

Kaden shook his head. "No, your truck is fine. There is no relationship with Riley or anyone else."

"So, he's available and on the market, is he?"

"Stay away from him."

"Hmm. So, what did you call for?"

"I need to change vehicles."

"I don't have another one."

"Nope. I have one in a storage yard about fifteen miles from my apartment. I need you to get it and meet me somewhere." Kaden shoved a hand through his hair, wincing as pain lanced his muscles.

"Why?"

"Got jumped."

"You got jumped?" Preacher asked, disbelief lacing his voice.

"Three on one ambush, yeah, it happened. Was driving a rental, but still, I don't want to take chances."

"Kid still alive?"

Kaden took a deep breath and blew out slowly before answering. "Yep."

"What kind of clusterfuck did you get yourself into? Now, will you follow the rest of us and leave the government jobs to other people. I'm not hiking my ass into that hellhole of a city you call home, or that District for that matter. I'll call Dez and meet him at the state line and you at—"

"There's one of those restaurant-truck stops just off the Interstate at Hawk Hollow. Place called Sandy's. Thursday. Twenty-two hundred."

"Three days? You want me to track Dez down and buy plane tickets to hell and back? Those don't come cheap."

"Book them on my card. Let me give you the numbers. Just email me the receipts."

"Your card or your uncle's card?"

"The uncle's."

"They'll hang you for that."

"Maybe. I have to get through shitstorm first." Kaden shrugged. "Besides, they should have played fair from the beginning."

Preacher laughed. It was a cross between a full-bellied laugh and sheer disbelief. "Yeah, that'll happen."

Kaden shifted the phone to his other ear. "I know, but my boss usually does. He looks better when he does."

Russell Lawrence was part politician, part pencil pusher, and at one time one of the best field agents the company had had. It was that field experience that made him a good supervisor and Kaden willing to trust him. Rumor had it that Lawrence's supervisor had been more politician than agent more interested in climbing the political ladder. He'd taken short cuts, given out unverified information, and had gotten people killed more than once, including Lawrence's last partner. According to the story Kaden had heard, Lawrence had returned from a failed mission, barely alive, and pinned the guy to the wall in the middle of a meeting. It had taken three men to pull Lawrence off his supervisor. He had been threatened with termination until he'd thrown the proof down on the table. The story was still a rumor. Lawrence had never volunteered the information and the only person dumb enough to ask him to his face had found himself on a shit detail in the Mongolian steppes in the winter.

Kaden knew their success rates were better than other departments, in part because of how Lawrence approached assignments. He wanted everybody alive that was supposed to be alive and nothing compromised. There hadn't been a reason to suspect Lawrence's information or his intentions. Until now. While Kaden was sure Lawrence had his reasons, or thought he did, whatever Lawrence had or whoever he was protecting, Kaden needed to know.

"You always did believe the best in people." Preacher chuckled. "Thursday, twenty-two hundred it is."

Kaden pulled the phone apart and stuck the pieces back in his duffel bag. There was nothing more that could be done until morning. He hoped Riley was still at the cabin and they had time to leave on his terms. The miles of protected forests of Michigan's Upper Peninsula coupled with few residents made finding anything that was off the beaten track difficult. It was a fact he'd gambled on when leaving Riley at the cabin alone. Kaden contemplated walking to the diner next door for dinner. Instead he opted to grab something from the gas station and eat in the car. Sleep was all he could do tonight.

* * * *

Kaden was up and on the road by five the next morning. Purple and orange smeared across the sky replacing clear gray. It promised to be a beautiful day. He grabbed a large cup of coffee and two breakfast biscuits from the gas station when he filled the truck's gas tank before heading across the bridge. The time it took him to get to the cabin crawled by, and he prayed to every deity that he could think of that Riley was safe. He alternated with wracking his brain to come up with answers to who was behind the attack on Riley and why they seemed to specifically target Riley and not the rest of the family.

Unholstering his gun as he slowed the truck, Kaden turned onto the nondescript gravel road that was more grass and dirt than anything actually resembling a driveway. After jumping out of the truck and unlocking the gate, he drove through, stopping long enough to wrap the chains back around the bars and secure them. He hesitated a moment before flipping on the motion sensor attached to the bottom of the gate pole. The extra minutes it would take to unlock the gates were minutes they may not have. However, it would also stop anyone who thought to drive through.

Climbing back into the truck, he weighed his options before putting the vehicle in drive and heading up to the house. Seeing no signs of life, Kaden pulled up behind the cabin. Gun drawn, Kaden burst into the cabin, searching each room. He found signs of life, but no signs of any sort of struggle. He walked into the bathroom just as Riley was stepping out of the shower.

Riley screamed and swore. "Don't you knock?"

"Are you alone? Have you had any visitors? Heard or seen anything unusual?" Kaden asked, trying to ignore the naked body in front of him.

"Are you high?" Riley asked, reaching for a towel. "Get out. Next time you want a show, go back to New Orleans. And stay there."

"Find me when you're dressed," Kaden ordered before turning and leaving the bathroom. Relief shot through him. Riley was safe and, at least for now, they had time. Walking through the cabin, Kaden reminded himself that he was a professional. Riley was not only an assignment, but was too young for him, and in way over his head. Kaden shoved a hand through his hair. He had eyes. He wasn't dead. Riley was model gorgeous. Not a type that usually appealed to Kaden, but he was still human. He could appreciate beauty.

Walking into the kitchen, he took off his jacket, tossed it on the back of the nearest chair and grabbed a bottle of water from the refrigerator, wishing it was something stronger. Cracking the top, he drank half of it before he turned and leaned against the counter. Maybe Preacher had it right. Maybe he should find someplace quiet and retire. He had a healthy bank account, one that would allow him to start over. He could probably find a job on a small-town police force to supplement what he had coming in, if he were inclined to.

"Who am I kidding?" Kaden muttered to himself. He had no skills outside of what it took to either keep someone safe or take them out. Pushing aside the train of thought, he focused on the mission at hand. His future would wait. Kaden unlocked and opened one of the upper cabinets, revealing several electrical components. He flipped on a set of switches. The cameras, motion sensors, and lights would pick up any movement outside of the cabin. Not only humans, but wildlife as well. It was one of the reasons he'd hesitated to turn them on before now.

"Why do you still have your holster on?" Riley asked, walking into the main room dressed in his sleep pants. "By the way, you need laundry soap."

Kaden raised an eyebrow and walked over to the front windows.

"So, what's up with the holster?" Riley asked, grabbing a bottle of water. "Did you bring food or beer with you?"

"No, I didn't stop at the store for groceries." Kaden faced the windows.

"So, what's—" Riley started to say.

Kaden turned at the silence, drawing his gun as he did. Riley stood in the center of the room, as though he'd started toward his bedroom then changed his mind.

"Put the gun away. Seriously, Kaden. There's no one around for miles." Riley walked over to him, grabbed his chin, and moved his face from one side to another. "Why are you bruised? Why are you moving differently?"

"I don't—" Kaden interrupted himself and laid the weapon on the end table. Pain was something that he pushed through. He acknowledged it and altered what he needed to in order to keep moving and working. Kaden swallowed. Telling his boss or Preacher he'd been jumped was different from telling the person he was supposed to be protecting. "I was ambushed after the meeting I had. I always have my holster on."

"No, not since we've been here you haven't," Riley answered. "So, how bad is it?"

"We'll leave in a couple of days. We'll meet Preacher and change vehicles at the Pennsylvania-Ohio-West Virginia border."

"Is that smart? Changing vehicles?"

"It's just a precaution."

"Like the gun?" Riley asked.

Kaden nodded. "A safe house may be the best option."

"My house is safe. Well, my family's is. It's gated, with guards," Riley answered.

"That could cause more problems."

"It could draw the people responsible out, though, right? Make it look like I'm an easy target, maybe they slip up?"

"I'm not using you as bait," Kaden scowled. He didn't think it would draw anyone out. It would only serve to put more innocent people in jeopardy.

"So, why did you ask if anything unusual happened?" Riley asked. "Does it have something to with you being ambushed?"

Kaden nodded. "The phone I used to call you was stolen. They may try to use it to find you."

"Shouldn't they have beaten you here then? Shouldn't we be leaving?" Riley's voice edged up slightly.

"I thought they might have arrived first, but the good thing about this area is the fact that if you don't know where you're going, you'll have a hell of a time finding it."

"GPS?"

"Only gets an approximate area. Up here, with few houses, fewer house numbers and street signs, it's a lot more difficult. I'm hoping we'll be okay until we have to leave."

"So, be ready to go at a moment's notice?" Riley asked.

Kaden nodded. "Listen, I'm going to take a shower and a nap. If you hear anything—I mean anything at all—wake me up."

"Sure man. I mean, no offense, but you look like shit," Riley observed.

Grabbing his duffel bag from the truck, he disappeared into the bathroom. He retrieved the tactical vest from the bag and swore. Two holes could be seen in the black fabric. He pulled the T-shirt over his head and tossed it on the counter.

"Damn it!" Kaden swore, anger raging through him.

Two small holes pierced his skin. One was two inches right of his heart and the other three inches to the left of it. Blood had pooled and dried over the wounds at some point, probably while he was unconscious, and stuck to his T-shirt. Small red trails appeared, crawling down the sides of his chest and down his abdomen. Picking up the vest and turning it over, he could see the crumpled tips of two bullets through the split material. He was going to first kill Lawrence, then the asshole who had issued him his equipment. He threw the vest at the door and slammed a fist into the wall.

"What is going on?" Riley demanded, opening the bathroom door.

"Nothing, don't worry about it," Kaden said.

"Really? Because there's a new hole in the wall," Riley said, bending down to retrieve the vest. "And this is what hit the door, I'm assuming."

"Don't worry about it. Let me have it back." Kaden held out his hand.

"Are these bullet holes?" Riley demanded, fingering the bullet holes in the front of the vest, then turned it over and ran his fingers over the sharp, protruding edges. "Isn't this supposed to stop bullets? Not let them through?"

"That's the general idea." Kaden took a deep breath and let it out slowly. He heard the rising panic in the other man's voice. "Yes. Like I said, I was ambushed. Three on one. I'm probably bruised in several places. I'll heal."

"So, why didn't this?"

"They didn't get through all the way." Kaden shrugged. "Some manufacturers took shortcuts, used inferior materials to save money. Most of the defective body armor went to the military. The rest were divvied up between civilians and federal, state, and city governments. Once the defect was discovered they were all supposed to be pulled from use."

"So, either somebody didn't get the memo or—" Riley looked up and stared. His mouth was slightly open and his face had lost all color.

"Or it was done deliberately," Kaden finished.

"You're hurt," Riley said quietly. "Somebody tried to kill you because of me? To get to me?"

Kaden stepped forward. "Because of you? No. To get to you? Maybe. I've made my share of enemies. Many of whom would probably like to see me dead."

Riley shook his head. "No. If you're dead, then I'm fair game to every asshole on the planet." Riley leaned against the counter, clutching the body armor. "I'm going to need a bodyguard for the rest of my life, aren't I?"

"For a few years, it probably won't be a bad idea. I'm surprised your father doesn't have security. Even if it's just for himself."

Riley continued to stare at the vest and shake his head.

Kaden took another step forward and gently but firmly removed the vest from Riley's hands. Laying the vest on the counter and pulled Riley forward and hugged him. Riley hesitated momentarily before wrapping his arms around Kaden.

Chapter Eleven

Riley blinked his eyes open and looked around him. He had a vague memory of Kaden helping him to his room and pulling a sheet over him. His last solid memory was of the supposedly bulletproof vest with holes in both sides.

Tossing the covers back, Riley sought out Kaden. Fear swamped him. Fear of being stranded. Of being abandoned. Of Kaden dying. He wondered what would have happened if Kaden had died. Would anyone have missed the other man? Who would have claimed his body? Would Preacher have raised a glass for him like they did on his back porch for their friends? Would the mysterious Ace have mourned Kaden's death? Not finding Kaden in the main room, he paused outside of Kaden's door. Riley was drawn to the bodyguard. He warred with himself. Blowing out a breath, he shoved a hand through his hair. He reached for the knob, resting his fingers on the scratched brass ball. Letting go, he crossed the hall to his room and leaned against the wall. He was being ridiculous, he chastised himself. He'd spent years alone. He was fine, he'd always been fine. He saw no reason why he wouldn't be fine now or in the future. Looking over at the empty bed, Riley pushed off the wall and left the silent room. Drawing in a deep breath, he opened the door and slipped into Kaden's room.

"Riley?" Kaden sat up in bed, covers pooled in his lap, his gun in his hand. "Is something wrong? Is someone here?"

"No one's here. I'm... I don't know, I'm being stupid," Riley answered, stumbling over the words. He didn't know what he wanted, only that he didn't want to be alone at the moment.

"Come on, you can sleep with me." Kaden slid over to the center of the bed and held the blanket up. The gun disappeared under the pillow.

"Thank you." Riley crawled under the covers. "I don't know what's wrong with me."

"Nothing's wrong with you. Fear is a normal reaction."

"Um — can you — "

Kaden wrapped an arm around Riley's waist and pulled him closer.

"I'm not — I don't — "

"Hush, we can talk later. For now, we both could use a human connection and a couple more hours of sleep."

When Riley woke up next time, the bed was empty, the sheets slightly cool to the touch. Stretching, he took stock of himself. Physically, he felt fine. More than that he wasn't sure. Part of him wished he could blame sleeping with Kaden on the alcohol — or lack of alcohol. This had been the longest stretch he'd gone without drinking, and the most recent. In the past couple of years he'd periodically stopped drinking to prove that

he could and give his body a rest. Those were the times
he went on vacations to places no one had heard of and
ignored everything and everyone, posting pictures of
places he'd been in the past in place of where he was.
No, if he was completely honest with himself, he didn't
really want to look to closely at any of the reasons. He
couldn't remember ever needing comfort or even
seeking it out before. He might have when he was a
small boy, but it wasn't something he could remember.
Truthfully, he also couldn't remember being that
scared before.

Blowing out a breath, Riley threw back the covers
and headed into the bathroom, making himself
civilized before joining Kaden in the cabin's main
room. Riley shoved a hand through his hair. His mind
drifted back to the bullet holes in the vest and the
bandage covering the center of Kaden's chest. He
wasn't sure how he was going to make it through the
next few days. The idea of Kaden or anyone else getting
hurt or killed because of him was almost more than he
could handle. Dressed in loose-fitting khakis and a light
blue button-down shirt, he headed for the refrigerator.
As much as he wanted to, he couldn't hide forever. In
his experience, it was always better to get any
awkwardness or embarrassment over sooner rather
than later. A beer and a laugh generally helped make a
smooth transition.

Riley grabbed a bottle of water from the fridge and
a banana from the counter.

"How did you sleep?" Kaden asked.

"Not bad, you?" Riley flopped down on the end of
the couch. He couldn't remember asking how Kaden
had slept before, it had never crossed his mind. Riley
looked over at the older man. His bodyguard looked

like hell, but seemed to be less stiff. *His bodyguard.* Riley tossed the idea around in his head. He'd never thought of Kaden as *his* anything. It didn't bother him. He half wondered why there was a change now, but not enough to pursue the line of thought. "You don't look like something a zombie threw up anymore."

"Thanks, I think."

"Did you sleep?" Riley smiled and peeled the banana.

"Some. Enough." Kaden glanced down at his laptop.

"What are you looking at?" Riley took a bite of the banana.

"Cameras."

"Wait. You have cameras and didn't tell me? I might have gotten more than a few hours of sleep every night."

"They're activated by motion. Every time a deer, raccoon, bear, coyote, or anything else big enough to trip the sensor walked by, it would have alerted you. Including, and especially, in the middle of the night." Kaden shrugged. "I turned the feed on shortly after I got up and already there have been three alerts. A coyote, a dog, and a very curious racoon."

Riley rubbed the back of his neck and wondered, again, if Kaden had actually gotten any sleep at all. "About earlier —"

"There is nothing to be ashamed of or worried about."

"I'm not used to feeling like…being in this position." Riley shook his head, trying to find the right words.

"I know," Kaden said, taking a drink from a plain white coffee mug. "Most aren't. Not too many people go looking for danger or feel the need to embrace fear."

"No, I get that. It's one thing to be told your life is in danger. It's another to see it first-hand."

"This wasn't the first time you saw danger, or even the first time bullets were used." Kaden set the mug on the end table.

Riley noticed the weapons harness and the butt of the gun visible over the edge of the computer. "I know that." His ribs still hurt from being kicked when he'd been kidnapped in New Orleans. He could still hear the echoes of the shots fired in the warehouse. This was different somehow. He just wasn't sure how.

"Give yourself time to process everything, you'll be fine."

"Would they have killed me?" Riley finished the banana. "If I had gone with you, would they have killed me?

"A possibility. You have something they need, or at least they think you do."

Riley opened the bottle of water and took a long drink. "I still don't know what they're looking for, though."

"Do you have anything special or unique that was given to you? Something like an heirloom or a good-luck charm? Something you were told either to not give away or to not show anyone?" Kaden asked, getting up and pouring himself another cup of coffee. "Do you want some?" Kaden lifted the pot in Riley's direction.

"No thanks." Riley closed the bottle and flipped it end over end in his hands. He didn't think he had anything that matched Kaden's descriptions. "How big are we talking?"

"I'm guessing not more than palm size since your attackers are assuming that you have it on you. Probably something common and unassuming. If we look at the time period, probably somewhere between the 1940s and the 1960s, airport security and customs were more lax than they are now." Kaden glanced at the screen as he sat back down in his chair. "Was your house ever broken into? The one you share with your friends?"

Riley cocked his head to one side before shaking it. "Not that I'm aware of. If they did, they didn't take anything. And I can't remember anything being out of place. We have a maid. I assume she would have told us if she noticed anything strange."

"You have a maid?"

Riley shrugged. "We can barely do our own laundry and dishes. The cleaning part is completely outside our skillset. We tried it. We found it easier to all pitch in and hire a maid to come in and clean twice a week."

"Can she be bought?"

Riley rubbed the back of his neck. "Maybe. We use a service. They guarantee discretion and satisfaction."

"How discreet?"

"They're more the we-won't-say-anything-if-you're-having-an-affair more than they are the hide-a-body-and-clean-a-crime-scene type."

Kaden nodded. "Have you ever found a secret compartment in any of the furniture in the house, or in some of the knickknacks around the house when you were younger? Found maybe some undeveloped rolls of film or files marked confidential, private, or anything like that? Did you ever get into things you weren't supposed to?"

Riley laughed. "Secret compartments, film, or anything spy-related, no, but get into what I wasn't supposed to? All the time."

"Any attention is better than no attention?"

Riley shrugged. Jumping to his feet, he dropped the water bottle on the couch and rushed into his room, grabbed his backpack off from the dresser and brought it back into the living room. "I don't know if this is what you're looking for, but it's the only thing I can think of."

Taking a deep breath, he dug into the pack and retrieved an antique-looking watch and a battered leather wallet. He'd never told anyone about them. He'd never mentioned they existed. The wallet went with him everywhere, something he wasn't willing to admit, but the watch only traveled with him when he was going on any sort of trip for more than a day.

"It's a starting point."

Riley hesitated before handing both items over to Kaden. "Nobody knows about these. Well, my grandmother knows about the watch, although I don't know if she actually remembers, but no one knows about the other."

"Tell me what I'm looking at."

"The watch belonged to my grandfather. My grandmother gave it to me when I was eight or nine. She said it was a good-luck piece and part of my heritage and that I needed to keep it safe," Riley explained, finishing the contents of his water bottle. "The other is just a couple of photographs, nothing important."

Kaden set the watch on the table next to him and opened the wallet. Riley picked at the label of the water bottle he'd been drinking.

Kaden removed the pictures, studied them, before turning them over and setting them down on his knee. "She's beautiful." Kaden smiled. "Who is she?"

"My mother."

"What do you know about her?" Kaden asked, inspecting the wallet.

"Not a lot." Riley shrugged. He knew only what he'd been able to piece together. "Her name was Elaine Catherine Greenwood. She married Charles when she was twenty, against her parents' wishes. They cut her off. She was sixteen years his junior."

"What happened to her?" Kaden replaced the photographs in their protective casing.

"She died three hours after I was born. Those are the only pictures I have of her."

"I'm so sorry, Riley." Kaden returned the wallet to Riley. "Where did you get those?"

"I was home on summer break, the year I stopped calling Charles 'Dad'. I was snooping around in closets, hiding from everyone, especially the nanny, Barbara, or something like that. She was tall, dressed all in black with her hair pulled back in a bun. She always smelled of too much perfume and alcohol. Anyway, in one of the closets, in the back, kind of hidden, was this shoebox with my mom's name written on it in black marker. I was curious and opened it up. It contained those pictures, along with some newspaper articles about her marriage and death, her death certificate, my birth certificate, court records from a custody battle, and a diary with two entries. One entry was those sono-picture-things pregnant women get, with my name written and 'it's a boy' written next to it. The other was a letter to me, with a promise to journal daily," Riley answered. "It was gathering dust, so I took it. No one was around, no one ever asked about it, and I never volunteered any information. When I went back to school in the fall, it came with me."

"Do you remember what the letter said?"

Riley nodded. "Mostly it was filled with how happy she was to have me, how she always wanted to be a mom. She did say that she had made a deal with the devil. She would ignore Charles' affairs in exchange for remaining married to him and raising me to be his heir. I'm not sure what she meant by that, but she said a divorce would be worse because her parents would never take her back, so staying was better than being poor and homeless."

Kaden shook his head. "I don't know about the heir part either. I know you said you didn't know any of your mother's family, but did you ever try finding any of them?"

"Yeah, but they weren't interested in me." Riley stuck the wallet in his backpack. He'd tried contacting his grandparents several times, but stopped when he'd received a letter from a lawyer who said that they wanted nothing to with him. The letter, along with everything else he deemed important, was locked away in a trunk in his closet at his family's estate.

"What about the watch?" Kaden asked, turning the antique over in his hands.

"My grandmother gave it to me just before I returned to school during Christmas break years ago. Pretty sure Charles was off with some chick in either the Caribbean or the Florida Keys the entire time."

"Is that common? For your father to miss holiday vacations?"

Riley shrugged. "Standard operating procedure. I never expect to see him. I stopped getting gifts for him years ago. In school, whenever we were instructed to buy or make gifts for our parents, I got something I wanted and kept it. Whatever Charles wants, he buys.

And if he doesn't want it and you give it to him, he'll throw it away."

"Is there anything special about the watch that you know of?"

Riley drew up one knee and shook his head. "No, not really. Just what I was told. But you know, I don't remember my grandfather ever carrying a pocket watch like that. He liked new and fancy gadgets. He was brand loyal on some things. He always wore tailored three-piece suits from the same shop and a Rolex watch." Riley jumped to his feet and tossed the banana peel and water bottle into the garbage before grabbing another bottle of water. "How do you do that?" he asked, leaning against the counter. "How do I remember stuff sometimes and not others?"

"Neither the watch nor the photographs are recent items that were given to you. Most people, when they're asked if they were given something in secret or something important, will first think of something recent. Something that may be valuable to them in their current role. If it's connected, even remotely, with something negative or considered harmful or evil, people will first assume that the person who gave it to them was also evil, and very few people are willing to believe that someone they know or possibly love is capable of evil. Those are things that happen to other people. To other families." Kaden sipped his coffee. "So sometimes rewording the question or asking different questions helps. Other times, a word or phrase will trigger a memory."

"I guess that makes sense." Riley sat back down on the couch. "But nobody knows I have these. Not even my friends."

"Not true. Your grandmother knows you have the watch, and it's possible that the box of your mother's things was left there deliberately for you to find, or someone knew it was there and when it came up missing either assumed you took it or that it was thrown away."

"The watch, yes. My mom's stuff, I don't think so." Riley peeled the label off the water bottle. "Nobody in the house talks about her. Ever. Not even the staff. I don't think Charles sees himself as a widower or checks widower on anything asking for marital status."

"I see. What's special about the storage room?"

Riley shook his head and took a sip of water. "Nothing. It was a closet. It had bunches of boxes and crates. I think there were old dishes in a couple of them. Trunks of old clothes, some sort of old-fashioned radio, and a clock. It was all smaller things. There was a large chest in the back, covered with stuff, but I never opened it. Honestly, at the time it looked like a lot of old, worthless junk. Some of it might be actually valuable to the right person now. Pretty sure there was a layer of dust on everything. Including my mom's box."

"Have you been back there since then? Somebody might have noticed."

"Yeah, the next time I was home, then a couple of years later. I remember being afraid they were going to notice the box was missing and demand I give it back or throw it away. Occasionally, I would look around and everything was the same. Still dusty. Nothing had been moved or added."

"Nothing in the box's place?"

Riley hesitated for a moment, trying to picture the storage room. "No, not that I remember. I know I was curious, or scared, to see if anyone would notice or say anything. No one ever did." Riley began peeling the label into small, thin strips. "I don't even know where she's buried. *If* she's buried. How sad is that? For someone to not know anything about their parents, including where they're buried. That has to make me the worst person in the world."

"It doesn't make you a bad person. However, it does make me wonder if you're being deliberately stonewalled or if the memories are too painful for people to talk about." Kaden opened the front of the watch, squinting at the engraving. "Sometimes people don't talk about things because they're afraid it'll distort the memory. I know Ace can find out what happened to your mother. If you want, they can dig up everything there is to know about her."

"I don't know—"

"You're her son. I'm sure she would want you to know." Kaden closed the front of the watch.

"Maybe, I—"

"What the hell?"

Riley looked up, dropping the shredded label on the couch. The back of the watch was open and a small bronze key lay in Kaden's palm. "What is that? Where was it?"

"Fell out of the back of the watch when I pushed the winding knob." Kaden set the watch aside and held the key up between his thumb and forefinger. "I take it you didn't know about this."

Riley shook his head. "No clue. Any idea what's for?"

"There aren't any numbers or words on it, so I don't think it's for a locker or safe deposit box."

Riley picked up the watch, leaving Kaden to inspect the key. Riley had looked at the watch hundreds of times before, finding nothing particularly interesting in the aged metal. This time he studied each line. The front was etched with swirling lines and some sort of flower. There were no decorative touches layered onto it, no intricate carved details. The back was smooth except for the name of the watchmaker engraved in small letters on the bottom near the hinge. It was lighter now than it had been before, but it looked the same. Like a well-cared-for pocket watch used by a man or men who wasn't well-to-do. Riley wondered about the man who the watch had originally belonged to. It wasn't something his grandfather would have bought or kept. The elder Hamilton had been an intelligent chemist and businessman, but he had been strict and cold.

"It's hard to imagine my grandfather using this, or even just hanging on to it. He wasn't the sentimental type. He was a scientist, not given to emotions."

"Not even anger?"

Riley cocked his head, drawing up his knee. "No, not really. He was strict. Cold. Blunt. I assume he shared emotions with my grandmother, but maybe not. They had separate bedrooms."

"Separate bedrooms?" Kaden raised one eyebrow.

"Yes. I didn't realize it wasn't normal for couples to have separate bedrooms until I was sixteen or seventeen," Riley admitted. There were a lot of things he hadn't known or realized until high school or college, but nothing else he was ready to admit. He'd learned a lot from his roommate his freshmen year, although he still didn't completely get the draw of a care package from home filled with some of the same things he could go get right off campus. "Do you think that is the key those goons were after?"

"That would be my guess. Either that or whatever that key goes to."

"If they have whatever it goes to, why would they need a key? Why not just pry it open or something?"

"You're assuming they have it. If they did, I think you would have noticed something missing. Unless it's not at your house, but at your family's estate. They may have only heard a rumor, and want to confirm the validity."

"This feels more and more like some sort of bad spy movie."

"You know what they say, truth is stranger than fiction." Kaden handed the key to Riley. "Best put it away. Less chance of losing it."

Riley examined the key before placing it back in the watch and closing it. The key looked like a normal key that could fit any number of things. Any of which could be in any of his family's homes.

Chapter Twelve

Kaden rubbed the back of his neck and headed into the kitchen. The cabin's open concept living area had the benefit of letting him see outside on three walls and keep an eye on Riley's comings and goings. The downside was that there was no place to comb through the tangle of thoughts and emotions that had embroiled him since he'd first removed the vest and seen the bullet holes. It wasn't the first time he'd been shot. It wasn't even the first time this year.

It wasn't the first time his body armor had failed, but it was the first time since he'd left the military.

Yanking chicken and vegetables out of the fridge, he busied himself preparing a meal for the two of them. He distinctly remembered Lawrence handing him the vest shortly after their meeting to replace his, which had come up missing. It happened occasionally, but not very often. Equipment would be picked up by someone else, usually by mistake. However, it almost always happened either during a mission or training exercise. It had never happened in the middle of the day from his office. Kaden didn't believe in coincidences. Not ever. He hadn't had a chance to investigate what had happened or find out who had swiped his vest or why before he'd had to leave. He still didn't know if it had been an accident or intentional. The former was bad luck. The latter amounted to attempted murder.

Chopping vegetables, he was beginning to think Preacher was right. Maybe he should look into another line of work. Unlike his friend, or most of their unit, he didn't have other skills he could channel into a civilian career. He'd wanted to be a soldier as long as he could remember. Everything he'd done was in preparation for a career in the Army. Even though he was no longer in the Army, he absolutely hated the idea of working in an office all day, every day, more than he despised the idea of working as a security guard for some rich person or politician.

An alarm pierced the silent room and red lights flashed, pulling him from his thoughts. Dropping the knife, he rushed over to his laptop.

"What the hell is that?" Riley demanded, jumping up from the couch. He'd been writing nearly nonstop for two hours in a spiral-bound notebook.

"The alarm system."

"It didn't do that earlier. I would have noticed both the sounds and the lights." Riley looked out of a window then back to Kaden. "I'm not that sound of a sleeper."

"I turned them on when I walked away from the computer."

"What is it?"

"Looks like a deer out back and someone turning around in the driveway."

"So what made the sound?"

"Both. Pulling into the driveway activates one set of motion sensors, while going through the gate sets off another. Then there are the sensors at various points around the property."

"This is going to be a long couple of days." Riley walked back to the couch and flopped down.

"Can you cook?" Kaden asked several minutes later, breaking the silence.

"Define cooking." Riley picked up the notebook and pen off from the floor where he'd dropped them.

"Anything more than ordering take-out or microwaveable meals." Kaden set the knife down.

"I don't need to cook. I have no interest in learning. I live within blocks of the best restaurants and bars in the area."

"Where did you learn self-defense? You know, the moves you used on me, but didn't use on your attackers?"

"In school somewhere." Riley shrugged. "I spend a lot of my time drunk, so it's not something I actually remember to use, plus, I've never needed them before."

"That makes sense. You also haven't had any alcohol since we left Preacher's."

"And?" Riley challenged.

"Observation." Kaden held up his hands. "You don't have any withdrawal symptoms and seem to be handling things okay out here."

"Yeah, not an alcoholic, James." Riley smirked. "Different stimuli. Less of some, more of others."

Kaden nodded. He wondered how much of Riley's nonexistent relationship with his father and hiding parts of whom he was contributed to Riley's drinking. "Come and give me a hand."

"Why?"

"Because you eat here too at the moment," Kaden answered. "Regardless of whether you want to or not."

"Not part of the deal."

"Or you can wash the dishes. I may be just a bodyguard, but I'm not actually a maid or cook."

Riley stood up, wincing slightly. "Not interested." Riley went out through the back door.

Kaden watched as Riley sat down in one of the Adirondack chairs. Returning the meat and vegetables to the fridge, he made himself a sandwich and ate it at the counter before washing his dishes. Satisfied, he picked up a book and opened it to where he'd left off. There was neither cable nor satellite dish connected to the cabin. He'd never bothered to bring in a television set or a movie collection. There was a radio that picked up a couple of local stations, but no CDs. The cabin was rarely used, so luxuries weren't a necessity. They were expenses he didn't want to deal with. The cabin was more of a bolthole than anything else.

Kaden peered over the top of his book, tracking Riley's movements as he looked toward the stove, shrugged, and grabbed a banana, an apple, and a bottle of water before disappearing into his room. Kaden wondered how long it would be before Riley offered to help with dinner. He briefly considered making Riley before scrapping the idea. His job was to make sure that Riley lived through this, not to teach him how to be self-sufficient and completely independent.

His mind drifted back to earlier. He'd been surprised when Riley had crept into his room. If he was honest with himself, he had enjoyed the way Riley fit against him as they slept. From the way Riley was acting both then and now, Kaden wasn't the only one. He wondered when the last time Riley had allowed himself to be that vulnerable, or when the last time was he'd been hugged. Kaden stared at the closed bedroom door, where he was sure Riley was naked. Kaden might not have spoken to his family since he was eighteen, but at least before his relationship with his parents deteriorated, they had hugged and kissed him and had always wanted the best for him.

* * * *

The alarms went off a dozen times over the next forty-eight hours. Each time, both men stopped what they were doing or woke up to see what triggered the alarm. Kaden rewound the footage on several occasions, verifying that either a deer or a wolf had tripped the alarm system.

Kaden looked at his watch and groaned. Rolling over, he hiked the covers up, hoping for a few more minutes of sleep. They needed to leave the cabin in a couple of hours. Next to him, Riley was still sleeping. Last night the alarms had sounded at two o'clock in the morning when a car had pulled up to the gates and sat several minutes before leaving. Riley had finally drifted off to sleep by pure exhaustion. Kaden had slept, but it had been far from restful. He wasn't sure leaving was a good idea, but it beat sitting in the cabin waiting for someone to show up. Being hundreds of miles from the action was not helping him figure out who wanted Riley or why. He still had no idea why he had been asked to protect Riley instead of someone from the FBI.

Kaden opened his eyes, wide awake. "I'll kill him," Kaden ground out, sitting up.

"Who are you going to kill?" Riley asked, sleep lacing his voice.

"My boss. Since you're awake, get up and get moving. We'll leave within the hour."

"Why kill your boss? I don't understand."

"It's what I suspect. I can't prove anything. Yet. But we need to find whatever that key opens."

"Why?"

"It can probably tell us who is after you and why, and probably why I'm involved."

"Because your boss told you to isn't a good enough answer?" Riley asked, climbing out of bed.

"No, it's not. Not anymore," Kaden answered, shaking his head. "Let's move. I'm going to grab a quick shower. Keep an eye on the alarms."

Riley nodded.

Twenty minutes later, Kaden stood dressed and refreshed in the center of the cabin's main room. His duffel bag sat on the corner of the counter. He only needed to shut his laptop down and stick it in the bag and he would be ready to go. The remainder of their groceries and water bottles were already out in the cab of the pickup truck.

Riley came out of the bedroom with his backpack slung over his shoulder, the weight of the past three weeks etched into his features. Kaden inhaled deeply, let it out slowly, and picked the HK45 up off the counter and handed it, butt first, to the younger man.

"Gee, you shouldn't have," Riley quipped.

"Yeah, well, you don't seem to be a diamonds-and-lace sort of guy, so I improvised," Kaden answered.

"I'll be a monkey's uncle. You have a fun side to you."

"Not that anyone will believe you." Kaden smirked. He didn't even quite believe the words he'd said. The carefree banter he'd once enjoyed with his buddies had ended with his military career. "Keep it close by, use it if you need to. Do you have that flash drive with you?"

"You mean the tracker? Yes, wait, why can't others use it to find me?" Riley asked, taking the gun from Kaden.

"Sources and resources." Kaden powered down his laptop.

"What the hell does that mean?"

"It means, that when I'm handed the shit I was, I bring a few of my own things with me."

"Isn't that illegal? Hell, this whole thing is probably illegal."

Kaden gave Riley a half-smile and shook his head. "At all costs. By any means. Wording is everything."

"Will you get in trouble?"

"There's always a chance that I can get in trouble. But then, so can the people I work for." Kaden shoved the computer into his bag and made one last sweep of the cabin. "Let's go." The pit in the bottom of his stomach opened up. What had been a simple babysitting job had become much more. Depending on more than a few details and the size of the scandal it caused, it had the potential to bring the agency to its knees. There was an election year coming up and anyone who was up for re-election was going to want to appear tough on corruption. He could lose more than his job, but it wouldn't be the first time. Aside from one or two people, there would be no one to mourn his death or be adversely affected if he ended up as a scapegoat spending the rest of his life in jail. Blowing out a breath, Kaden led the way out to the truck.

Leaving the relative safety of the cabin, he was aware of their vulnerability. He'd purposely parked the truck so Riley could get in without being seen from the treeline. Kaden ran around the front of the truck and climbed in, tossing his bag in the back. Adrenaline surged through him. He wanted to push the truck as hard and as fast it would go, but drawing attention to them in any way would do more harm than good.

"When we get to the gate, slide over and pull the truck through, while I unlock it."

"I can get the gate," Riley offered.

"I'd rather you stay in the truck."

"Why? I'm not an invalid. I'm not going to break." Riley crossed his arms over his chest. "I promise, I'm not that fragile."

"It's not that you can't handle the gate," Kaden said, exasperated. "It's that this truck is bulletproof."

"Wait, what?"

Kaden smirked. "Preacher is a bit overzealous on safety. All of his vehicles, including Mary Jane, are bulletproof. Those odd ventilation windows on the doors are for shooting out of. There's actually a mount for a machine gun in the bed of the truck. Currently, cleverly disguised as a trailer hitch for a fifth wheel."

"Seriously? People really do that?" Riley asked, disbelief threading through his words.

"Yeah, people really do that."

"That's got to cost a ton of money."

"A bit, that's for sure, and it takes a specialized skill set. However, depending on where you are in the country, you could run into more than a few modified vehicles, with a varying degree of security features."

"Why? Surely that many people don't distrust society."

"Actually, more do. However, for some, it's more of a show of masculinity."

"Fantastic." Sarcasm dripped from Riley's voice.

"Actually, right now, it works. Because it makes this truck blend in better." Kaden slowed down as he approached the gate. There hadn't been anyone there the last time he looked, but that could have changed in the last handful of minutes.

Rounding the bend in the driveway, he breathed a sigh of relief. There was no one in sight. Pulling to a stop, he unholstered his gun and hopped out of the truck. He stood for a moment listening for anything that shouldn't be there—or an absence of sound. Moving quickly, he removed the chain and opened the gate, waving Riley through. Once through, he threaded the chains through the bars, padlocked it closed, and turned off the sensors.

He had just climbed back into the cab when a black SUV passed them, stopped, and did a U-turn in the middle of the two-lane road. Kaden threw the truck into gear and rolled forward, prepared to force the truck to its limits if needed. He watched the SUV pull off onto the side of the road and stop at the edge of the driveway. Kaden pulled his weapon from his holster and laid it on his lap.

"Brace yourself in case we have to move fast," Kaden whispered.

"Thought you said this was bulletproof."

"It is, but that doesn't mean it's completely impenetrable or will last forever, despite what the movies show."

"Great. Just great. We should really head for my family's house."

"That might require a small army to guard you there," Kaden replied as the passenger door of the black SUV opened and a middle-aged woman stepped out. She turned to say something to the driver before walking over. Kaden watched. She'd left her purse in the car, but carried several pieces of paper with her. Beside him, Riley put his ball cap on and pretended to read the *National Geographic* magazine he'd taken from the cabin.

"Excuse me! Excuse me!" she called out, waving to them.

Kaden tensed. She looked like a lost tourist. However, it could be a distraction. She could be waiting for him to open the door before shooting him and taking Riley. He hoped Preacher had been prepared for that kind of scenario.

The SUV hadn't moved, it was still on the edge of the driveway. If he needed, Kaden could get through without hitting the other car or the woman. He also knew that if he needed to, he could push the SUV out of the way. Kaden wound the window halfway down as she approached.

"Can you help us? I think we're lost."

"Well, I can try." Kaden gave the woman a fake smile.

"We're looking for Ta-que-mon falls, but I think we're going the wrong way. My fiancé thinks we're on the right road."

"Tahquamenon."

"What?"

"It's pronounced tuh-KWAHM-in-uhn," Kaden repeated.

"Oh. Okay. Are we close?"

"You missed the turnoff. It's about an hour east. There will be a sign for Tahquamenon Falls to the north. However, there is a small town fifteen miles to the west, where you can get a great breakfast at the North Star Café and fill your tank."

"Oh. Should we get gas first?"

"Yes, I recommend you fill up whenever you can, just because there are so many back roads with nothing on them for miles. Easy to get lost up here."

"I noticed. We're taking our daughter up to Marquette for college, thought we'd make it a family trip."

Kaden nodded and gripped the weapon tighter. "Enjoy your vacation."

"Thanks again."

Winding the window up, Kaden waited until the woman was in the car before holstering his weapon. He waved and turned out of the driveway toward St. Ignace and the Mackinaw Bridge. He watched the rear-view mirror. She seemed genuine, but he was taking no chances. He didn't relax until the other vehicle did another U-turn in the middle of the road and drove off in the direction of the small town he'd indicated. Kaden held his breath. A similar tactic had been used in another assignment, another mission, and two of his friends had been killed.

"Do you think she was who she said she was?" Riley asked several minutes later, sitting up in his seat.

Kaden checked his weapon and nodded. "I think so, yes. She seemed genuine. Otherwise, she's a phenomenal actress and is in the wrong career field."

"Where are we headed?"

"South for now. Probably east. But right now, I'm not sure."

"Well, wake me when we get there or it's time to stop." Riley pulled the cap down to shade his face and slouched back down in his seat.

Kaden nodded and turned the radio on low. He started to relax the farther from the cabin they were.

The drive to the Mackinaw Bridge was uneventful. He saw nothing to make him suspect that they were being followed or that the woman who had stopped them was anything other than who she claimed to be. Scrubbing a hand over his face, he admitted that Riley was right. They would need to go to his family's house. The answers were there. Either in whatever that key opened or in the secrets that no one wanted to talk about.

Kaden flexed his fingers and paid the bridge attendant, grateful that Riley's face was hidden. He didn't know if heading to Riley's family home in New York was the smartest or safest choice, but it was the only course of action he saw for them. He needed to talk to Lawrence to see what the other man knew or was hiding. Sorting through the situation, Kaden crossed the expansive bridge, continuously checking for anyone following him. His gut said that shit was about to hit the fan. It was usually right, even if he didn't know what would hit or how bad it would be.

Leaving the bridge, he pulled into the first gas station and stopped in front of the pumps. Riley stirred as he turned the truck off.

"Where are we?" Riley asked, sleep crawling through his voice.

"Mackinaw City. I need gas and to stretch my legs. You should too. We'll stop to eat in a couple hours," Kaden answered.

"Okay, I'll go in with you. I could use a drink."

Kaden filled the truck's gas tank then waited for Riley to join him before going into the store. They were paying for their purchases when Kaden saw Charles Hamilton's name scroll across the screen of the small TV the gas station attendant was watching behind the counter. Kaden swore silently. Beside him, Riley stiffened.

"I have a call to make," Kaden ground out as they left the store. "Get in the truck. I'm going to park around back."

Riley nodded and climbed into the truck, yanking his hat down farther.

Kaden pulled the truck behind the gas station and dug out his phone. Putting it together, he climbed out, slamming the door shut behind him.

"Lawrence."

"Damn it, Lawrence, you were supposed to handle the family. All of the family. Now, there's a rolling scroll bar that Charles Hamilton issued a plea for help looking for his son."

"It was handled. I have no idea what happened."

"Fix it."

"Tennison—"

"What did you find out about those names?"

"They don't exist."

"Both IDs are forgeries. Good ones."

"What the fuck? Did you find anything out that is remotely useful?"

"There is no—"

"Who's the double agent?"

"There is no d—"

"Find out who the double agent is. It's someone in his family. And they have or had something that someone is willing to kill this kid over."

"I have no idea—"

"Who is the fucking double agent?" Kaden demanded.

"I don't know what you're talking about."

"Stop with the bullshit. I'm not some rookie. A double agent is the only explanation on why I'm handling this and not—"

"Tennison," Lawrence cautioned.

"Who is the double agent?"

"I don't know."

"An innocent life is in danger. 'I don't know' is *not* a viable answer," Kaden shouted. He shoved the phone in his pocket, climbed into the truck, and sped out of the parking lot.

Chapter Thirteen

"What's going on?" Riley asked several tense minutes later.

"While this is all speculation until there's proof, I could be a hundred percent wrong."

"But you don't think you are." Riley mentally braced himself for whatever new bombshell Kaden was going to spring on him. At this point, Riley wasn't sure anything Kaden said would actually surprise him. Every family had its secrets. Things people didn't want anyone else to know.

In junior high one of the teachers had assigned a family tree project with bonus points given for presentation and if you went back more than four generations. He had turned in his on a plain sheet a paper with a family tree design he'd found online with the information he knew and made up the rest with semi-believable answers. One of his classmates, a boy with bright red hair, freckles, and pale white skin, had turned his project in on a huge piece of poster board, saying that the assignment had caused a huge fight in his family over the holidays. It turned out a great-grandmother had married a black man who was descended from runaway slaves. The kid's revelation at home had caused accusations of lying and threatened the unity of his family. At school, it caused the teacher to go into a week-long civics lesson on racial issues in the country and state over the century.

"Am I going to like this new theory of yours?" Riley still wasn't sure how he felt about the idea of his family being Russian spies, but it did make more sense than the idea his grandparents had just sprung up fully formed and all grown up in the city, which was the basic story he'd always heard.

"Probably not."

"Well, at least you're honest about it."

Kaden raised an eyebrow. "By all rights, I shouldn't be involved with you, I—"

"You aren't involved with me. You're supposed to babysitting me or acting as my bodyguard," Riley grumbled, "which I suppose really does add up to be about the same thing."

Grinning, Kaden shook his head. "That's just it. I shouldn't be the one acting as your bodyguard. That is actually someone else's job. Different area altogether. This whole situation may have gotten a whole lot messier. We need to get you safe and figure out what they're all after."

"All? They're after the key. We found that," Riley said, shifting in his seat. "Maybe I should just give them the key. I can get back to my life, you can find a boyfriend and take off that edge you have."

"I don't have a boyfriend. I already told you that."

"No, but you need one. That means you'll have sex and will get rid of that ultra-serious, stick-up-your-butt side."

"We'll see. That stick-up-my-butt side, as you say, makes me good at my job." Kaden flexed his fingers around the steering wheel. "Besides, I don't think giving them the key is the answer. Then they have the key and whatever secret and there is no reason to keep you alive any longer."

"What is so important that someone would kill over it?" Riley shook his head. He couldn't think of anything that was so important he'd kill for. "Nothing is that important."

"Depending on who you ask."

"Well that's cryptic and not at all helpful."

"No, it does. For a drug addict, an ounce of heroin or gram cocaine is enough. That greedy bastard in the news a couple of months ago decided that killing his wife for her life insurance and marrying his much younger mistress was enough. For a spouse who has been cheated on, getting cheated on again is enough," Kaden explained. "Money, drugs, and power are generally the three things people kill for."

"You forgot revenge."

"Yep, revenge is the fourth. Unless you, your father, or grandmother are dealing or using drugs, that doesn't apply. Someone might kill you for the money in your pocket or rob your house for money or things that can be pawned, but they aren't the kind to hire thugs to kidnap you. A planned kidnapping like this takes money and resources. Most people don't have the money or resources to pull something like that off, or are willing to, unless it's for revenge."

"Kidnapping is easier than that. It just takes a van, someplace to hide, and a moment of distraction." Riley shook his head. "They were after me, but anyone in New Orleans could have been targeted. Hell, there are hundreds of people that go missing every year. Some of them are held for ransom."

Kaden looked over at Riley and raised an eyebrow.

"Just an article I read somewhere. Or maybe it was one of those random video news stories." Riley shrugged. Kaden knew more than enough about him. He wasn't ready or willing to let him know any more than he already did.

"You have a point there. Kidnapping as a means for ransom or to use someone as a bargaining chip, that does require additional resources, and either specialized knowledge or power. Or both."

"Most people don't know who I am," Riley pointed out. He preferred staying out of the news even if his father might not mind the spotlight. "So the ransom plot isn't a good choice."

"Very true. It could be revenge — a past lover of your father's. However, I—"

Riley laughed, the sound hollow. "No, just no. Even if it was one of Charles' exes — and to be sure, there are a lot of them — they would be more successful going after Charles' business than me, which is something everyone knows. Even ex-business partners know that if you want to hurt Charles, attack his business, not his family."

"So, if it's not revenge, then it's either money or power, or both. And Charles may or may not have anything to do with it. It could be one of your grandparents or their siblings."

Riley relaxed against the seat and tossed the information around in his head. "But why go after me when I didn't know either of my grandparents had siblings? Neither one talked about their family. At all. Ever."

"How long have you and your father lived with your grandmother?"

"Pretty much my entire life, although Charles has a small place in the city too. Why?"

"What do you know or remember about their habits? How they live?"

"Ah — boarding school, remember?"

"I do, but you were there sometimes. So, what do you remember?"

"Um, I don't know. They slept in separate rooms. They went to the symphony and saw shows on Broadway. My grandfather liked wine, collected it. I'm pretty sure there are still bottles in the wine cellar that he bought. Grandmother liked to travel, still does. She goes to Paris, Milan, and London at least once every year. I remember being fascinated by her traveling. I'm pretty sure she's been to almost every country. I know she's been everywhere in the Americas, most of Asia, and all of Europe, although I don't know if she meant all of Europe or just Western Europe."

"What about daily or weekly habits?"

"I don't know that I really paid attention. I know my grandfather went out to some club every Saturday night. My grandmother had some sort of ladies' club meetings on Tuesday and sometimes Thursdays. But what those are or were, I have no idea," Riley answered, shoving a hand through his hair. "To be honest, though, I don't know if she still goes to them or if those were code names for going someplace else. I didn't care enough to ask, and even if I had, I probably wouldn't have gotten an answer."

Kaden nodded and flexed his fingers around the steering wheel. "That doesn't really narrow a whole lot down."

"Plus, they both worked."

"Wait, your grandmother continued to work after she got married?"

Riley nodded. "It came up during one of those brunch deals that my grandmother has or goes to occasionally. She usually pulled me in during one every year or so starting in high school and introduced me to her friends. I stayed as long as it took to be polite without being rude or until the conversation went to places I didn't want to hear or know about. One time, one of the women was complaining about how her husband had told her she couldn't do something. Another woman said to do it anyway and the woman responded that she'd been informed that since she wasn't working, she didn't have any of her own money. My grandmother said that was why she continued to work after she got married and still worked. There were comments made in the past about my grandmother working like some common woman. I think she had moved to the company's Board of Directors at that point. I left at that point. " Riley rubbed the back of his neck. "I haven't thought about that in ages. Huh. Is it important?" Family was something that had never been important to him, legal guardians who never really cared where he was or what he was doing unless it made them look good or bad. He knew details because it made getting what he wanted easier, either with or without permission. He hadn't really cared what he'd been told.

"Maybe, but it might just be weird. It certainly was uncommon for a woman to work, especially when they didn't have to."

"It could have something to do with her being a perfumer."

"What would she have done as a perfumer?"

"Perfumers, at least now, deal with scents. They generally have powerful scent receptors and can smell things that most people can't. A lot of times they can detect the layers of scent in a mixture. Technology has helped a lot, but there are some things that a computer or lab can't do."

"I thought you didn't want anything to do with your family's business."

Riley shook his head. "No, not really. But having access to pretty much anything I wanted or needed made the homework in some classes extremely easy."

"Isn't that the same as cheating?" Kaden asked.

"Ingenuity." Riley shrugged. "Besides, sometimes having the data was only part of what was needed."

"So, you fake not knowing anything."

"No," Riley answered. "I don't hide what I know. I don't flaunt it. I simply don't care. It's not like Charles and I sit and talk about business or I ask him questions. But following conversations, trends, and thought processes is important."

"What does your grandmother think about your disinterest in the family company?"

"I don't know. I didn't ask. It's not overly important to me. And most likely I'll end up there anyway. I'm just putting off the inevitable."

"You know, you don't have to follow the direction they're pointing, just because they're family."

"And exactly what do you suggest I do, James? I don't have sole control over my trust fund." Riley crossed his arms over his chest and stared out of the window. "I assume you're an expert in defying parents."

Kaden sighed. "An expert, no, but experienced? Yeah, that I am." Riley turned from the window. There was something about Kaden's voice that made Riley cringe at the tone he'd used. Aside from being in the military, he didn't really know anything about Kaden.

"I grew up in a very conservative, pacifist family, with a fairly normal, mostly happy childhood. My father wanted me to be an accountant like him and become a deacon in the church. I want nothing to do with offices, listening to people complain because they didn't plan for the taxes they owed, or greedy assholes wanting the laws changed, bent, or broken so they didn't have to pay something or could swindle more people out of their money. I knew I wanted to join the Army, to be a hero like the guys I saw on TV and in the parades. So that is what I worked toward. I played sports that would help me give the strength and ability to do the things that they showed in movies and documentaries. Things I wasn't supposed to watch anyway." Kaden finished the coffee he'd bought at the gas station. "I enlisted in the Army when I was eighteen, told my parents I was out with friends and in processed. I managed to keep it a secret until two weeks before I was to report for boot camp."

"What happened when they found out?"

"They pretty much stopped speaking to me. I wasn't allowed to eat meals with the family, or go to church."

"That is seriously messed up. Wait, they had a problem with you being in the Army, but not being gay?"

"No, they had a problem with me being gay too. They found out after I came home from my first tour in Afghanistan. I thought that might change the way they felt about me being in the Army. Somehow they found out I was gay and called me out about it. That ended like you would expect, the 'you're not our son, we didn't raise you this way' spiel."

"You haven't seen them since? How old were you?"

"No. Twenty."

"Why isn't there a prick test or something for parents?" Riley asked, shaking his head.

"A prick test?"

"Yeah, you know, a test that determines if you're an asshole or not. If you're an asshole you don't get to be a parent."

"There would be a lot less people. And not everyone starts out being a prick."

"Sure they do, it's always there. Some people are just better at hiding it than others," Riley argued. "Besides, it would cut down on the overcrowding issues, and possibly on child abuse and neglect. Then maybe the asshole gene wouldn't get passed on nearly as much."

Kaden chuckled. "It doesn't work that way."

"It should." Riley pouted. "It's a good idea."

"Maybe, but you'll have someone asking who decides who's a prick and who isn't. Some people are simply obeying the tenants of their religion."

"Yeah, religion is a bad idea to base anything off. There are too many to choose from and some contradict others." Riley thought about it for a minute. "I've got it.

You have to pass a business and bio-medical ethics class."

"A business and bio-medical ethics class? Don't most people pass those?"

"I know of three people in my class that failed, and one that finally passed on their third time through."

"How the hell do you fail an ethics class?" Kaden asked, looking over at Riley like he'd grown an extra head.

"Not realizing that ethics, morals, and values are different things. Or just not having any." Riley shrugged.

"Possibly."

Kaden shook his head and Riley returned to staring out of the window. Watching the passing scenery, Riley wondered what Charles' statement or press release said. He also wondered if he should have at least told Brock the truth or some portion of the truth. Whatever Charles said, it was bound to complicate matters. He just hoped it didn't cost him his life. Or Kaden's.

* * * *

Kaden swore and slammed on the brakes as traffic on the two-lane highway came to a stop. Riley bolted awake.

"What the hell is going on?" Riley demanded.

"No idea. Went from sixty to zero," Kaden answered, turning the radio on and looking for a local station that might explain the backup. After finding nothing but top forty or country music, Kaden turned the radio back off. Traffic crept forward.

They were directed off the road and given directions to get back on the highway on the other side of the town.

"Since we have to go through town, can we stretch our legs?" Riley asked, donning his ballcap.

"It would be better to stop at a rest stop than in town. Even a small one." Kaden shook his head.

"Rest stop, like the one we passed five miles ago?" Riley quipped. "It'll be another seventy-five to a hundred miles before the next one. Besides, I have to pee and I want to get a drink."

"You need to stay sober."

"Jesus, you're a fucking tight-ass prude," Riley countered. "No shit I need to stay sober. Thank you, Captain Obvious. Way to jump to conclusions, James. Not to mention, you're completely wrong. I'm thirsty, I want something to drink. Not water or gas station coffee either, which by the way is plain horrible. How the hell do you drink that stuff? Wait, don't answer that. I don't want to know."

Kaden rubbed the back of his neck. "We'll stop at the next gas station and you can get a drink there while I'm getting gas."

"Can't we stop at a real coffee place?"

"First, I don't think a town this small has anything like a Starbucks or even a local coffee shop. There probably isn't anything outside of a small mom-and-pop-type diner."

"Which means no.".

"Riley—"

"I get it. I do. Still sucks. I still want to kill the son of a bitch who is trying to kill me or kidnap me or whatever his game plan is."

"Hopefully it won't be too much longer," Kaden said, turning onto the small town's main street. A banner strung across the road proclaimed it to be Oak Corners Pioneer Days Celebration. Police barricades were erected after the next intersection. It looked like the town's entire population and then some were behind the barricades celebrating. "Damn it." Kaden pulled into the gas station. "What do you want to drink?"

"Uh—Coke is fine. I thought places like this were extinct." Riley leaned forward in his seat. All of the buildings were brick two-stories with large front windows. He couldn't make out any coffee shops, but he did see a couple of restaurants, a pizza place, a movie theater, and a bowling alley along with a hardware store, photography studio, a feed and tack store, and a grocery store. It looked like all of the small-town life painting and photographs he'd seen.

"What do you mean?"

"These postcard-perfect small towns."

"They have them up and down the Eastern Seaboard. Some within driving distance of your home."

"No, those are tourist destinations that cater to the rich. Places that pass a multitude of ordinances to keep things looking a certain way." Riley stared out of the window. "This is like the real deal. Small-town America."

Kaden nodded his head slowly. "I'm not sure I see the fascination. Small towns are everywhere. We've passed several of them."

"Passing on the outskirts isn't the same as driving through them."

"You know, they aren't bugs in a jar to be studied and analyzed."

"Bugs, no, but studied and analyzed, yes," Riley argued.

"And you know this how?"

"Seriously? Four years of college and damn near every single class starts out with some version of tell me your name and what your major is. Some also want to know where you came from and where you plan to go," Riley answered. "A girl in one of my sociology classes wanted to study small-town life in Middle America. She did this basic compare-and-contrast demographic presentation on it for class."

Kaden nodded, turned off the truck, and climbed out. Taking a deep breath, he pulled a credit card out of his wallet and slid it into the pump. While he had no intention of staying anywhere long enough to be found, he also didn't want to be followed. He might not trust his agency, but he trusted Ace. The researcher had never let him down. Eyeing his surroundings, he filled the truck's tank. A county sheriff vehicle pulled into the gas station. Kaden swallowed, his breath catching in his chest. Movement in the cab caught his attention. Riley pulled his hat down farther and wrapped a blanket around him. He looked like he was sleeping. Kaden smiled and nodded.

The sheriff's deputy walked into the gas station. Blowing out a breath, Kaden stayed where he was and watched the officer and the crowd. Once the tank was full and the cap replaced, he walked into the gas station, inclining his head at the officer and attendant. He grabbed two bottles of Coke and two bottles of water and headed up to the counter.

"Will that be it for you?" the teenager behind the counter asked him.

"No, can you give me one of the dollar scratch-offs." Kaden sat the drinks on the counter. "What's going on in town?"

"Not from around here, are you?"

Kaden forced a smile and shook his head. "No, just passing through."

"Pioneer days. Town was settled one hundred and fifty years ago this year, so it's kind of a big deal," the attendant replied. "Everyone for probably twenty miles is here. The state police are helping the sheriff's department with crowd control. Lots of food, games, and live music. You should check it out. It'll be a lot of fun."

"I might," Kaden said noncommittedly, paying for his purchases. "Thanks. You don't happen to know what happened on the highway do you? Hit a dead stop. You might be getting more traffic this way if it keeps up."

The guy nodded. "Car-semi accident. Highway will be shut down for a bit. State police are taking care of that."

Kaden raised an eyebrow.

"Police scanner." The kid smiled. "You learn some pretty interesting things with that thing."

Kaden smiled and nodded. "So do your neighbors."

The kid shrugged and Kaden thanked him again before grabbing his purchases and leaving the store. He handed the drinks in to Riley before walking around and climbing into the other side. Riley was going to have to wait a little longer to get out and stretch his legs. Between the people and the added law enforcement officials, he planned on spending no more time than was absolutely necessary in this area.

"You didn't pay with cash," Riley stated, handing two of the bottles to Kaden.

"No, they shouldn't be able to trace it."

"Shouldn't?"

"Just because it's on television or in a movie, doesn't mean it's real."

"Yes, but tracking credit card purchases has been around a long time. Along with tracking ATM movements."

"True. But first they have to know where to look and who to look for. And that will take some time." Kaden wasn't sure how long they would have once they started looking for him as well, but it wouldn't be as long as they needed, though. At the moment, he was banking on the fact that no one, except Lawrence Russell, knew he was involved.

Riley turned to stare out of the window as Kaden maneuvered the truck through the small town's blocked off and pedestrian-filled streets.

"Damn it!" Kaden swore and pulled into the parking lot shared by the post office and a pharmacy.

"What? What's wrong?"

Kaden forced himself to take a breath and pause before replying. He could hear the near panic starting to rise in Riley's voice. Shoving a hand through his hair, he needed to watch what he said and how he said it. At the cabin, Riley's edginess and near panic wasn't as obvious. Kaden mentally kicked himself for not seeing it sooner.

"I need to use the GPS. Between the construction detours, this festival, and the accident on the highway, it's not as simple to find my way south compared to the last time I was here."

"Gotcha." Riley nodded. "Wait a minute. Who knows you're with me?"

Kaden plugged his GPS in, swore, and waited for the system to boot up. Ignoring Riley's question, he punched in the destination before pulling back out onto the road.

"Kaden, answer me!" Riley demanded. "Or stop the truck and let me out. Who knows you're with me?"

"We've been through this before."

"No, this is new. Different. You said they would have to know who you were, who to look for. The implication is that no one knows we're together. So, once again, who the hell are you? Who knows you're with me? And who or what do you work for?"

"Riley, we've —"

"No! Not good enough!" Riley pounded a fist on the dashboard. "I want the truth. I deserve that much. You're asking an awful lot out of me. Not to mention your reaction to seeing Charles on TV," Riley shouted.

"Riley, we — I —"

"No. You aren't dodging me anymore. Tell me what I want to know or let me out. Now."

"There isn't anything around here."

"There's a parking lot. Pull over there. Now. It's empty. I need to stretch and you need to tell me the truth!"

Kaden pulled into the parking lot of the abandoned factory that Riley had suggested. Weeds poked through cracks in the asphalt. The grass behind the rusted chain-link fence stood almost two and a half feet high. Three stories tall, the metal and brick building looked like it had been built in the fifties and added onto haphazardly before being deserted. Several windows were broken out, others had been boarded over. Kaden drove through the neglected terrain to a spot in the back. There was a driveway leading farther back into the plant off to one side. Kaden parked the truck by the fence, positioning it so he had the best view of their surroundings.

Riley jumped out as soon as the truck came to a stop.

Kaden threw the truck into park, turned the vehicle off, pocketed the keys, and scrambled out after the younger man. Riley stood by the fence, his back to Kaden. "Riley—" Kaden began. "Do you have to do that now? Here?"

"I could have peed in the truck. However, I don't think Preacher would appreciate that."

"Riley—"

"I want answers."

"I can't tell you or anyone else who I work for."

"You keep saying that!"

"Because it's the truth!" Kaden walked over to Riley and grabbed the man's shoulders. "More lives are on the line than just mine. So no, I'm not going to tell you."

Riley broke free and stalked off. He stood, facing away from Kaden, arms crossed over his chest. "You still haven't answered the rest of my questions."

"One."

"What?" Riley spun around. "What did you say?"

"Only one person is supposed to know I'm with you. My boss."

"And that is—"

"Way above your need to know."

"What about Ace? They know."

Kaden nodded. "Because I didn't know everything *I* needed to know."

"And all the James Bond shit you know?" Riley demanded.

"Riley, enough. I was in the military. Now I'm not. Now I work for someone who wants you kept alive. More than that—"

Several black SUVs rounded the corner and pulled to a stop.

"Get in the truck now!" Kaden ordered. He pushed Riley toward the truck. "Don't run, don't look at them. Don't stop."

Windows opened. Time crawled by. Muzzles of weapons appeared. Kaden blew out a breath and reached for his weapon, following Riley at a slower pace. Riley opened the passenger door of the truck. The first shots rang out, pinging off the metal. Riley screamed.

"Shit!" Kaden swore. Bullets pinged off the metal frame of the truck. Kaden thanked every god he could think of not only that had Preacher had agreed to loan them Bubba but also that he had remained overly cautious after leaving the service. The door slammed shut. Kaden withdrew his weapon from its holster, ran toward the truck, and began to return fire. If whoever was after Riley didn't know about Kaden's involvement, they would soon.

Tires squealed. Kaden counted four black SUVs all with tinted windows. If he could get into the truck, Kaden knew they would have a fighting chance of surviving.

The attackers formed a half-circle in front of their truck. Kaden took a deep breath and let it out slowly. There was no way to tell how many gunmen each vehicle held other than the four barrels he could see. He would have preferred a rifle and semi-safe spot where he could pick them off. He didn't have either. Climbing up on to the bed of the truck, he lay down on the leather cover, making himself as small as possible. Undoing the snaps took time he didn't have.

Kaden he took several deep breaths, forcing his heart to stop racing. Taking aim, he fired his Glock 19. He took out two gunmen. Engines revved. Two of the SUVs pulled out and turned around, windows down. Sunlight glinted off metal. Bullets ricocheted off the truck's body and ripped through the leather. Kaden took in a deep breath and let it out slowly. A bullet hit the glass near his head, bouncing away from him. Kaden said a silent prayer of thanks and hoped his luck held out. Shifting his position slightly, he squeezed off another round. The front windshield of one of the black SUVs shattered.

Kaden weighed his options. He could get in the truck and try to continue to fight or run and risk a chase, possibly at high speeds, definitely putting innocent lives at risk, or he could use the pickup as cover. That came with its own set of problems. Staying out in the open was not an option. Kaden blew out a breath. He wasn't sure who he was dealing with — hired thugs, gang members, drug dealers, or the people after Riley. Kaden ignored the constant pinging of bullets off the truck. He aimed at the vehicle with the missing windshield and squeezed the trigger. The glass in the rear window shattered. A body slumped forward.

Slowing his breathing, Kaden aimed at the next vehicle and fired. The glass shattered. The driver slumped forward. The SUV continued rolled forward until it hit the cement base of a tall light. The pole groaned and fell, crushing the vehicle. A passenger climbed out of the wreckage. Kaden squeezed off another round, and the man took two steps before falling to the ground. Another passenger in the backseat prised his way out, bringing an Uzi Submachine gun with him. Kaden fired. The man's hand exploded. The weapon clattered to the ground. Kaden fired again. This time the shot entered his forehead, spraying blood and brain matter all over the side of the SUV.

Engines revved. Tires squealed. Kaden swore, aimed, and fired at the next vehicle in line as they drove for them. The windshield shattered. The driver fell backward. Riley screamed and slid into the driver's seat. Kaden barely made out the order to hang on. Gripping the leaver cover, Kaden lurched as Riley put the truck in gear and drove. He swerved to miss the SUV just before it hit them. Riley pulled to a stop a hundred feet beyond the group.

A bullet whizzed by his head. Kaden rolled over and off from the truck. Kaden continued to fire, hitting more than he missed, taking out the remaining gunmen and the driver of the second SUV. A passenger climbed out of the third SUV, his Uzi spraying bullets everywhere. Kaden rolled under the truck, belly crawling to the back. He aimed and fired, hitting the man in the knee, causing him to drop to the ground. Kaden aimed for the head and fired again. Blood splattered the ground.

The fourth SUV turned around and headed for them. Kaden crawled out from under the truck and took out the windshield and back window. There was a driver and two gunmen remaining in the last SUV. This group knew what they were doing, however, they didn't seem to want Riley alive, if the number of shots fired was any indication. If they were even after Riley, Kaden reminded himself.

Kaden crouched by the bed of the pickup. He needed to get inside the truck while their attackers figured out what they were going to do next. He was almost to the door when the gunman opened fire. Kaden returned fire until he heard the click of an empty chamber. He peered into the cab. Riley was crouched down in the front seat.

Kaden yanked open the door. "Give me the magazine from the center console!" Kaden demanded. "Stay down."

The magazine appeared in his line of sight, shaking slightly. Kaden released the magazine and slammed the new one home, and chambered a round. Turning, he aimed and fired, killing the driver causing the vehicle to veer away. From the main driveway, a line of cars and trucks pulled up, spreading out as they neared.

"Damn it!" Kaden swore. "Where the hell did they come from? Who the hell are they?"

"They aren't your people?" Riley asked, rising up off from the floor of the truck enough to peek out of the back window.

Kaden shook his head. "Not mine. They wouldn't risk you getting injured or killed in this mess. These people don't seem to care." Kaden returned his attention to the remaining black SUV. Leveling his weapon, Kaden fired. The gunman slumped over. The car rolled forward, veering off toward the newcomers.

Kaden climbed in, slammed the door shut, and opened the small side window. He threw the truck into gear. "Give me your gun!"

"My what?" Riley climbed into the seat.

"The gun I gave you, my spare. Give it to me!"

Riley pulled the sleek black HK45 out of its hiding spot and handed it over to Kaden. "No unlimited supply of bullets?" he quipped. "How come you don't have more than two magazines for your gun with you?"

"Character flaw." Kaden shrugged, stepping on the gas. He headed away from the remains of the first attackers and drove toward the newcomers. Vehicles skidded to a halt. Men, dressed head to toe in black, poured out and opened fire.

"Son of a bitch!"

Kaden fired as he drove by. He contemplated taking one more pass, decided against it and sped off down the road. In the rear-view mirror, he saw another group of vehicles approach from the hidden drive. The sounds of gunfire continued to fill the air. Sirens wailed in the distance. Kaden slowed down to just under the speed limit as two police cars drove past them.

"It's safe," Kaden said, turning on to a main road. "Bubba is completely bulletproof."

"Thank Preacher's paranoid heart!"

Kaden laughed.

"Ah, it wasn't that funny," Riley said when Kaden continued to laugh.

"Nope, but adrenaline does weird shit to you," Kaden answered, taking a deep breath.

"The fact that the glass didn't shatter and the bullets bounced isn't as reassuring as I thought it would be."

"I don't think anyone finds it reassuring," Kaden admitted. "I didn't think we'd run into any gunmen yet." More attackers were simply a matter of time. He'd hoped they would've had more time. "Good driving, by the way."

Riley buckled his seatbelt. "They were trying to kill me, which I don't understand. I thought they wanted me alive. That just doesn't make sense."

"For that, I have no answers. Believe me, I wish I did."

"Who were they?"

"I think there were two, possibly three different groups there. I'm just not sure how they found us," Kaden answered. That was what worried him the most. How had they found them? And who were they?

"Are you sure they were after me? Maybe it was a wrong place and time sort of deal."

There was a chance that they were random thugs making drug or arms sales, but that would be one hell of a coincidence. One that didn't seem likely. They were between Lansing and Detroit, so neither could be completely ruled out. Kaden shoved a hand through his hair. The second group of arrivals looked like they could be law enforcement, given how they deployed. Their shots were scattered and didn't appear to hit anything. But there were no lights, sirens, or more importantly, anything labeling either the vehicles or the occupants as having any part of any agency. There were no decals saying police, FBI, ATF, or DEA. The colors of the vehicles didn't match either. The third group was a complete unknown. He hadn't been able to see anything that might help him identify who they were. He heard sirens and pulled over to the side of the road. A pair of police cars screamed by them, heading toward the plant. He couldn't be sure what they would find. Instinctively, he didn't think it would be a lot. Right now, there were too many unknowns. He had more questions than answers.

Riley scrubbed a hand over his face then rubbed the back of his neck. "So, I guess the question is, do they know about you?"

"If they didn't before, they do now. And they can probably guess that the truck is bulletproof."

"Is that bad?" Riley asked, turning in his seat to look out of the back window.

"It could be," Kaden conceded.

"Great. Now what? You didn't plan for this, did you?"

"Nope, this is new. We're going to go meet Preacher, then we may have to head to your family's home."

"And who am I supposed to introduce you as? My boyfriend? Because a security guard in the family's business won't actually work this time."

Kaden rolled his shoulders and flexed his fingers. "A boyfriend would definitely explain the long absence, enjoying yourself yet simultaneously worried about what your family would think. However, it would most likely cause your father and grandmother some embarrassment, and it doesn't go with what you told your friends in New Orleans. Although, you could argue embarrassment with them too," Kaden replied. "Bodyguard is probably a better idea."

"I forgot about Brock. I wonder if that's why Charles is making a big deal out of me disappearing. Although embarrassing Charles has its merits, and my grandmother could weather the fallout, it may not be the smartest idea. I don't see why Charles is going through the trouble of acting as if he cares."

"Have you disappeared like this before?"

"Sort of. Not really, but he doesn't know that," Riley answered. "Pretty sure he assumes that I leave for wherever I want at a moment's notice."

"Do you?"

"Sometimes. However, partying is much better with friends, so I rarely actually go alone." Riley shrugged. "Besides it's not like he has ever once informed me of his plans. We don't talk. He doesn't miss me. Hell, he doesn't even like me. And the feeling is mutual, I might add."

"Would one of your friends have questioned him? Demanded to know why he called you home early?" Kaden asked, looking over at his passenger.

"No, not that I know of. I mean, like I said, Charles has pulled this before," Riley answered, cracking open the bottle of water. "Brock is the only one who might say anything, and that would be more of a side note or in-passing remark to his father."

"Who is Brock's father?"

"Gaylord Richard Wetherby Kingston the Fourth, owner of Kingston and Owen Investments. Brock's mother is Patricia Avery, a highly respected and very powerful corporate attorney, who didn't change her name." Riley smiled.

Kaden glanced over at Riley, who shook his head. "And what? His mother didn't approve of an attorney as a daughter-in-law?" Kaden asked, merging onto I-96. They would take that to just east of Brighton, where they would head south on Highway 23. The highway would take them just outside Toledo, Ohio on their way to Hawk Hollow.

Riley chuckled and shook his head. "Brock said his father's parents were livid and threatened to cut him off without a dime. He laughed at them and said go ahead, he would have a million dollars in his bank account by New Year's Eve and they would miss out on any grandkids. They relented, but tried to get them to give their kids traditional family names. Instead, they ended up with Brock, Lysander, Autumn, and Taryn."

"What the —"

"Pretty much." Riley laughed. The sound filled the cab.

Kaden's gut clenched. He hadn't heard Riley laugh like that. As though they were taking a road trip instead of trying to save his life. He could get used to the sound.

Ruthlessly, he slammed the door on the idea. Riley was his assignment. The mission was to keep the younger man alive, not try to seduce him. Besides, Kaden reminded himself, Charles wouldn't stand for Riley dating a man. Riley had said that himself. The fact that Kaden was on the lower end of middle class wouldn't help his cause. Definitely not with Charles, and monetarily wise, there would be no way he couldn't compete with Riley's way of life.

Kaden pressed the heel of his palms against his eyes. Regardless of what Riley said, the younger man wasn't ready to leave the safety of the wealthy lifestyle he was used to. He probably never would be. To be fair, though, Kaden couldn't blame him, even if it did appear to be a very stifling world.

Chapter Fourteen

Riley stirred as the truck pulled to a stop. "Where are we?" he asked, rubbing sleep from his eyes. The radio was playing a song that he thought was from the eighties or maybe the nineties. "Sorry, I fell asleep on you."

"I'd say you needed it, but it's a fairly boring drive."

Riley nodded and pulled on his hat. "Yeah, and I can't read or anything in cars, so I get bored easily. It's one of the reasons why flying is better."

"Except for that whole government ID thing."

"Yeah, except that. Which, by the way, was never a problem before," Riley said, getting out of the truck. He shrugged into a plain gray zippered sweatshirt and followed Kaden into the building. Glancing around the parking lot, he was relieved there were no police cars in sight. There were a handful of cars, most with Ohio plates, but there were a couple from Michigan and one from Wisconsin.

There were a half-dozen choices for food and coffee and one place selling Ohio souvenirs. The sitting area with a dozen tables and chairs was off to one side.

Mounted on the walls were four large-screen televisions playing a baseball game, a race, cartoons, and some sitcom Riley had never seen before. At least people appeared to be more interested in their phones or the baseball game and race instead of the news.

"What is this place?" Riley asked, raising an eyebrow.

"An Oasis," Kaden explained. "We're on the Ohio Turnpike."

"A what?"

"They're the rest stops along a toll road."

"Weird." Riley shook his head.

"Just imagine everything you miss by flying everywhere."

"You say that like it's a bad thing." Riley frowned, laughter and mock horror edging his voice. "I'm going to the restroom then get a cup of coffee. Hopefully, it's decent."

Kaden nodded.

Twenty minutes later they were back on the road. A comment by one of the baristas at the Coffee Hut had made them both edgy, with Riley suggesting he should color his hair as they climbed back into the truck. Kaden had agreed. They began looking for an exit that looked like it would have a store that would carry hair dye. Riley wanted something dark, either a brown or even black, that would give him a completely different look.

Kaden took the next exit, paid the toll, and followed the signs to the left.

"Why did you get off here?" Riley asked. "It looks like cornfields. Lots and lots of cornfields."

"Sign for a hospital. Most of the time hospitals are found in areas with larger populations. That means a drug store or grocery store that will carry hair dye."

"A motel sounds good."

"The motel or just getting out of the car?"

"Yes," Riley answered.

Kaden laughed. "We're meeting Preacher in a couple of hours, so no motel yet."

Beside him, Riley stiffened.

"You don't like Preacher?"

Riley shrugged. "It's not that I don't like him, I just don't know him. He's dangerous."

Kaden nodded. It was a fair assessment.

"You thought he sold you out or something."

Kaden shoved a hand through his hair and shrugged. It had been an easy jump to make. He could blame it on the present circumstances he found himself in, but there was more to it than that. Preacher viewed laws, rules, and regulations as suggestions more than something hard and fast that he needed to follow. "It's one of two guiding principles that I have."

"Like one of those warrior codes of conduct deals? First, do no harm?"

"That would be the medical profession, but yes."

"So, what are these fantastic guiding principles you have?"

"What?"

"You heard. I want to know what the guiding principles of the man tasked with protecting me are." Riley crossed his arms across his chest. "Just to be clear on where I fit on the food chain."

Kaden sighed. He really needed to remember to think first around Riley. The man had an uncanny ability to get him to reveal things he had no intention of sharing. "First, trust few, verify all. Second, everyone has a price."

"That's a fairly cynical view of life. Not everyone can be bought. A fact that has pissed Charles or his cronies off more than once."

"I thought you said your father didn't spy on other companies."

"I don't know about any spies *Charles* may or may not employ or their tactics, nor do I care," Riley replied flatly. "There are probably a dozen reasons why Charles or any other wealthy businessman may need to pay people off. Avoiding a scandal would probably be the first choice. Things like sex with either a man or women, especially with men, mistresses, pedophilia, unwanted children or pregnancies, marriages that should have been annulled or otherwise ended, but weren't. There are the classics like drugs, drinking, drinking and driving, public intoxication, sexual harassment, causing an accident or death, fleeing from an accident. And don't forget good old-fashioned bribery. For any number of reasons."

"All of which just illustrate my point."

"No, your point was that everyone has a price," Riley argued. "I said that no, they don't. Many businessmen have lost more than money when someone couldn't be bought. For example, that pair of Wall Street stockbrokers who were arrested three months ago for running a prostitution ring out of their firm. They had both male and female prostitutes, but specialized in young males. They were outed, so to speak, after trying to first bribe then threaten a security officer."

"And—?"

"The bribe was for a half billion dollars. More money than that security guard will see in his lifetime."

"And you know this how?" Kaden asked skeptically. "That wasn't released to the public." He remembered the story. He made a point to follow the news, reading the same stories on multiple networks or newspapers so he had a more complete picture of what was going on. There was a possibility that the ring was part of a larger international sex-trafficking ring. The occupation and identity of the whistle-blower had been kept out of the news, as had the amount of the bribe. The identity of the security guard matched up with what he'd heard. However, he wasn't prepared to swear to that as a fact.

"People talk. Rich people gossip too, just about different stuff."

"Sounds like the same stuff, just more of it." Kaden shook his head. Riley continued to surprise him. He found himself looking forward to what he was going to discover next about the other man. Kaden pulled into a spot near the front of the store and left the truck running. "I'll be right back. Then we need to find a place where you can color your hair."

"A hotel? Hot shower. Soft beds."

"A truck stop with a shower would be better. It will take a few minutes for the dye to set."

"And you know this how?" Riley asked.

"Bodyguard one-oh-one. Hair dyes and beards are the easiest way to change appearances."

"You want me to try to grow out a beard too?" Riley turned and raised an eyebrow.

"The idea has merit."

"Okay, no. That so isn't going to happen," Riley answered.

"Why not?"

"Two reasons. One, every time I've tried to grow a beard or moustache it has come in scraggly and pathetic. Second, I hate the way my face feels. And really, it takes forever to grow. Like I can shave every three days or so. It takes that long to grow."

Kaden nodded. "I'll be right back."

Inside the store he scanned the aisle of hair color, overwhelmed by the variety of women's hair dyes. He spotted the small section of men's hair dye and chose a midnight blue-black. Riley's light brown hair should take the dye without too many problems. He paid cash for the box and returned to the truck. Kaden put it in reverse and sped back out of town toward the highway and the nearest truck stop. Thirty-five minutes later, he found what he was looking for. The sign boasted a restaurant with real home cooking and showers in addition to a gas station and convenience store.

"Shower."

"Um, no offense, but I'm not taking a shower with you." Riley shook his head. "Anyway, you have that rule about not mixing business and pleasure."

"You can go in under the pretense of taking a shower and color your hair. Take a shower after to rinse off all the dye. Don't forget to change your clothes."

"Joy."

"We don't have a lot of time nor do we have a lot of options. I want to make it another hour or so past our meet-up with Preacher before we stop for the night." Kaden pulled into a parking spot and turned the truck off.

"That can't come soon enough." Riley sighed, climbed out of the truck, and grabbed his backpack. "These showers cost, right? So I assume you're paying."

Kaden nodded, pulled out a credit card from his wallet, and stuck it in the front pocket of his jeans. They walked through the building to the showers. Kaden paid for the shower and waited until after Riley ducked inside and locked the door behind him before he wandered through the small store. He picked up a copy of the newest Alpha Centauri Colony book and two red sweatshirts with the word Ohio emblazoned on the front. One for Riley and one for his youngest brother, Aiden. His birthday was next week. It was stupid. A stupid move. But it was done. The last email from Braydon had said that Aiden was going through a really rough time and his brother didn't think Aiden would make it if something wasn't done to help him. Kaden hadn't been sure how he could help, but he reminded his brother that they were both welcomed at his home anytime. Shoving a hand through his hair, he sat down in the restaurant where he could keep an eye on the hall leading to the showers and ordered a cup of coffee.

Kaden briefly considered taking the second sweatshirt back, but decided against it. His youngest brothers, Braydon and Aiden, were the only members of his family that he had any contact with anymore. Kaden sipped on the coffee and glanced down at the plastic bag before turning his attention back to the hallway leading to the showers.

Riley walked down the hall, his baseball cap pulled down low over black hair. Kaden held up a hand, catching Riley's attention. Kaden tracked Riley's progress into the restaurant as a state police officer walked into the store.

"The crap stinks!" Riley said, sliding into the booth across from Kaden. "Can't they make it stench-proof? Damn."

"I think it only comes in stench and extra-stench."

Riley grinned. "Are we eating here?"

"Hadn't planned on it," Kaden answered, tilting his head in the direction of the state trooper, who had been joined by a second one. "Are you hungry?"

"Yes. We have time, don't we?"

Kaden looked at his watch. They didn't have the time. Not really. The detour for hair dye and gun battle had taken time he hadn't planned on. He liked getting places early if he could help it. Most of the time, it gave him the advantage. But they hadn't eaten much the entire day and the sense of normalcy might help Riley regain some of his equilibrium. Kaden nodded. "We can't take too long, though."

"Awesome!" Riley said, opening up the menu.

The waitress came by and took their orders, returning shortly afterward with a glass of water for Riley.

"So, what's in the bag?" Riley asked.

"Sweatshirts. Here, put it on." Kaden pulled both sweatshirts out, looked at the tags then put one back. "I felt the inside of it. It feels really soft. Softer than most of the ones I have." He had never taken the time to feel the inside of a sweatshirt before. He'd felt the insides of all three styles they had and went with the one that felt the softest. He hoped it was good enough for Riley.

"Um, thanks." Riley held it up. "It's a bit baggy."

"Just enough to hide your shape."

Riley nodded, pulled off the tags, and slid it on. "It's soft at least."

"Good. I never paid attention to the feel of things before, so I was guessing."

"It's a good guess. Who's the other one for? Your friend Ace?"

Kaden laughed and shook his head. "No, Ace wouldn't be caught dead in something as mundane as an Ohio State sweatshirt."

"Sounds…um…kinky…weird…"

"Ace has a blue and purple Mohawk with bits of silver and probably glitter. Their casual wear is more clubwear, sometimes there is a tie or button-down shirt, but it's never boring."

"So they look like a rainbow threw up on them?"

Kaden thought about it for a moment. "No, it's a little more tasteful than that, just not what most people would call normal."

"So, who's the sweatshirt for then?"

"One of my brothers."

"You have brothers?"

"Yes, five of them in fact. You sound surprised."

"I am. I guess I just never pictured you with a family. I mean, you mentioned family earlier, I just never actually pictured you with, you know, siblings."

"I don't. I have two brothers I write to occasionally."

"How — why — You know, never mind, that's a personal question." Riley shook his head and sat back as their waitress set their food on the table.

"It is." Kaden nodded. He wasn't sure he wanted to tell a virtual stranger his life history. "Braydon and Aiden."

Riley raised an eyebrow. "Braydon, Aiden, and Kaden? You know your names all rhyme, right?"

Kaden made a sound of disgust. "I think that was my mother's idea."

"Anyway, you were saying."

"Braydon found me a few years ago and sends letters and messages from Aiden occasionally."

"It's cool that he's talking to you regardless of what your parents think." Riley looked over at him. "Thanks for telling me. I know you didn't have to."

Kaden smiled, nodded, and bit into his burger.

They finished their food and paid the bill in cash, leaving extra on the table for a tip. The police officers had left shortly after the food had been delivered. A pair of county sheriff officers walked in as they were walking out. One of the officers stared at Riley, who smiled and grabbed Kaden's hand and pulled him over to the rack of postcards, stating he needed to send one to his mom.

Kaden paid for the postcards and tossed the coins in the charity jar sitting next to the register.

"What was that about?" Kaden asked when they were in the truck.

Riley shrugged. "I didn't like the way that officer was looking at me."

"Which was—"

"Like I was either someone they were looking for or their next meal. I don't know which, and I'm not really interested in finding out."

"Fair enough. Let's go, before we're late meeting up with Preacher." Kaden pulled out of the parking lot and headed toward Hawk Hollow.

"Who names these places?"

"What places?"

"You know, places like Hawk Hollow, Dry Gulch, Hickory Corners, Oak Creek. That one didn't even have a creek near it. No river or anything else."

"You'll want to take it up with their founders." Kaden smiled. "If you want to see something really interesting, you should take a road trip down Route 66."

"I've heard of that. That still exists?"

"Most of it, yes."

"Huh." Riley pulled off the hat and ran his hands through his hair. "Do you know there's a cop following us?"

"Yep. I'm hoping it's a coincidence."

"And what are the chances of that?" Riley asked, looking in the side mirror.

"Fifty-fifty," Kaden answered flatly. Kaden continually glanced in the mirrors and carefully monitored his speed. The last thing he needed was to get pulled over for any reason. Riley sat in silence, his gaze fixated on the truck's side mirror. Tension filled the space between them, pushing everything else out.

Kaden held his breath as they passed a sign indicating the highway on-ramp was three-quarters of a mile ahead.

"I feel like I should be praying we make it," Riley said, barely above a whisper.

Kaden simply nodded. Without a clear view of the patrol car, it was nearly impossible to tell the difference between the local and state police.

Red and blue lights flared. The siren pierced the cabin.

"Shit!" Riley swore.

Kaden flipped the turn signal on and began to pull to the side of the road. The patrol car slid into the other lane, speeding up as it passed them. Kaden let out a breath and slumped back in his seat.

"Holy shit!" Riley shouted before bursting into laughter.

"Pretty much." Kaden shook his head. Flipping his flashers off, he stepped on the gas.

"The only thing I could picture was getting stopped and going to jail. I'd be dead before they could straighten this whole mess out." Riley shoved his hand through his hair.

"They wouldn't put you in jail," Kaden said, looking over at Riley. The idea of the younger man in a cell with a real criminal made the bottom drop out from his stomach.

"No," Riley agreed. "They would put you in a jail cell and me in some sort of interrogation room without any protection until they got a hold of Charles or, more likely, Charles' lawyers, who would arrange for someone to pick me up. And by the time the officer got back from making that call, one of those people who can be bought would either have slit my throat or kidnapped me."

Kaden swallowed and nodded. He had to hand it to the other man—he had a fairly accurate grasp of the possibilities. "You're awfully calm."

"Scared shitless." Riley shook his head. "But screaming or reverting to some sort of babbling idiot is not going to actually help me. I have no intention of dying now or anytime soon really, nor do I intend to let a bunch of goons kidnap me for whatever 'it' is. Hidden key or not."

"Let's get to Preacher."

"Why are we meeting him again?"

"Change vehicles," Kaden reminded him.

"Is that smart?" Riley asked, cracking a bottle of water. "I mean, this thing is bulletproof. Which is totally cool by the way."

"And depending on whether anyone who survived caught the license plate number, could be wanted by the police."

"How? There weren't any police at that—that—whatever the hell that was."

Kaden reached over and squeezed Riley's knee. "Gun battle or firefight are probably good descriptors, however, unexpected is a better word."

"I still want to know who they were."

"That may be something we never know." Kaden merged onto the highway.

Riley nodded and turned to stare out of the window.

The remainder of the drive to Hawk Hollow was uneventful, the silence broken by discussion about books, music, movies, and myriad other topics that were superficial. Light conversation purposely designed to avoid reliving events. The sun had nearly disappeared below the horizon when they pulled into the back of the gravel parking lot of a large truck stop. The flashing red and blue neon 'open' sign clashed with the brown and gold 'Old-West inspired' sign declaring the restaurant Sandy's and home to America's best meatloaf and home cooking.

"Black Dodge Charger?" Riley asked, raising an eyebrow. "That's subtle."

"That's not mine." Kaden shook his head. "The Mustang is mine. The Charger, I don't recognize. Shit. Yes, I do." Kaden tightened his grip on the steering wheel and mentally cursed Preacher.

"Another Army buddy?"

Kaden nodded. "Yep. Let's get this over with."

Kaden turned the truck off and pulled out the keys. Weapon drawn, he climbed out of the truck and made his way to the pair of men leaning against the Charger, pausing briefly for Riley to join him.

"This is an unexpected surprise." Kaden glared at Preacher.

"You're late," Dez snarled. The six-foot three-inch tall black man crossed his arms over his muscular chest. "I had to eat truck stop food and listen to his whiny ass go on and on about Bubba. You'd think it was a damned lover the way he went on."

"You're the one who wanted to come." Preacher shrugged and stepped away from the car.

"Do they always argue like old women?" Riley asked Kaden, pointing a thumb at the pair.

Kaden laughed.

Chapter Fifteen

"Just watch who you're talking to, boy!" Dez said, and straightened out his six-foot three-inch muscular frame.

Kaden felt Riley stiffen beside him.

"Yes, as a matter of fact they do." Kaden chuckled and stepped forward. "New job not work out?"

"I take it he's yours," Dez sneered, nodding at Riley.

"In a manner of speaking, yes."

"What manner?"

"Nothing that concerns you." Kaden folded his arms over his chest. "Why are you here, Dez?"

"Preacher said that you got your ass into two shit tons of trouble with your fancy—uh—job." Dez stepped forward, his body tense. The need to fight flowing off him in waves.

"Yeah, thereabouts." Kaden nodded. "But I really just needed a different car."

"Why are there dents in Bubba?" Preacher demanded.

"Got caught between two gangs of possible drug or arms dealers."

"Gunrunners in Michigan? Seriously?" Preacher asked in disbelief. "There's less there than in the corn states. I still can't understand your fascination with the place. I mean really, aside from some decent fudge, there isn't anything there. And the good fudge is only on the one island, Mackinaw, isn't it? Place where cars aren't allowed."

"And lakes that freeze between one country and another," Kaden countered. He refused to go into details with his friends. He'd bought the property years ago, after he'd joined the military. He'd fallen in love with the area when he was a kid on one of the few family vacations they'd taken. First he'd planned on using it as a hunting cabin, then it had become a refuge from the world after the years of war, then it became his bolthole and personal safehouse.

"So what happened?" Dez asked, his weight shifting slightly. His eyes narrowed. Jaw clenched.

Kaden knew the look, the stance. Dez was an amazing tactician. The man had the uncanny ability to put patterns together, he was a wealth of random and sometimes useless information.. It had saved their asses more than once. At one time Kaden wouldn't have hesitated to tell his buddies everything. Too much had happened, though. Too many years had passed, and at the same time not nearly enough.

Long moments passed. Kaden's past and present warred. Tension increased. A hand lightly touched the small of his back. Riley stepped into his line of sight, withdrawing his touch as he did. Kaden let out a breath and reached for a decision.

"The short version is, this is Riley Hamilton."

"As in the missing heir to the Hamilton fortune?" Dez whistled. "Official reports say that Charles Hamilton contacted the FBI, supposedly after he received an anonymous tip that his son had been kidnapped. He went public with a plea for information. I've heard that not everyone in the *family* is on the same page with that."

"And the unofficial report?" Kaden pushed.

"Feds went to him."

Kaden nodded. He'd thought about not revealing Riley's identity, but knew from experience that inaccurate information cost lives and could mean the difference between a mission's success and failure. Dez's emphasis told him that there some sort of disagreement between agencies, not within Riley's family.

"Riley, this is Dez, otherwise known as Desmond O'Shaughnessy," Kaden said, introducing the tall, muscular black man.

"Nice to meet you." Riley shoved his hands into his pockets. The formality of the tone was not lost on Kaden.

"How do you know all that?" Kaden asked.

Dez smiled. "I know someone who knows."

"That'll get them fired."

"It could. But, probably not."

"Any idea when Charles' received this *tip*?"

"Three, three and a half weeks. A Friday night, I think."

Kaden stiffened. That was the night that Riley had been kidnapped.

"You kidnap the kid?" Dez asked.

"I was told to keep him alive at all costs," Kaden said, "because someone was after him. Now the kicker is, I wasn't told who. Just 'someone'. I think the Russians are behind it, but why they would be after the grandson of a possible Russian sleeper cell is beyond me."

Dez rubbed the back of his neck. "You're stating you believe that someone in the Hamilton family is or was a spy for the Russians? That family is very small, moderately well known, and very wealthy, and they also travel all over the world."

"It gets better. After I met my boss, I was beaten, tied up, and left under my rental truck. By three men with FBI badges and guns," Kaden explained. "The dents, those come from a gun fight. We stopped at an abandoned warehouse to stretch our legs, when we were attacked by men in black SUVs. Four of them, ten to fifteen assailants. Then just as that fight was ending, a second group of vehicles approached. Mixture of SUVs and cars, spreading out in flanking maneuvers."

"That sounds like law enforcement or military." Dez cocked his head to one side.

"Possibly," Kaden agreed. "But it could also have been drug dealers or gun runners."

"I don't know, man." Preacher scrubbed a hand over his face. "It sounds like you kicked up some seriously heavy shit. Are you getting support or not?"

"That's unclear." Kaden hesitated.

"Or a no, not at all. Considering the bulletproof vest nearly didn't do its job," Riley spat.

"Defective vest? That sounds planned." Preacher folded his arms over his chest.

"The question is, who planned it? Who knows?" Kaden asked. "That's one of the things I need to figure out. The other is who is behind this. I can't see the

Russian government caring about the grandson of a spy."

"But someone closer would," Dez said slowly.

"Agreed." Kaden rubbed the bridge of his nose.

"Like who?" Riley asked. "Who wants me dead?"

"Kidnapping isn't dead," Preacher said flatly. "It may lead to death, and generally does. But kidnapping first is about obtaining something someone wants."

"Yeah, we figured that part out. But them shooting at me means they now want me dead." Riley stepped forward. "Seriously, Kaden? These are the best resources you can find? We'll be dead by morning."

"Watch it, kid." Dez lowered his voice.

"Time's up." Kaden stepped between Dez and Riley. Riley was no match for Dez. And Dez's posturing was eating up valuable time. "We need to leave."

"Well she's gassed and ready to go."

"She?"

"Your car. She. Name is Bella, short for Isabella. Nice, pretty ride," Preacher chided. "What is it with you and refusing to acknowledge spirit, man?"

Kaden rubbed his forehead. "It's a car, Preacher. It's just a car. A hunk of machinery, sleek and powerful maybe, but it's still a machine."

"Poor delusional soul. Maybe if you had respected and acknowledged the spirit of your vehicles more, yours wouldn't have been blown up all the damned time," Preacher said.

Kaden opened and closed his mouth. There was no reason to point out that IEDs were buried or snipers were hidden. Preacher had driven the same roads, although it was actually only Kaden's vehicles that had seemed to be consistently lost.

"*Her* name is Bella. Be good to her. And if there is any permanent damage to Bubba, I'll send you a bill."

"That's fair. Shouldn't be more than dents and a couple of holes in the bed cover," Kaden replied. "Change the license plate, though."

"What makes you think I would do anything illegal? I'm shocked at your suggestion." Preacher pretended to be horrified. Riley laughed and shook his head. "Oh, and Rowdy, your bike, is in Bella's garage."

Kaden rolled his eyes. Riley supressed a laugh.

"Look me up if you need help." Dez clasped forearms with Kaden. "Don't be a damn stranger. Stop by Scotty's Tavern sometime and have a drink with me. We'll catch up. Hash everything out."

"No promises, Dez."

"Kid, you bring this old codger with you and come down for a proper visit," Preacher said to Riley, while clasping forearms and hugging first Kaden then Dez.

Riley nodded and followed Kaden back to the truck. They grabbed their gear and tossed Preacher the keys before heading to Kaden's car.

"Ladies first!" Kaden yelled, sliding into the car and turning it on.

"What was that all about? And is this thing bulletproof?"

"Unfinished business. The glass is and the doors are reinforced, but that's it," Kaden answered, waiting for Preacher to finish his inspection of his truck. Kaden would leave after Dez and Preacher. Dez would return to Washington DC, Preacher would head back to Texas. Kaden wanted distance between them.

"Not as spacious as the truck. Doesn't look fast either." Riley set his bottle of water into the cup holder.

"Okay, can we now, please, go find someplace to sleep. Preferably with a pool so I can swim."

"Swim?"

"Yes, swim. It's seen as a form of exercise. I need to stretch my muscles. Besides, I'm going to get out of shape."

"A couple of weeks won't hurt you."

"Three and a half," Riley correct. "Maybe. Maybe not, but let's not try it. I'm not used to staying put. I need to get out and move."

"I don't know," Kaden said, hesitating.

"Look, I'm not trying to get caught or killed, I just need to move. To relax. I won't be there long. Hotel pools stink of chemicals worse than just about anything else. You can check it out beforehand. If there aren't any people around, I can swim. If there are, I don't. If they come in once I'm in the pool, I get out. Easy."

"Maybe. If we find a hotel with a pool. And if it's open. And if you have something appropriate to wear."

"Who did the anonymous tip come from?"

"What?" Kaden blinked and looked over at Riley as Dez's and Preacher's taillights disappeared into the night.

"Who did the anonymous tip come from?" Riley repeated with exaggerated slowness. "Distracted much? How exactly do you manage to get anything accomplished?"

"I don't know, but I'm damn sure going to find out."

"How? Why doesn't law enforcement track everything?"

"Some would like that. However, there is that whole freedom without Big Brother that this country is known for argument. And that constitutional law thing that gets in the way."

"Very funny. But seriously, it would make finding the bad guys easier."

"True, but on the other hand, if that were the case, then those bad guys we're trying to avoid would already have you and possibly have what they want."

"And me dead."

"Probably."

"Great." Riley stretched and yawned. "So, how come this car isn't as tricked-out as Preacher's truck? I may need to invest in a car like that."

"Preacher and I don't have the same resources or connections. Not only that, this is actually only a back-up car."

"Yep, definitely need to get a car with all of the security options as well as a powerful engine." Riley cocked his head and turned toward Kaden. "Can anyone get the machine gun mount or is that reserved for special customers?"

"You're having way too much fun with this."

"Exhaustion, discomfort, and leftover general terror from getting shot at will do that to you. Humanities one-oh-one. You know, in case you forgot how to be a human in all of your super spy cum military action hero training."

"That's—"

"You may be used to getting shot at, Kaden, but for most people it's a new and rather unnerving experience. You can process it however you need and want to, and I'll do the same, thank you very much." Riley pulled his hat down over his eyes and slid back in the seat.

Chapter Sixteen

"Wake up."

Riley blinked awake. He stretched and pushed himself upright. His muscles protested the movement, as well as the awkward and uncomfortable sleeping position. He'd dreamed. Riley wasn't sure if his proximity to his bodyguard had made things worse or better. His dreams were spliced with memory, experience, and a horrifying mixture of fantasy and reality, leaving him more than a little unsettled. "Where are we?"

He recognized the name of the hotel chain they were parked in front of. Riley raised an eyebrow. The hotels ran from barely functioning with questionable bedding and optional cleaning to the high end of the mid-range hotels. It was not a luxury hotel, but he doubted they could pay cash for a room here, and a questionable credit card most likely wouldn't work.

"Pool is open until ten, which means you have just over an hour to swim."

"Yes! Thank you!"

"We're on the first floor."

Riley nodded and got out of the car, stretching again before grabbing his duffel bag and following Kaden into the side entrance of the hotel. Kaden handed Riley a white plastic key card.

"Room one-fifteen. Vending machines are halfway down the hall across from the elevator." Kaden opened the door to the room and stepped inside.

Riley followed Kaden into the room and stopped at Kaden's signal, waiting while the other man checked out the bedroom and bathroom, even opening the door of the closet and all of the drawers. Riley was on the cusp of reminding Kaden that people weren't actually small enough to fit in the drawers, when Riley realized that he was also looking for bugs. Riley shivered. He wasn't sure if Kaden was being paranoid or if there was actually a reason to worry.

"Please tell that was a precautionary measure only."

Kaden stood, turned around, and raised an eyebrow. "And what do you think I was doing?"

"Looking for bugs." Riley crossed his arms over his chest. "You don't think they've found us already, do you?"

"No, I don't think they've found us already. However, if I know what things look like beforehand, it's easier to figure out what has changed," Kaden replied. "Do you have swim trunks with you? I can't imagine the hotel will be thrilled with a skinny dipper in a family pool."

"Yes. Although, come to think of it, I don't think I've gone skinny dipping before. That sounds like fun. Something I definitely need to try."

Kaden shook his head. "By the way, where were those? I've seen inside your backpack."

"Snagged them from the suitcase in New Orleans before we mailed it back."

"Wishful thinking?"

Riley shrugged. Honestly, there wasn't a good reason why he'd kept the swim trunks. They had fallen out when he'd added another change of clothes to his bag. He'd shoved them into the pack without really thinking about it. He still wasn't sure if he'd grabbed them because he hadn't believed Kaden or if he'd wanted the other man to be wrong. Riley yanked out the trunks and headed into the bathroom to change.

Stepping back out into the room, Kaden tossed a hunk of black fabric at Riley, causing him to drop his clothes and the towel from the bathroom.

"What the—" Riley sputtered. "At least warn a guy before you throw something at them, geesh. Seriously, Kaden, you need to work on your manners."

"My manners are fine."

"If you say so." Riley picked up his clothes and the towel, depositing them on the bed. "Why do I need a T-shirt? And one of yours? Are you concerned for my modesty or some such crap? Doesn't modesty go against the whole spy-code thing? I mean, James Bond beds every woman he meets, or tries to at any rate."

"I am not James Bond."

"Probably not, because I'm pretty sure the gay version of James Bond would have tried to fuck me already."

"I prefer my men willing, completely," Kaden growled. "The shirt is for you. In the case of cameras, there is less of a chance of you being recognized."

"I thought that's what the hair dye was for, which stinks by the way."

"It is, but everyone has tell tale gestures and movements. Bodies can be similar, and someone who has intimate knowledge of you might be able to identify you."

Riley laughed. "That would imply that someone gives a rat's ass about me more than what I can do for them, and I can guarantee you, there isn't a soul alive who matches that description. Now, can we go swimming before my entire night is ruined?"

Kaden nodded, grabbed his new book and gestured to the door.

* * * *

Riley treaded water in the deep end of the pool watching the interaction between Kaden and a newcomer. Kaden was tense, looking more out of place than he already did. The newcomer, a middle-aged man, had come in with his wife and three kids. His wife had taken the smallest with her and had left almost instantly. The other two were in the shallow end of the pool and the man had sat down at the table across from Kaden. Riley had heard enough of the conversation to know that Kaden had explained that he didn't know how to swim, but they were newlyweds, so he didn't want to be too far away. It wasn't until Kaden waved at him that he realized that the other man had been hoping he heard the conversation. Either that, or that Riley would just be go along with whatever he was doing. Anger coursed through him. Riley smiled, hoping it appeared genuine, and waved back. He dove under the water, swimming as hard as he could from one side of the pool to the other. Kaden would have to know that he wasn't going to blindly go along.

Riley surfaced as the man's wife, a beautiful Indian woman, walked in with the little one wearing bright-pink blow-up plastic arm bands. The conversation between Kaden and the other man was drowned out by the giggling and squealing from the kids, the noise reverberating off the walls. Riley swam to the shallow end of the pool and climbed out.

Taking a deep breath, he smiled and walked over to Kaden, half-jumping in the other man's lap. He chuckled and shook his head, making sure to get the other man wet.

"I'm sorry for interrupting." Riley turned to the other man and stuck out his hand. "I'm Jay."

"Harish, nice to meet you," the man said, shaking hands. "You are passing through?"

"Road trip. I want to see both sides of Niagara Falls." Riley reached over Kaden, grabbed a towel and dried off his hair. "Can I have the key? I'm tired."

Kaden pulled the plain white key card from his back pocket and handed it to Riley.

"Nice to meet you, enjoy your vacation." Riley stood, careful not to disturb Kaden's jacket and the gun it was hiding. He was almost to the door when Kaden caught up him. Riley smiled, but stayed quiet. He wasn't sure if the family believed the story that Kaden had told or not. He didn't care. Slamming open the door, he didn't wait for Kaden to check the room out before storming inside.

"Wait—"

"You couldn't come up with any other story?" Riley asked, grabbing his pack.

"It's nine-thirty at night. I certainly didn't expect a family with young kids to show up, or someone who wanted to talk."

"We couldn't be friends or brothers on a road trip?"

"Friends and brothers don't watch someone from the deck, fully dressed. It's never done. That wouldn't have been believable. But I'm glad that you were able to hear what was being said."

"Until the kids started making noise."

"Without admitting to being a bodyguard, and having to explain a reason for that, newlyweds was the only real choice I had."

"And the boner?"

"You *did* jump in my lap and you *are* a hot guy," Kaden explained. "Why did you do that by the way?"

"Pool parties."

Kaden raised his eyebrows. "What?"

"Pool parties. Invariably, there is some chick, or a guy the last time, come to think of it, that is dating some stick in the mud that doesn't want to get wet, so they run and jump into the date's lap soaking wet."

"This is a thing?"

"It is at parties with teenagers and college students, or at least college-aged people instead of fuddy-duddy, stuffy backyard barbeques filled with middle-aged people and families," Riley smirked. "I'm going to take a shower and go to bed."

It had been impossible to miss Kaden's cock starting to harden. It hadn't bothered Riley as much as he'd thought it would. Not that he wanted to think of the bodyguard in any sort of sexual way, but it was satisfying to know that he had been responsible for the reaction. Riley stripped and turned on the water. He had always considered himself on the straight side of bisexual. He'd experimented, dated, and had sex with both men and women, but invariably found himself more attracted to women than men.

Riley lined his bath products along the edge of the tub, removing the small bottles of cheap shampoo and soap. Stepping into the shower, he admitted it wasn't impossible to see himself dating someone like Kaden. The other man was cute with dark hair and eyes. Cute was a fun one-night stand, maybe a weekend. It wasn't a long-term relationship, and it certainly wasn't one that would be sanctioned by either Charles or his grandmother. While he wasn't sure he cared what either one truly thought, he wasn't willing to give up his lifestyle for something that under normal circumstances would have been little more than a one-off, if that.

These weren't normal circumstances.

Riley let out a frustrated, angry scream and pounded his fist on the shower wall. He wasn't sure what he wanted more — to punch Kaden for where he was now, the idiot who had targeted him, or, if Kaden was right, the family-member who is actually a traitor. He wanted his normal life back. At least being Charles' pawn came with benefits like the best cars, trips, sex, and houses. Blowing out a breath, Riley shoved a hand through his hair. He was sure Charles would figure out a way to leverage the whole situation into more money for himself.

Relaxation slipped away. Riley's muscles tightened. Promising himself a long vacation that included a masseuse and alcohol, he turned off the water and stepped out of the tub.

* * * *

"What are you watching?" Riley asked a short time later as he walked into the room.

"News. Senator Jeffrey Abrams out of New York just announced his intent to run for president in the next election."

"Hey, I know him."

"You know a senator?" Kaden asked in disbelief.

"Technically, no. I saw him at the house over the years when I was younger. Holiday parties are excuses to drink, have sex, and schmooze. Not necessarily in that order." Riley dropped his backpack onto the floor next to the bed and sat down. "Politicians have rich friends."

"Most of them are also rich. Like goes with like."

"Yes, but politicians like to have friends that give them money. Like those who host or attend benefit dinners or holiday parties. Rich people, well, those who want to make friends of politicians who are more likely to give them or their interests special consideration."

Kaden nodded. "Lately?"

Riley shook his head. "I haven't seen him since I was fourteen or fifteen. He's creepy, by the way. I think he was more my grandfather's friend than my grandmother's."

"Creepy is nice and specific."

"Yeah, which means I didn't go looking for him."

"Does either your grandmother or father still host those benefit dinners or parties?"

"Sometimes. Not as much. My grandmother sits on the boards of a bunch of charities and organizations in addition to ours. Charles hosts parties occasionally, but I try to avoid those, so I couldn't tell you who is at them or anything else. His secretary probably has all of that information. I know none of the women he's involved with seem to be capable of planning a party like Charles throws."

"Meaning?"

Riley raised an eyebrow. "Seriously? Charles isn't looking for a companion, he's looking for an adoring trophy. One that is slightly disposable."

"Here." Kaden tossed a bottle of water at him. "Does his secretary have information on these women as well?"

Riley shrugged. "Yeah, probably."

Kaden nodded and scribbled notes on a pad of paper Riley hadn't noticed before. "Well, this could be an interesting election season."

"Wait. She's familiar. Who is she?" Riley pointed at the screen with the closed bottle of water.

"How do you know her?" Kaden asked.

Riley cocked his head to one side. "I don't. I think she was at some function my grandmother went to." Riley shook his head. "Her secretary and personal assistant work together when she hosts things —"

"Do you have names?"

"Elizabeth Miller is Charles' secretary. Older woman, married. She's been there for sixteen years. Maybe longer."

"He doesn't hire future exes?"

Riley laughed. "I think he did for a while. Until one of those girlfriends caught him cheating on her with a future ex and screwed up a bunch of stuff. Nothing illegal. Just made a mess. Maxine Cook is my grandmother's personal assistant and Jackson Kelly is her secretary."

"You have no problems handing over their names?"

"I was shot at. People want me dead. Or that key. Charles' stunt put me in their crosshairs. I'm not feeling particularly familial at the moment."

"Fair enough."

"So, who is she?"

"Army Major General Amelia Mathers. She's seen combat."

"I didn't think they let women in combat."

"Rules have changed. Women saw combat before the rules changed. She's one of them. Has a wife I believe."

Riley nodded as the news footage cut away to yet another press conference where Connecticut Congressman Richard Peterson was announcing his candidacy. "Well, as fascinating as the trip from death to politics may be, I'm going to bed. Can we not get up at the ass crack of dawn?"

"Alarm is set for six."

Riley groaned and flopped back on the bed. "You're a sadistic asshole, Kaden."

"Probably."

Chapter Seventeen

Riley turned and scowled at Kaden. "How is this a good idea?" They had driven ten hours almost straight. They'd stopped for gas and little else along the way. Riley's body was cramped and he was tired of being in a car. If he never took another road trip it would be too soon. He wasn't sure why people liked them.

"It's not."

"Then why are we here?" Riley demanded as they turned into the drive leading to his family's home. His stomach rolled. This was the last place he wanted to be at the moment. He just couldn't decide if it was because he was catching Kaden's paranoia or because he would have to deal with Charles and explain Kaden's presence.

"The answers we need are here?"

"And what if the bad guys are too?"

"What do you mean?" Kaden pulled to a stop at the gate.

"What if it's someone who knows my grandparents?"

"May I help you?"

"We—"

"Hey, Frank, can you let us in?" Riley leaned over the seat and waved at the uniformed guard.

"Where have you been? Your father has the FBI looking for you!"

"It's a long story, but do me a favor—don't let anyone else in."

"Don't know that I can do that, sir."

"I don't want to be disturbed or answer questions."

"That's up to your father."

"Which means there will be a press conference tonight, not that Charles actually gives a damn about me." Riley sat back in the seat.

The guard hesitated for a moment before nodding and opening the gate. Riley didn't miss the look of pity the older man gave him. He hoped Kaden had. Charles' disdain for him was an open secret. Nobody talked about it, but everybody knew.

"You'll keep your gun on you, won't you?" Riley shivered as they neared the house. There was a single SUV parked in front that he didn't recognize. At least it didn't appear that a contingent of FBI agents were around.

"Shit!" Kaden parked the car in front behind the SUV. "It's bigger than I thought it would be!"

Riley burst out laughing.

"Share with the rest of the class."

"Sorry, the only thing I could think of is that shirt that says 'That's what she said'."

Kaden shook his head. "Junior high humor? Really?"

Riley shrugged. "Whatever works."

"Keep that thumb drive on you at all times. If we get separated for any reason, I can use it to find you again."

"You may not follow me into the shower or my bedroom."

"Shower, no. Bedroom, we'll see."

"Seriously, *James*? It's my own house." Riley opened the car door.

"Yes, and Charles was told not to call the FBI." Kaden stepped out of the car.

"By your employer?" Riley joined him at the front of the car.

Kaden nodded. "So, tell me about the house."

"Apparently, it was built by a lumber baron or shipping magnate. It was abandoned during the Great Depression. My grandfather had it completely renovated. It's been updated a few times since then." Riley blew out another breath. He'd grown up here. While the house had never been particularly warm and receptive, tonight it felt downright sinister.

"Impressive."

"Why shouldn't Charles have called the FBI? I still don't understand. Aren't they supposed handle kidnappings and the domestic stuff?"

"The guys that jumped me had FBI badges. Not sure if they were fake or not, couldn't get a close enough look," Kaden answered quietly. "And yes, normally, under some circumstances anyway, the FBI does handle kidnappings and the like."

"Why do I feel like we're walking into the viper's den?"

Kaden reached for his weapon and stopped.

The door opened. An older man with white hair and dressed in a black suit opened the door. "Mister Riley, your father is waiting for you." The man paused and swallowed. "And your guest in his study."

"Thank you, Benjamin. I'm sure Charles is anxious for my return," Riley said sarcastically. "Benjamin, this Kaden Tennison, my bodyguard and friend. He gets to go everywhere with me."

"Your father—"

"I don't give a shit what he wants or says. Kaden is *my* bodyguard and not employed by Charles, so what he wants doesn't matter. It's not like he missed me."

"Your grandmother did," Benjamin replied softly.

Riley nodded at the reproach. He watched Benjamin head toward the kitchen. Cocking his head to one side, he wondered what the older man did what he wasn't answering the door or running errands for the family. Riley shoved a hand through his hair. Benjamin had always been kind to him, now that he thought about it. Mentally chastising himself, Riley led the way to Charles' study. He wondered why he hadn't thought about Benjamin before.

"Is this normal? Your father isn't waiting here for you?"

Riley stopped and turned. "He's waiting in his study."

Kaden raised his eyebrows and shook his head.

"You're acting like that's weird."

"It is. I have never once seen a parent of a kidnapped child to not only not be waiting, but running out of the door as soon as law enforcement pulled into the driveway."

"Those parents care. Big difference." Riley steeled himself for the meeting ahead.

"I'm sorry, I—"

"No worries. I'd say Charles would make for a fascinating behavior case study, but I'd be lying," Riley quipped. "Brace yourself."

Riley knocked once and opened the door.

"What is the meaning of this?" Charles demanded. "Who are— What did you do to your hair?"

"Riley James Hamilton?" a white man with graying brown hair and dressed in a black suit and a blue shirt asked, stepping forward. He wore an FBI windbreaker and held his left arm in the same manner as Kaden held his right arm.

"Seriously, Charles, if you didn't want me home, then you shouldn't have gone on air demanding my safe return from whatever evil monster was holding me. What is it that you said to me?" Riley dropped into the nearest chair, aware that Kaden was right behind him. "Oh, yeah, I remember. That I was worthless, hopeless, and not wanted even by my mother. That my only value to you was in a good marriage."

"I—" Charles turned red, his chest puffing in anger.

"Which, by the way, no one was holding me."

"Where have you been then? The police have—"

"Oh please. The police have not actually been looking for me. One, because I'm an adult and I can freely travel wherever I feel like it. And two, it's hardly the first time I've gone off without telling anyone. If you ask any number of the staff, they'll tell you it's a regular occurrence."

"I am your father. You will respect me!"

"Seriously? The FBI is here and *now* you want to play father of the year. That's rich. Considering you've never been a father, and I haven't called you 'Dad' since I was seven and you decided that spending Christmas and New Years with that blonde bimbo was more

important than being home with your only child!"
Riley snapped. "So, why are you here?" Riley turned to
the black-suited strangers. "I'm not an important
enough person to justify wasting taxpayer dollars on."

"That's need-to-know information," the FBI agent
who'd asked him his name stated. "We have some
questions for you. Without your friend."

"I'm not interested in answering anything you have
to say. I wasn't missing. I'm twenty-two, so an adult
everywhere."

"Where have you been since you left New Orleans?"
Charles demanded.

"Having the time of my life. Not here."

"You told your friend Brock I had you brought
home."

"I'm surprised he said anything." Riley shrugged.
"Huh." God knew none of his friends could actually
stand Charles any more than he could.

"Riley James Hamilton, where were you?" his
grandmother demanded, walking into the room. "And
why wasn't I told he had been found? And you are my
grandson's bodyguard?" Margaret Hamilton asked,
looking over at Kaden.

Kaden nodded.

"I wasn't missing, Grandmother."

"The FBI have been looking for you. They received
an anonymous tip that you had been kidnapped. Then
when you didn't return home with your friends, we
thought the worst."

"I'm sure you're the only one, Grandmother.
Charles couldn't have been bothered."

"Your father—"

"Said I was worthless and useless, so not someone
the FBI actually should have been wasting time on. I

want to know who called them and why they actually believed it," Riley said, interrupting his grandmother. He refused to discuss his family and Charles' love, or lack thereof, in front of Kaden or the FBI. While he didn't really care what the FBI thought of him or his family and Kaden already knew, Riley didn't want it thrown out in public. The last thing he wanted from anyone was pity.

"That is —" Charles began.

Riley looked the three agents up and down. "If you are unwilling to answer my questions, then you can leave."

"This is *my* house, they don't have to go anywhere, and you will answer their questions."

"Technically, the house and the grounds belong to Grandmother and by law, I don't have to answer any questions. And, I absolutely won't answer them without my lawyers present. Both of them. And as one of them is out of town, that could take some time."

"Your lawyers are mine," Charles sneered.

Riley shook his head. "I have dealt with others, and in this case, yours will be biased against me. I'd rather have people on my side." Riley jumped to his feet. The FBI agents reached for their guns. "Don't shoot inside the house. Your combined salaries for three years couldn't replace the antiques in this room, let alone in the rooms surrounding us." Riley walked over to Charles' mini fridge and grabbed a bottle of water. "Did you know people name their vehicles? For instance," Riley checked to make sure the bottle was sealed, flipped it upside down and squeezed, "one of my lawyers, the one on vacation, has a sports car named Mary Jane."

"I don't care if some asshole names their cars," Charles shouted.

"And I don't care why the FBI wants to ask me questions. I want to know why they thought I was kidnapped in the first place."

"We had reliable information," one of the agents stated. He was a tall black man who looked like he'd played football at one time. "I'm Agent Wilkins and—"

"They lied." Riley shrugged, opening the bottle of water.

"I'm Agent Wilkins," Agent Wilkins repeated. "And these are Agents Cobb and Johnson. Do you know why someone would want to kidnap you?"

"You, I like." Riley smiled, pointing the bottle at the man. He saw something floating in the water and set the bottle down on the corner of Charles' desk. "You don't have that slimy, used car salesmen vibe. But that is a question, and I don't feel like answering questions from the FBI." Riley returned to Kaden's side. "Now, if you don't mind, we're going to bed. I'm exhausted."

"It's barely seven."

"Yes, and I'm exhausted. I really do hate mornings."

"Your friend can sleep in the blue room," his grandmother said, nodding.

"Actually, he'll be sleeping in my room."

"Oh, I didn't realize he was *that* kind of a friend."

"He's both my boyfriend and my bodyguard." Riley smiled and shrugged. He prayed he knew what he was getting himself into. There wasn't a relationship or anything else between them, but two out of the three agents in the room rubbed him the wrong way and he didn't want Kaden out of his sight.

"You're gay?" Charles demanded. His face turned red and his cheeks puffed out. "How—? Why—? What about all of those girls?"

Riley leaned on the back of the chair he'd been sitting in and shook his head. "I'm bisexual, not gay. It means I like both men and women, Charles."

"You can't—how dare you—" Charles sputtered.

"Think of it this way, with a bisexual son, the company can look progressive and hire the best talent. You might even be able to make more money that way. Being LGBT friendly and all." Riley grabbed Kaden's hand and headed for the door.

Margaret Hamilton stepped forward and stopped them, placing a hand on his cheek. "I'm glad you're safe."

"I'm home. For now," Riley replied. Kaden squeezed his hand and Riley stepped back. "Excuse us, please."

"I want to meet with you and your young man at breakfast tomorrow."

"How about lunch instead? I hate mornings."

"Lunch it is. Twelve-thirty."

Riley nodded and pulled Kaden out of the study. Kaden insisted on retrieving their bags from the car before going to bed. Riley relented. He took the time to explain where they were, what each room was for and some of the artwork as they walked to his room. He knew Kaden would be able to piece enough of the information together to find his way around the house if needed. Once in his bedroom, Riley waited while Kaden searched the room. He found two bugs along with a hidden video camera.

"What the fuck?" Riley was livid. "I don't get it. Why—"

"Quiet," Kaden whispered in Riley's ear. "You have a role to play. One I didn't think you wanted to try."

"Made it up as I went along." Riley shrugged. "Now what do we do?"

"Make it as believable as possible."

"I'm not an actor," Riley protested.

"So, awkward in a relationship with another man for the first time, at least as far as your family knows, is normal." Kaden kissed his cheek and rubbed a hand down his back.

Riley shivered, nodded, and stepped back. "I'm going to take a shower. Did you get all of the unwanted visitors?"

Kaden shrugged. "I'll look again."

Riley grabbed his bag and disappeared into the en suite. He needed to figure out what he was going to do now. There was something definitely off about at least one of the FBI agents, possibly two of them. He didn't trust the agents any more than he trusted Charles. At this point, he also wasn't sure if trusted his grandmother. Riley slid the small leather wallet from the hiding spot in his backpack and stared at the photos of his mother. Briefly, he wondered what she would have thought. What she would have done. Taking a deep breath, he closed the wallet and replaced it in his bag. He wasn't sure he could act like Kaden's boyfriend.

Scrubbing his hands over his face, he stripped and turned the water on. Hopefully, he could go back to his own place tomorrow. Riley pushed the thought aside. Kaden wasn't about to allow that. Showering quickly, Riley turned the problems over in his mind and still found himself circling back to the same questions with no obvious answers. Wrapping a towel around his waist, he walked out of the bathroom and over to his dresser.

"Where is—"

Riley let the towel drop, pulled out a pair of clean sleep pants, and stepped into them. "Where is what?" he asked, turning around.

"The—um—" Kaden stuttered and shoved a hand threw his hair. "Please do me a favor and try not parade around half-naked. Shit."

"I'm not naked." Riley walked over to the queen-sized bed and pulled back the covers. It didn't look like his bedding had been altered in any way. "I take it you checked everything out."

Kaden nodded, pointing to the pitcher of water with several metal and plastic pieces lying on the bottom of the container.

"Go take a shower. You kind of stink. I'll give you a tour of the place tomorrow."

"Do not—"

"I got it. Go!" Riley shook his head as Kaden retreated to the bathroom. Riley turned in a circle, arms crossed over his chest. He was certain the room was as secure as Kaden could make it. Knowing that people had been in his room and that everyone had a price, he picked up the chair from his desk and wedged under it the knob to the bedroom door. The curtains had been arranged to completely hide the window. Riley cocked his head and turned back to the chair. Blowing out a breath, he ran his hands through his hair. Kaden might trust the agents, or even other law enforcement, but he wasn't about to. Nor, would he trust the locks on any of the bedroom doors. He wondered what bothered Kaden more, his family, who Kaden believed were Russian spies, or the FBI agents. If they *were* FBI agents.

He didn't think law enforcement, in general, should give off a slimy vibe.

Scrubbing a hand over his face and rubbing the back of his neck, Riley walked around his room. It didn't look like a lot had changed. Things had moved slightly, but that was normal. He wasn't as worried about it. He worried more about the people after him and how much Charles and his grandmother knew. If Kaden was right.

Riley flopped down on the bed. He retrieved the pieces of his phone from his backpack and reassembled it before shoving it back in his bag. What did that mean for him if Kaden was right? He wasn't a spy. Would he have to leave the US? His friends? Would he have to go live in Russia? Hadn't Kaden said he was American because his mother was?

"Riley?" A hand touched his shoulder.

"What the—" Riley jumped, hitting his head on the headboard. "You scared me."

"I noticed. You have to be aware of your surroundings. At all times."

Riley rubbed his head. "Isn't that what I have you for?"

"Yes, but you have to be aware also. Know where you are, who's around you, and where the danger is."

"I'm at home. Aside from a couple of FBI agents that give off a weird vibe, my life already has a full array of people who want to use me for their own gain. Or at least use my money. Danger is relative."

"I'm talking about life or death danger, not making or losing money in the stock market or betting on a game." Kaden walked around to the other side of the bed and sat down.

"People kill for less. I think I saw a story on the news about a man who attempted to kill his girlfriend because he *thought* she was looking at another man. Not that she was cheating on him, but because she was *looking*, or he assumed she was looking. She wasn't. He was cheating and paranoid. If people didn't get hung up over stupid stuff, the police would be out of a job."

"I don't think that would be a bad thing. Kind of sounds like paradise."

"No, paradise is white sandy beaches, clear blue water, and good music."

"And here I thought you were going to say free-flowing alcohol."

Riley shook his head and crawled under the blankets. "Paradise is a place where the alcohol isn't needed."

Chapter Eighteen

Kaden snapped his eyes open, slightly disoriented with the warm body coiled tightly into him. He hadn't expected Riley to seek him out in the night, or how right the other man felt next to him.

"Kaden?" Riley asked, his voice husky with sleep.

"Quiet," he ordered. He lay still, trying to seek out what had woken him up. Slowly, he reached up beneath his pillow, withdrew his Glock 19 and slid it under the sheet, placing it on his stomach.

Riley's hand moved down his body, stopping at the weapon.

"Where was this? Why do you have it? What's going on?" Riley demanded, whispering.

"Shh. I don't know yet."

They listened in silence. The doorknob jiggled.

"There are two men trying to get in," Riley said. "They're looking for the key or they have a key. It's muffled, but they aren't being quiet about it. They must think or know everyone is asleep and on the other side of the house."

Kaden nodded. "Or both." Grateful for Riley's sensitive hearing, he slipped out of bed. He first checked the windows before moving to the door. At least one of the voices sounded like it belonged to one of the FBI agents. Kaden shook his head. Someone was going through a lot of trouble to get to Riley. He needed to find out why. He needed to find out everything he could on the Hamiltons.

The knob jiggled again. One of the men swore. Kaden chambered a round. Quietly, he moved the chair from under the knob. The door burst open. Kaden hit the first man on the head with the butt of his weapon, sending him sprawling across the floor. The second man through the door, Johnson, swung at Kaden, knocking the gun from his hand. Johnson rushed Kaden, slamming him into the wall. Pictures rattled. Kaden doubled his fists and brought them down across the agent's neck. The man dropped to the floor. Kaden moved for his gun. Johnson shook his head and scrambled to his feet. Kaden kicked him in the gut, pushing him into a heavy wooden desk that sat in the corner of the room. A lamp and a pen holder fell over. Johnson picked the lamp up off the desk and swung. Kaden ducked. The lamp hit the wall with a thud, the bulb shattered. Johnson punched him in at the face then in the gut, pushing him backward. Kaden stumbled, stood, and smiled before striking back. The pair traded blows, Kaden giving as he received. He pinned the man against the desk. The agent groaned. Kaden reached into the man's jacket and pulled out a gun, tossing it toward the bathroom.

"Kaden!"

He turned in time to see the agent introduced as Cobb scramble over the bed, gun drawn, after Riley.

Riley grabbed the lamp off the nightstand and swung, knocking Cobb to the floor, the gun skidding under the bed. Kaden spotted his gun by the foot of Riley's bed. He slammed Johnson's head against the wall and launched himself. Kaden grabbed the weapon and jumped to his feet.

"Behind—"

Catching a glimpse of Johnson in the mirror coming up behind him, Kaden waited the span of a breath then shot his leg out, sending the man stumbling backward.

Moving, he positioned himself in front of Riley. "Stay behind me!" Kaden demanded. He felt a tentative hand on the small of his back.

"You can't fire on federal officers!" Agent Cobb shouted, pushing himself up.

"Hand over your weapon," Kaden ordered.

"Over my dead body."

"That's original," Riley quipped.

"I can arrange that." Kaden smiled.

"You can't kill both of us!"

"Actually, I can. And my money is on the fact that you aren't real officers."

"You saw our badges!"

"No, we didn't. You didn't show them to us when you introduced yourselves or when you demanded to take Riley for questioning. And you certainly didn't show them or announce yourselves as federal agents or even law enforcement officers—per FBI protocol— when you barged into our room in the middle of the night as we were sleeping," Kaden replied, weighing his options. "If you're FBI, you're dirty."

"How dare you! You'll pay for this!"

Kaden shrugged. If the two men were real agents they were dirty, willing to kidnap and murder to get a hold of Riley. Alone, the information didn't provide him with anything new. It could be a matter of simple bribery that had them working for Riley's unknown enemy, or something more nefarious.

The second agent moved.

Kaden fired, shooting the wall an inch away from the man's head. "Next time, I won't miss."

"What in the world is going on in here, Mister Riley?" Benjamin demanded, barrelling through the door.

"Benjamin, please call the cops. These two men broke into my room and were trying to kill me. Or kidnap me."

"They're FBI agents, sir."

"Maybe. Maybe not. Please call the police. They can sort it out."

"Riley!" Margaret Hamilton called from the hallway. Kaden recognized the twin emotions of terror and worry.

"I'm fine. Kaden is protecting me. But we need someone to call the police on these two. They tried to kill or kidnap me."

"Of course," Margaret replied. Her voice was cold. Either she was a master of disguising her emotions or she was some combination of angry and worried that only mothers seemed capable of. It was the tone of voice that promised they were going to rip you limb from limb for hurting their precious baby.

"Do your guards have handcuffs?" Kaden asked.

Benjamin shook his head. "No, they've never been needed before."

"They should start. And be on the premises at all times from now on."

"Do you have any idea how much money that will cost?" Charles demanded, pushing his way into the room.

"Get out!" Kaden yelled. "Everyone. Out. Now."

The hand moved from his back.

"Riley, don't move."

Riley's hand returned to its previous position.

"This is my house!" Charles shouted.

Cobb started to move. Kaden fired, hitting the man in the knee. Turning, he fired a second shot by the head of the man identified as Johnson.

"Don't do it," Kaden ordered. "Mr. Hamilton, you are a distraction and a potential hostage. Please remove yourself and your mother from the immediate area. Benjamin, please get me a dozen zip ties and let the police know there is an injury."

"You'll never get away with this!" Johnson shouted.

"Maybe. Maybe not." Kaden carefully sidestepped his way to the bedroom door, his weapon fixed on the agents. He wanted Riley closer to the room's only real exit. Long minutes passed before the zip ties and a pair of guards arrived.

"Bind the hands and feet of both men." Kaden indicated the agents with the end of the gun.

"You'll regret this!"

"He sounds like one of those cops on TV that always turn out to be crooked," Riley said. Kaden heard the nervous laughter in the other man's voice.

"It's probably all of the training he's had."

"I want to know who hired them."

"I do too," Margaret Hamilton said from the hallway. "The police are on their way. One of the staff heard the shots and called it in."

"I'm not telling you anything!" the second agent spat.

Kaden walked over and dug his fingers into the wound on the other agent's leg. "Who hired you?"

The agent howled.

"That's a federal officer you're torturing," Johnson shouted.

"I'm not torturing anyone. I doubt either of you are federal officers or any sort of law-enforcement officers. I want an answer."

"Hampton City Police, put the weapon down!" a gruff voice ordered as eight police officers swarmed into the bedroom, guns drawn.

Kaden's weapon was seized.

"Kaden!" Riley called out as a uniformed officer tried to grab him.

"Do. Not. Touch. My. Grandson!" Margaret Hamilton ordered. The calm, feminine voice cut through the chaos. The police officer reaching for Riley hesitated then stopped.

Kaden forced his body between the officer and Riley. "He's the one they were after."

"You will come with us," an officer said, reaching for Kaden.

"Riley, go to your grandmother," Kaden said. A pair of officers grabbed his arms and forced him against the wall, cuffing his hands behind his back.

"He's my bodyguard," Riley protested. "He's doing his job!"

"Just your bodyguard?" Charles sneered.

Riley spun on his heel, facing Charles. "What in the hell do you care? You've never given me a second thought. This whole mess is all your fault, plastering my photo all over the country. Not like you actually care."

"Why should I?"

"Charles, that will be enough," Margaret said. "Riley, please accompany me to the library."

"Ma'am, he can't leave," one of the officers stated, his voice soft but firm.

"He is joining me in the library of my own house. You may talk to us both downstairs. However, as Riley has stated, Mr. Tennison is his bodyguard. His job is to keep him safe by any and all means possible. Now, you will excuse us."

"Ma'am—"

"You." Margaret pointed at a young black officer holding on to one of the agents. "You look trustworthy. You can guard the door to ensure we don't run away. Satisfied?"

"Jamison and Hernandez, go with Weston. Take the rest of them with you." A red-haired, middle-aged man and a Hispanic female joined the group.

Kaden watched the group leave. Five officers remained with the two federal agents and himself. Kaden growled as the two officers led him out of the door. Agent Johnson jumped to his feet as the zip ties on his feet were cut, pushing one officer to the floor and running past a second. Kaden broke the free from the easy grip of a sandy-haired officer and hurled himself at Johnson, sending the man down the staircase.

Two police officers surrounded him. Two more rushed after Johnson.

"Let's go, asshole! You bought yourself—"

"I'm a fucking federal agent," Kaden argued as he was pushed against the wall near the staircase. "ID is in the black duffel. Hidden compartment in the bottom."

"Like we're going to believe you."

"Check it out," Kaden demanded. If anything happened to Riley because he wasn't there, he wouldn't stop until everyone responsible was eliminated. Kaden tried to force himself to calm down. Riley was simply an assignment, not his lover, no matter what charade they were playing for his family.

"Count on it."

Time stood still. Kaden clenched his jaw as he was handcuffed and led out of the house and forced into the back of a police car. A call to Lawrence had the potential to ruin everything. Kaden flexed his fingers as he tried to figure out his next steps. They still needed to know what they were after, figure out who was ultimately responsible, and keep Riley safe. He'd taken a chance, exposing himself, but he couldn't risk going to jail. That would leave Riley completely unprotected. He didn't trust Charles Hamilton any more than he trusted the FBI agents.

"Where's Kaden?" Riley demanded as a middle-aged man in a black suit walked into the library. The officers had already talked to everyone in the room, but had steadfastly refused to answer any of his questions.

"Mr. Tennison is being detained for further questioning."

"Why? He didn't do anything wrong! He saved my life," Riley said.

"Chief Montgomery," his grandmother said quietly. It was the polite, reserved tone that his grandmother used whenever she was displeased with something or someone.

"Good evening, Mrs. Hamilton, I'm sorry to disturb you at this time of night."

"Will this take much longer?"

"I apologize, ma'am, but we do need to figure out what happened here."

"I already told the officers what happened," Riley snapped. "We woke up to the sounds of those agents or whatever the hell they are trying to break into my bedroom."

"I thought he was your bodyguard."

Riley silently wished he hadn't said anything in the first place or that Kaden, or the very least Preacher, were here to help. "Yes, he's both my bodyguard and my boyfriend."

"I see."

Riley wanted to punch the man and his condescending tone.

"Chief Montgomery, whatever the proclivities of my grandson and your antiquated opinion, he is *my grandson*, and I presume you will do your job to the best of your abilities as will every member of your department," his grandmother stated. She narrowed her eyes and pursed her lips. "Mr. Tennison is the *only* reason that my grandson is still alive. He does not need to be charged with anything."

"With all due respect, ma'am, we have to get to the bottom of this," the chief said, swallowing.

Riley shoved a hand through his hair. "Kaden moved a chair, they busted through the door. Kaden hit one with his gun, I think, then fought the other guy."

"Shots were fired?" the older man asked.

"Yes." Riley scoffed. "Because they wouldn't stop coming after me. One grabbed me, left a bruise."

"He threatened one of my officers."

"Your officers were going to grab me and probably arrest me too. His job is to keep me safe, at all times,"

Riley answered. "And, for the record, I don't like being touched."

"They're doing their job."

"And those two agents claimed to be doing theirs, but were breaking into my room while everyone in the house was asleep, or getting ready for bed. After I already told them I wouldn't talk to them without my lawyer present." Riley paced the room. He wanted to see Kaden, to know the other man was okay.

"How well do you know Mr. Tennison?"

"I met him a couple of weeks ago, in New Orleans, when he saved my life the first time."

"Did he? How much do you know about Kaden Tennison?"

"I know that he saved my life."

"I don't think so. I think he wanted you to believe—" The old man shook his head.

"Multiple broken ribs from being kicked, bruised damn near from head to toe from where some assholes had kidnapped me!" Riley spat. "I seriously doubt that was his idea of wooing me for whatever reason you seem to think. Because, until tonight, I hadn't admitted I was bisexual to anyone. Ever."

His grandmother gasped and the police chief sputtered. Riley didn't care. He knew he'd said too much, but Kaden was the only person he knew he could trust at this point.

"Most likely, he'll be released tomorrow."

"He shouldn't have been arrested in the first place!" Riley shouted.

"He's not being arrested. He's simply being detained while we determine exactly what happened."

"Is all of this really necessary?" Margaret Hamilton asked, her voice firm and clipped. "We've been over everything multiple times already. It's late. We've talked to your officers alone, and now to you as a group, without our lawyers present, I might add. I see no reason why this has to continue at this point. There is no reason for holding Mr. Tennison for any reason. My grandson's safety is of upmost importance."

"I'll leave a couple of officers out front for additional security."

Margaret Hamilton nodded. "Riley, stay in the Rose Room tonight."

"Yes, Grandmother. Benjamin, as soon as Mr. Tennison arrives, please send him up."

"Of course, Mister Riley."

"He won't be—"

"There is no reason to keep him, so there is no reason he needs to wait until morning to be released," Riley said, walking toward the door. "Unless of course, you and your officers also want to see me kidnapped and killed."

"That's quite an accusation, young man."

"Two federal agents, which by the way, where is the third one? Have you even looked for him? Two federal agents, or imposters, tried to kill me an hour ago. Less. More. You'd be a little suspicious of law enforcement too."

"You're accusing men, good men, of accepting bribes."

"Everyone has a price," Riley said. "Grandmother, excuse me."

"Jamison, please escort Mr. Hamilton to his room. Unharmed," Chief Montgomery ordered.

"I do not need an escort. Especially not from strangers." Riley clenched and unclenched his fists. He wasn't going anywhere with any of the police officers.

He had no reason to trust anyone on the force. He didn't know them. He didn't know if they could be or had been bribed or might even be inadvertently passing information on to the people who either wanted him dead or kidnapped for whatever reason.

"There is no need for your officers to waste their energy on something trivial," Benjamin said flatly.

Chief Montgomery hesitated before nodding once.

Riley stormed out of the room, aware that Benjamin had followed him. A pair of uniformed officers stopped their conversation as he neared them. Mentally Riley dared them to stop him. He wanted to argue. To fight. To rip some poor asshole apart. The men watched his progress, but said nothing to him.

"Really, Benjamin, I don't need an escort," Riley said as they neared the grand staircase.

"All the same, I'll walk with you," Benjamin said quietly. "Alone, your grandmother will worry for your safety."

"Grandmother doesn't worry about me."

"You'd be surprised, sir."

Riley rubbed the bridge of his nose. He was too tired to argue with the older man. He stopped by his room and retrieved his backpack and Kaden's duffel bag before heading to the guest room his grandmother had assigned him. The Rose Room was closer to his grandmother's and Charles' bedrooms than his bedroom. It was decorated with delicate, antique furniture and pale pink roses. It was one of the more feminine rooms in the house.

"Have a good night, sir."

"Good night, Benjamin." Riley smiled and walked into the room. It was as he remembered it. A large mahogany Queen Anne four-poster bed dominated one wall, flanked on either side by large curtained windows and matching nightstands topped with Tiffany lamps. The right nightstand held a digital clock and a white handheld phone. A mahogany armoire and a pink and white rose-covered wingback chair and matching ottoman filled the wall on the left side of the bed. On the right side were a pair of matching doors. Between the wall and the second door sat an antique writing desk and chair. On one corner of the desk a slender crystal vase held a pair of silk pink roses, a matching vase with identical roses surrounded by an assortment of pink and white candles sat in the center of the dresser that faced the bed. A search of the dresser produced a chain ladder. The room smelled of roses. However faint it might be to others, it was still slightly overpowering.

Riley walked around the room, looking for anything out of place. He searched through the armoire and looked behind the pictures of still-life roses. The windows provided a good view of the front lawn. He would be able to see anyone that drove through the gates. One door led to a bathroom, where the rose theme continued. A claw-foot tub surrounded by a rose-covered shower curtain stood in one corner. A white pedestal sink and ornately framed mirror stood against the adjoining wall. The other wall held a linen closet and the toilet.

The other door in the room led to a walk-in closet. He almost missed the small door tucked behind curtains that were hanging and pushed all the way back. The door led to a room and locked from the inside.

Riley smiled. It wasn't a panic room, but he was starting to wonder if his grandmother had one of those somewhere also. There were several places in the room he could hide if he needed. The bedroom windows opened, and appeared to be connected to the security system. Shoving a hand through his hair, he pulled the chair from the desk and stuck it under the doorknob.

He moved both bags to the side of the bed, pulled out the silver-gray gun he had used before, and laid it on top. Undressing, he tossed his clothes over the weapon and slid into bed.

Chapter Nineteen

Kaden sat on the edge of the cot in the jail cell, clenching and unclenching his fists. The urge to hit something or someone crawled through him. Calling on his training, he pushed the anger aside and relaxed his body and mind. He'd been in worse situations in worse places for longer than he should be here. The thin blue mattress offered little in the way of comfort. The stark white-painted walls were devoid of graffiti, in contrast to the stained gray concrete floors. There was a faint smell of sweat, urine, and bleach. He didn't want to know how many people had sat in the same cell. Kaden rubbed the bridge of his nose. He was taking a risk, but he didn't see that he had much choice. There were more rules, more gray areas. The presence of possible FBI agents changed things. He needed to get out of here. He wasn't sure who could be trusted, and the list of possible suspects continued to grow.

Charles Hamilton didn't need the money, nor did he seem to have any sort of relationship with his only child, but he wouldn't have been the first person to use their children to further their own interests. Kaden rubbed the back of his neck. He knew for some people they were only concerned with how something affected them, looking at their children as commodities. He was certain that even if this was the view that Charles held, it didn't appear to be one that Margaret Hamilton shared. Kaden slid back on the bed and leaned against the wall and closed his eyes.

* * * *

The door rattled and clanged. Kaden opened his eyes. The clock on the wall read eight o'clock. A pair of uniformed police officers walked in. They were similar in height and build. One was a black man by the name of Robinson, and the other a Hispanic man by the name of Hernandez. They were different than the officers who had arrested him. He wasn't sure if they had heard his claim or not and whether or not they believed him — their body language was impossible to read. Kaden assumed they would err on the side of caution and assume he was guilty and dangerous. They had families they would want to get home to at the end of their shift.

"Stand. Turn around. Hands behind your back."

Kaden obeyed the officer's directions.

"Back up."

Kaden cautiously walked backward until his hands touched the bars. Metal cuffs snapped onto his wrists. He was ordered to turn around and was led through the holding area and through a small maze of corridors to the glassed-in office belonging to the chief of police. Kaden glanced around the room, studying the contents.

The slightly worn path on the carpet indicated the door was normally kept open. A glossy, dark wooden desk dominated the office. A name placard sat at an angle on the left. On the right side of the desk, a small cup held pens, pencils, highlighters, and a permanent marker. A file organizer and a small stack of folders were on the left. A monitor, keyboard, and mouse sat on the right side of the desk. A lone file and notebook lay in the center.

A pair of tall, matching black bookcases flanked a long, narrow cabinet. Certificates of appreciation and diplomas from two different universities declaring the recipient had degrees in Criminal Justice and Business Management hung on the wall. The top row on the left bookcase held plaques and a unit photograph. Books, binders, and labeled magazine holders filled the remaining shelves. An overflowing file organizer lay on the right side of the cabinet. Photographs were grouped together on the other side. Two were of couples with children, one was of an older couple, and one was of a couple by themselves. The man sitting in front of him wasn't in any of the photos.

A pair of blue and gray chairs sat in front of the desk. A low bookcase full of books was pushed against the only other solid wall. A well-used coffeepot stood on the top next to plastic containers of sugar and creamer. A tall, black metal filing cabinet wasin the corner of the brick wall behind the glass door.

"Release him," the chief ordered. "Have a seat, Mr. Tennison."

Kaden turned so Officer Hernandez could unlock the cuffs. Rubbing his wrists, he perched on the edge of the seat.

The chief waited until the officers left and the door was closed before continuing. "Your friend is hard to get a hold of."

"Boss."

"I'm sorry?

"Russell Lawrence is my boss, not my friend."

"Yes, either way, he only responded twenty-five minutes ago confirming your identity."

Kaden looked through the window to the clock hanging high on the wall. Seven-fifteen. Lawrence had taken his time. On purpose. Kaden clenched his jaw and dug his nails into his palms.

"He wasn't very forthcoming with information. How about you tell me what you're doing with Riley Hamilton and why you're in my town."

Kaden played out all of his options. "There is very little I'm allowed to tell. However, I can tell you I was told to keep an eye on Riley as there was a very serious threat to his life."

"Why is your agency involved?"

Kaden rubbed the back of his neck, shrugged, and leaned back in the chair.

"Where were you and why did you come back here?"

"New Orleans. And we came back because Charles Hamilton went on national TV and demanded to know Riley's whereabouts, which actually put his life in greater danger," Kaden replied, hoping he wasn't making a bigger mistake. "Have you found anything out about the supposed FBI agents?"

"Not yet—"

The song *Lady in Red* blared from the personal mobile sitting on the desk, interrupting the chief.

"Rachel," the older man said, answering the phone, "I take it you got my message?" There was a brief pause. "I'm going to put you on speaker. Agent Tennison is in my office."

"I'm only doing this because I trust your gut."

"I appreciate it, Rachel."

"Agent Tennison, what do you know about the two men you shot last night?" a woman's voice crackled over the phone.

"Only that they claim to be FBI agents," Kaden answered. "And had been staying at the Hamilton estate for some time."

"Badges might have been real, but those men aren't. Agent Johnson's real name is Eduard Cestmir Dvorak and Agent Cobb's real name is Gustav Ivan Simek. Eduard Dvorak is the son of a low-level Czech crime boss by the name of Josef Dvorak. Simek is Dvorak junior's friend and bodyguard."

Kaden pinched the bridge of his nose. "What in the hell am I dealing with? And more precisely, who? Ma'am, what can you tell me about them?"

"Josef Dvorak immigrated here legally at the age of seven with his parents, two older brothers, and a sister. His father, Cestmir Dvorak, had claimed to be a professor at Charles University in Prague, until he was forced out of a job when the university shut down during World War II."

"I take it that wasn't the case." Kaden leaned forward.

"No. His brother, Patrik, was the professor. He was arrested as a political prisoner. Cestmir Dvorak was a factory worker and thief. He seems to have had a legitimate job for about three years before he fell in with a local gang. He was killed by a rival gang."

"Why is the DEA interested in Dvorak?" Chief Montgomery asked.

"Peripheral interest only at this point."

"Street-level thugs are easy enough to come by, but people who can and will impersonate others for a period of time isn't as easy, especially when it means infiltrating the FBI." Kaden shook his head.

"The question is, who would want to bankroll that?" Rachel asked. Kaden could hear the click of computer keys.

"How many people can afford that?" Kaden asked. "Not to mention the thugs we ran into in New Orleans."

"What is so special about this kid?" Rachel quizzed.

Chief Montgomery shoved a hand through his hair. "From everything I've seen and the times I've run into him, he's an average trust-fund kid."

"Agent Tennison?"

"Ma'am, we have no idea why they're after him. How likely is it for the Czechs to work for the Russians?"

"Since the second world war," Chief Montgomery answered. "They were part of the Eastern Bloc, communists allied to Moscow and Russia."

Kaden jumped to his feet and began pacing. Everything seemed to be going back to Russia and the Cold War. He needed to move Riley. Again. "Who has the most to lose?"

"Pardon?" Chief Montgomery asked.

"Agent?" Rachel questioned.

"It's not about money." Kaden shook his head. "It's about who has the most to lose or gain. They're using money gained either legally or illegally, or both, in order to protect something or someone. Or even several people. My money is on themselves and the life they created here."

"Russian spies? From the Cold War era?" Chief Montgomery asked incredulously.

"It's the only thing that makes sense."

"Shouldn't they have been called back to *Mother Russia*?"

Kaden stopped and faced the half-empty bullpen and spun around on his heel to face the police chief. "Not if they were in a position that made staying worth more."

"What are you thinking, Agent?"

"Business or politics, ma'am. The right industry that works on government contracts — or almost any level of government — would be worth letting someone stay."

"Good luck, Agent. Joe."

"Thanks, Rachel."

The line went dead. Kaden resumed his pacing. They needed to find whatever it was they thought Riley had, then they needed to move. Kaden saw two paths before them. A life on the run or standing and fighting. Neither option was good. Both had higher chances of failure than success.

"Agent Tennison, I believe you're in the wrong location," Chief Montgomery said, sliding Kaden's identification, cell phone, holster, and weapon across the desk.

Kaden slipped the holster around his shoulders. He hadn't realized they would have found his phone or thought to grab it along with his wallet and identification. There was a quick knock on the glass before the door opened.

The officer Kaden recognized as Weston stepped into the office. "The two feds you shot at the Hamilton estate are dead."

"What?" Kaden demanded. "From what?"

"Throats slit. Both of them. Nurses doing rounds found them this morning."

Chief Montgomery pinched the bridge of his nose. "Let the feds know. Shit. Feds were pulling security too." He waited until Weston left and the door closed behind him. "I suggest that you talk to whomever you need to. Security was left with those two men."

Kaden nodded and holstered his Glock 19.

"Tennison, while no one will ever accuse Mrs. Hamilton of being mother of the year or even a doting grandmother, I've seen the look she gave me and my officers before. She'll skin somebody alive if Riley is harmed."

Kaden nodded. So would he. "They wouldn't even see it coming." Kaden excused himself, pulled out his phone, and walked out of the building.

A black Chevrolet Grand Traverse pulled to a stop in front of him. Kaden looked up and slid his phone into his back pocket.

The black-tinted passenger window opened. "Get in," Lawrence ordered.

Kaden sat in silence as Lawrence drove them out of the police station and down to the beach. They stopped at a section devoid of people and vehicles. Kaden was ordered out of the SUV. He followed Lawrence down to the water's edge.

"What a clusterfuck you got yourself and me into."

Kaden counted to ten. "It was a clusterfuck from the moment you handed me Riley Hamilton's file with two pieces of paper in it. One of them was his flight information to New Orleans! I asked you for more information. I told you my suspicions. Someone should have been sent out to the Hamilton residence from the beginning. That would have eliminated Riley and me walking into that trap!"

"Why did you go to the Hamilton estate? Why didn't you stay wherever in the hell you were?"

"I was ganged up on and knocked out by a group of federal agents posing as thugs. Riley's safety was compromised."

"You didn't know that."

"You weren't willing to confirm that it wasn't," Kaden spat. "And it was. We ran into issues a couple of different times. Then we see Charles Hamilton on the news with the FBI standing with him asking for Riley to be returned to his family. National fucking television."

"We didn't—"

"Please. You knew or suspected. Someone knows. People are deliberately playing dumb. Now those two agents are dead. Only they weren't agents. They were Czech. Low-level Russian mob thugs. And the other agent that remained is missing. Probably dead."

"How did you find all of that out? We only learned they were dead an hour ago."

"I asked. I went to jail. Seems local law enforcement still doesn't appreciate federal agents playing in their jurisdiction without letting them know. Tell me everything I need to know about Riley and who is after him. Who is afraid of him, or more to the point, something he has?"

"I can't get any answers."

"That's bullshit."

"Maybe. But I haven't been able to reach the — ah — person — who wanted you assigned to this case."

"So this isn't agency sanctioned."

"It is," Lawrence said hesitantly.

Kaden heard the unspoken *now*. It hadn't been. Which meant he had been operating without proper authority. Kaden swore. "This is my last mission."

"Ten —"

"Last one. I'll make it official when I'm done," Kaden answered. "What did you say?"

"You stumbled across possible Russian spies on vacation and are following up."

Kaden shook his head and swore. "And they bought it?"

"Mostly. Just don't screw up or we'll both be fucked. Royally."

"Joy. This person better be worth it. I'm really not in the mood to go to jail or die for some idiot."

"He's not an idiot. He's a friend."

"Then you're an idiot."

"It was supposed to be a simple babysitting job."

"He lied. He probably knowingly lied."

"Are you sleeping with the kid?"

"First, he's an adult. Second, it doesn't matter. I will do what I have to do to get the job done."

"And the fallout? The Hamiltons will bury you."

Kaden shrugged. Admitting he would hate himself more than anything the Hamilton family could possibly do to him was something he wasn't going to admit out loud to any one, especially not his boss, when he wasn't sure he could completely trust the other man.

"Where do you need me to drop you?"

"Hamilton estate," Kaden answered as they headed back to the car.

"You're going to need to move again."

"Tell me something I don't actually already know." Kaden shrugged and kept moving. He would get in touch with Ace. For now, Riley might be safest at his place.

Chapter Twenty

"Riley!"

Riley groaned and sat up. The clock on the nightstand read ten-thirty in the morning. He flopped back on the pillows. He hadn't slept more than fifteen minutes at a time all night. Instead he had alternated between pacing the room, staring out of the windows, and tossing and turning in the surprisingly comfortable bed. Riley had been taken aback at how much he missed Kaden's presence, not just nearby, but in bed. He couldn't remember enjoying sleeping in the same bed with someone before.

The pounding on the door continued. The knob jiggled. "Riley, open up, it's me."

Riley slipped out of bed and retrieved the gun from where he'd hidden it under his clothes. He briefly debated on getting dressed, but decided against it. It sounded like Kaden, but he wasn't completely sure.

Carefully moving the chair and unlocking the door, he opened it part way, aiming the weapon through the crack.

"What do you want?" Riley demanded.

"It's me, Kaden." Kaden held up both hands. "I'm alone, sweetheart."

Riley pulled the door open a little farther, making sure the other man was indeed alone before yanking it open and pulling his bodyguard into the bedroom.

"This is" — Kaden said, paused before continuing — "different."

"Grandmother's choice. There are hidey-holes, and an escape ladder. So I'm okay with it."

Kaden grabbed Riley's face and looked down at him. "How much sleep did you get?"

"Um, probably more than you did."

"Let's take a nap before we have to meet your grandmother for lunch, then we can see if we can figure out what these creeps are looking for."

Riley nodded and handed Kaden the gun.

"Are you going to put on clothes?"

Riley shook his head.

Kaden swallowed. It was going to be a long day. Riley padded back to the queen-sized bed and slid under the covers.

"This is an interesting room." Kaden scanned the room before walking around it.

"Check this out." Riley sprang out of bed and opened one of the doors.

Kaden raised an eyebrow. He didn't see how a closet was important. Riley may have seen places to hide, but Kaden saw easy access points and obvious hiding spots. He looked in the closet as Riley disappeared. There was a trapdoor hidden behind yards of fabric. Pulling a flashlight out of his pocket, he peered through the opening. It was a small, narrow room that held a dust-covered cot with what looked like plastic-wrapped sheets on the edge of the bed. It looked like there was another door at the far end of the room, but he couldn't make out enough detail to be certain.

"I'd want to know if there is another way out before using it. Otherwise, it could become a death trap."

"There is a ladder to get out of the window. Looks long enough to reach the ground."

Kaden nodded. "It was a good choice for you, then. How about we take a nap, then you need to show me around this house?"

Riley shrugged and climbed into bed. "So did the police just let you go?"

"Yes, they generally don't hold people without a good reason," Kaden answered, kicking off his boots.

"Then why didn't they let you go last night? They knew then you didn't do anything wrong."

"They have a job to do, whether we like it or not." Kaden tossed his jacket over the arm of the chair along with his T-shirt. He hesitated before adding his jeans to the pile. He'd spent the better portion of the night tossing and turning on a mattress that stank of beer and piss and God only knew what else while the police chief checked out his story. To Kaden's surprise, Lawrence had verified his identity while insinuating that Kaden was on a mission of international significance. Kaden followed enough of the police chief's explanation and apology to figure out what Lawrence had probably told him and what details he could fill in.

"You shot those two assholes. Which reminds me, I need to find out what happened to the third guy."

"Not now you don't." Kaden slid into bed next to Riley. "Set the alarm for an hour. That should give us enough time to rest before we have to meet your grandmother."

He was willing to bet the third man was either dead or long gone. The other two needed to answer some questions. Even Lawrence was in agreement. The drive from the police station back to the Hamilton estate had been intense as he'd filled his boss in on some of the information they had pieced together. Kaden's responsibility to the mission and his need to know Riley was safe weren't at odds at the moment, but his developing feelings were beginning to the blur the lines of acceptability. It was a complication and a distraction that he couldn't afford. They came from two different worlds, even if Riley was willing to date him or commit to anything long-term.

Riley nodded and set the alarm before pulling the covers over them.

Kaden smiled as Riley shifted closer.

* * * *

The shrill ring of the alarm cut through Kaden's dream, pulling him sharply back to reality. Riley's firm ass was pressed against Kaden's cock. At some point during their nap, he had wrapped Riley in his arms. Kaden carefully tried to disentangle himself from the younger man. Scooting backward on the bed, he tried to pull away from Riley, reminding himself that the other man might not be happy with a hard cock pressing against his ass. Riley moved back with him, protesting the movement.

"Riley, stay put," Kaden ordered.

"What's going on? Are you okay? Um, what...what..." Riley stilled. "Why are you holding me?"

"Everything's fine. The alarm went off."

"Why are you—"

"Hard?" Kaden smiled, finishing the question Riley seemed to be stumbling over. "Because not only are you attractive, you didn't seem to want to let me go and you were snuggled up against me. Nude, I would like to add."

"Um, wow, okay." Riley shifted positions and turned over. "I'm not upset, just surprised. I didn't expect it."

"What, that someone would react to you?" Kaden raised an eyebrow. "You're a bit of tease, you know what you're doing."

"Mostly, I just go with the flow." Riley shrugged.

"Are you saying you didn't know what you were doing? That you didn't mean to tease? Garner a reaction, any sort of reaction?" Kaden asked, forcing his jaw to relax even as the rest of his body tensed and his cock started to soften.

Riley shook his head and propped himself up on his elbow. "No, I meant to tease you, I just didn't think far enough to realize that you might actually respond. That you might actually like me like that."

Kaden hissed as Riley's other hand brushed his cock. "Stop."

Riley's hand stopped moving, but didn't leave his cock. "Why? Because you think I don't know what I want or what I'm doing or because you have a real reason? Sex isn't against the law. I'm sober and over twenty-one. I'm not actually a virgin."

"Sex with women isn't the same as sex with men," Kaden answered. He needed to stop this before it went too far.

"I've had sex with a man before. It was awkward and a first time for both of us. I would like to try it again. Not because I'm curious, I mean I am, I'm assuming sex with someone with more experience will be better than figuring things out the first time or even first few times. But, I like you. I want to have sex with you."

Kaden groaned, silently wishing for an interruption. Riley's hand started to move again. Kaden grabbed his wrist, intent on stopping him. Riley squeezed his cock through his underwear. "You are going to be the death of me."

"I hope not!" Riley exclaimed in mock horror.

"You're—"

"Sober. And I know what I'm doing and what I want. It's not because you saved my life or went to jail and I feel guilty or anything else. I want to try it. So, show me how this done." Riley slipped his hand under the fabric. "I have condoms."

Kaden swallowed a groan and rolled them over so that Riley was trapped beneath him. "If you say stop at any time, for any reason, I will stop."

"Just like that? You'll stop?"

"Yes. And probably go take a cold shower."

Riley nodded, rubbing Kaden's cock. It was smooth, velvety, and hard as steel. It had been years since he'd touched someone else's penis. Kaden's cock felt bigger and thicker than his own. For a moment he wondered if it would fit or if the pain would be too much. "So, show me how this is done."

Kaden smiled and leaned down to kiss him. Kaden's mouth slanted over his. Riley inhaled sharply. He hadn't expected that. To be kissed. He didn't fight it. Kaden's tongue pushed into his mouth. Kaden shifted and some of the weight was gone. Riley missed it immediately. Kaden shoved one hand through Riley's hair and tweaked a nipple with the other.

Riley moaned and arched up into the feeling. It didn't hurt. It sent unexpected pleasure racing through his body. Kaden kissed a trail from his mouth to his nipples, laving first one then the other. Riley's cock hardened at the sensations. He wasn't sure how much more he could take before he exploded.

Kaden wrapped a hand around his cock and began fisting it.

"Holy shit! I'm going to come"

"Not yet." Kaden squeezed the base of his cock and balls, stemming the pending orgasm. "Condom?"

Riley shook his head. He didn't want the lose the pleasure running through his body. "Feels great."

"Still need a condom." Kaden smirked.

Kaden straddled his legs, their cocks rubbing together as he leaned over the side of the bed and dug in his duffel bag. A small bottle joined the condom on the bed.

Riley took the opportunity to run his hands over Kaden's chest. Healed knife and bullet wounds decorated the other man's torso and left arm. A small scab was all that remained of the wound where he'd been shot when Riley had been left alone in the cabin.

"What are all of these from?"

"War is messy and brutal for those who actually have to fight it," Kaden replied. The tone was cold and flat and didn't match the sensations his hands created as they danced over Riley's body.

Riley nodded and glanced over at the jacket. Even without the seeing all of the patches, he knew the Purple Heart was sewn onto the front. He didn't want to ruin the mood by bringing up things that were better left unsaid. He lifted his head and tentatively lapped at one of Kaden's nipples. Kaden held his head in place with one hand while rubbing their cocks together.

Riley moaned. Kaden released him and he fell back to the bed. Kaden shuffled back and swallowed Riley's cock down. The wet heat enveloping him sent a torrent of pleasure through Riley. Kaden's hand clamped around the base of his cock. Minutes passed into eternity. Pleasure built at the base of his spine and raced through his body. His orgasm pushed forward.

Kaden released him and sat back.

"What—no—" Riley protested, moving his hand to his cock to bring himself off.

"No." Kaden shook his head and rolled the condom down his shaft. "Trust me."

"I'm so close." Riley dropped his hand, frustrated.

"I know."

"You're evil."

Kaden smiled. "So it's been said." Kaden reached forward and grabbed a pillow. "Lift your butt up."

Riley raised his eyebrows, but complied with Kaden's request. Kaden shoved the pillow under his ass, keeping his hips elevated. Riley moaned as Kaden cupped his balls, squeezing the gently. Kaden licked his cock, blowing across the head before taking one of his balls in his mouth. Riley arched his back and gripped the sheets. He wasn't going to last if the man kept this up.

A lubed finger circled his hole. Kaden turned his attention to the other testicle while his free hand slowly jerked Riley's cock. Riley gasped. A single digit slid into his ass. Senses on overload, Riley let the pleasure roll through him. The finger fucked him leisurely. He wanted more.

"More," he demanded. The finger wasn't fat enough, wasn't big enough. It drove pleasure through him, but wasn't enough to get off on. "Please."

"Shh," Kaden said. He moved, kissing Riley as he added a second finger to Riley's hole.

"Oh! More. It's not enough," Riley said, trying to meet Kaden's thrusts.

"Preparations first," Kaden whispered, nipping his jawline.

"I—I—I'm not going to last." Riley was panting, his breath coming in gasps. Wave after wave of ecstasy pushed through him.

An eternity passed before Kaden added a third finger to his hole. He needed more. He wanted all of Kaden. Now. Kaden clamped down around the base of his cock, stemming his orgasm.

"More. You. More."

"Do you like that, love?"

"Love it. Yes. More."

Kaden pulled out his fingers.

"No!"

"Relax." Kaden sat back and lifted Riley's legs onto his shoulders. "Push out."

"Want you."

"You'll get me. Just do as I say."

Riley nodded and forced his body to respond to his lover's request. The tip of Kaden's cock tapped at the entrance to his body.

"Push out. Let me in, baby."

"Trying."

The head of Kaden's cock slipped in.

"Oh. Oh. Oh," Riley repeated, grabbing Kaden's arms.

Kaden slowly pushed forward. Riley closed his eyes. Full. He was full. Pain quickly morphed into more pleasure. He needed more. His body fought between pulling Kaden in and pushing him out.

"More." Riley panted.

"You've got me all," Kaden answered. Riley could hear the smile without opening his eyes. "Get used to me."

"Oh. My. God. So full."

"Good?"

Riley shook his head. It was better than good. "Great."

Kaden pulled back before pushing forward again. Riley moaned. He'd never felt anything like it. Pleasure and pain rolled into one. Kaden's hand had wrapped around his cock again. Kaden pistoned in and out. Pleasure and pressure built in Riley's body as Kaden continued to fuck him.

"More. Faster. Harder. Please."

"Feel good?" Kaden asked, wrapping Riley's legs around his waist and bracing himself over Riley.

Riley nodded, looking up in Kaden's dark brown eyes, the gold highlights sparkling as Kaden obliged. Kaden slammed into him again and again, pushing pleasure through him. Riley clamped a hand over his mouth to keep from yelling out. He'd never shouted before during sex.

"Move your hand," Kaden ordered.

Riley shook his head, moved his hand, and clamped his mouth shut. "Going to come," he said between gasps. "Don't want to yell."

"Then come." Kaden pushed into him, kissing him.

Riley shouted into the kiss, coming hard. He shivered. Black spots appeared before his eyes. Kaden's cock pulsed in his ass, and he could feel Kaden's essence filling the condom between them. In that instance he hated the barrier. Relaxing his grip, Riley's limbs dropped to the bed. Kaden's weight rested on him momentarily before disappearing.

"Where—" Riley started to ask when Kaden returned, and a warm washcloth wiped at his stomach and cock. Riley shivered. Every nerve in his body seemed to be on fire.

Kaden slid back into the bed and pulled him close.

"Holy shit," Riley panted, fighting to regain control of his body.

"It gets better." Kaden chuckled, kissing Riley's ear. Riley shuddered.

"What's going on?" Riley asked, concern filling his voice.

"Aftershocks, they'll pass."

"I—that's never happened before."

"And it doesn't happen all of the time or to everyone."

"But—"

"Enjoy it." Kaden dragged his fingers across Riley's nipples, eliciting a gasp.

Long moments passed in silence as they lay there, Riley slowly relaxing and regaining control of his body. "I'm going to feel that for days."

"Sore?" Kaden asked, bending over and lapping at the nipple closest to him.

Riley nodded. "Too. Much."

Kaden lay down and pulled Riley into his arms. Riley shivered again and snuggled deeper into the arms wrapped around him. "Do you regret it?" Kaden whispered, kissing his shoulder.

"No. It was better than I imagined it would be."

"You thought about it?"

"Not a lot, and not until recently. It was easy to ignore what I wasn't supposed to have it," Riley shrugged. He couldn't explain it. He hadn't been with another guy since Christian Howard in high school. Awkward kisses and even more awkward blow jobs and sex were easy to push out of his mind, especially against losing everything. He hadn't loved Christian. They had been interested in each other, but looking back at it, there was no chemistry between them. Riley wasn't sure he loved Kaden, but the sex had been better than he could have imagined.

"When do we need to meet your grandmother?"

Riley looked over at the clock and groaned. "Twelve-thirty."

"At least we only have to go downstairs. We have enough time to shower and dress."

Riley blew out a breath and nodded. "Fine, you can go first."

"Be here when I get back," Kaden whispered.

"No place to go right now."

Riley rolled over and pulled the covers up to his chin. He wanted privacy. His ass was sore, but it didn't hurt. With the euphoria wearing off, his body was sore, but he wasn't in pain. He'd done it. He'd had sex with a man. It had been intense. And one of the most satisfying experiences he'd ever had.

* * * *

The events were still replaying themselves in Riley's mind twenty-five minutes later when they walked downstairs in search of his grandmother and lunch.

"Mister Riley," Benjamin said as they walked into the dining room. "Your grandmother sends her apologies, but she must postpone your lunch date until tomorrow. She was called away unexpectedly."

"Where did she go?"

"She didn't say. She said she would be back tonight and would have lunch with you tomorrow."

"And where is Charles?"

"He has returned to the city."

"In other words, I'm home so he can go back to doing what he wants."

"He wasn't told he couldn't leave."

"Benjamin, what happened to the third FBI agent?" Kaden asked.

"He hasn't been seen since the night Mister Riley returned home," Benjamin answered.

Riley turned and walked to the edge of the dining room. "Someone is screaming. What rooms were the agents given?"

"Agent Wilkins was given the green room, Agent Johnson was given the white room, and Agent Cobb was given the Lincoln Room."

"Why were the agents staying in the house?" Kaden asked as the trio ran up the stairs. "They shouldn't —"

"The FBI insisted that agents should be here at all times in case the kidnappers called. Mrs. Hamilton offered them rooms to sleep in after the first few days. She is a very formidable woman," Benjamin replied as they reached the room at the end of the hall.

Kaden pushed passed the two men and rushed into the room, his weapon drawn. A young woman sat on the edge of the bed, being comforted by an older woman. The older woman simply pointed to the bathroom. Nodding, Kaden quickly searched the bedroom before moving into the bathroom. The room was similar in size to the one connected to the room he and Riley had shared. The green floral décor carried into the bathroom from the bedroom. The tub was a newer built-in model with whirlpool jets. A large wicker basket sat in the middle of the floor, piled with green and white sheets and white towels. Kaden opened the door with one hand. Still dressed in his black suit, FBI agent Wilkins' body was shoved into the bottom on the linen closet.

"Damn it!" Kaden holstered his weapon and knelt next to the body, checking for a pulse. "Fuck." Standing, he pulled out his phone and called Lawrence. "Send a wagon. The third agent is dead," Kaden said as soon as his boss answered the phone. "How did they miss him last night?"

Riley shrugged. "Benjamin, didn't they search the rooms for him after I said something?"

The older man shook his head. "Apparently, the police chief didn't believe it was necessary. He thought the other agent had returned to headquarters."

"Seriously? Wonder if the dead body of an FBI agent rates the front page of the paper?" Riley asked. "The chief needs to be replaced. He can retire to the Caribbean or something. You know, maybe the whole force. Since you weren't released until this morning, even though everyone, including Grandmother, said it wasn't necessary for you to be arrested."

"No, it wasn't necessary," Kaden agreed. It hadn't been necessary to keep him in jail. The local police were pissed off that federal agents had operated in their jurisdiction without bothering to let them know or consult them. At this point, Kaden didn't care whose feelings got hurt or who was pissed off, he needed to find out who was after Riley and why. If the agents were here and insisted on staying, it could mean that whoever was after Riley thought whatever he had was on the family's estate.

"Are you going to call the police?" Riley asked, following him back into the bedroom.

Kaden shook his head. "Law enforcement have been called, though." Kaden knelt in front of the two women. "Ma'am, can you tell me what happened?"

Both women were white and dressed in plain black slacks and light gray button-down shirts with white collars and sleeves. Their shoes were also the same, plain black thick-soled work shoes. The older one had salt-and-pepper hair pulled up into a tight bun, with piercing green eyes, and looked to be in her fifties. The younger woman looked like she was in her early twenties and had curly red hair that just touched her shoulders and brown eyes that were puffy from crying.

"You don't believe she killed that man and stuffed him in the closet, do you?" the older woman demanded.

"I think that would take either a lot of power or a lot of trust and manipulation. But I need to know what happened if I have any chance of keeping Riley safe. Ma'am, please answer the question."

"I heard Brianna yell when I was leaving Mrs. Hamilton's rooms."

"She left earlier this morning."

"I never clean Mrs. Hamilton's rooms before ten o'clock. I have several other responsibilities that need to be taken care of first. This is not a hotel or a television show, there are not an infinite number of staff here."

"Do you always clean Mrs. Hamilton's rooms?"

"Yes, I'm the only one who does."

Kaden nodded. "Brianna? Tell me what happened."

"Since Mister Riley is home and those agents left last night, I was finally able to clean their rooms. I was going to pull out the laundry basket that's in the linen closet. I opened the door and he was—he was—crumpled up in the bottom of the closet." Brianna cried, fresh tears streaming.

"Did you clean either of the other two rooms?"

Brianna shook her head. "I came in late this morning. I had a doctor's appointment. I had two other bedrooms and three bathrooms to do first and—"

"And catch up on what happened overnight," Kaden filled in.

Brianna sniffed and nodded, glancing quickly over at Riley before turning her attention back to Kaden.

"Thank you." Kaden stood. "Officers will be here in a moment and they'll ask you the same questions, as well as several others. Just tell them the truth like you told me and they'll get to the bottom of this." Kaden longed to keep pushing and digging information out of the younger woman, but he had a feeling that as long as Riley was present she wouldn't say too much more than she had. Kaden shoved a hand through his hair. Plus there was only so much he could say without giving away who he was. It had taken less time than he had assumed it would to get the local police department's cooperation and guarantee to not release the information to anyone for any reason.

Nodding first to Riley then to Benjamin, Kaden walked out of the bedroom, stopping when he was several feet away.

"There is no way that Brianna could get that asshole into the closet," Riley spat.

"No, not on her own." Kaden shook his head. "Benjamin, when did those three agents become the only remaining agents in the house?"

"Thursday last. The lead agent said that due to Mister Riley's age and the amount of time that had passed, they couldn't keep agents here indefinitely."

Riley rubbed the back of his neck. "That's odd, isn't it? I mean, the FBI are the ones who said I was missing in the first place. Or kidnapped. So why would they leave after what, two weeks?"

"There are a whole lot of things that aren't adding up at this point," Kaden answered, pinching the bridge of his nose.

"So what are my options?" Riley asked, shoving his hands in his pockets. "Whatever you think of my family, our home should have been safe."

Kaden's heart sank. He pulled Riley into his arms and hugged him tight. "First, we see if we can find what everyone seems to be looking for. Starting with —" Kaden paused at the sound of approaching footsteps. "Make it the second thing."

"What?" Riley pulled away and spun around as several police officers and a pair of EMTs appeared. "They can't be freaking serious? What a bunch of incompetent buffoons."

"They're doing their job," Kaden admonished.

"Not very well."

"It was your father who said they left, and no one besides you contradicted him."

"Charles would sell me off in half of a heartbeat," Riley scoffed, "if it gained him money or power. Preferably both. Hell, he's already trying to."

Kaden glanced from Riley to Benjamin and back again. That the older man didn't contradict Riley told Kaden all he needed to know about Charles Hamilton. "A fact that most people, especially other parents, wouldn't think was possible. Even among the rich." Kaden shook his head.

"Excuse me." A middle-aged white man with thinning blond hair dressed in a navy-blue suit walked up to them.

"What in the hell do you want?" Riley demanded, crossing his arms over his chest and drawing himself to his full height.

"I'm Detective Greenway. I need to ask you some questions."

"No."

"Excuse me?"

"Riley, love, they have to ask. Either here or down at the police station," Kaden said, laying a hand on Riley's shoulder. "A man is dead."

"No. They were here for over four hours last night. In the middle of the freaking night. They kept you in jail until this morning because you did your job, which pissed somebody off. And if they had listened to me then they would've found Agent Wilkens at that time. Maybe even alive!" Riley shouted.

"Mr. Hamilton, there is no need to get—"

"Stop. There is no good way to finish that sentence." Kaden shook his head.

"To what? Get hysterical? Cry? Shout? Upset? Weak? Feminine?" Riley finished. "Which word were you going to use, *Officer*?"

Kaden swallowed. Riley made the word 'officer' sound like it was little more than a piece of dirt to be wiped off the bottom of his shoe. To be fair, the detective was going for all of the stereotypes.

"Mr. Hamilton, there's no need —" Chief Montgomery walked up to the small group.

"Your officer implied that because I'm bisexual, I'm somehow weak and prone to hysterics like I'm some freaking damsel in distress from the eighteenth century or those ridiculous Saturday morning cartoons," Riley shouted. "Am I'm hysterical or weak? No. Am I upset? Yes. There is a *dead body* in that bedroom." Riley pointed toward the bedroom. "He was probably killed *in this house*. Had any one actually listened to me last night, the man might still be alive. Not to mention the trauma it's caused our staff. This house. *My* house. *My family*. When it's *your* house and *your* family, you can feel however the hell you want! Until then, you can all back the hell off."

"Mr. Hamilton, I understand your frustration. However, if you tell Detective Greenway what you know, we can leave you alone and figure out what happened to Agent Wilkins," Chief Montgomery said flatly.

"Fine." Riley huffed and crossed his arms over his chest.

Kaden held his breath.

"We came down for a lunch meeting with my grandmother at noon, but she had to go out of town this morning. Then we heard the maid, Brianna, scream. We ran upstairs. She was sitting on the bed crying. Ms. Ava Williams, Head of Housekeeping, was with her. They pointed to the bathroom. We went in and saw him shoved into the bathroom closet."

"Did either of you touch the body?" Detective Greenway asked, looking at them as he scribbled notes in his pad.

"I did." Kaden nodded. "I touched his neck looking for a pulse. He was already dead."

"Did you notice anything out of place?"

"It's a guest room. It smelled like shit." Riley crossed his arms over his chest.

"That's normal when a person dies," the detective sneered.

"It looks sterile, like it's been recently cleaned," Kaden commented.

"The maid was in there cleaning." Detective Greenway flipped through his notebook.

Kaden shook his head. "No, the FBI and those fake agents had been here for two weeks. If you look in the other two bedrooms, you'll find toiletries, dirty towels, suitcases with clothes, and probably more than a couple non-government issued weapons. In there? Nothing. Like it had been completely and deliberately cleaned."

"It didn't smell clean, though." Riley turned to Kaden. "It smelled different."

"Different how?" Kaden and the detective asked at the same time.

Riley tilted his head to one side and closed his eyes momentarily. "More chemically. It must have faded. It wasn't overwhelming."

"And you know this how?" Chief Montgomery asked, skepticism dripping from his voice.

Riley shrugged. "I have an extremely sensitive sense of smell."

"Mrs. Hamilton has the same issue. It was how she met Mr. Hamilton," Benjamin cut in. "She used to be one of his employees. Her sense of smell was so delicate that she worked as a perfumer for him. A very high-paid and in-demand position in the perfume industry. Her recommendations and skill propelled Hamilton Perfumes well ahead of their competition here in America."

"I thought they met at some sort of dance or fancy dinner." Riley cocked his head to one side. "At least, that's the story I heard."

Benjamin shook his head. "No. As I remember it, she made several suggestions, her boss at the time, a man by the name of George Arnoldson, had said they were worthless then made some others. The product was a dud. When Mr. Hamilton came down to find out what happened and fire your grandmother, she pointed to her notes and recommendations and the report she'd written and told him that it was her boss's fault. And if he didn't like her work, she'd go work for the competition. Since she already made him a lot of money before, he let the manager go instead."

"Interesting, but back to these cleaning products," Detective Greenway said, interrupting. "How long does it take for that kind of smell to fade?" Detective Greenway asked.

"I don't know. I don't keep track," Riley quipped.

Kaden shot Riley a disapproving look. He knew his lover was frustrated and angry, but antagonizing police officers who are trying to do their job wouldn't help them go away and could cause them problems in the long run, not to mention pissing the officers off to the point where they start looking for reasons to arrest him.

"Several hours, probably." Riley stepped closer to Kaden, so they were touching. "It's an enclosed space, the windows weren't open, and the fan wasn't on. I don't know. I don't use that crap."

"Assuming that the smell is due to cleaning products, they wouldn't have been used in the house?" Detective Greenway probed.

Riley clenched and unclenched his fists. "I don't—no. The stuff our staff uses smells different. Less chemically. Less offensive."

"We will need a list of the brands used here."

"I can get that for you. Ava does the ordering," Benjamin confirmed. "If you'll follow me."

Detective Greenway nodded. "I think that will do it for now, Mr. Hamilton, Mr Tennison. Stay available for questioning."

Both men nodded and the detective turned to a uniformed officer as the police chief walked away. A pair of EMTs pushed a stretcher carrying an oddly shaped bundle covered in black plastic.

"What does that?" Riley asked, nodding toward the body.

"Any number of things, why?"

"No, I meant, what can kill somebody that quickly and quietly?"

The detective turned back around and stepped toward them.

"Poison probably," Kaden replied. "There's no blood anywhere. No evidence that a gun or knife of any kind was used. Even a silencer makes some noise. And if he suspected his fellow agents weren't who they said they were, they would have a harder time sneaking up on him with a weapon drawn."

"So not necessarily quick, but quiet."

"Actually, with all of the commotion last night, then being held in the library until well past two in the morning, he could have made a lot of noise, just not enough to be heard over everything else that was going on and through a closed door," Benjamin interjected.

"Convenient," Riley spat.

"Mr. Hamilton—" The detective stepped forward.

"No. Tell me I'm wrong," Riley challenged. "It's convenient that possibly the only legitimate agent in this whole mess was killed, or at the very least poisoned, at some point before the pair of wannabes broke in and tried to kill me in my own freaking room. Then while people could help, he was dying. And no one heard or thought to check on him. Bloody. Freaking. Convenient." Riley began pacing. "How many more people have to die because of me?" Riley demanded. "Do you have any idea what it's like to know that people are dead because of you and without any idea why? It's bad enough to know that people want me dead, but others? Truly innocent people? I'm done. I've answered all of the questions I'm going to. I've talked to all of the law-enforcement people I'm going to." Riley turned and walked away.

"It's not his fault." Benjamin sighed. The detective looked at him.

"No, Benjamin, it's not his fault." Kaden watched Riley leave. "He's being used as a pawn. Someone wants him, apparently dead or alive now, instead of just alive."

Kaden turned and followed Riley through the house, keeping the younger man in sight, but staying far enough back to give him some privacy. They passed through a large room filled with heavy antique mahogany furniture and floor-to-ceiling bookcases that were filled with books ranging in a variety of subjects and dates, onto a large columned covered porch. Riley sat in an oversized cream-colored loveseat tucked into the corner.

"I don't need a lecture on manners."

"I think I have an idea how you feel," Kaden said.

Riley drew up a knee and looked at Kaden before returning his attention to the well-manicured lawn.

Kaden leaned against the railing and shoved his hands in his pockets. "I've made decisions, made choices, that meant people, good people, may not go home."

"Killing bad guys in war, that you volunteered for, is hardly the same thing."

"Maybe. Maybe not. They were my people. Even though we volunteered to go, knew we may not come home, it still eats at you, at your soul, until you wonder if you have any soul left."

"Were you kicked out then?"

"No. Finished my tour, then got out when my time was up. Like I said, not quite the same thing, but I think I have an idea of how you're feeling."

"What do we do now?" Riley hesitated before continuing. "I don't want any more innocent people to get hurt."

Kaden arched his eyebrows and nodded. "What about those who may not be innocent?"

"They aren't my concern."

"Even if it's your family?"

Riley shrugged. "If they were innocent, I wouldn't be running for my life."

Kaden studied the other man for a moment. Grim determination had replaced the boyish innocence. Riley appeared ready to face the truth, regardless of how uncomfortable it made him.

"Show me where you found your mother's things. Maybe there's more information there. Then we can check out Charles' office. Does your grandmother have an office in the house?"

"Sort of. She has a sitting area that she also uses as a study off from her room. I believe she had it redecorated after my grandfather passed away. She also has a parlor with a writing desk that she uses. Mostly, when she's meeting with other people. What are you looking for?"

"Anything that can help us keep you safe. What about your grandfather's things?"

Riley shook his head. "I don't know. She probably kept some stuff and gave the rest away."

"Let's start with the storage closet."

Riley pushed himself up and out of the chair. Shoulders set, jaw clenched, he looked every bit like a warrior instead of the only son of a wealthy business magnate. His green eyes had lost their sparkle. The snarky, snide remarks disappeared, replaced by the solid stoicism of a man determined to do the right thing no matter the cost.

"This room, who used this? There are no—"

"No women's books?" Riley chuckled. "This was my grandfather's library. My grandmother's rooms have her books, at least the ones she kept."

Kaden nodded and looked around. There were four plush, solid, dark-green wingback chairs, each with its own round table and reading light. Bookcases completely filled three of the four walls. The fourth wall containing the glass doors leading out to the porch had a bench seat built between a pair of bookcases and under the room's only window. On the other side of the doors, tucked into the corner, was an antique mahogany and glass cabinet. He moved to inspect the bookcases by the door.

"What are you doing?" Riley stopped and turned. "I thought you wanted to see the storage closet."

"I do, but we're right here."

Riley sighed and started to look through the nearest shelf of books. After an hour of searching, Riley shoved the book he'd finished flipping through back onto the shelf and turned in a slow circle. He couldn't actually recall his grandfather ever reading. Some of the books he'd looked through he was sure had never actually been opened before. He remembered his grandfather sitting in a chair near the fireplace, reading the paper and drinking a glass of brandy. There had usually been a decanter and a pair of glasses in the cabinet next to the door.

The cabinet held an empty decanter and a pair of upside-down glasses. In addition to the glasses there was a pair of tattered black books and several old maps. Riley flipped through the top book and inhaled sharply.

"What's wrong?" Kaden asked, shoving a book back in the shelf.

"This is Hebrew."

"And?"

"First, my grandparents are Christian. Well, I assumed they were. We celebrated Christmas, but we've never gone to church. I couldn't even tell you a denomination. But this, I can't read it, but I recognize it. I had to take a comparative religions class in high school. This is Hebrew. I don't know if it's like a Torah or the other book. I don't remember the name." Riley pointed out the writing. "My grandfather hated Christmas and Easter. Refused to celebrate them. I thought he just had bad memories or thought they were a waste of time." Riley carried the books over his grandfather's chair and sat down. "What if he hated them because he didn't believe in them? Because he had to hide his true identity. Or because it signified everything evil or at least reminded him of what he'd lost. What if he lost family to the Nazis?"

"It's possible. His wouldn't be the only family to have hide who they were in order to survive." Kaden picked up the second book. Both books were old and worn, but were in fairly good condition given their age. Kaden laid the book on the table and took several pictures with his phone of the first few pages, as well as the last few. Leaving Riley to look through the book, Kaden pulled out the small drawers found in the side tables. They all held the same things. Two letter-size pads of lined heavy white paper and three plain black pens.

Paper crinkled as he pulled the last drawer out of the table where Riley sat.

"What was that?" Riley asked, setting the book down.

"Don't know. There isn't anything different in this drawer than any of the others, though," Kaden stated.

"Pull it all the way out."

A square, yellowed envelope floated to the ground.

"And here I only thought secret letters and compartments happened in the movies," Riley quipped, picking up the envelope. "William R. Smith, esquire."

"Who is that?"

"A lawyer friend of my grandfather's. I think."

Riley pulled out the single sheet of paper and scanned the note. "Okay, this is weird. It's dated for

June 7, 1987. Charles and Amethyst divorced finalized quietly. Fifteen million dollars paid in settlement. Then what looks like an initial. A 'w' maybe."

"Who is Amethyst?" Kaden asked.

"I have no idea. This says they divorced. So there should be records of that, right? And of their marriage. Maybe even something in the paper."

"Possible. Although, it may have nothing to do with you or why people are after you."

"I know. But it could. And I want to know what kind of woman divorces for a fifteen-million-dollar settlement when she could have gotten like half the company."

"I'm sure she had reasons. Let's take this and find this storage closet you mentioned."

Riley nodded and placed the letter back in its envelope and stuck it into the first page of the book he'd been going through. Carrying both books with him, Riley led the way through the art-filled hallways, a nondescript door, and down an empty hallway lined with doors on either side to the last door on the left.

"How many doors and hallways are in this place?" Kaden asked, staring down another hall of doors.

"No idea. Benjamin probably knows, though. He's been here forever."

"So what did we just go through? And how do you tell the difference?"

"I was a nosy kid. Kids shouldn't be seen or heard. At least I wasn't supposed to be. Benjamin and Ava each have a room here. One of the doors leads to the garage where they park and one leads to other service areas of the house."

"And nothing has changed since you were a kid?"

"A few things. The main kitchen and staff quarters were renovated about ten years ago, but the overall layout hasn't changed. I think the house is old enough now that if we wanted to make external changes we'd need to get permission from the city. That would incur extra fees, which I doubt Charles would want to pay."

"And this place?"

"All storage."

"All six rooms?"

"Yes. Where else are we supposed to store everything? That one is for Christmas decorations." Riley pointed to each room as he named them. "That one is for kitchen and dining room storage. That one is for other household decorations. Those two are for furniture. This last one is for pretty much everything else. This is the one I found my mother's things in."

Kaden stepped in front of Riley and opened the door. It moved quietly and easily. Kaden walked in and the lights turned on. Riley pushed past Kaden and led him between two sets of shelves to the far back corner. They searched the storage closet for nearly two hours before admitting there was nothing there that would help them.

"I'm hungry. Let's get something to eat, then search Charles' study and my grandmother's rooms." Riley picked the books back up. "And I need to get my backpack. I want to put these in there."

Chapter Twenty-One

Riley scanned the hallway one more time. The late lunch gave them a chance to ensure both his grandmother and Charles were away from the house for the remainder of the day. Taking a deep breath, he pushed open the door to his grandmother's room. He'd been in the rooms before, but he'd never *snuck* in. There hadn't been any reason too. He'd gone through Charles' office and bedroom on occasion looking for more information on his mother and come across porn and little else of importance to him.

"This is officially weird." Riley stood in the middle of the room. It didn't look like it had the last time he'd been in the room. Bright white-painted wood furniture replaced the heavy, dark furniture he remembered.

"What is?"

"It's my grandmother's bedroom. It's weird."

The walls were painted in a medium gray from the baseboard to the white chair rail, and painted in a pale purple the rest of the way. Black and white prints of

Parisian landmarks and original oil paintings of *Sacre Coeur* and the Eiffel Tower graced the walls. A large king-size bed dominated the far wall, flanked on either side by matching nightstands and white and gray lamps. An alarm clock and a framed print of the Eiffel Tower lay on one nightstand. A dresser and full-length mirror were propped up against the wall to his left. A single gray lounge chair sat in opposite corner of the room next to a nightstand that matched the rest of the furniture. The table held a lamp, phone charger, and a hardback copy of Mark Twain's *Adventures of Huckleberry Finn*.

Riley searched through both nightstands before crossing through the double doors into his grandmother's sitting room. Painted in the same shades of gray and purple with white trim, the light gray carpet flowed from the bedroom into the sitting room. In the far right corner was a Queen Anne-style dark wooden desk and a dark gray office chair. The desk held a pair of monitors and a computer docking station as well as a mouse and mousepad. The drawers contained an assortment of office supplies and both personal and professional letters, some recent and some older. None of which appeared to be of any use. White bookshelves standing three feet high were pushed against the wall. In the middle of the room were a couch and two chairs. The walls were full of artwork and a medium-size flat-screen television, but no photographs.

Riley walked back into the bedroom. "There are no photographs in that room, not even the artistic shots of Paris that are in here. There are no people in any of these."

"No, but I did find this." Kaden held up a large, plain yellow envelope.

"What is it?"

"Read it for yourself."

Riley pulled out the stack of papers and read through them. "I don't understand. This says I have a brother."

"An older brother." Kaden nodded. "I took pictures, these need—"

"To come with me. Screw that," Riley finished.

"Fine, but we should probably be going. We don't want to be discovered in your grandmother's rooms."

Riley shoved everything back into the envelope and followed Kaden out of the bedroom and back to the Rose Room. Flopping down into the chair, Riley drew up a knee and pulled the papers from the envelope. He read the letter two more times before setting it aside in favor of the pile of photographs. The first was a headshot of a young man with short spiked dark brown hair and bright blue eyes. The second was the same man and an older woman. The pair looked enough alike, that Riley assumed the woman was the man's mother. Clamping down on the pang of jealousy, he flipped back to the letter looking for a name to put with the face.

"Dante Abraham Sterling MacKenzie." Riley leafed back through the photos. The next one showed Dante holding another man's hand. "He's gay. Huh."

"And?"

"Pretty sure that would piss Charles off even more. One of his sons is gay and I'm bi—"

"You've said that several times."

"It gets easier each time. It also makes it real. You know?" Riley shrugged and flipped to the last photo.

An older man had joined them at the table. The photos seemed to have been taken from a distance without the knowledge of the subjects. They seemed to follow Dante and his lover into a well-known restaurant where they were joined by his mother and another man.

"Do you recognize any of these people?" Kaden asked, reaching for the photographs. "Or the restaurant?"

Riley shook his head. "I never knew he existed. Do you think — I — were his mom and Charles married? Maybe she's the Amethyst from the letter. Do you think he knows about me?" Riley tried to censor his thoughts. Growing up he'd always wanted a brother, either older or younger, he hadn't cared. The moment of selfish panic was pushed aside in favor of the realization that he had a brother.

"I don't know. I can have Ace do some checking."

Riley drew in a breath and let it out slowly. "Maybe it would be better, you know, more responsible, to talk to his mom first. If he doesn't know Charles is his father, me showing up would be an unwelcomed shock."

Kaden nodded and handed the photographs back.

"Shit!" Riley sprang from his chair. "What if the assholes after me go after him?"

Kaden pinched the bridge of his nose. "The letter addressed to your grandmother is dated from four days ago. My guess is that is what someone paid to find out. These are surveillance photos."

"My grandmother. It's the only possibility."

"It does look that way."

"First, I learn my family or someone in it are probably Russian spies, then one or both of my grandparents is or was probably Jewish, not Christian like I always thought, and now a brother, who someone went to a bit of trouble to find out where he was. How many more secrets are we going to uncover?"

"That is a very good question."

"What if the same people that are after me, went after her first? Maybe that's why she paid someone to make sure Dante was okay?"

"It's a possibility. Let's see what turns up in your father's office," Kaden suggested.

Riley nodded and placed the photographs and letter back into the envelope before sticking the packet into his backpack. Shoving the bag under the bed, he let out a deep breath and led the way to Charles' office, scanning the area to make sure they weren't being watched or followed.

The search of Charles' office produced a copy of his will, a framed black-and-white photograph of two young boys in matching school uniforms, a copy of the divorce agreement between Charles and Amethyst MacKenzie, the unsigned divorce agreement between Charles and Riley's mother, Elaine, and a variety of business files including one on a possible merger.

"Is your father not sentimental?" Kaden asked as they entered the Rose Room, closing the door behind them.

Riley shrugged. "I don't know. Honestly, I never cared." Riley laid the photograph and the stack of papers on the dresser.

Kaden picked up the frame. "I assume one of the boys in the photo is your father. I'm not sure who the second one is, though."

"His brother. I think." Riley stretched out on the bed. "Mind you, I've never met the man and he's never discussed. But my understanding is that he was caught kissing another man or he was caught in a police raid kissing another man. I'm not sure which. The stories are confusing. Either way, I guess there was an argument and he refused to stop seeing the guy. My grandparents kicked him out. Disowned him completely. Charles tried to talk some sense into him. Make him straight. But it didn't work."

"Do you know where he is now?"

Riley shook his head. "I don't even remember his name."

Kaden carefully removed the photograph from its frame and flipped it over. "It's faded, but you can just make it out. Charles and Daniel, 1966. It's a name."

"Maybe Ace can find him too?" Riley shrugged. "I'm going to owe Ace a lot after all this is said and done."

Kaden lay down next to Riley and pulled him into his arms. Riley stiffened then relaxed. He wanted to laugh at the absurdity of everything. He was lying on the bed cuddling with a man he was starting fall for while his life still in danger by an unknown group of assailants.

"It's interesting, though," Kaden said, pulling him from his reverie.

"What is?"

"Your grandmother appears to be more interested in her grandsons than either of her sons. The timing is…suspicious."

"Are you suggesting my grandmother is a Russian?"

"I'm saying that the timing is suspicious." Kaden rubbed Riley's arms.

"It's my *grandmother*. Maybe the fact that the FBI showed up on her doorstep claiming I had been kidnapped was enough to worry her about her other grandson. I seriously doubt Charles gave either of us any thought past how it would impact his business."

"A distinct possibility." Kaden kissed the top of Riley's head. "You know your family has secrets. Your grandmother may have some of her own."

Riley chuckled. "I doubt it. She isn't the type to have affairs or pass secrets to the Russians. And what kind of spying would either her or my grandfather have done? The latest techniques or ingredients in making perfumes?"

"Industrial spying and sabotaging happens in almost every industry and area of research," Kaden answered, kissing the back of Riley's neck.

"Perfume is not worth killing anyone over. It's a luxury item." Riley shook his head slightly, not wanting to dislodge Kaden. "Distracting me with sex?"

"Hmm. I don't know. Is it working?"

"Isn't there some sort of rule in place about mixing business and pleasure?"

"Hmm, probably." Kaden nuzzled the side of Riley's neck and lightly flicked his nipple.

Riley gasped, bit his lip, and rolled over. "Seriously, are you going to get into trouble?"

"Could I get in trouble for having fantastic sex with you?" Kaden repeated. "Depends. If I've really screwed up, it would be one more nail in my coffin. Among many others. If I don't screw up, my boss will probably look the other way. So long as you aren't coerced in any way, shape, or form."

Riley heard the unspoken statement. If Kaden really screwed up, one or both of them would be dead. The thought instantly killed his mood. "How abnormal is it that there are no family pictures up?"

"I'm sorry?" Kaden blinked and pushed himself up into a sitting position.

"Earlier you acted as though it was weird that there are no family photos hanging up in the house. So how weird is it?"

"That came out of —"

"It's better than imagining either of us dead."

Kaden squeezed him tighter. "Most people have photos in their offices and homes of the people who matter most in their lives. Parents, grandparents, siblings, cousins, children, grandchildren, and even friends. There's nothing visible here. Your grandmother's rooms have a single small photograph of you and a box of photographs hidden in her closet. Under a stack of blankets. Charles had a picture of him and his brother. Also hidden. It's as though the people in this family are ashamed of either the people or their emotions. Or that it's a job and personal photographs muddy the waters."

"You forgot the painting of my grandparents in the foyer."

"That is a portrait painting showing status and ownership. A nearly identical painting hangs in the corporate offices of Hamilton Perfumes. There is nothing that says a family lives here. Certainly not a close one."

"Maybe it's cultural," Riley suggested quietly.

"What do you mean?"

"I remember when my grandfather was alive and even up until I started college, we used to dress for dinner. Like dress up. When I was a kid, if I wanted to eat dinner with the adults, which wasn't often, I wore a suit with a tie and had to sit still and be quiet. They would talk about business, politics, and social gossip.

Once I went to boarding school I rarely came home. Even when I went home with friends, there were always trips to fantastic places, but there was always a nanny to keep an eye on us while the adults did their own thing. Houses are filled with artwork and antiques. Private areas may have photographs of family, but not always," Riley explained.

"But there is nothing in their private areas either."

"Not everyone marries for love. And what if instead of spies, they were running from their pasts?"

"You mean like a business arrangement."

Riley nodded, rolling onto his back. "They probably came over around the time Hitler was running rampant through Europe. Anti-Semitism was present here too. All over, to hear one of my teachers tell it."

"It's possible. It would certainly explain some things, but it doesn't answer the questions about who is after you or why."

"My family being spies doesn't really either." Riley held up a hand. "I'm just saying."

"More questions certainly don't help us at all."

"No, but it is infinitely more interesting than being stuck in an office all day." Riley smiled and wrinkled his nose. "Do you have any idea how smelly and noisy offices can be?"

"Then why go to work for the family company?"

Riley shrugged. "No choice."

"What would you do if you could choose?"

"What is wrong with lying on a beach all day and drinking? Watching the scenery."

"That's not really a career goal. It certainly doesn't pay the bills. And your father doesn't strike me as the type to foot the bill for you to be a beach bum."

"No, probably not."

"So, what would you do?"

"If I could do anything?"

Kaden nodded. "Yep."

Riley shrugged. "I think I can name maybe a dozen guys I went to school with who actually thought about what they wanted to be that was different than what their family wanted. Only one had the courage to do it."

Kaden shook his head before laying his forehead against Riley's. "I've heard of parents like that, but I've never met someone whose parents actually made them follow study what they wanted."

Riley rolled over to face Kaden. "No one you know has a father that was determined that his son was a miniature version of himself? That he would go into the same field or industry, or take over the family business? Be a lawyer, accountant, or doctor either because he was or because that's what he wanted to be and wasn't. Or play football or whatever because he had."

"When you put it that way, yes, a few. I'm sure it was more common twenty or thirty, maybe even sixty years ago, but even among those who claimed their son was going to follow in their footsteps, no one was forced to. No one, at least that I'm aware of, was ever threatened with being disowned or disinherited for following a different career path or playing a different sport or not playing sports at all."

"But you probably know how to work, do laundry, cook, and even do without something. Those are scary prospects for those who've never done them. That's like jumping without a parachute." Riley pushed up on his elbow and looked into Kaden's eyes. The man had stumbled over the last part of his answer. "Some people shouldn't be allowed to have kids. No one should be disowned because of who they love or how they believe."

Kaden shrugged and pulled Riley into his arms. "It's the way some churches and parents are. It's seen as either a fall from the true faith, or being corrupt, or a handful of other explanations meant to keep from tainting a pure family."

"Can we send Preacher to look in on my brother and uncle? To make sure that they're truly okay and not in any danger."

"Contacting them if they aren't known or sought after could alert who is after you about them and put them in danger."

"I know. But Preacher isn't a known friend or associate of mine. If we can get a hold of him without anyone knowing, maybe he can check on them. Discreetly."

"I'll ask him." Kaden hesitated.

There was a sharp knock on the door moments before it opened.

Benjamin stepped into the opening. "Sir, your grandmother called, she will meet you both at Russo's for dinner in an hour."

"Thank you, Benjamin."

The older man nodded, turned, and left.

"I'm not sure if that is a smart idea," Kaden said once the door was closed. He trailed his fingers up and down Riley's arm.

"Going to Russo's?" Riley asked. "It's an exclusive restaurant and—"

"Exactly. Going out in public, exclusive restaurant or some out-of-the-way hole in the wall shack isn't a smart idea. That your grandmother even thinks that this is a good idea is nuts," Kaden protested.

Riley clenched and unclenched his fists. He knew Kaden was right, but Russo's was his favorite restaurant and he hadn't been in there in years.

"What are you thinking about?"

Riley shrugged. "It doesn't seem to matter what I want, does it?"

"Riley—"

"Look, I get it. I understand. I'm just saying it sucks. Big time."

"I know. My job is to keep you safe. Alive."

"I can't live in a cage forever."

"It's only been three weeks, it hasn't been forever."

"Long enough when you can't do anything, go anywhere, or see anyone. Besides, while this is your *job*, which means you're getting paid, it's my life. And it's been completely interrupted. And I still have no idea why. Besides, by now half the city is going to know I'm home."

"You have a point. I seriously disagree with this completely, though."

"Fine, but you can disagree over the best Italian cooking on the Eastern Seaboard." Riley rolled off the bed and jumped to his feet. "I'm going to take a shower. We need to be presentable for dinner."

"I don't like this." Kaden glanced around. "This is a security nightmare."

"You're sounding like a broken record, James," Riley quipped, bringing the flashy red Porsche to a stop in front of a valet parking sign behind a silver Miata and a large black SUV. "I'm beginning not to care."

"I am not James Bond."

"*Hrumpf.*" Riley eased the car forward as the SUV pulled away.

"Bond would already have the blueprints of the building and all of the surrounding buildings, known all of the weakness and exits, and who or what he would be facing."

"Gee, thanks for the warning."

"Can we at least park—"

"Valet parking." Riley turned the car off, opened the door, stepped out of the car, and handed the keys to the attendant.

"No, this is—"

"Welcome home, Mr. Hamilton. It's been a while since you were here. We were surprised to hear you were missing."

Riley smiled and took the claim ticket. "Thank you, Michael, but it was all a misunderstanding. I was on vacation."

"Damn it! Wait a bloody minute!"

Riley clenched and unclenched his fists and stepped off to the side, not caring if Kaden followed him or not.

"Riley—"

"Let me make this very simple for you. I do not drive subtle vehicles. Ever. And whenever possible, I *always* use valet service and I tip very well. To do anything different would draw more attention to me. I actually know my world and my place in it. What you're suggesting won't work. And could get me killed."

"Being out—"

"Is damage control."

"Now is not the time."

"Now and later." Riley sighed. "When a story breaks, it plays out the longest and the loudest to those it impacts directly and indirectly."

"I know that."

"I'm local. My family has been here long enough to be known. Not only that, our company is very successful," Riley muttered. "My grandmother is trying to limit the damage to the company."

"At the expense of your life."

"If the company goes under, twenty-five hundred people all over the country lose their jobs." Riley led the way into the restaurant.

"Sympathy is good for business," Kaden quipped, placing a proprietary hand on the small of Riley's back.

"Mr. Hamilton, right this way." The maître d' smiled and led them to a semi-private table where his grandmother was already sitting.

"Sympathy only works if it's genuine, which means there can't be any secrets."

"Maybe." Kaden looked around the restaurant.

"Is there a problem, Mr. Tennison?" Margaret Hamilton asked, standing.

"Possibly."

"What do you mean possibly? You don't care to dine with me?" The elder woman sat back down at the table.

"No, ma'am, I disagree with a public dinner," Kaden answered as he and Riley sat down.

"I want to find out about the," Margaret Hamilton paused, "the man who seems to have captured Riley's attention."

"Mrs. Hamilton, a quiet dinner at the house would have been better," Kaden argued.

"People need to see that my grandson is alive and well," Margaret Hamilton said tersely. "We have a business to run. Whether Riley wants to or not."

Riley fiddled with the edge of his napkin as Kaden silently slipped his weapon from his holster and laid it across his lap. Riley followed his attention and swallowed. All of the tables were covered with bright white linen tablecloths and had the same small white floral bouquet and glass salt and pepper shakers in the center. Several couples sat at tables facing each other. Groups of businessmen and women gathered around other tables. Three families with older kids sat on the far side of the restaurant. He didn't see anything out of the ordinary, but he trusted Kaden's instincts. "Grandmother, there isn't a lot to tell. We met in New Orleans."

"There seems to be a lot that needs to be explained about your *extended* vacation." Margaret folded her hands and set them on the menu.

"Not here there isn't," Kaden ground out.

"We met in a bar," Riley explained, his leg bouncing up and down. "He kissed me. I kind of liked it even though I knew I shouldn't."

"Why did you let a strange man kiss you?"

"I was drunk. Why didn't you —"

Kaden held up a hand and picked up the floral centerpiece and examined it. He swore and pulled a small black rectangle with an antenna out of the arrangement.

"What in the world is that?" Margaret gasped.

Kaden grabbed the glass of red wine sitting in front Margaret Hamilton and dropped the small electronic into it. "That is a bug. And we are leaving. Now. Once we get back to the house, we will need to go through everything to see if there are any more."

"A bug? Like the kind spies use?" Riley asked, holding the wineglass up.

Kaden nodded.

Riley swallowed and set the glass down. His stomach rolled.

"How did that get there?" Margaret asked. "*Why* is it there?"

"Both good questions. Neither of which I'm to going to answer right now." Kaden holstered his weapon. "We need the check. We're leaving. Now."

Margaret and Riley nodded. Riley raised a hand to get the waiter's attention. He explained that there was some urgent business that came up and they needed to leave.

"I'm sorry to see you leave already, but of course we understand. Do come back again." The waiter handed a slim black book to Margaret Hamilton.

Riley nodded as his grandmother paid the bill, leaving a generous tip. Riley put a hand on Kaden's knee and squeezed. Kaden simply glared at the waiter, while constantly looking around as though he expected an attack at any minute.

Riley forced himself to breath normally. "Do we keep it to find out who it belongs to?"

"We'll drop it by the police station and let them see what they can find out about it. But honestly, it looks like something that can easily be bought off of the Internet."

"You can get pretty much anything online." Riley shoved a hand through his hair.

"You can." Kaden nodded. "Which is both a good thing and a bad thing."

"The police can find out who bought it from the company," Margaret said, standing.

"Only with a warrant. And only if they find the right company," Kaden replied. "Eavesdropping isn't illegal, merely unethical."

Kaden retrieved the listening device from the wineglass and led the way out of the restaurant, waiting impatiently as both vehicles were brought around. He dropped the bug to the ground and smashed it with the heel of his shoe.

"I should have known you would drive this one." Margaret smiled.

"We will see you back at the house." Riley kissed his grandmother's cheek and held the door for her as she slid behind the wheel of a black Mercedes Benz. He closed the door of the car before paying the valet and climbing into his bright red Porsche.

The silence in the car on the drive over to the police station was deafening, adding to his anxiety. Kaden finally turned the radio on and gave him directions to the station. Riley pulled into the first visitor's parking spot he could find and put the car in park.

"Let's go." Kaden reached for the door handle.

"Really? Why do I have to go?"

Kaden raised an eyebrow.

"This is ridiculous. We're in the parking lot of a police station!" Riley shouted and turned the car off. "You're going to be, what, ten minutes?"

"There was a bug on the table of the restaurant we were told about just over an hour beforehand."

Riley opened and closed his mouth without saying anything. Mentally kicking himself, he followed Kaden into the police station. They were shown to a small windowless room with a two-way mirror to wait while Chief Montgomery was called.

"Can't they at least have a decent waiting area?" Riley stretched out his legs. "These chairs are uncomfortable."

"Most people don't come here voluntarily. Comfort isn't really their goal. Information is."

"*Hrumpf.*"

Minutes ticked by, Riley crossed his arms, wishing he'd brought his phone with him. It would at least have given him something to do. Standing, he paced the small room before throwing himself back into the chair. The door finally opened just as he was about storm out.

"Now what is so urgent that I needed to come in immediately?" Chief Montgomery asked, walking through the door. "Mr. Tennison. Mr. Hamilton. Follow me."

Riley stood and followed the police chief through a maze of desks to a large glassed-in office.

"Now, again, Mr. Tennison, why was it so important I come down here? Why couldn't you talk to one of my officers?"

"This." Kaden slammed the destroyed listening device onto the desk.

"Where did that come from?" Chief Montgomery dug a rubber glove out of his desk and put it on.

"The centerpiece at Russo's," Riley answered.

"And you think it was meant for you?" Chief Montgomery held the device up and examined it.

Kaden nodded. "Russo's seems to be very busy despite being overpriced. We only knew to be there about an hour or so before we got there." Kaden sat back in his chair. "I don't believe in coincidences."

"Who arranged the meeting?"

"It was dinner. And my grandmother."

"Maybe she put the bug in there."

Riley scratched his head. "Not likely. First, I'm her grandson. There is no reason to record our conversations. Especially, a personal one. Second, she not only didn't know what it was, she was horrified when she found out."

"I don't know what we can do with it, but I'll have it processed." Montgomery dropped the smashed electronic into a plastic evidence bag. "The hospital has confirmed it wasn't an employee of the hospital that killed Dvorak and Simek."

"Who are Dvorak and Simek?" Riley cocked his head to one side.

"The fake FBI agents. They were killed this morning." Kaden rubbed the back of his neck. "That could cause a gang war."

"What do you mean a gang war?" Riley demanded, standing. "Who were those guys? How do they tie-in to the assholes after me? Are gangs after me?"

"They were part of the Russian mob. More than that, we don't know." Chief Montgomery shook his head.

"Russians? More Russians?"

"Technically, they aren't Russians, they were Czechs. They only worked for the Russians," Chief Montgomery explained.

"Is that important? That distinction?"

"Could be. Depends on who ordered them dead. It could be cause for retaliation," Kaden supplied.

"Okay, so, how does this affect me? Why should I care if a few assholes kill each other?" Riley jumped to his feet and paced the office.

"It can make everything messier with more people after you. And they don't necessarily care if you're alive or dead. Especially if you being dead screws over the people responsible."

"Freaking great."

Kaden nodded. "It complicates matters."

"Do you have a plan?" Chief Montgomery asked.

"Yes."

"Good. Let's get you two on your way then." The chief leaned forward in his chair. "Let me make a call. What vehicle is yours?"

"The red Porsche," Riley answered, leaning against a bookcase.

The chief raised an eyebrow and picked up the receiver and punched in a five-digit number. "Captain Martin, I need your team to do a sweep of the red Porsche sitting in the visitors' lot."

"What kind of sweep?" Riley asked, sinking into the chair. "Like looking for more bugs or bombs?" His life seemed to mirror some sort of horror movie. He should be with his friends, commiserating over their loss of free time, not trying to stay alive in a war between spies and mobs.

Chief Montgomery folded his hands on his desk and nodded. "Captain Martin is the head of EOD."

"I swear, when I find the person responsible — "

"You will let the law handle it," Kaden interrupted.

"You can't imagine what it's like to be hunted. To lose everything. And not know why." Riley jumped to his feet and resumed pacing. He pretended to be interested in the various decorations and clenched and unclenched his fists.

"No, but I've seen what happens when people go off half-cocked against someone with more experience and less morals. It's not pretty." Chief Montgomery shook his head.

"Innocent people are dead because of me!" Riley shouted. He stopped and turned to Kaden. "You said fake agents. So they weren't FBI? They were only pretending to be? How in the hell does that happen in this day and age? Computers and smart phones are everywhere."

"No idea," Chief Montgomery said. "But somebody will probably lose their job over it."

"That's reassuring," Riley quipped.

The phone on the desk rang twenty minutes later. The car was clear. Kaden thanked the chief as they followed him out of the office. Riley's stomach pitched and rolled as Kaden spoke with the EOD Captain. No explosives had been found, but they had found a tracking device stuck to the bottom of the car. Riley's sigh of relief was followed by the realization that not only could the car still be bugged — more people's lives had been put in danger because of him. The idea that the police chief and department were mixed up with whoever wanted him dead crossed his mind as well. There was no way to tell who was a friend and who was an enemy.

"I don't stand a fucking chance," Riley muttered. "Can we go? If I'm going to die, I'd like to do it drunk and at home." Riley climbed into the sports car and turned it on. He contemplated leaving Kaden at the police station. "Damn it!" Riley pounded a fist onto the steering wheel. He put the car into gear and waited for his bodyguard to climb into the car.

The ride back to the estate was silent and tense. Both Kaden and Riley checked to see if they were being followed. Riley relaxed as the gates closed behind them. He parked the car in the garage and was halfway to the house before Kaden caught up with him.

"Hold on a damn minute! Riley! We don't know where we picked up the tracking device. The car may be bugged also."

"I get that. I actually thought of that. I get that anywhere that those idiots went too may also be bugged. What I want to know is why are you all of a sudden buddy-buddy with the chief of police. The same man who had you arrested not twenty-four hours ago," Riley demanded. "Did you even spend the night in jail or did you and Montgomery laugh and joke about having to babysit me. A spoiled brat, I believe is what you called me. Several times."

"I spent the night in jail with some idiot who couldn't handle his alcohol and not only pissed all over himself, but threw up multiple times, while they figured out whether or not they wanted to believe me. This morning the chief and I learned who those two men were. There is nothing wrong being diplomatic and getting their help. There is nothing unique about that bug. So I will gladly let them use their resources, resources I don't have by the way, to help figure out who is after one of their citizens," Kaden explained. "While I would much rather have been with you, where I can see you, I also have a job to do."

"Are you any good at your job?" Riley asked flatly, looking Kaden in the eyes.

"The best."

"Let's hope you're right."

Kaden nodded and pulled Riley into a hug. "Is there anywhere else we need to check?"

"Check for what?"

"Information. Bugs."

"No, not that I can—wait, yes. My closet. I have a few things hidden there. But the police have it sealed off still."

"Let's go look. While we're there, you can pack a bag."

"Great. At least I can bring my own stuff." Riley led the way into the house. "They didn't leave a cop to guard the door."

Kaden pulled a knife out of his pocket and carefully sliced through the police seal and opened the door. "Touch only what you need." Kaden stood aside and let Riley slip inside before closing the door behind them.

A search of the room turned up a bug and a camera. Kaden destroyed both items while Riley knelt in the back of the large walk-in closet in front of a large black metal footlocker with a built-in combination lock. Flipping the dials to the proper sequence, he held his breath and opened the lid. He'd never shown the contents of the trunk to anyone. Ever. He wasn't sure he was ready now, but he also knew there was little chance that Kaden was going to leave him alone. Riley shoved a hand through his hair. The idea wasn't completely unwelcomed. He was tired of being chased. Tired of having to be on guard all of the time. Most of all, he was tired of never knowing who to trust.

It had been several years since he'd opened the trunk, but he remembered everything in it. There was an assortment of ribbons, trophies, and certificates intermingled with his favorite stuffed bear from childhood, as well as a battered, much-read copy of *The Sword of Shannara*. Nothing in there was important to anyone but him. They were his memories.

Kaden squatted beside the chest as Riley dug through the box, carefully stacking things to one side or another. He handed an ornately painted box to Kaden before sitting back against the wall.

"It's not what I was looking for, but I found that box with my mother's stuff. I don't know if it's hers or not, but I put the rest of her stuff in it," Riley said, staring at his hands. "There wasn't much left of hers. I left it here — I didn't — it seemed weird bringing important things with me to school."

"What were you looking for?" Kaden asked slowly, opening the box.

"There was a box that came with my grandfather's watch. I kept the watch with me, but the box was ugly so I put it away. I thought it was in here with the rest of my things." Riley bit his lip and got to his feet. "I hoped it might help us figure out what the key goes to."

Kaden sat down and looked carefully at each item. Riley pulled down a plain white box from the top shelf of his closet and opened it as he sat back down cross-legged on the floor. Tucked into one corner was the box that his grandfather's watch had come in, as well as photos and letters from pen pals he'd had when he was in grade school. There was also a small battered wrapped box with the tag still on it. It was the last gift he'd ever bought for Charles. He'd bought a pair of cufflinks and a matching tie-tack and had them wrapped at the store. After Charles had left, he'd thrown the gift in the trash. It had ended up on the corner of his desk. He'd thrown it away several times. Each time it had ended up back in his room. Finally, he'd stuck it in a box to keep from looking at it.

"What is in that box?"

"Things I didn't want but couldn't get rid of."

"Why not throw them away? Why keep them if you don't want them?"

"I threw things away all the time, but some things would end up back in my room time and time again. I don't know what possessed the maids to go through my garbage, but they did. All the time. So I hid them away instead."

Kaden nodded and frowned. "Your mother's journal doesn't have a lot in it."

"I don't think it's her first one, but I've never found any others. Maybe she started one because she was pregnant."

"It's possible. Have you looked in the library for them? That is where I would hide something if I wanted to hide it in plain sight."

"No." Riley shook his head. "I don't see her as the type to hide something like that in the library. That was my grandfather's room when he was alive. He was always either there, in his bedroom, or the dining room when he was home. At least, those are the only places I ever saw him in."

"What room was your mother's? Did she share a room with Charles?"

"I don't know which one was hers. I'm sure I asked at some point in time, but everyone pretends she never existed. Probably on Charles' order. Benjamin or Ava would know though. Why?"

"Maybe, like the hidey-hole in the Rose Room, her bedroom had someplace secret where she could stash things she didn't want found."

Riley sprang to his feet. "We need to find out."

"One thing at a time. Do you know where this box came from?" he asked, setting the other items aside. "It looks old. Antique maybe."

"It could be. My grandparents liked antiques." Riley slid back down to the floor. "Someone once said it was because they were new money and were trying to legitimize their wealth and place in society."

"Legitimize their wealth? That's a thing?"

Riley shrugged and nodded. "Some people think that if you haven't had money from like the Civil War or some such shit, then you aren't good enough to attend their parties and stuff."

"Who said that?"

"Classmate. Earned me a week in detention and bruised knuckles."

Kaden chuckled. "And the other kid?"

"Stanford Elias Bradford Weatherby the Third. Two years older than me. Ended up with a black eye, a split lip, and a couple of loose teeth. His mother said that was happened when the school opened its doors to everyone who could pay."

"And?"

"And what?"

"You can't tell me you walked away from that."

Riley smiled. "Nope. I said something to the effect of at least we earned our money honestly and that a two-bit money-grubbing whore with less brains than God gave a gnat and who did nothing more than try to look pretty had no place to talk. Earned me another week's detention and a lecture from the headmaster."

"Did you ever get kicked out of school? Try to?"

"Thought about it, but Charles would have just found another one to send me to. It was easier to stay put." Riley pulled out the watch box. He examined the box, but nothing about it suggested that there was a secret compartment of any sort. Heaving a sigh, he gave it to Kaden and watched the other man examine the wooden box. Kaden turned it over in his hands, opening and closing it several times before pulling out a pocketknife.

"Whoa! What the hell are you doing?" Riley protested, jumping to his feet.

"Pulling the velvet up," Kaden explained. "Here, look. The inside isn't as deep as the outside."

Riley sat back down next to Kaden, trying to see what he meant.

"Secret compartments in chests and trinket boxes are always a popular item for young women, lovers, and spies. Especially those who love someone they aren't supposed to," Kaden continued.

Riley held his breath as Kaden carefully pulled up a corner of the red velvet lining. There was a rip in the corner of the fabric and edges were frayed and worn from where it had been lifted and shoved back into place repeatedly.

"Do you have the key?" Kaden asked, revealing a small keyhole.

Riley shook his head and leaned over. "It's in my backpack. A false bottom with a lock. I never —"

"They were popular several times over the course of history."

"I'll be damned."

Kaden nodded. "If you're traveling, a handful of lady's jewelry would easily disguise the height difference. Especially at a cursory glance."

Chapter Twenty-Two

"Let's go get it and see if it fits. Then you need to pack a bag and we need to get out of here."

"Do I have time to let my grandmother know we have to leave?" Mentally Riley added *again*. He knew they needed to leave. They had to find someplace else for him to hide. He didn't want to leave. He didn't want to hide. He didn't want to pack. He wanted to go back to his life.

Kaden raised an eyebrow. "Do you normally?"

Riley clenched and unclenched his fists. No, he didn't make a habit of telling anyone anything, but this was different. They both knew that. "I don't normally have people who want me dead actively hunting me. So no, it may not be normal, but nothing about my life right now is normal. For anyone."

"No details."

"Duh. I'm not a complete moron, *James*." Riley put everything back into the box and chest, taking the time and care to make it look like it was beforehand. He didn't think anyone would look in there, but he wasn't certain and he didn't want to make it obvious.

He shoved clothes into a large, black canvas duffel bag before adding his hygiene products from the bathroom. Kaden followed him back to the Rose Room, holding the box, covered with several pairs of pants and shirts on hangers.

"Is everything okay, Mr. Hamilton?" Ava asked, glancing at the items in their arms. "Do you need help with anything?"

"Yes, Ava, I just wanted to bring some of my clothes and things down to the Rose Room. I know the police unsealed my room, but it needs to be cleaned and repaired before I'll be comfortable staying there."

"Of course, sir."

"How is Briana doing?"

"Not very well. She's worried about her job and what the police will think."

"Her job is safe. She needs to see a counselor. We'll pay for it. Her experience would shake anyone up," Riley answered. "As for the police, I'm sure they know she had nothing to do with it. They just have to make sure and figure out who's responsible."

"Nobody in this family," Ava said adamantly.

"I agree, I don't think it was anyone that actually belongs here." Riley nodded. "Ava, do you remember my mother?"

"Sir, that is not something I can talk about." Ava shook her head, tears welling in her eyes.

Anger roared through him. He was tired of being stonewalled. "I'll kill Charles!" Riley spat. "I don't care why you aren't supposed to talk about my mother or who gave the order. I have a *right* to know about her.

At All Costs

The same as I had a right to know that I have an older brother!"

The housekeeper gasped. "How did you—"

"I know. That's enough." Riley shrugged. "What room was hers? My mother's?"

"Her room?"

"I can't imagine that Charles actually shared a room with his wife."

"They did. For a couple of months. But then she moved into the Rose Room. It looked different then. Your mother wasn't a fan of flowers. She preferred white lace and linens."

"Thank you, Ava." Riley led the way back their room.

"How did you know that your parents didn't share a room?" Kaden asked when they were out of earshot of the housekeeper.

"First, my grandparents didn't share a room. Second, if my parents shared a room then Charles would have had to pay for a hotel room to screw whatever woman he was interested in at the moment, and he doesn't like to be obvious. It's bad for the company's image as a 'family company' to be seen constantly cheating on your wife, especially a pregnant wife." Riley dropped the duffel bag on the edge of the bed.

Kaden nodded and tossed the clothes next to the bag. "That makes sense."

Riley dug the antique watch out of his backpack, pushed the button and released the key from its hiding spot. Excitement and nervousness raced through him. Taking a deep breath, he let it out slowly, forcing himself to relax. The answer to who wanted him dead could be in the ornately carved box. What was worth killing him over? And why were they after it now? Why not before?

Hands shaking, he took the box from Kaden and sat on the edge of the bed. Inhaling deeply, he inserted the key into the slot and turned it. The gears creaked and clicked as they moved. The false bottom sprang partway open. Riley prised it open all the way.

"What the hell?" he exclaimed. A tarnished gold lipstick tube lay next to a shaving cream brush on top of a beige cellophane envelope containing what looked like photographs. Riley shoved the box at Kaden.

"Ingenious."

"I don't get it."

"One or both items can be used for smuggling. The photograph may tell us who."

"Smuggling what? Like film?"

"Exactly like film."

"Seriously? Like in the James Bond movies with the gadgets, mini-cameras, pen bombs, and shit."

Kaden nodded. "Probably a lot less glamorous, though."

"What would these pictures be of? A lot has changed in the last forty or fifty years. The process and ingredients used in making perfumes and colognes is completely different. Some of it isn't even legal to use anymore."

"You're assuming that whoever hid these were company rivals."

"What else would there be?" Riley jumped to his feet and began to pace the room.

"Depending on when and where these were taken, it could be anything. Allied troop movements or anything that could have helped the Nazis or the Russians win the war against the Allies. Later, it could be just about anything related to space race or building and keeping nuclear weapons. Or even chemical and biological warfare."

"Aren't you a bucket of fun. I can't begin to imagine why you're still single, James," Riley quipped. He stopped his pacing and turned. "But it could be the other way, too, right? Stealing from the Russians or the Nazis and passing them to the Allies."

"Yes, it could."

"So, how do we figure out what it's in there? And which side they were working for? Whoever *they* were. Or are."

"Maybe an answer as to who is after you and why." Kaden shoved a hand through his hair. "Ace can help us."

"Does Ace have a safehouse?"

Kaden chuckled. "No, Ace has a two-bedroom apartment perfectly positioned between their favorite club, restaurant, and coffee shop."

"Job?"

"Ace works from home."

Riley flopped down onto the bed. "It doesn't look like we have a choice. I don't like it."

Kaden nodded and pulled Riley close to him. "Honestly, there isn't a good answer. Until we figure out who's behind this and why, you'll never be safe."

"I know. I'm not arguing. Just stating a fact." Riley blew out a breath. "So, when do we leave? Where are we going?"

Kaden dragged his fingers along Riley's arm. "I'd like to leave within the hour."

Riley nodded, stood, and stretched. "I want to check out the secret room again before that. Maybe we'll find something useful."

"Can't hurt."

Riley repacked his things before leading the way into the secret room behind the closet. A cursory search of the room uncovered a handful of empty hiding spots, a book of poetry, a gold and diamond ring, a handful of *National Geographic* magazines, and magazines of scantily clad and nude women.

"That was a bust." Riley shouldered his backpack and grabbed a blanket out of the closet.

"Maybe not."

"There was nothing in there."

"Except a book of poetry in plain sight, possibly a lady's ring in the seat cushions, and some poorly hidden porn. Recent stuff. It's possible that the truly valuable stuff was moved or is still hidden. And we don't have time today to look for it," Kaden sighed.

"Poetry I can kind of understand, a private space for a lonely woman. But the porn, that's just plain weird."

"You don't have porn?" Kaden asked as they made their way downstairs.

"Yes, but I keep it in my room. In the nightstand under a couple of *Men's Health* magazines. Or on my computer," Riley answered. "It doesn't do me any good in another room."

"And it was a lady's room."

"So was it deliberate then?"

"I think so. But why? Why set up a hidey-hole that no one would know about or look for?"

"Can I help you, Mr. Hamilton?" Benjamin asked, meeting them at the foot of the stairs.

"Where is my grandmother?"

"You're leaving. Excuse me, sir, but is that wise?"

"Kaden seems to think it's the only choice we have."

The older man shook his head. "I don't understand. The estate is fenced in. We've brought the security guards full-time on site. There are — "

"The estate is huge and there is only one of me. There are too many variables and people coming and going," Kaden challenged. "There is also the matter of the listening device found at dinner and a tracking device on Riley's car. I don't suppose you know anything about that, do you?"

Riley cringed at the accusation. Benjamin had been with his family as long as he could remember.

"No, I don't. I would never do anything to hurt Riley, first of all. And second, I have nothing to do with the garage and the cars." Benjamin sniffed, his chest puffed out. "I resent that accusation, Mr. Tennison. If that is your real name."

Kaden stepped forward. "I can prove my identity in a court of law. Can you?"

"How dare you?" Benjamin exclaimed, his face turning red.

"What makes a man serve a family as a live-in butler for twenty or thirty years?" Kaden asked, cocking his head to one side.

"Forty-seven years, if you must know. Loyalty. A trait that is sorely missing in the world today. Now, unless you plan on calling the police, I have things that I must attend to."

"Where is my grandmother?" Riley asked. "I need to say goodbye before we leave."

"In the solarium, Mr. Hamilton."

They walked in silence through the house to the solarium. Even though it was the right thing to do, it still felt weird to Riley to seek anyone in his family out to say goodbye or even let them know where he was going or what he was doing.

"He loves you, you know," Kaden said softly, stopping outside the door.

"Who?"

"Benjamin. Does he or has he ever called you by your first name?"

"No. Not that I recall."

"He called you Riley when he got angry. He sees you as a son or grandson."

"I— How did I not know?"

"He didn't want you to know."

"Still." Riley pushed open the door. "Grandmother?" Riley called out, walking into the large glassed-in room. Flowers and decorative trees filled the walls of the room and comingled with the pale blue and yellow overstuffed furniture. Margaret Hamilton sat in a light blue wing-backed chair, one leg crossed over the other. Her elbows rested on the arms of the chair, fingers laced together.

"Riley, I didn't know you were back."

"I assumed Benjamin would have told you." Riley sat down in a pale yellow and blue floral chair opposite to hers. "But we can't stay. *I* can't stay."

"Nonsense. Of course, you can stay. I don't mind your...your boyfriend."

"It has nothing to do with Kaden."

"I'm not the same person. We were wrong, you know. Parents disowning a child because of who they loved. We thought it—it doesn't matter what we thought. I have learned a lot in the past few years."

"No, Mrs. Hamilton, Riley can't stay here. He isn't safe here."

"That's absurd. We have security."

"And yet, two men impersonating FBI agents were allowed to stay here. They killed the third man, an actual FBI agent. In. This. House. The police found a tracking device on Riley's car. It was placed in it either while we were here or at the restaurant. There was a listening device on the table of the restaurant where we met *you* for dinner. And those fake FBI agents tried to kill both of us." Kaden stepped forward and put a hand on Riley's shoulder.

"Are you accusing me of trying to kill my grandson?"

"No, I'm saying that there are too many coincidences to ignore. My job is to keep Riley safe. From everyone. Even family if needed."

"I don't think I like your tone of voice, young man."

"Ma'am, with all due respect, I don't give a rat's ass if you care or not. This family is more like a group of strangers with too many secrets and not enough love or trust," Kaden declared.

"Kaden—"

"No." Kaden turned to face Riley. "Your father, who doesn't care if you call him by his first name, announcing to the entire world that you were missing has caused this mess. Three more people are dead, your family's home is shot up and its security undermined. The fact that neither your father, who left as soon as you returned, nor your grandmother seem to care where you are until money is involved tells me that the emotional connection that families—have and should have—is missing. Completely. This is more like a job than a family. We need to go."

Riley drew in a deep breath and blew it out again, nodding. "No family is perfect. Even yours."

"True enough. And if anyone approached my family now saying I needed help or was in trouble they would slam the door in their face. I'm as good as dead to them. But, growing up, even as reserved as my dad could be, we always knew he loved us."

"Where are you going?" Margaret Hamilton demanded.

"A safehouse, Mrs. Hamilton," Kaden replied. "That is all you need to know."

"How dare you!"

"I dare because Riley may pay with his life for something someone else, possibly someone who never had the time for him, did. I dare because it's my job. I dare because I actually give a damn about him!" Kaden spat.

Riley blinked and let Kaden pull him to his feet. "Care...like...friend...or..."

"Care as in I'm falling for you. In ways that aren't professional by a long shot." Kaden pulled him into his arms, crushing him to him, and kissed him.

"I don't understand." Riley shook his head when they parted.

"Neither do I, not really," Kaden admitted. "But right now, it isn't the time or place to discuss it."

"Shouldn't I be the one falling for you? Isn't that the way it goes?"

"In the James Bond films you're so fond of quoting, Bond seduces women on the wrong side of the law in order to get what he wants. He doesn't care for those women. They're simply a means to an end. Me, I can keep you alive without seducing you or falling for you. I'm not after anything you have. And I most certainly have never fallen for or even started to fall for somebody I was working with."

"Not even when you were in the Army?"

"There were very few dating options in my career field." Kaden shrugged.

"Preacher said—"

"Civilians. I'm pickier about my partners than Preacher has ever been."

Riley laughed.

The sound relaxed the tension building in Kaden. He hadn't been sure what Riley's reaction was going to be after his impromptu confession. He hadn't meant to rail against Riley's grandmother—the old woman probably had no real clue about the true danger they were in. He would need to talk to Lawrence about getting a detail attached to the family as well.

"I suggest both you and Charles hire bodyguards until we know who and what we're dealing with," Kaden suggested, turning to the family matriarch.

"I—I will make no promises about what Charles does. Given the circumstances I can see your point. I will check into it today." Margaret Hamilton pushed herself to her feet. "Once this mess is over, Mr. Tennison, and my grandson is safe, I would appreciate a report, in detail, about the security issues you have found in my house. Now, if you will excuse me, I have some calls to make."

"Of course, Grandmother."

"And, Mr. Tennison, bring my grandson home safe," Margaret Hamilton said before leaving the room.

Kaden looked over at Riley and cocked his head to one side. "That doesn't seem to be the same woman."

Riley shook his head. "I think you threw her. I don't think anyone has ever said anything like that to her before."

"Probably should happen more often."

"So, where are we going?"

"Someplace safe." Kaden shoved a hand through his hair and swore quietly. He knew several different safehouses where he could stash Riley, but he wasn't sure he could trust them. Blowing out a breath, Kaden followed Riley to the garage where his car was being kept. It took several minutes to locate Seth Richardson, the Hamilton's mechanic and chauffer.

"You're in charge of all of the vehicles, right?" Kaden asked as Seth unlocked the door to a small office at the back of the multi-stall garage.

"I take care of them, yeah."

"And what does that entail?"

"I drive Mr. Hamilton or Mrs. Hamilton wherever they need to go when they're here. I wash the cars, keep 'em filled, do minor maintenance. Things like that. What's this about?"

"And are you the only one who has access to these vehicles? Can someone get in here without your knowledge?"

Seth stopped what he was doing, turned, and crossed his arms over his chest. "I don't like your tone of voice or the questions you're askin'. I don't think that's any of your business."

"Seth, people are trying to kill me. Kaden isn't blaming you for anything. He's trying to figure out how easy it is for someone to tamper with our vehicles without anyone's knowledge."

"I lock the garage at night when I go to bed, but anyone can get in. I'm here most of the time, but not always."

"Have you seen anyone around here that shouldn't be. Or noticed anything out of place?" Riley asked.

"Just those FBI agents. I don't think they were ever here when I wasn't. I didn't trust them." Seth pulled a set of keys from the peg board. "Here are your keys."

Kaden nodded, took the keys, and made his way over to his car. "Wait here." He pulled a small flashlight from his duffel bag and set the bag on the ground by Riley's feet. He circled the vehicle slowly before lying on his back and scooting under it to look at the undercarriage. Satisfied that nothing had been done, he moved his examination to under the hood and in the trunk before looking inside the vehicle.

"Okay, let's go," Kaden said finally, retrieving his bag.

"I know I've asked before, but seriously, are you like this *all* of the time?" Riley asked, shaking his head. "Definitely a mood killer."

"Only when I have to be," Kaden replied.

"So all the time. Gotcha." Riley smirked and tossed his bag into the back seat.

Kaden shrugged. He wasn't going to apologize for doing his job. He didn't always have the luxury of checking a vehicle out first. Usually he relied on clues to let him know something was amiss.

"And here I thought we were done with the road trips." Riley sighed and slid into the seat.

"Not yet."

"You're not even phased by any of this."

"It's my job. I'm good at my job. You might as well as get some sleep, we have long a drive ahead of us."

"Fine. At least turn the radio on." Riley pushed the button and adjusted the dial until he found a station that he liked. He unfolded his blanket and pulled it up to his chin. He grabbed his ball cap off the dashboard and put it on, pulling the brim down until it covered his eyes.

* * * *

Just after one in the morning Kaden pulled off the highway and followed the signs to the Super 8 Motel. He'd contemplated just pulling into a truck stop or rest area and parking for the night, but had changed his mind when a highway patrol officer had continued to follow them. The drive from Long Island to Washington DC was one he'd made often enough to know that he could do it in one day—had they left earlier in the day instead of ten o'clock at night. He still wasn't sure if going home was the best decision he could make, but he didn't see any other option. His first stop tomorrow morning was to see Ace and hope they could figure out what, if anything, was in the lipstick tube and shaving brush.

Scrubbing a hand over his face, he left Riley sleeping and went in to pay for the room. He climbed back into the car and smiled. Riley hadn't moved. Kaden backed out of the guest spot in front of the office, and parked in a spot three doors down from their room. They had gotten the last room available, a king in the middle of the building on the first floor.

"Riley, wake up." Kaden gently shook Riley's shoulder.

"Huh?" Riley pushed himself up in the seat. He pulled the cap off and rubbed his eyes.

"Wake up."

"Where are we?" Riley asked, his voice rough with sleep.

"A motel for the night. I'm exhausted."

"I don't know why we couldn't have waited until morning to start this road trip. Well, I mean I do, but I don't." Riley readjusted the ball cap. "Does that make any sense?"

Kaden nodded. "I know what you mean."

Kaden grabbed the duffel bags while Riley untangled himself from his blanket. Scanning the parking lot, he waited for the younger man on the sidewalk. Locking the vehicle as soon as the door was closed, he sidestepped so Riley could get by him and led the way to their room.

"Well, it looks like it's a couple steps up from the last place." Riley shook his head and took the duffel bags from Kaden and slung them over his shoulder.

"Complete with indoor plumbing, running water, and electricity," Kaden quipped, drawing his weapon from the holster. He pulled the flashlight from his pocket and turned it on.

"Smart-ass. Here, give me the key."

"I—"

"I can open it from the side. You need both of your hands free."

Kaden nodded and handed the key card to Riley. Kaden held his breath. Riley slid the key card into the slot, removing it when the light turned green. Riley turned the handle of the door. Kaden slammed it open and stepped through it. He swept the room, searching under the bed, behind doors, and in the closet and bathroom before holstering his weapon and crossing back to Riley. Riley had stepped inside the room, closed the door behind him, and stood against the wall between the door and the window.

Kaden closed and locked the door and took the duffel bags from Riley.

"Thank you."

"No big deal." Riley shrugged. "At least it doesn't stink."

"Stink? None of the places we've stayed in have stunk."

"Not to you, maybe. But to me, a few of them absolutely did. On a scale of one to ten, some were at a three and others were at a six or seven. This is a three and a half."

Kaden nodded. "You should've said something. It's easy for me to forget."

"Kaden, I've been dealing with this my whole life. Trust me, if it was really bad, I'd have said something."

"You shouldn't have to just deal with it you know."

"It is what it is."

"Benjamin didn't seem surprised earlier when you mentioned the difference in chemical smells."

"I didn't notice that, but you're right."

"Maybe he's suspected all along?"

"Possible." Riley tossed his ball cap onto the small table and scratched his head. "Why is there only one bed? I mean, I don't mind sleeping with you and the sex was great and all, but, um, why?"

"Thanks. I think." Kaden pulled Riley into his arms.

"Hey! I was giving you a compliment. Geez, you don't need to act like a barbarian."

"I know," Kaden whispered against Riley's ear. "I'm *your* barbarian, though." His tongue flicked the sensitive lobe. Kaden slanted his mouth over Riley's, his tongue pushing forward, seeking entrance. Riley gasped and opened, returning the kiss. Kaden deepened the kiss and pulled Riley closer to him.

"Seriously, why is there only one bed?" Riley asked, laying his head on Kaden's shoulder.

"Apparently, there are two different sports events, regionals or something, as well as, some sort of pageant thing, on top of the usual crop of tourists. The attendant said pretty much every hotel room in ten square miles has been rented. We have the last one they had due to a last-minute cancellation."

"Gotcha. It's a good thing I don't mind sharing a bed with you then." Riley smiled. "I'm going to take a shower."

Kaden secured the room and double-checked the parking lot before pulling his toiletry bag out of the duffel. He had just finished cleaning his weapon when Riley finally emerged from the shower, hair still damp and dressed in a pair of loose, low-hanging light-gray sleep pants.

"Sexy." Kaden smiled.

"You need to take a shower and I need to sleep." Riley kissed Kaden on the cheek.

Kaden grabbed Riley and pulled him into him, capturing his mouth in a kiss. "You look gorgeous."

"You're not so bad yourself. You still need a shower."

"Hmm. Spoilsport."

"Nope, tired. And you smell like road, car, and police station. Not a flattering combination."

Kaden chuckled, released Riley, and headed into the shower. "Good night."

* * * *

Riley blinked open his eyes and stilled. It took him a moment to realize where he was and that Kaden was wrapped around him, pressing against him. Riley opened his eyes wide. Kaden was hard.

"Um, Kaden," Riley whispered.

"Yes, I'm hard. Yes, it's normal. And yes, it's due to you." Kaden kissed the back of his neck.

"Oh." Riley swallowed. He'd never woken up in the same bed as another man before meeting Kaden.

"Let me untangle myself and take a shower. Go back to sleep for a bit." Kaden hugged Riley tight before releasing him.

"Wait. Um. Can't we, um, can we... Bond would've had sex."

"True, he would have, but then, he has different ideas about relationships than I do."

"I know. That's why I like you. Well, part of the reason." Riley rolled over in Kaden's arms. "What I'm trying to say, to ask, is," Riley inhaled deeply, "can we try it again? Sex. Can we try sex again? You know, to make sure I still like it and that you're not a complete barbarian or anything." Riley stared at Kaden's chest and cupped his cock.

"Any time you want. Well, almost any time. You know there's nothing to be ashamed or embarrassed about wanting or enjoying sex with another man."

"I know. I—I don't know what I'm doing. Not exactly."

"What do you mean?" Kaden rubbed one of Riley's nipples between his thumb and forefinger.

"I know how sex works with women. How to approach them, seduce them, get them off. Men are different. This is different. And new. I don't know this. How to do any of this."

"You're. Doing. Fine." Kaden punctuated each word with a kiss.

Riley bit his lip and pushed Kaden onto his back. Straddling him, Riley traced the curve of Kaden's biceps with his fingers, leaned down and captured his mouth. Tentatively at first, he reveled in his lover's strength. The confidence and pleasure Kaden did nothing to hide. He ground his hips against Kaden's groin. Riley's cock hardened. Briefly, he wondered how it would feel to fuck Kaden. Releasing Kaden's mouth, Riley sat up and gently played with Kaden's nipples. There was no fear of being caught, no awkward fumbling, only pleasure and desire. Kaden pulled Riley back down to him. The move brought their cocks in contact. Riley kissed Kaden along his jawline. Kaden's hand slid beneath Riley's sleep pants and grabbed his ass, one finger tapping his hole.

Riley gasped as Kaden's finger entered him. Kaden rolled them over and kissed Riley deeply before trailing a line of kisses down to Riley's cock, divesting him of his clothes as he went. Riley arched his back. Kaden swallowed his cock down to the base.

"Shit! Holy shit!" Riley fisted the sheets, fighting the instinct to grab Kaden's head.

Kaden pushed a second finger into Riley, his tongue dancing around his cock. The combination threatened to overwhelm his senses. Kaden lifted off Riley's cock and blew a breath lightly across the head.

"No more!" Riley gasped out. "I want to come with you in me. Then I want to fuck you."

Kaden chuckled and withdrew his fingers. Riley moaned his displeasure at the emptiness. He bit back a protest as Kaden climbed off the bed and retrieved a condom and lube from his bag. Riley didn't want the barrier between them. Refusing to examine the meaning behind it, he sat up and kissed the scars on Kaden's shoulder and arm taking the time to trace the muscles down to Kaden's cock and balls. Kaden hissed as rolled the heavy balls between his fingers.

Kaden's head fell back. The bottle of lube rolled onto the floor. Pleasure sang through Riley's body. Breathing deep, Kaden pushed Riley back before retrieving the bottle. Riley drew up his knees. Kaden poured lube on his fingers before turning his attention back to Riley's hole. Kaden slanted his mouth over Riley's as he inserted a finger, fucking Riley with it. Riley moaned into Kaden's mouth positive he would die of pleasure. A second finger joined the first. Kaden's other hand rubbed one nipple between his thumb and forefinger. A third digit was added. Riley's breath came in pants and gasps. Kaden pulled out. Riley whimpered and watched through half-closed eyes as Kaden tore open the wrapper and rolled the condom on, using the excess lube on his cock. Riley swallowed. Kaden's cock looked positively monstrous. His hole twitched in anticipation.

Riley held his breath. Kaden grabbed Riley by the knees and pulled him closer, pressing forward and sliding into him at the same time.

"Yes!" Riley shouted before quickly cramming a fist in his mouth.

Kaden smiled and hitched Riley's legs over his shoulders. Slow and gentle movements melded into hard thrusts. Riley reached up and tweaked one of Kaden's nipples before running his hands down the ridged abdomen. Kaden hissed his response. Riley arched his back, wanting more of Kaden. His own cock oozed pre-cum. Pleasure-pain built in the base of his spine and raced through his body. Kaden built his momentum, his thrusts becoming harder and deeper. Riley bit back a scream as he came, shooting ropes of cum over the both of them. Kaden thrust one more time and came. Riley shuddered. Kaden pulled out of him. He was vaguely aware of his lover moving beside him as waves of pleasure continued to drive through him before he was wrapped in Kaden's embrace.

Chapter Twenty-Three

"Time to wake up, sweetheart."

Riley smiled and rolled over. He was perfectly content to lay in bed with Kaden for the rest of the day and not move a muscle. His body was deliciously sore. He loved the way sex with Kaden made him feel.

"Mm-mm." Riley shook his head.

"I know, but we have to get moving."

"Spoilsport. I wanted a turn."

"At fucking me?"

Riley nodded. "Never done it before, want to know what it's like. If it'll feel as good."

"We'll do that next time. I'm assuming this means that you liked it enough to want to do it again."

"Yes, just not now. Pretty sure that would overload my system."

"We'll avoid overloads for now," Kaden said, kissing Riley's ear. "But we do have to get moving. Checkout is in about an hour and we both need showers."

"Ohh, shower sex. How does that work? We have to try that."

"Not today we aren't."

"Meanie." Riley stuck out his tongue and pulled the covers over his head.

Kaden laughed and tugged the blankets down. "Come on, sleepyhead. We have to meet Ace."

Riley grumbled and crawled out of bed. They quickly showered and dressed. Riley waited in the car while Kaden went into the office to check out. Riley sat slumped back in the seat, with his ball cap pulled down low over his eyes. Bored, he fiddled with the controls for the passenger side mirror until he could see the parking lot. The emblem for a black Mercedes Benz glinted in the late morning sun.

"What the hell?" Riley pushed himself up and tried to get a better look.

The alarm beeped and the locks disengaged. Riley glanced over at the driver's-side door as it opened and Kaden climbed in.

"We need to drive through the parking lot. That way." Riley pointed toward the back parking lot.

"Why?" Kaden asked, starting the car.

"Because there's a brand-new black Mercedes parked over there."

"And?"

"And this is a cheap motel. Anyone who can afford that car isn't going to bypass the Hilton or even the Holiday Inn over there," Riley answered, pointing at the hotel signs peering over the hill. "Those look way more impressive than a run-of-the-mill motel."

"You think they're here for you?"

"Even if they aren't, they aren't here for business that's on the up and up."

Kaden nodded and drove toward the vehicle. Riley pulled out a small video camera.

"Where did you get that?" Kaden asked, looking over at the camera.

"My bedroom. I thought it might come in handy. I have a regular camera too. I've had them for years, but never use them anymore."

"Convenient."

Riley shrugged. "No, I want proof of the assholes who want me dead. This will work. And no GPS to give my position away. Never thought I'd use it again, though. Phones are way more convenient."

"Is there anything else I should know?"

Riley shrugged. "I still have the tracking device on me. It's small enough I can put in my shoe if I need to. Hopefully not, but that was good to know."

"Uncomfortable?" Kaden asked as Riley trained his video camera on the Mercedes Benz.

"Yes, but if it came down to it, I could live with it."

"Do you have what you need?"

Riley nodded and turned toward Kaden. "I do. What has you freaked out?"

"Not freaked out, just uncomfortable. Like a nagging suspicion that something isn't right."

"Okay. Let's go then. Just don't speed. We don't need a ticket to add to our troubles."

Kaden pulled out of the motel parking lot and onto the main road. A line of police and SWAT vehicles passed them, turning into the motel.

"Um, shouldn't they be going lights and sirens?"

"Not if you don't want people to know you're coming."

"They aren't after us, are they?"

Kaden shook his head. "I don't think so, sweetheart. There's no reason to send SWAT after us. Besides, the

FBI called off the search. You've been seen in public and even answered a couple of questions."

Riley scowled and crossed his arms over his chest.

* * * *

The ride into Maclean was quiet and tense. Riley doubted that everyone bought the story the news was reporting. He still had more questions than answers and he wasn't completely convinced that this Ace person had the answers he needed either. He trusted Kaden, but no one else. There were too many unknown variables. He'd begun to wonder at the history of the company and his grandfather's business affairs. He'd founded the company, growing it from the ground up.

"Where are we?" Riley asked as Kaden pulled off the highway. The area appeared to be an upscale, artistic neighborhood filled with coffee shops, boutiques, and locally owned restaurants.

"Ace's."

"Ace lives here?"

"Single person who's a computer genius, they can afford it." Kaden shrugged. "They don't need to hide out in some basement warehouse or something like that. Technically, they can afford more, but they like the artistic and inclusive vibe they get here. Or something like that. It's more woo-woo than I normally deal with."

"Woo-woo? Is that like a technical term?" Riley quipped.

Kaden scowled and whipped into a curbside parking spot as another car left. Riley looked around, hoping he would spot something unusual and at the same time praying time he wouldn't. Taking a deep breath, Riley left the relative safety of the car. He grabbed his backpack and closed the door, leaning against the side, waiting for Kaden to join him, slinging his bag over his shoulder. They passed a restaurant, a women's clothes boutique, a bookstore, bakery, and coffee shop before Kaden stopped in a doorway between a coffee shop and a vegan restaurant and pressed the bottom buzzer.

"That looks like it's part of the stonework," Riley whispered.

Kaden nodded. "Ace has made some special modifications to the area."

"I noticed."

Kaden pressed the buzzer again. "It's Kaden. Just the two of us."

The lock clicked and Kaden opened the door. He let Riley go in first and closed it behind them. "Up the stairs. Door on the left."

"Where does the other one go?"

"Technically, the third floor."

"Does that belong to Ace also?"

Kaden smiled and nodded. "They own the whole building and the one beside it. Bought them on auction and renovated them. Rents out the first floor of both buildings and the two apartments in the other building."

"I thought they were into computers or something."

"Diversification."

Riley looked up at the unexpected voice. It was soft, firm, and sounded neither male nor female. Riley smiled and swallowed. The owner of it was slender with waist-length hair dyed purple and turquoise with silver glitter throughout. A hot pink bra strap peeked out from under a Deadpool tank top. They wore short black shorts and their fingernails and toenails were painted bright turquoise.

"Um, you must be Ace," Riley said, stumbling over the words and holding out his hand.

"He's got manners at least," Ace mused, black eyes sparkling.

"Ace—"

"Hold your tits, eesh. Goddess, you're testy. You obviously need to get laid." Ace ushered the pair in. "Yes, I'm Ace. Nice to meet you." Ace shook Riley's hand then locked the door behind them.

Riley took a step forward and looked around the room. The walls were painted a light gray and the furniture was modern and black. Brightly colored pillows and blankets were strewn everywhere. Posters and paintings covered most of the free wall space. A small bookshelf filled with books sat at one end of the living room. A large-screen TV hung on the wall opposite of an L-shaped couch, taking up most of the space. An array of video game systems and games were stacked neatly in the cubicles under the television. Another large bookcase held hundreds of board games, most of which Riley had never heard of. The dining room table had six matching chairs tucked around it. He turned slightly. He didn't see a kitchen, bedroom, or computer.

"Not what you expected, is it?" Ace asked, leading them through the open room.

"No, it's not. It's less—more—put together."

"Hmm. Nice save. But no, it's not a collection of leftovers and hand-me-downs. When I upgrade, I do it right. It also helps having friends who are interior designers and are willing to help."

They stopped in the middle of the room. Ace crossed their arms and glared at Riley. Riley mimicked the move and waited.

"I'm taking a big chance here, Kaden," Ace said finally.

"I know, Ace."

"He worth it?"

Kaden nodded. "He is."

"Trustworthy?"

"I'm standing right here," Riley protested.

"People lie to get what they want. Your opinion on your own trustworthiness isn't to be trusted. You're an unknown variable. A complication I don't want in my life or in my house."

"I have no reason not to trust him, Ace."

"Hmm. Fine, this way."

Riley followed Ace and Kaden through the main room. Behind the dividing wall was a kitchen and a staircase. The same gray color punctuated by random brightly colored accents continued from the main living area into the kitchen. The stairway led to a small landing and hallway. There were three closed doors, all the same old brown wood. The walls were painted bright teal with brown trim. Everything was neat and clean. Nothing matched with what he'd pictured for a computer genius-hacker. He'd expected messier, more haphazard. Or even still living in their parents' basement.

Halfway up the stairs, Riley spotted a camera on the ceiling, pointing down at them. Riley ducked his head and pulled the ball cap down farther. "What's with the camera?"

"*Cameras.*"

"That's what I said."

"No, you said camera — as in one camera. There isn't one camera, there are multiple *cameras*. One can never be too careful."

Riley raised an eyebrow but said nothing as the trio filed into a large office. There were two separate workstations with eight different monitors, as well as a variety of electronic equipment that Riley wasn't sure he'd seen before. The room was cooler than the rest of the house.

"Do not touch anything." Ace sat in a plush black office chair and turned to face them. "What do you have for me?"

"How do you know —"

"I've known Kaden a lot longer than you have."

"Give Ace the brush and lipstick tube."

Riley nodded and dug into his backpack and retrieved the jewelry box and key. Reluctantly, he opened the secret compartment and dumped the contents into the researcher's hands.

"Cute. They look like they're from the sixties or so." Ace turned the items over in their hands, inspecting them. "Innocuous. They wouldn't make it through security nowadays, though. But why am *I* looking at these? Shouldn't you take them to that job you're so fond of? This is not my area of expertise."

"Probably the forties," Kaden corrected. "We need to open them and see what's in there. Could be the key to this whole thing."

"I'll take a look and get back to you."

"We'll wait." Kaden leaned against the wall.

"And your other options?"

"There aren't any."

Ace nodded. They turned on a work light with a magnifying glass, set down a plain white towel, and pulled out a small zippered tool case. Ace donned two pairs of rubber gloves and picked up the shaving brush. Time passed with infinite slowness as Ace first examined both the lipstick and the brush before opening the shaving brush first. A small roll of microfilm landed in the palm of Ace's glove. They set it aside and began working on the lipstick tube. A second roll of microfilm was removed from a secret compartment in the base of the tube.

"Brilliant." Ace held up both rolls of film.

"Fuck me sideways." Riley sat down on the small stool.

Kaden put a hand on Riley's shoulder and squeezed. "Can you tell what's on them?"

Ace nodded. "Probably. They appeared to be developed. But I don't know how decipherable it will be. Film, like most other things, degrades over time."

"We—I—I need to know. People are trying to kill me." Riley's stomach dropped. Developed. That meant either one of his grandparents, or possibly both, knew what was on the film.

"That's—" Ace grimaced and nodded, rubbing the back of their neck.

Kaden pulled Riley into a hug. "Let's find out what we're dealing with before we start worrying about anything."

"Easier said than done." Riley allowed himself to be comforted for a moment before pushing Kaden away.

"Kaden, grab the stools from over there. This is going to take a bit."

Riley watched Ace pull a rectangular device forward from the back of their workspace. The film was loaded into the tray and slid into the machine. Ace began processing the images. Riley alternated between sitting on the stool and watching Ace work and pacing the office, occasionally looking out of the windows. The lack of breakfast or lunch that morning was starting to wear on Riley as hour after hour passed.

"Holy shit!"

"What? What is it?" Riley demanded.

"See that?" Ace asked, pointing to a photograph of several rows of odd-looking characters handwritten onto lined paper on the computer screen.

"What is it?" Riley asked. His stomach dropped. He knew the answer before he asked the question. "Please tell me it's not what I think it is."

"No can do, love. Sorry," Ace apologized.

"That's Cyrillic. Russian," Kaden said flatly.

Riley clenched and unclenched his fists. "Is there any way to tell what all of that means and who wrote it?"

"The translation will take time. I'll make a copy and start working on it. I can't tell you who wrote it or why."

"Make a copy of both rolls of film. Email me a copy and put at least one copy away for safekeeping."

"Can we do the thing they do in the movies?" Riley asked. "You know, where a copy is set to be automatically sent to the papers if something happens to me. You. Us."

"That actually might be a good idea, depending on what Ace finds."

"I can't believe you're actually saying that." Ace shook their head.

"FBI agents tried to kill me. Either rogue or fake FBI agents killed a real agent and tried to kill Riley on his family's estate. Someone domestic is trying to get to Riley. That changes the game."

Ace raised an eyebrow and turned back toward the screen. Several more hours passed before Ace returned the microfilm to their containers, handing them back to Riley. "I have copies. It may take a couple of days to go through them. I will need to look at every frame. Some of the photographs are blurry, but I may be able to clean them up. Skimming through it, it almost looks like a vacation trip. Random places and people from Europe. My suggestion, Kaden, is to get your people on this ASAP."

"I don't trust my people. I don't trust anyone outside of this room at the moment."

"What about Chief Montgomery?" Riley asked, crossing his arms.

"Who?"

"Chief Joseph H. Montgomery. Police Chief in East Hampton," Riley answered. "You trusted him with plenty."

Kaden nodded. "Trusting him with some information is *not* the same as trusting him with you or information that can kill you."

Ace turned back to the computer and began typing furiously. "Joseph Hendrick Montgomery. East Hampton department for seventeen years. Transferred over from the Newark, New Jersey, police department. Before that he was in the Marines. Force Recon. Served during the first Gulf War. Divorced. Ex-wife's name is Rachel Louise Williams. No children. But she works for the DEA. Jesus-fucking-Christ." Ace closed the screen and typed another set of commands and several windows popped up.

"Trustworthy?" Kaden asked.

"Looks like your gut was right. Again." Ace nodded. "But what in the holy hell are you messed up with?"

"That's what we're trying to figure out," Riley answered.

"Kaden, sweetie, you need a better line of work. Maybe you should go back to school for accounting."

Kaden wrinkled his nose. Riley laughed.

"Seriously, think about it," Ace prodded.

"You keep telling me that."

"And one of these days you'll listen to me."

Kaden chuckled. "Pack up, Riley. We need to be moving."

Riley nodded and returned the lipstick tube and shaving brush back to their box and stuck them in his backpack. "We need food."

"We need —"

"Food. Now. I haven't eaten since lunch yesterday. It's past dinner. Food. On the way. Drive through someplace."

"We —"

"Were distracted this morning and dinner was interrupted before it even started. We've been here most of the day."

"Good thing today is Saturday or you would have a ticket waiting for you," Ace quipped.

Kaden scowled. "Fine. We'll get something to eat on the way."

"Stop at the first edible restaurant." Riley slung his backpack over his shoulder.

"Go out through the back door," Ace said. "Too many people out front." They pointed to the far-right screen and the multiple security footage views.

"Yep. Do you have a view of the alley? I don't want to be surprised." Kaden stood, looking over Ace's shoulder.

"Here you go." The screen changed and several different views appeared. "A pair of cops two blocks east and another pair three blocks west."

"How many cameras do you have?" Riley asked, shaking his head.

"Enough. I like to know who's around me."

Riley whistled and shook his head again.

"Okay, so we can take the alley through the back of coffee shop and down that way." Kaden leaned in and looked at the screens closer.

Ace nodded and led the way back downstairs and through the kitchen and into the pantry. The wall of shelves slowly swung forward. Kaden squeezed through the opening. Riley slid in behind him and the shelving unit closed, locking them in. Riley grabbed a belt loop on Kaden's jeans. Kaden took a step and a small light came to life on the side of the stairwell.

"Is Ace paranoid?" Riley whispered as they descended into the inky darkness.

"Careful. Paranoid suggests that the source of fear is imaginary."

"That's not quite comforting."

Kaden shook his head. They reached the landing and a small viewing screen came to life, showing them a wide-angle view of the immediate vicinity. Taking a deep breath, Kaden pressed a thumb to a small electronic pad on the doorframe. Locks clicked and the door opened. Riley felt Kaden's body shift and knew the other man had reached for his weapon. Riley followed Kaden through the door and stepped to the side. Kaden closed the door behind them and led the way down the alley.

Swallowing, Riley followed him through a glass door and down a hall that opened up into a coffee shop. Kaden stopped at the counter long enough for them to each order a coffee and a muffin and pay for it before exiting onto the main street. Riley walked next to Kaden in silence, half watching his surroundings and half paying attention to the cranberry-orange muffin and mocha latte he'd ordered. He'd finished his muffin and his coffee before they reached the vehicle. Kaden walked around the vehicle, dropped his coffee cup, and looked under the car before they got in.

"So, where are we going now?" Riley asked. "Another safehouse?"

Kaden shook his head and looked in the rear-view mirror. Kaden was quiet and drove through the streets and highway, past office buildings and hospitals, before turning into a gated apartment complex. Pulling up to the gate, he punched in a code and waited for the tall, wrought-iron gate to open. Riley looked out of the window as Kaden drove through the maze of roads and driveways and pulled into an empty slot under a carport.

"Where are we?" Riley asked when Kaden turned off the car.

"My place."

"Wait. Your place? As in your *home*?" Riley opened the door and jumped to his feet. "Is this safe? Seriously?"

"Keep your voice down," Kaden ordered. "No, it sure in the hell isn't. But I'm out of options at the moment." Kaden grabbed the duffel bags out of the car and withdrew a small wallet from a zippered compartment. He produced a single key and shoved the wallet in his pocket. "Let's go."

Riley rubbed the back of his neck and followed Kaden across the parking lot and to the middle of three doors in a large three-story building. They went up to the second floor and the first door on the left of the stairwell.

"What a clusterfuck." Kaden handed the bags to Riley and withdrew his weapon and flashlight.

Kaden turned the light on and unlocked the door. Riley turned the knob and pushed. Kaden shoved the door open and stepped through. Riley slipped inside and closed the door behind him, preferring the confines of the apartment to the unprotected openness of the hallway. The flashlight swept across the walls and furniture before disappearing from view. Riley forced himself to breathe normally, waiting for Kaden to return. Long moments passed before Kaden walked back to him, turning lights on as he did.

"Safe."

"For how long?"

"Hopefully long enough to figure out who we can trust and who we can't. Otherwise, probably three days max."

Riley pressed a hand to his growling stomach. "We didn't stop for food."

Kaden nodded. "Let me give you the tour. You can take a shower and I'll order pizza and breadsticks."

"Order? You don't cook?"

"I do, when I'm home and know I'm going to be home for a while. Right now I don't have anything in the house. Not edible at any rate."

Riley shook his head and followed Kaden through the apartment. There was one bathroom, kitchen, living room, dining room, and one bedroom that Riley could see. He guessed Kaden's home office or weapons room was probably behind the locked door. There were photographs on the wall of people, some in uniform, and places that Riley had only seen on the news. In the bedroom was a large framed photograph of a group of young kids.

"Your siblings?" Riley dropped the bags on the bed.

"Yes." Kaden pulled off his jacket and hung it on the back of the bedroom door. "Why don't you take a shower and I'll order food?"

"Where am I sleeping?"

"You have the choice of the couch, which doesn't pull out, or in the bed with me. I don't have a spare bed."

"The couch doesn't pull out?"

"Into a bed. Some couches pull out into beds."

"They do?"

"Some do. Mine doesn't."

"Why do they do that?"

Kaden scratched his head. "Because some people want an extra bed in case they have company but don't have a guest room."

"Oh. Okay. I'm going to take a shower."

* * * *

Kaden set the pizza, breadsticks, box of cannoli, and two-liter bottle of Coke onto the coffee table and was retrieving glasses and plates when Riley walked out of the bedroom dressed only in a pair of dark-blue sleep pants. "Day-um."

"I take it you approve?"

Kaden nodded. "You look better every time I see you." Stepping forward, he wrapped his arms around Riley and pulled him in for a kiss. A knock on the door had them jumping apart. Kaden set the dishware on the chair and picked up his weapon, motioning for Riley to go back to the bedroom. He waited until Riley was in the master bedroom before heading toward the door. There was another knock at the door. Kaden looked through peephole and swore. He unbolted the door and yanked it open.

"Aiden? What in the hell are you doing here? Get your ass in here." Kaden peered out of the door before shoving the gun back into his holster. He locked the door behind him and walked toward the living room.

"Sit on the chair in the living room." He continued on to the bedroom. "Riley, love, it's fine."

"Who's here?" Riley asked, coming out of his hiding spot.

"My brother. One of them."

"I take it this is unexpected."

"Very."

Kaden retrieved another plate and glass while Riley went into the living room.

"Riley, this is my youngest brother, Aiden. Aiden, this is Riley." Kaden handed both the plate and the glass to Aiden and sat down. "You might as well eat with us. What in the hell are you doing here? If Mom and Dad find out, they'll kill you."

"It's Alia, not Aiden."

Kaden dropped the piece of pizza he'd grabbed onto the box. "What?"

"Alia. Not Aiden. I'm — I'm — not a boy."

"Well, Alia, it's nice to meet you." Riley shook the teenager's hand.

"Holy shit." Kaden rubbed the back of his neck.

"Um, yeah."

"How —"

"I'll explain everything, but can we eat first? I haven't eaten anything in a couple of days."

"Dig in." Kaden filled the glasses, grabbed a slice of pizza, and sat back against the couch. He resisted the urge to pull Riley into him. He wasn't sure what the other man would think or do. Kaden was pretty sure that there hadn't been enough cuddling or touching in Riley's life. He also didn't know what his brother — sister, he mentally corrected himself — would think. He hadn't seen Aiden in eight years. Not since he'd come out to his family. His parents had disowned him and had warned him not to have anything to do with his siblings.

They ate in strained silence. Kaden glanced between his sibling and his boyfriend before closing his eyes. He needed time to wrap his head around what had been said and to figure out the next move with Riley. Bringing a friend or a boyfriend back to his apartment was very different from bringing back a client. Kaden blew out a breath and contemplated his options.

When the food was gone and the dishes cleared, Kaden sat back down on the end of the couch and rubbed the bridge of his nose. "Now, tell me what's going on and how do you know that you're Alia instead of Aiden?"

"Kaden—" Riley started to say.

Kaden shook his head. "I haven't seen any of my family in over eight years. No one should know where I'm at, let alone my youngest brother—I mean sister. I need answers. To know how they reached the conclusion they did. Especially since it's not something they would have been exposed to."

"Don't be—"

"It's okay." Alia drew her knees up to her chin. "At first I thought I was gay. I like boys more than girls. I never wanted to chase the girls or try to kiss them. I always envied their pretty dresses and toys and stuff. I thought I would grow out of it. You know, learn to like boy stuff. I thought that I didn't like sports because they were violent, and we're pacifists. But, my brothers did. Cheyenne didn't. I was going to ask you about it the last time you were home. You always took the time to answer my questions. Do you remember, you were supposed to take me for ice cream, but instead you had that fight with Mom and Dad and left?"

"I remember. I still kick myself for taking the bait instead of taking you for ice cream or just walking away."

"You left and there wasn't anyone else I could talk to. I kept waiting for you to come back. But you didn't. And I hated you for it. Braydon is the one who finally told me what happened. Cheyenne and Mace still believe being gay is a choice and evil and all that other bullshit. Zander's girlfriend and best friend have re-educated him."

"And Braydon?"

"Um, he lives with his boyfriend at school."

"Shit, Braydon's gay? I take it Mom and Dad don't know."

"No, they think they're roommates. I know. Zander knows. I think Braydon is waiting until he's out of school before coming out. He won't be able to finish otherwise. That leaves me." Alia wrapped her hands around her knees. "The family might be conservative, but Denver is diverse. I found an LGBT youth center and was able to ask questions."

"And how did you find me? And get out here?"

"Braydon. He has your address and phone number. He bought me a one-way ticket on the Amtrak. Then I used Lyft to get here."

"How did he get it? The community is gated."

Alia shrugged. "Slipped in at night when the gate opened. Then into the building when the pizza guy came up."

"Kid's determined." Riley shrugged and leaned against Kaden. "Do your parents know where you're at?"

"Sort of. Braydon and Zander helped me box up what was important and they each have some of it. I left a note saying that I knew I was transgender and that I

371

knew they weren't going to approve, so I left to save us all a scene."

"You can't just run away, Aid — Alia. I'm sorry, it's going to take me some time to get it right," Kaden said, shaking his head. "The cops will make you go back. And I'm not home enough to fight for custody."

"A lawyer can do the custody stuff. I'm fourteen, not a baby. I don't actually need a babysitter anymore."

"I know a lawyer that can help." Riley squeezed Kaden's hand. "Or should be able to."

Kaden shoved a hand through his hair. "Call Braydon."

He spent the next hour talking to both Braydon and Zander and catching up on all that had happened. It had been several months since he'd emailed his younger brother. But even then, Braydon hadn't said anything about Aiden's thoughts of either being gay or trans, nor his own sexuality. Kaden swore. Maybe his brother hadn't mentioned them because he hadn't asked or brought it up.

"Apparently, I suck as a big brother." Kaden hung up the phone.

Alia shook her head. "Just out of practice."

Riley pulled away from Kaden and slapped him in the arm. "Go hug your sister. Because I doubt you did it before."

"No, I think I surprised him." Alia grinned.

"Just a bit. I — we weren't due home for a couple of days, so, that was good timing."

"Were you on vacation? How long have you been together? You are together, right?"

Riley laughed and pushed Kaden forward.

Kaden stood and hugged his sister. "I'm glad you're here."

"Braydon said you'd be a safe place for me."

"I'll do my best, kid." Kaden hugged Alia once again before releasing her. "For now, I'm going to take a shower. The two of you can do the dishes. Tomorrow I'll need to go grocery shopping and check into schools."

Kaden dragged Riley into the bedroom with him and began pulling bedding out of the closet that his sister could use. "Will you be okay sleeping in here with me?"

"Hmm, I don't know. I mean, sleeping with you is such a hardship." Riley smiled and shook his head. "No, I don't mind. Though it probably would have been weird if I wasn't already sleeping with you."

"I can always try and figure something out if we need to," Kaden offered.

"I know your sister showing up out of nowhere threw you for a loop, but I'm fine. Honestly. I like sleeping with you. Yes, it was weird at first, but I like it. At least, I like *sleeping* with you. And the sex is good." Riley smiled.

"Well, that's something then."

Riley chuckled. "Get Alia settled in and take your shower. I'm going to bed. Wait, is your bed soft?"

"It's comfortable for me, but—"

"It's fine. It still has to be better than any of those hotel beds or even the bed at the cabin."

Kaden shook his head and left the bedroom. Life with Riley would never be boring. It was probably just what he needed. Maybe Ace was right. Maybe it was time to find a different job. Especially if he wanted a relationship with Riley, as well as to gain custody of his sister. Even if the court continued to see Alia as Aiden, Kaden was going to need a bigger place and a job where he was home regular hours.

Chapter Twenty-Four

Three days turned into two weeks. Riley was climbing the walls with a need to get out of the apartment. Kaden had gone out to get groceries, swap vehicles, and to visit Ace twice. At Riley's suggestion, Kaden had asked Ace to come talk to his sister and the pair had gone shopping for more appropriate clothes. Riley was certain Kaden was glad he didn't have to try to deal with women's underwear and could just scowl or nod in approval at the clothing the pair had bought. Riley had been surprised at the modest clothing Alia had chosen.

"I need out. I don't care where. I don't care for how long or how many security guards you have around me, but I need out of this apartment."

"Riley, love, it's not safe."

"It's never going to be safe. Why can't Ace tell you what kind of issues they ran into with the translating? I need out. Let's go out to eat."

"We could go see a movie," Alia offered.

Riley cocked his head to one side. "Or that."

Kaden's phone vibrated. "Riley, love, it's not a smart idea." Kaden picked up his phone and read the screen.

"I know. But I'm going nuts. It's worse than at the cabin. At least there I could go outside. You don't even have a balcony to sit on. Ace hasn't been able to tell us anything. I can't stay inside any longer."

"Fine, we'll go see a movie and get something to eat," Kaden said finally. He sent a message back before pocketing the device.

"Yes!" Alia shouted.

"Thank you, Kaden." Riley kissed Kaden. He had an idea of how much it had cost Kaden to concede to his request. His lover seemed to be always warring between safety and giving what he could to the people he cared about. Riley jumped to his feet and went to change his clothes. He disconnected the tracking device from its charging station on the dresser and slid it into his pocket.

"Please, Riley, don't—"

Riley shrugged into the oversized Ohio sweatshirt. "Love, I know how much you don't want to do this. I'm grateful. I'm not going to intentionally do anything that will either draw attention to myself or put my life in jeopardy. Especially not with your sister with us. We haven't heard anything or seen anything. From anyone. And I'm going to guess you know or have a way of finding out what is going on not just around here, but anywhere else you want to."

Kaden pulled him into his arms, kissing him deeply. "Thank you." He rested his forehead against Riley's. "I'll be right out."

Riley nodded and joined Alia in the kitchen. "Ready to go?"

Alia nodded. "Why is Kaden so squirrely? Like bordering on paranoid."

"It's his job."

"His job? I don't understand."

Riley shoved a hand through his hair. "Some people want me dead. It's his job to make sure that doesn't happen."

"Wait? What? Should we be going out, then?"

"No, but apparently I'm not the sharpest crayon in the box today." Kaden scowled. "Let's go."

The trio made their way to Kaden's car. Riley and Alia waited while Kaden checked the car before letting them get in it. Alia kept up a steady stream of conversation as they left the apartment complex and headed toward the movie theater. Riley was staring at the mirror when he thought he noticed a white car following them.

"Um, Kaden—"

"I see them."

"The white car?"

"What? Fuck. No. There's a green SUV three cars behind on the left." Kaden glanced at the other mirror. "Sedan?"

"I think so. They've mirrored us. Maybe it's a coincidence. Someone else going to the movies too."

"Maybe, but I'm not a big believer in coincidences." Kaden glanced in the rear-view mirror.

"Shit." Kaden handed Riley his phone. "Hit reply. Say nine-one-one. Detouring."

"Kaden, what is going on? Who did I just text and where were we going?"

"Ace. I was going to meet Ace at the movies. They have information we need."

Kaden increased his speed and maneuvered the Jeep Grand Cherokee through traffic, swearing as both the green SUV and the white sedan kept pace with them. Kaden left the crowded city streets for the highway, hoping to gain speed and lose them long enough to at least get Alia someplace safe.

"Damn it!" Kaden pounded a fist on the steering wheel. One semi-truck passing another cut off his progress. A dented, plain white van cut in front of them. Kaden slammed on his brakes to avoid hitting the other driver. The green SUV pulled up alongside them. The white sedan boxed them in from behind. "Son of a bitch."

"Riley, is there anything on the shoulder?" The van began slowing down.

"Empty!"

"Hang on!" Kaden jerked the wheel to the right. Hitting the rumble strip, he pressed his foot on the gas and flipped his hazard lights on. Passing the semi-truck, he cut back onto the highway. The white sedan continued their pursuit. Kaden tried to put distance between them and the sedan. He glanced in the rear-view mirror. The semi-truck had pulled behind them. Kaden swore again. The green SUV caught up to them. Ahead of them, another pair of semi-trucks blocked his way. The sedan passed them on the shoulder, swerving sharply and cutting back in front of them.

They were forced to slow down and move to the shoulder of the road. Kaden yanked the wheel and took them into the grassy area next to the highway. The SUV hit them in the side, pushing them out of control.

"Hang on!" Kaden yelled. The car careened through the grass, coming to a rest at the bottom of the embankment a hundred feet from where they'd left the highway with a lurch.

"Alia, get on the floor!" Riley shouted.

Kaden rubbed his head and withdrew his weapon. He thought he heard sirens somewhere in the distance. Shots were first at the front window. The passenger door opened and Riley's arm was grabbed. Riley fought with the assailant. Kaden shot across his lover, hitting his mark. Blood sprayed the interior. Someone swore. Someone else yelled about Riley's seat belt. Kaden shot again as Riley's seat belt was undone and he was dragged from the car. Kaden ducked for a better shot and saw the barrel of a silver nine-millimeter pointing at him.

"Freeze! Put the weapon down!" a male voice shouted.

The shooter changed positions. Kaden tried unsuccessfully to open his door. He watched in horror as Riley was dragged to the waiting van. Two shots rang out. Kaden aimed and shot through the open window, winging the man holding Riley as he climbed into the van. Out of his peripheral vision he saw the shooter fall to the ground.

"Driver, put down your weapon."

"Son of a bitch!" Kaden laid his weapon on the dashboard and held up his hands as the van sped away. "Alia, are you okay?"

"I'm okay. But they got Riley."

"Passenger, hold up your hands."

"Do as the cops say." Kaden forced a calm he didn't feel into his voice. The fact that Riley had his tracker on him didn't make him feel any better. He wanted answers and he wanted them now. Several more police cars, sirens blaring, pulled up to them.

With weapons trained on them, they were instructed to leave the vehicle one at time. They were handcuffed as soon as they exited and separated.

"Please tell me you are looking for that white van," Kaden demanded.

"How about you answer some questions first? Name."

"Special Agent Kaden Tennison, Central Intelligence Agency. I was tasked with keeping Riley Hamilton safe."

"The millionaire's kid that was on vacation instead of missing?" the police officer asked dubiously.

"Yes."

"He wasn't on vacation, was he?"

Kaden shrugged as his identification was verified.

"Who's the kid?"

"My little," Kaden paused, "sister."

"You don't know if you have a sister or a brother?" The officer raised an eyebrow.

Kaden blew out a breath and prayed for the best. "She's transgender."

"And?"

"And she needed a safe place to stay."

"And home isn't safe?" The officer's voice softened slightly.

"Only if you're straight and a pacifist. Oh, and go to the right church and marry the person our parents want you to." Kaden glanced over at his sister. "I'm planning on meeting with a lawyer in the next couple of weeks to start the process of gaining guardianship."

Minutes ticked by into eternity as they were questioned and re-questioned about the chase, accident, and shooting. Emergency personnel had been unable to save shooter and the police had begun their investigation.

"A BOLO has been issued for the van." The officer released Kaden from his cuffs. "Your weapon is evidence."

Kaden rubbed his wrists. "The van was probably stolen along with the plates."

The officer nodded. "Good luck getting Mr. Hamilton back."

"Thanks." Kaden pulled Alia in a tight hug. "Are we free to go?"

"I can get an officer to take you back to the station," the officer replied.

Kaden shook his head. "If it's all the same, I'll have a colleague pick us up. I need to go after Hamilton."

A tow truck arrived to remove his vehicle. Kaden pulled Alia with him and walked over to the car. Holding up his identification, he assured the officers that he only wanted to see the inside of the car. After they had come to a stop, Riley had ducked under the dashboard. Kaden needed to make sure that the tracking device was still on Riley and not in the car. It was the only way he had of getting the younger man back. Kaden looked in both the front and back of the car without finding what he was looking for. Their phones and Alia's bag had been returned to them and there was no trace of Riley left in the car.

Kaden shoved a hand through his hair and rubbed the back of his neck. He was going to kill whoever was responsible for the nightmare his life had become. First, though, he needed to get a hold of Ace. He needed answers. .

"Will the cops get Riley back?" Alia asked, pulling Kaden from his thoughts.

"They'll try. But they weren't looking for him or us. They were just there at the right time and place."

"Good thing too. Would they have killed us?"

"Me, yes. You, only if they saw you. They weren't after you."

"I like Riley. He's different. That weird mixture of someone who knows a lot about some things but is completely naïve about others."

"That about sums it up."

"You like him, don't you?"

"I do. I want to date him properly, see if we can make a go of it."

"Good. He likes you too. What about his family? Are they okay with it?"

Kaden scratched his cheek then cocked his head to one side. "At one point I would have said no, but I think they're coming around."

"Can you get him back?"

"I hope so, pipsqueak. I hope so."

"You know, you're the only one who ever called me that."

Kaden smiled, pulled out his phone to call Ace, and led the way back up to the side of the road. He needed his friend to pick them up and hopefully they would have answers for Kaden. Another forty-five minutes passed before Ace's black Nissan Rogue pulled over on the side of the road.

"This is new," Kaden said, getting into the passenger side of Ace's SUV.

"Picked it up from the dealer on Tuesday. Got a huge bonus from a client," Ace confessed. "Did they get van?"

"No. It's probably been dumped already."

Ace nodded. "I have news you aren't going to like."

"I figured as much."

"Where to?" Ace pulled out onto the highway at the police officer's direction.

"Your place. I'll get what I need later. Alia needs to stay with you for a few days."

Ace nodded.

"I need my clothes and stuff," Alia protested.

Kaden sighed. "My place first."

They drove in silence back to Kaden's apartment. The hair on the back of Kaden's neck stood on end as they neared his building. He reached for the empty holster and swore. "Damn it. The police have my gun."

"You can take mine. It's in the back pocket of my purse."

Kaden retrieved the weapon and inspected it before chambering a round. "Stay here. If I'm not back in ten minutes or you see anything remotely hinky, get the hell out of here."

Ace nodded.

Kaden jumped out of the SUV and walked quickly to his building. Taking the stairs two at a time, he paused at the top of the stairwell. The door to his apartment was barely open. Drawing his gun, he pushed the door open with his foot. His apartment was in total disarray. He quickly searched the apartment before holstering the borrowed weapon. His office door had a bullet hole in it but was otherwise still locked.

He sent a message to Ace, then called the police. It was another hour wait while the police took down his statement and began their initial investigation. Kaden shoved a hand through his hair as he walked through the apartment with an officer. The only thing that appeared to be missing was Riley's backpack and duffel bag. He made a point of going through every room except for his office and opening closets and cupboards. The towels in the linen closet were askew and Kaden could see the corner of the wooden box. Heart pounding, he couldn't wait for the police to leave so he could grab the box and go find Ace and his sister.

Once the cops left, Kaden raced to the bathroom and pulled the box and key from their hiding spot. He wasn't sure when Riley had removed them from his backpack, but Kaden was grateful he had. He shoved the box, his laptop, and a second weapon and ammunition into a backpack, hiding both under a change of clothes. Locking the door behind him, he ran back down the steps and flagged Ace.

"How bad was it?" Alia and Ace asked as Kaden slid back into the passenger seat.

"Nothing destroyed. It was made to look like a robbery."

"What was missing?"

"Riley's backpack."

Ace swore. The drive back to Ace's was silent. Once inside, Ace showed Alia their video game collection before leading Kaden up to his office.

"What did you find?"

"Did they get the film?" Ace demanded.

Kaden shook his head. "Riley must have hidden it sometime after we got to the apartment. In the bathroom of all places. They didn't look there, though."

"Thank the goddess."

"What did you find?"

"That film contains a list of Russian spies, both their Russian and American names, places of employment, meeting places, and in some cases their missions and handlers."

Kaden sat down hard. "Holy shit."

"There's more. One of the names is Jeffrey Michael Abrams from New York."

"They will kill him to get a hold of this." Rage and terror coursed through him, flooding his emotions. Kaden jumped to his feet and began pacing the room. "Abrams just announced he was running for president. Ace, Alia needs to stay here. Get her whatever she needs. I'll pay you back."

Ace nodded. "First, you have to be a US citizen to be president. Second, what you going to do?"

"Forged birth certificate. Or it's real, but he took the place of the real Jeffrey Abrams." Kaden shoved a hand through his hair.

"You can't just replace someone like that." Ace shook their head.

"Car accident and amnesia. Face bones crushed. Plausible excuse given the technology in the forties and fifties. Especially if the people involved were young." Kaden shrugged. "As for what I'm going to do? Talk to my boss and get Riley back. He has a tracking device on him. I also need to go see his family."

"Are you sure he had the tracker on him?"

Kaden scrubbed his hands over his face. "Yes. I saw him stick it in his pocket."

"Hmm, so at least not a death wish. Maybe not as much as of a spoiled brat as you thought."

Kaden headed back to the living room. "Alia, I need you to stay here with Ace for a few days. I have to go after Riley."

"Why can't the cops do that? They had guns. They were shooting at us."

"It's my job."

"Your job?" Alia jumped to her feet and stormed across the room. "What kind of job do you have that you get shot at and don't seem to be bothered by it? That you have to go hunting for someone?"

"I'm in security. That's all I can tell you. It's my job. Riley's safety is my job," Kaden answered. "You'll be safe here with Ace. They will get you what you need to until we can get back to the apartment."

"You need a new job."

"I told him the same thing, sister." Ace smiled.

"We'll talk about it later," Kaden said, exasperated.

"Go bring your boy home." Ace motioned him through the door.

* * * *

Kaden hailed a cab and took it to the storage area where his mustang, the one Preacher had named Bella, was stored. After retrieving the vehicle, he pulled into the parking lot of a nearby fast food restaurant and called his boss.

"Lawrence," Russell Lawrence said, answering the phone.

"Coffee Shack. Twenty minutes."

"Tennison? What in the hell?"

"Coffee Shack."

"I am heading home. We have plans—"

"Change them," Kaden growled.

"This had—"

"Trust is a two-way street. Twenty-minutes."

"Fine."

Kaden hung up the phone and drove to the small coffee shop. The Coffee Shack was owned by two women. The unique blends of coffee they served were a particular favorite of Kaden's boss. Rolling his shoulders and flexing his fingers, Kaden prayed he wasn't making a mistake. Neither he nor Ace could find anything that pointed to his boss being anyone other than who he said he was.

Sitting in his car, Kaden waited and watched, looking for anything out of the ordinary. Pulling out his phone, he called Margaret Hamilton, grateful Riley had given him the older woman's cell phone number.

"This is Margaret Hamilton. May I help you?"

"Mrs. Hamilton, it's Kaden, Riley's boyfriend and bodyguard."

"They got him, didn't they." The voice was flat, not a question but a statement of fact, as though she had been expecting the news.

"Yes, I need to see you tonight." Kaden forced himself to remain calm. Anger wouldn't help either him or Riley at the moment.

"I'm heading to DC now, it'll — "

"I'll meet you there. Where will you be?"

"Mr. Tennison, my grandson may have hired you — "

"Riley did not hire me. But I am responsible for his safety. And I need answers. Tonight. Now, where will you be?"

"I have a room at the Jefferson. You will find me at Plume, the hotel restaurant. Eight-thirty."

"I will be there." Kaden ended the call and watched Russell Lawrence pull into a parking spot two doors down from the coffee shop and get out of the car. Kaden waited until Lawrence was in the building before joining him.

Lawrence raised a hand when he walked into the restaurant. Kaden acknowledged him and ordered a coffee before sitting down across from his boss.

"What in the hell is so damned important that you called me? Where is Hamilton?"

"Kidnapped. We were run off the road around lunchtime. A state police officer happened to be in the area and saw what happened. Didn't get there in time to keep them from taking Riley, but did keep me from getting shot."

"Where were you going?"

"Doesn't matter. I was in my personal car, not a rental or loaner. My apartment was ransacked. These people know who I am and where I live. And probably where I work."

"Great. Your job was to keep Riley Hamilton safe."

"You know, I've been trying to figure out who would want to get to the son of a millionaire without an ounce of political clout outside of reasonably sized donations. With the kind of financial backing it would take to travel over half the country and be willing and able to kill an FBI agent, bribe at least one agent and plant two more."

"I don't know."

"Bullshit, Lawrence. Whoever handed you this assignment knows what's going on or knew that it could. They also know why."

"And you know this how?"

"Because I know why." Kaden set the small duffel bag on the table. "Now, I have copies. And I have translations. But have someone you trust, implicitly trust, run these. They'll get the same things."

"What is it?"

"Details of a long-term Cold War spy ring. Names. It goes almost all the way up." Kaden pushed the bag toward his boss.

"Cold War?" Lawrence shoved a hand through his hair and whistled. "So, Cyrillic?"

Kaden nodded. "I'm heading back to the Hamilton Estate. I have questions that need to be answered. I need to find Riley."

"This is going to take more than a day, you know this."

Kaden shook his head. "Time is our enemy. More than twenty-four hours and Riley will be dead."

Lawrence sighed. "Do you know where he is?"

"Heading north," Kaden answered. "And, Lawrence, don't double-cross me or the entire thing is released to the public. En masse. Internationally."

"I wouldn't—"

"Who hired you? Who gave you this assignment?"

"I can't—"

"You can. You're choosing not to. I'm choosing not to trust you. Or anyone else."

Kaden pushed away from the table, stood, and strode out of the door. Dashing to his car, he plugged his phone in and placed it in the holder before he pulled out into traffic and headed to Washington DC. He wanted to get to the hotel before Mrs. Hamilton. Kaden blew out a breath, shoved a hand through his hair, and kept one eye on his phone and the map showing Riley's location. It was a direction that surprised him. Everything screamed they should be heading back to New York, not Washington DC. There was no valid reason to explain away Riley's presence there if he were to be discovered there. Kaden clenched and unclenched his fists. Unless there was no intention to letting Riley live. It was a thought that had crossed his mind more than once. He'd dismissed the idea, reasoning that with Riley dead, then there would be no reason for whoever had been threatened originally to toe whatever line they were supposed to. Kaden pounded his fist on the steering wheel in frustration. Pushing the multitude of scenarios streaming through his head away, he focused on his driving.

Chapter Twenty-Five

Riley groaned and fought to not throw up. Refusing to open his eyes, he tried to take careful stock of himself and his environment. His wrists were tied with rough, scratchy rope, but his feet were free. For the moment. He was moving, probably in the van that had cut them off. Were Kaden and Alia still alive? Two men had tried to pull him from the car. He knew Kaden had shot one of them. Riley had tried fighting them off, but being belted into the truck had been more of a disadvantage than he'd thought it would be, especially against the pair of larger men determined to kidnap him. His ears were still ringing from the shots fired inside the vehicle. He wasn't sure who had fired when, only that the attackers had shot first. Once they'd neared the van, he'd tried to run, but they had hit him on the head.

Riley flexed and contracted his muscles, hoping for give. He'd stuffed the small thumb-drive-looking gadgets into his shoe while Kaden was driving. He'd been certain they would search him looking for the key and find the tracking device. They would have made it if the semi-trucks hadn't blocked them in. As long as his captors didn't find it, Kaden had a fighting chance of finding him. If Kaden was alive. If the device had a long enough range. If it had enough power. Riley mentally chastised himself, wishing he'd thought to ask Kaden about the range and capabilities of the tracker or what he should do in this situation.

They hadn't talked about what would happen, what he needed to do or not do if he was kidnapped again. Riley squeezed his eyes tighter. Obviously, Kaden hadn't thought this would actually happen. They had been careful. He'd stayed in the apartment, away from the windows. Kaden had only given him a burner phone that afternoon. Riley searched his memory for what kidnapping victims in the movies and television did, carefully keeping his thoughts away from the worst-case scenarios. The vehicle bounced twice and slowed down before coming to a stop.

"Is he awake?" a gruff male voice demanded.

"No," another voice answered a moment later.

Riley forced himself to stay where he was. He needed to save his strength until he could escape. If they bound his legs, he wouldn't be able to run when he needed to. Time slipped into infinity. Riley let himself be pulled out of the vehicle and dragged.

Head hanging down, he barely opened his eyes. A black sedan sat ten feet in front of them. He was surrounded by buildings and concrete. There were plenty of places to hide until he could find either the cops or Kaden. Biting his lip, he inhaled deeply and planted his feet. The action was enough that the grip on his arms lessened. Riley broke free and bolted, making a dash for the first open door.

Shots rang out. Riley zigzagged toward the building.

"Don't use bullets, you ass!"

Riley stepped through the open door and pain radiated through his body. He fell to the ground. The electricity swamping him stopped. Riley lay on the ground, trying to catch his breath. He needed to move. His muscles and his mind refused to cooperate. Pain exploded in his head. Riley forced himself to stay awake. He was dragged back toward the van and shoved in the trunk of the black sedan. Riley flexed his foot against the uncomfortable feeling of the small tracking device in his shoe. It's presence filled him with relief. Kaden would find him.

He lost track of time and direction as the car constantly stopped and started, slowing down and speeding up. Aside from the occasional pothole, it sounded like they had stayed to paved roads. The car stopped and the trunk opened. Riley squinted against the bright light. He was forced out of the trunk and into the backseat of the car in between two large men, both with guns trained on him. Both wore dark sunglasses and New York Yankees baseball caps. The driver sat alone in front and also wore dark sunglasses, but no ball cap. Riley tried to memorize as many details as he could of the men, the car, and his surroundings.

His heart sank as they turned onto the road leading to a small airport, surrounded by trees and farms. A sign pointed in one direction to the airport and the opposite direction for an aircraft rental company. The driver turned toward a black-and-white sign proclaiming Smith Pierce Aviation. The men holstered their weapons, cut the rope binding his wrists, and reminded Riley not to run. He was forced into the back seat of a small, white jet engine airplane. The words Citation Mustang were printed on the side. The man who had been sitting on his left, taller than him and blond, sat in the back seat with him, his gun hidden from view and trained on Riley. The man who had been on his right, his height with short, dark brown hair, sat in the front seat next to the pilot, a bald white man who had shaken hands with his captors. Riley wondered if they were friends, business partners, associates of some other sort, or if this was simply a chartered flight. If he had to guess, it was a chartered flight. Private planes were cost prohibitive for most people. Otherwise they would've left him bound. Riley filed the information away for later. He stared out of the window as the pilot steered the aircraft to the end of the tarmac. After receiving clearance from the tower, he throttled the engines and started down the runway. Riley's heart sank as they took off.

Looking out of the window, Riley wished he knew where they were going and how long they had been in the air. The combination of gas, two different kinds of cologne, and the body odor of all four occupants was almost more than Riley could handle. Breathing through his mouth, he stared at the landscape below. None of it looked familiar.

Riley rolled his shoulders, resisting the urge to rub the welts on his wrists. He needed a drink. Something to take the edge off from his senses. Resting his head against the back of the seat, he closed his eyes. That he hadn't had a drink since they were at Preacher's surprised him. So did the fact that he hadn't wanted one since the cabin. Riley clenched and unclenched his fists, taking long slow breaths. He hadn't thought about it before. Kaden had adjusted things so that they didn't bother him as much. He'd gotten used to the accommodations Kaden had made for him.

The plane started its descent into an equally small, grassy field as the one they'd left from. Riley's stomach dropped. Something this small probably wasn't known to anyone, except maybe as a line entry in notebook somewhere. There was no way Kaden would know about this or where he was at. Once the plane landed, he was forced into the back of a black Cadillac Escalade with dark-tinted windows. A black cotton sack was placed over his head and cinched. His hands were tied behind his back. He leaned back against the seat at an awkward angle as they drove through winding roads. When they finally stopped, he was pulled from the SUV and manhandled up a set of stairs and pushed down onto a floor.

"Where is it?" a gruff male voice demanded.

"Where is what?" Riley asked, trying to get to his feet.

"Don't play dumb with me, boy," the man bit out.

Riley was pushed down and kicked in the side. "I don't know what you want."

"I can't kill you, but there's a lot of room for pain before death." The man chuckled.

Riley focused on what his senses could tell him. There were three attackers. All men by their scents and how they walked. He didn't hear or smell appliances, and there was a slight echo in the room. He guessed it was an unused bedroom.

"Tell us what we want to know."

Riley shook his head. "I don't know what you want." He was kicked, punched, and Tasered while three different voices demanded the location of 'it', before one of them mentioned the word 'key'.

"What key? The only keys I have are for my house!" Riley shouted. A knife was drawn across his arm. Blood flowed from the wound.

"Give us the key and maybe you won't get hurt anymore." The voice was male, rough and with an accent he couldn't place.

"They're in my backpack," Riley screamed as the blade sliced through his flesh again. "Front pocket!"

He heard the contents of two different bags hit a table and more cursing followed by a hard kick to his back. Riley groaned and squirmed before blacking out. He woke as he was tossed into another room. He hit his head and shoulder on the floor and lay where he fell.

Moaning, Riley shifted positions.

"Welcome to hell."

Riley lifted his head in the direction of the voice. "Who's there?"

"Dante MacKenzie. And you are?"

"Riley Hamilton. Your brother."

"I don't have a brother." His voice was bitter and tense.

"Technically, I'm your half-brother." Riley tried to sit up and failed. The jarring movement sent new waves of pain rolling through him. His stomach pitched and rolled and he threw up before passing out.

* * * *

Kaden sat in a chair near the fireplace in the sitting area of the lobby of the hotel and waited for Mrs. Hamilton to arrive. He stared at his phone, scrolling through the screens while scanning the lobby. The green blip representing Riley on the map was static, someplace in upstate New York, and he was anxious to get up there. He'd booked a ticket on the ten o'clock flight into New York. Preacher would be waiting for him.

The doors slid open and Mrs. Hamilton walked in. She was dressed in a black pantsuit and carried a large black leather bag over her shoulder. She was pulling a small, plain black suitcase. Kaden waited until she had finished checking in before standing and pocketing his phone.

"Mrs. Hamilton." Kaden joined the elderly woman at the elevator.

"I do not appreciate meeting this way."

"I don't appreciate being lied to, so I guess we're both out of luck."

"I don't know what you mean."

Kaden raised an eyebrow and followed her onto the elevator. The ride up to the fourth floor was silent and tense. As they neared the end of the hallway, Kaden drew his weapon.

"Really, are weapons necessary?" Mrs. Hamilton asked, opening the door.

Kaden let her enter first and shut the door quickly behind him. "Yes, it appears they are." He chambered a round, grabbed her by the arm, and pointed the gun at her head. "Show yourself."

"Who are you —"

"Show yourself or she dies."

A man in a black suit stepped from behind a partially opened door, holding up his hands.

"There's no need —"

"All listening devices, cameras, and weapons on the coffee table. Now." Kaden gripped Margaret Hamilton's arm harder. "I don't care if I spill the blood of a spy. Especially a *Russian* one."

The man deposited a micro-recorder and Smith & Wesson nine millimeter on the coffee table as well as a badge.

"Sit. Both of you." Kaden released Margaret Hamilton. The pair sat across from each other. Kaden turned the chair from the desk around, picked up the badge, and sat down facing the pair.

"What is this about?" the man demanded.

"James Daniel O'Riley. Retired from the Company." Kaden cocked his head to one side. "Huh. Now that is interesting."

"What are you talking about?" Margaret Hamilton demanded. "You said Riley is missing."

"No, I didn't. You knew that before I called." Kaden shook his head and pointed the gun at Riley's grandmother. "Interestingly, you said 'weapons' instead of 'gun' or 'that'."

"What is this all about?" O'Riley demanded.

"As a *professional* courtesy, it's about the fact that Riley has been kidnapped. That my home was ransacked and that we were run off the road. Now, amazingly enough, no one knew that I was involved until we were at the Hamilton estate. So now the question is, where are the moles. And how many are there."

"What do you mean?" Margaret asked. "You're making no sense."

"I want answers. I want to know why, when you," Kaden pointed to O'Riley, "asked my boss for a favor, you didn't bother to tell him that Riley was your grandson or that she" — he pointed over to Margaret — "was a Russian spy. Well, technically, a double agent. Knowing who was after Riley from the start might have meant that they would be in jail or dead now. Instead both Riley and your other grandson, Dante, are now in the hands of Senator Abrams' thugs or partners. I don't think it's just Abrams. I'm betting it's the whole cell, or what's left of it."

"Don't be absurd—"

Kaden shook his head and sat down in a floral wing back chair. "Stop, please. Families don't appear out of nowhere. With no history. No nothing. We guessed Russians, but the hidden Torah gave another possibility. Running from Germans during the war."

Margaret shook her head. "Those are my husband's, if you—"

"A marriage of convenience." Kaden shrugged. "Not love."

"What do you mean Dante is missing also?" James O'Riley asked.

"I had someone *I* trust keep tabs on Dante as soon as we found out he existed."

"Riley knows?" Margaret asked.

Kaden nodded. "Found the report and pictures while you were out of town. Kind of despicable."

"I—"

"Let me clarify." Kaden held up a hand. "*Charles* is despicable. Although, disowning his older brother because he's gay makes you just as bad." Kaden rested his left ankle on his right knee and leaned back. "We all make dumb decisions. You will have to live with yours. What I want to know is where they would have taken Riley and Dante. And also, why you didn't turn over the microfilm containing the list of names of Russian spies years ago."

"What microfilm?" Margaret and O'Riley asked at the same time.

"Cute. The film hidden in the jewelry box. The one that was in with Riley's mother's belongings. The pitiful few that there were."

"It was where?" Margaret asked, defeated.

"Riley had it. He found it with his mother's things. The key hidden in the watch you gave him opened a secret compartment."

"I thought you said Robert never knew," O'Riley stated. "You told me the film was destroyed."

Margaret shook her head. "I didn't think he did. I found the remains of the lipstick tube and shaving brush in the fireplace along with pieces of film. I never doubted Robert. He said one of the maids had done it. He'd fired her on the spot."

"This is nice. You two can talk about it later. I need to know where I can find the senator."

"He's not going to get his hands dirty. Not this late in the game." Margaret crossed her ankles, folding her hands on her lap.

"Senator Abrams is a Russian spy?" O'Riley asked. "We knew there were sleepers. But still in the country? After all these years? Are you sure? He's married. Has kids and grandkids."

Kaden nodded. "We have the film."

James O'Riley shoved a hand through his hair and blew out a breath. "He just made a bid for the White House."

"That can't happen," Kaden said.

"His has family place in the Adirondacks. Or he did," O'Riley answered.

There was a sharp knock at the door. "That's my cue." Kaden stood and crossed the room, opening the door for his boss, Russell Lawrence, and two other agents. Kaden stepped aside, letting the trio in.

"And Hamilton?"

Kaden shook his head. "Adirondacks."

"We'll keep this quiet."

"It's the only way to get Riley and his brother back alive."

Margaret Hamilton's phone rang.

"Go ahead and answer it," Kaden ordered. "Do not let anyone know what we talked about or know, or both of your grandsons could die."

Margaret nodded. "Margaret Hamilton, may I help you?" Margaret paused. "Benjamin? What is Amethyst doing there? No, I'll speak to her."

Kaden looked at his watch and swore. "I have to go." Kaden looked back at Margaret Hamilton and swore again. He wanted to know why Dante's mother was calling Margaret Hamilton and not the police or Charles.

"There will be a team waiting for you," Lawrence said, interrupting his thoughts. "Call this number. You're flying commercial?"

Kaden nodded, took the proffered card and envelope, turned, and left. He sped through the city streets to the airport. He cleared security, making it to the gate just as they were getting ready to board. Kaden spoke quickly to the attendant at the desk and showed his badge and clearance papers. Boarding first, he spoke with the pilot and head flight attendant before taking his seat. Once situated, he opened the app on his phone relieved to see that Riley was still in the same location. It would make picking up his trail easier. He nodded as Dez sat down next to him.

"Preacher will meet us at the airport," Dez whispered. "Do you have an address?"

"Not yet. I'm working on it."

"Do you know where they went to?"

"Adirondacks."

"That's a lot of ground to cover."

Kaden nodded. "Yep, but I'm working on narrowing it down."

"So the kid?"

"He's a man." Kaden eyed the boarding passengers. "Young. Naïve."

"Less so now."

"Are you two a thing?"

"What difference does it make?"

"You're asking us to take a huge-ass risk."

"You can always say no."

"Doesn't work that way, man. But emotions can fuck everything up."

Kaden nodded. "And they make everything worth living and dying for too."

"So, you two *are* a thing." Dez cocked his head.

"I don't know if 'thing' is the right word, but yes, we're involved."

"If it comes out…"

"Already thought about it. Don't care."

"Desk jobs require a lot of political diplomacy."

Kaden shoved a hand through his hair. "I hate both."

Dez laughed and nodded.

Kaden shook his head and stared at the window. Hopefully, he could get an address for the senator's family home by the time they landed. They would have the drive up to make plans before meeting up with the Company agents.

"So, is your boss providing assistance?"

"Yes."

"Reliable?"

Kaden shrugged. He hoped so, but they were people he'd never worked with before, so he wasn't sure.

* * * *

"What proof do you have that we're brothers?" Dante demanded.

"Divorce papers between our father, Charles Hamilton and your mother, Amethyst MacKenzie, and a letter from a private investigator from a couple of weeks ago stating that you and your family were fine." Riley wriggled into a sitting position. He had no idea how long he'd been out and his brother wasn't very forthcoming with information. Nothing that he would consider helpful at the moment anyway. "Didn't your mother ever tell you about Charles?"

"No. She did tell me once that my sperm donor was a womanizing bastard and that she got the better part of the deal. She met my dad, Stephen Chambers, when I was seven. They were married a couple of years later. I wasn't interested in someone who never had time for me."

"She sounds like a smart woman."

"Wait. Charles Hamilton. He's the guy from the news. The FBI said you were missing. Kidnapped."

Riley chuckled weakly before coughing. "Hiding."

Hours passed in silence. Riley slept fitfully, exhaustion claiming dominance over pain and fear. The doorknob jiggled. Riley woke with a start and held his breath.

"Let's go, you!"

Riley was picked up and dragged out of the room, the door slammed shut behind them. He recognized the smell of the room as the same one he had been in before.

"Where is the key?"

"I don't know what you mean. What key? The only keys I have are for my house and car," Riley answered, praying he could last until Kaden arrived. Pain ricocheted through him. Electricity coursed through his body. Riley fought as he was tied to some sort of table. His head was higher than his feet. A fist connected to his groin. Riley gasped and tried to curl in on himself. His limbs were stretched and tied to the sides of the table.

"Where is the key to the lockbox?"

"I don't have one!"

Water poured through the cotton hood. Riley sputtered and gasped, trying to breathe.

"Where is it?"

"I don't have it!"

The whisper of water spilling from the bucket was all the warning Riley had before it landed on him. He'd been able to hold his breath, but the ice-cold water caused his chest to constrict.

"We know they gave it to you!"

Riley shook his head, repeating his denial. He prayed Kaden arrived soon. He wasn't sure he could hold on much longer.

"Tase him!" someone argued. It wasn't a voice that Riley recognized.

"He's drenched. That'll kill him, you ass. We don't get paid if he's dead."

"The son of a bitch isn't going to pay us anyways. He'll pay —"

"Go check the cameras."

"One more time, boy. Where is it?"

Riley shook his head and swore he didn't have any other keys. More water poured over his head in a slow, steady stream so he couldn't catch his breath.

"Take off his shoes. Let's try something else."

Riley's shoes were removed. The thumb drive hit the floor. Riley swore silently. If they figured out what it was or crushed it, there would be no way for Kaden to find him.

"We have visitors." The voice belonged to the man who had wanted to Taser him.

"Get rid of them. I'll take him."

Riley was released from the table only for his wrists and ankles to be tied together with zip strips. He was tossed over someone's shoulder before being thrown into the trunk of a car.

* * * *

Kaden and Dez waited until everyone had left the plane before leaving. They found Preacher sitting in the black truck he'd named Bubba.

"Well this is fun," Preacher quipped.

"Not how I was planning to spend my night or day." Kaden climbed into the passenger seat.

"Speaking of that, what in the hell happened?"

Kaden filled Preacher in on the major details of what had happened after they'd parted at the Pennsylvania-Ohio border. His phone dinged. Ace had been able to get the senator's address. Kaden plugged the information into the GPS on the dashboard.

"Two-and-a-half-hour drive," Dez said from the backseat. "Did you at least bring weapons?"

"Yep. Weapons and ammo are next to you. Food is up the road on the left."

Kaden turned around when Dez whistled. Dez held up a Glock 19 with a silencer and an AR-15.

"Enough firepower to stop a small army."

Kaden nodded. "We'll need it. They aren't going to just give up."

"They might. Especially if they don't know exactly who they work for."

Kaden shook his head. "If they're holding Riley and his brother, they're trusted. They know. Or they suspect. They have too much to lose if they get caught." Staring at the phone, he shoved a hand through his hair and sat back against the seat. No, they may not know they work for a Russian spy or that carrying out these orders could be construed as treason, but he wasn't willing to take a chance. The senator had too much at stake. So did everyone else on that list.

The trio stopped at a park fifteen miles from the address they had been given and slept for several hours. Just after eight a.m. they pulled into the rendezvous location. After short introductions, Dez and Preacher were cautioned against actually entering the building where Riley and his brother were held. There were several outbuildings on the property in addition to the main building that needed to be searched. It was another hour before they received the go ahead. Twenty minutes later power to the property was cut as the caravan crashed through the gates, splitting up as they did.

Preacher parked the vehicle and the trio scrambled out of the truck. Kaden had chosen a small guest house for them to search. He didn't expect to find Riley and Dante in the main house or the nearby barn. There was a hunting cabin farther back on the property, but it appeared to lack basic utilities. Kaden inhaled deeply and let it out slowly. Silently, they ran through the woods toward the guest house.

Shots rang out. Kaden swore. Off to their left glass broke and more shots were fired. In the distance an engine revved. Tires squealed. More shots fired.

"Stupid fuckheads," Dez swore. "Going to get everyone killed."

Kaden nodded and sent each one to a different area. Preacher and Dez would go through the back, he was going through the front. Behind them a twig snapped. The trio stopped and dropped to the ground. A young man named Williams, from the group they'd met up with, stood frozen. Kaden launched himself at the stranger, holding a gun to the side of his head, the elbow of his other arm pressing against the newcomer's throat.

"What are you doing here?" Kaden demanded.

"Harrison. He sent me to keep an eye on things. Civilians enter and we don't have a case."

"Fucking politicians." Preacher checked the sight of his weapon.

Kaden nodded. "You're with me. If you betray us, you won't see daylight."

Keeping an eye on the newcomer, Kaden made his way toward the front of the house. The building was dark. He didn't believe that the guards had slept through the gunfire. Grabbing a smoke grenade, he pulled the pin and lobbed it through the window. It exploded, smoke filling the room and wafting out of the window. The door opened and a man stumbled out. Williams tackled the armed man, knocking him out. They took cover behind a tree and an SUV.

Shots were fired from inside the house. Kaden and Williams returned fire, aiming for the muzzle flash. The third shot was rewarded with a scream. Kaden signaled and Williams ran to the open front door. He went in low while Kaden went in high. Shots rang out from his left. Kaden turned and fired. A body dropped to the floor. He heard more shots from the back of the house. Williams shot another assailant. A door opened. A weapon fired. Kaden took aim and shot, followed by a thud.

"Clear." The voice came from the back room.

Kaden and Williams searched the front room, adding their own report of clear before moving on to the next room.

"Don't shoot!" a male voice yelled.

Kaden flipped the red flashlight on and scanned the room. In the corner of the room, behind a toppled dresser, crouched a hooded man. The body was wrong for Riley. This was probably Dante. "Target two acquired," Kaden said into his mic, crouching down by the figure.

"Not so fast," Williams ordered.

Kaden stiffened. He guessed that the other man was about five feet behind him based on the way his voice carried.

"Let me see your hands."

Kaden turned on his heels and raised his weapon. Taking aim, he fired. The bullet struck Williams in the knee. Williams screamed and collapsed on the floor. Kaden jumped to his feet, kicked the handgun across the floor, and stepped on Williams' neck.

"Dante MacKenzie, are you okay? Where is Riley?" Kaden aimed his weapon at Williams' head.

"They took him out earlier. He was screaming. They're after some sort of key."

Three members of the team Kaden had ridden in with entered the bedroom. "What the hell is going on?"

"Tried to shoot me." Kaden shrugged. "He's alive. For now. Hamilton, however, is missing."

"Williams? Shooting one of our own?"

"Fuck you. I have my orders," Williams rasped.

"Who do you answer to?" Kaden demanded, pressing down harder.

"We should take this..." The team leader nodded toward Dante.

Kaden nodded. "Can you walk?"

"Y-yeah," Dante stammered. "How do you know who I am?"

"Riley."

"How? I never even knew he existed."

"Long story. Preacher and Dez will protect you until Riley and I can join you."

The team captain nodded and moments later Preacher and Dez appeared in the doorway.

"Let's go, kid," Preacher ordered

Kaden watched Dante pick his way out of the room. "Now, where were we? Oh yeah, who do you work for?"

"Fuck you."

Kaden fired a shot into Williams' shoulder. "Try again."

"There's a Taser out there. Let's try that."

Kaden nodded.

Fifteen minutes and another skirmish passed before Williams revealed the names of his contacts and everything he knew. Stripping off his gear and tossing it into the SUV, Kaden watched a large black truck pull up and begin to load bodies. A second one appeared and took the two prisoners that remained alive. He'd found the tracking device lying in a pool of water. Crushed. Scanning the area again, he took in the details he'd missed before. The table. Rope. Blood. Upturned bucket. Balling up a fist, Kaden punched a hole in the wall.

Blowing out a breath, he climbed into the driver's side of the SUV. Kaden flexed his fingers. His arm twinged where a bullet had grazed him. His phone rang.

"Get your ass back here immediately," Lawrence Russell shouted into the phone.

"Riley—"

"They think he was in the SUV that screamed out of the area. I'm well aware that Jake Shannon and Desmond O'Shaughnessy have his brother under protection. You're needed back in DC now."

"Fuck. Fine."

Kaden tossed the phone into the cupholder and swore again.

"Problems?" the team leader, Taylor Harrison, asked, climbing into the truck with Kaden.

"Yep. Company calls."

"Back to DC?"

Kaden nodded.

"Plane's waiting in Lake Placid. We're both due there. Fucking clusterfuck if you ask me."

Kaden raised an eyebrow but said nothing. He drove to the airport, where a private jet waited to take both of them and three other members of the team back to Washington DC. Five hours later they landed at Reagan National Airport. Three black SUVs waited for them. Kaden climbed into the SUV with Lawrence and leaned back against the seat.

"What in the hell is going on?" Kaden demanded as Lawrence pulled out of the airport. He held on to his anger, letting it fester and build. Even if no one else was ready to admit it, he was. He'd failed. This was recovery, not rescue. Revenge, not justice. "There's a leak in the office."

Lawrence looked over at him before turning his attention back to the road. "Mrs. Hamilton has agreed to confront the senator about his involvement with Riley's kidnapping."

"What? Why? We have the microfilm."

Lawrence shook his head. "Sixty-year-old microfilm isn't enough."

"Whose idea was it?"

"Hers, actually. Apparently, she thought the film had been destroyed. She was trying to turn it over to O'Riley when she was in a car accident. When she got out of the hospital two weeks later, she came across the remains of the film and the containers in the fireplace. Her husband told her it was the maid's fault."

"Was it?"

"Don't know. Maid was fired. She was found floating in the river three months later."

"So this is her way to make amends?"

Lawrence shrugged. "If she can't get him to confess, we don't have a lot to go on."

Kaden nodded.

"Hamilton?"

"The brothers were kept in the guest house on Abrams' property." Kaden ejected the magazine from his gun. "He can claim they broke in, that it's a vacation house and he hasn't been up there in a couple of years. At least one, possibly both, were tortured." Kaden counted the number of rounds left before slamming the magazine home.

Lawrence quirked an eyebrow. "How so?"

"Looks like they drew blood, used a Taser, and waterboarded Riley."

"We operate under the assumption this is still a rescue," Lawrence said flatly. "If you can't do that, you *will* sit this part out."

"I'm a professional." Kaden shrugged. "Any hits on Riley?"

Lawrence shook his head. "No. My guess is he's on his way to DC. Senator Abrams has a long reach."

* * * *

Ignoring the stiffness in his joints, Kaden checked his weapon one last time. Mrs. Hamilton's voice floated effortlessly between English and Russian. The male voice responding to her moved from feigned surprise to accusation to compromise.

Three days. It had taken three days for Margaret Hamilton to get through to Senator Abrams and for them to get a plan and team together. An internal investigation had quietly begun in multiple agencies to see how many people were involved and what information had been compromised. Kaden wondered how Riley was doing, if he'd ever see the other man again. Lawrence still insisted it was a rescue mission, but Kaden could tell that even his boss was having doubts. It hadn't taken long for word to circulate that Riley was the grandson of one of their own. Even to those who didn't know James O'Riley, it made a difference to each of the men and women that stood ready in a multitude of positions. Local law enforcement had given their assistance, and publicly the operation was being called a 'training exercise.'

Senator Abrams house was on a cul-de-sac in an upper class neighborhood in Arlington, Virginia. They had used an empty house two blocks over as a staging area. Three SUVs would be needed to drop everyone off at the residence, including the entry team. They needed a confession on tape. The conversation played out in a mixture of Russian and English with subtle threats and offers of agreements and compromises batted around. Two doors down from Abrams' house, Kaden and Lawrence listened carefully as Mrs. Hamilton held her own, her voice never wavering.

"Really, Ivan, guns are not necessary." Margaret Hamilton sighed.

"My name is Jeffrey Abrams. I'm a senator in the US Congress."

"No, it's not. Your birth certificate says Ivan Dominick Petrov. Or have you forgotten?"

"How did you know?"

"Vehicle approaching," a female voice crackled in Kaden's ear. "Not a match. Reported stolen from Lake Placid."

"Let it pass," Lawrence ordered.

The car passed them and headed for Abrams house.

"Don't shoot it. Hamilton could be hidden in there." Kaden forced his voice to stay flat, refusing to acknowledge the glimmer of hope that appeared.

"Go check it out." Lawrence nodded at Kaden.

Kaden slipped out of the vehicle and made his way through the trees lining the road and driveway. The car pulled to a stop in front of the garage. Kaden crept toward the vehicle. The driver was talking on his mobile. Through his earpiece, Kaden heard the phone in the senator's office ring.

"I'm busy. Handle it," Senator Abrams bit out.

"They sounded angry," Margaret Hamilton mused after Abrams hung up the phone. "And Russian. Your handler perhaps? Or a friend. Although friends that threaten to shoot people for you are probably not friends you want to keep."

Kaden smiled and stifled a chuckle. The car door opened and the driver stepped out. Kaden edged his way forward. The man walked to the back of the car, weapon drawn.

"Tennison, hold. We need more," Lawrence ordered.

Kaden swore.

The driver popped the trunk and pulled someone out. They groaned, letting out a yelp as they hit the concrete. Kaden's stomach dropped. He recognized the voice. *Riley*.

"It's Hamilton," he whispered into his mic. "Alive."

"Do not interfere."

Kaden swore again, watched the driver force a stumbling, hooded Riley into the back door of the house.

"How did I know what?" Margaret Hamilton asked, sounding as though she were bored. "I know a great many things. Including the fact that both of my grandsons are missing."

"Don't play dumb with me. No one knows who I am."

"I do."

"Who else knows?"

"A good many people will know if I don't return to my family. And my grandsons with me."

"You would ruin everything I've worked for? Everything your family worked for? False marriages. Children. Grandchildren. All expendable. All part of the job. Mother Russia pays your salary and mine."

Margaret chuckled. "No, she doesn't. I was a child when my parents came to the US, bringing my brothers and me. While I was told it was my duty to help Mother Russia, I've never been paid by her."

Kaden listened. Tension mounted. Time passed slowly. Margaret Hamilton kept her voice calm and steady, weaving stories, getting the senator to reveal more and more.

"Does it exist?" Senator Abrams demanded suddenly.

"Does what exist?"

"The microfilm? Neither of your grandsons had it on them. It wasn't among their possessions." Abrams exploded. "Everything points to you. You had the film. The proof. The list of agents. I know it was in the watch you gave your grandson. Riley, by the way, can apparently withstand a lot of torture. At least he *could*. Even he has his limits. Especially now that his bodyguard, the CIA agent, is chasing his tail all over New York City. Give me the film."

"That is not how you do business with me," Margaret replied flatly.

"Fine. I'll remove the evidence of your family's involvement."

"As well as your own, I assume."

"Naturally. And in return, I'll see to it both of your grandsons are returned to you. Alive."

"I don't make blind deals, Ivan. You know better than that."

"At least your emotions don't override your sense of duty," Senator Abrams stated.

"Tonight, Ivan," Margaret ordered.

"Go! Go! Go!" Lawrence shouted into his mic.

"It will take days to—"

"Ivan, I'm not a fool. I'm sure you have the number in your phone. Handling dynamite is always best left to those who know what they're doing."

Kaden moved with the entry team.

"What is the meaning of this? You were told to deal with the problem, Mikail. Why did you bring him here? You fool!" Senator Abrams yelled. "Put that gun away!"

"Riley?"

"Grandmother?" Riley asked, his voice weak. Kaden's heart skipped a beat.

"Torturing children, Ivan?" Margaret Hamilton asked, her voice deadly calm.

"You owe us money. And you owe me for my brother's death. You said nothing about the CIA or the FBI being involved," Mikail argued.

Kaden tried to place the accent and the name. It was a New York City accent with a Russian lilt. "Lawrence, the newcomer, I think it's Mikail Ivanovich. His brother was probably one of the kidnappers shot in New Orleans."

"Federal agents!" federal agents shouted as they burst through both the front and the back doors.

"What was that?" Abrams asked. "Twenty-two. Hardly a child. Besides, if you actually cared about him, you wouldn't have let your son send him away or use him as a pawn."

Kaden and four others swept through the first floor, heading straight for the office. They paused outside, listening. Other teams cleared the rest of the house.

The team leader signaled for them to move.

"Federal agents! Freeze!" The group burst through the door. Kaden glanced around the room, taking in the scene. Senator Abrams stood next to his desk, his cell phone next to him. Riley lay on the floor several feet in front of the driver, who clutched a black cloth bag.

Margaret Hamilton sat looking like an elegant lady, light glinting off the silver edging on her purse.

"What the— How dare you? Do you know who I am?"

"Put down your weapon!" The entry team leader shouted.

Abrams fired a small pistol at them. The bullet lodged in the wall behind them.

"Take him alive!" Kaden ordered.

Abrams smiled and fired again. The bullet hit the center of Kaden's Kevlar vest. A single shot rang out. Abrams yelled and collapsed, clutching his hand.

Kaden rushed to Riley's side. Margaret Hamilton knelt next to him. "Riley, love, are you okay? I've got you." Kaden pulled Riley into his arms and looked over at the family matriarch. "Mrs. Hamilton, are you okay?"

"Yes, Mr. Tennison. What about Dante? Where is he?"

"Dante is safe. He's with friends of mine. Men I trust."

Kaden helped Riley to his feet. Abrams continued to wail.

Margaret stopped and turned. "Ivan, shut up. The bullet hit the gun, not you. Exactly how have you managed to remain alive and an agent all this time?"

Kaden bit back a chuckle. "Let's go." Kaden wrapped an arm around Riley. The younger man shook his head and collapsed.

"Thank you for rescuing my grandsons." Margaret Hamilton smiled. "Riley, you're safe now. We need to go."

"No thanks to you."

Kaden swung Riley up into his arms. "Riley—"

Riley shook his head. "You knew. You knew and said nothing and did nothing."

"Ma'am, you need to come with us." Russell Lawrence walked up with a pair of agents.

"How—"

"We have questions for you."

The matriarch nodded and followed the three men out of the room.

Tense silence filled the air. Riley turned to Kaden. "Do. Not. Ever. Leave. Me. Again."

Kaden squeezed Riley closer to him and kissed him deeply. "Okay."

"Are Ace, Alia, and Dante okay?"

"Everyone's fine."

"Mr. Hamilton, you need to come with us," a man in a dark suit said, walking up to them.

"No."

"You need to go to the hospital, and they have questions they need to ask. There are questions we all have to answer."

"No."

"It'll be okay. I promise."

"We'll take it from here," the man said, waving in a pair of agents.

"No," Kaden growled. "I'll bring him out."

"Don't leave me," Riley pleaded.

"Tennison! Let's go!" Lawrence shouted.

"We don't have any choice right now. I'll see you as soon as I can."

Kaden's phone beeped.

Target secured?

Kaden shoved a hand through his hair and sent back a single word.

Accomplished.

He couldn't wait to see Riley. To take the man on a real date. To see if they had a chance at real happiness.

Chapter Twenty-Six

Eighteen months.

It had been eighteen long months since Kaden had spoken to Riley. Things had finally fallen into place and Kaden was finally able to find his lover. Kaden pulled the zipper of his black leather jacket up against the biting wind and side-stepped into an alley. The man he'd been following shoved up the sleeves of his sweater, adjusted his laptop bag, and walked into the coffee shop. Ten minutes later he sat at a small table by the wall and the front window and pulled his computer out. He had a routine. Kaden blew out a breath. Routines made people feel comfortable. Secure. It also made them easy to find.

Gravel crunched. Someone stopped.

Kaden looked past the stacks of boxes and debris down the alley. A middle-aged man stood four feet away. Dressed in blue jeans and a blue winter coat, he didn't look out of place. Kaden's gut clenched. He glanced across the street at his target. The man at the coffee shop had opened his laptop. Kaden turned his attention back to the newcomer. He recognized him. William Bradford. Anger screamed to the surface. The career Kaden had wanted had been cut short because of the man standing nearby.

A whisper of metal against plastic caught Kaden's attention. Kaden stepped around the boxes and in front of his former friend. "Looking for someone?"

"None of your— Tennison." William Bradford sneered and pulled out his gun. "No body armor or friends to save you this time. What are you doing here?"

"Bradford. So are you high or just selling to kids?" Kaden crossed his arms over his chest.

"They never caught me."

"No, they couldn't prove you were the dealer. It was still enough to get you kicked out of the Rangers and the Army."

"You cost me my career!"

Kaden shook his head. "No, you did that by selling drugs, by convincing Kennedy to sell for you. On base. Off base. To the military. To fucking kids. How many innocent lives did you ruin with your fucking greed?"

"Not enough. I'm going to kill you and everyone you love!"

Kaden laughed, the sound hollow. "Newsflash, asshole. In case you forgot, I don't have a family." It had come out to the men he served with that his family had disowned him. At first he'd simply told them that it was because he was in the Army and his family were pacifists. Preacher was the first to ask him about his orientation and the first to guess that was the rest of the reason his family wanted nothing to do with him. That he had reconnected with his sister and two of his brothers wasn't something he'd shared with anyone aside from Ace and Riley.

"You have friends. And that pretty boy across the street."

"Assignment. Friend. Singular. You go after Preacher and they'll never find your body."

"He knows I was innocent."

"No, that was Dez who *said* you were innocent. Because he felt indebted to you. Life-for-a-life sort of deal." Kaden relaxed his body. "I don't have that kind of gratitude, guilt, whatever the hell you want to call it."

"Saved your life too."

Kaden nodded once. "Yep, but you cost me my career, so we're even."

"I lost everything because of you!" Bradford waved the gun at Kaden. "Why couldn't you have kept your mouth shut? Everyone else did."

"Kids died." Kaden watched the man's hand.

"You would still have your career if you had just minded your own business!" Bradford shouted.

Kaden lunged forward. Grabbing the barrel of the gun with his left hand, he moved out of the line of fire. The gun went off. Kaden slammed his right hand against Bradford's wrist, breaking the hold and disarming him. The other man shouted and swung. The gun clattered to the ground. Tires squealed. Sirens filled the air, reverberating off the brick work.

"Better run while you have a chance," Bradford sneered. "You were always good at running."

Kaden shrugged. "It's my word against a drug-dealing junkie."

Bradford tried to kick him. Kaden recognized the attempted martial arts move, caught his ankle and pushed, sending the other man sprawling on the ground.

"Police! Freeze!"

Kaden stopped and raised his hands. "His gun is on the ground five feet from us. Mine is in my left shoulder holster. Identification is in my wallet. Inside jacket pocket. Left side."

Bradford pushed himself off the ground and scrabbled for the gun. "I'm not going alone, Tennison!"

"Freeze! Don't move."

Time slowed down as Bradford wrapped his hand around the handgun.

"Put the gun down!"

"Bastard! You deserve to die!"

"Maybe. Maybe not." Kaden shrugged and stepped back. He itched to reach for his gun, but with the weapons trained on him, he didn't want to give the police any reason to shoot him.

"Put the gun down!"

"Don't do it, Bradford." Kaden took another step back.

"Suspect stop moving!"

Kaden froze.

Bradford pointed the gun first at Kaden, then turned toward the police. Shots rang out. Kaden fell to the ground. Officers swarmed them. He was searched and his weapon and wallet removed before he was handcuffed and led out of the alley. Glancing at his attacker, he shook his head.

"Why did he want you dead?" the officer asked him.

"He blamed me for ruining his career."

"Did you?"

"My job is to protect people, even from my co-workers if necessary."

"Who was he?"

"William Robert Bradford. Ex-Army Ranger. Drug dealer."

"Kaden!"

Kaden stiffened. "Stay back, Riley!"

"Why are they arresting you this time?"

"Don't go anywhere. Please?"

Long minutes passed as his identification and permits were checked and his statement taken before he was released and his weapon returned. Blowing out a breath, he made his way toward the crowd, searching for Riley.

Kaden held up his hands. "I can —"

Riley punched him in the jaw. "An excuse or a reason, no matter how good, doesn't give you the right to drop off the face of the earth! It's been eighteen months!"

"Can I buy you lunch and we can talk about it?" Kaden asked, trying to move them away from the crowd.

Riley crossed his arms, turned, and walked away.

Kaden hurried to follow. "Where's your bodyguard?" he asked, catching up to Riley at the entrance to the coffee shop.

"He has the day off today, if you must know."

"That's convenient. And no alternate?"

Riley shrugged. He packed up his belongings and took care of his dishes before turning back to Kaden. "So where is the wonderful place you want to eat at?"

"It's an Indian place, about twenty miles away."

"What's so special about it?"

Kaden remained silent as he led the way out of the building and toward the Subway station.

"Kaden! Answer me!"

"Ace gave me the address where your mother is buried."

"They couldn't send it to me themself?"

"I wanted to give it to you in person."

"This year, last year, or next year?"

Kaden shoved a hand through his hair. "There were rules. Things that had to be cleaned up and dealt with."

"Is that supposed to make me feel better?"

"No. I hadn't intended to stay away."

"So why did you?"

"Because I had no choice."

"Convenient."

Kaden shook his head and scrubbed his hands over his face. "We went after the rest of the cell."

"You what?"

"We knew there were more." Kaden rubbed the back of his neck. "Fuck." He was in trouble either way. The only question was who mattered more.

"Kaden? What in the hell are you talking about?" Riley grabbed his arm and stopped. "What about that other guy? The one the cops killed?"

"His name is William Bradford, and we served together until he was dishonorably discharged."

"Why was he trying to kill you then?"

"He was discharged because of me. He was after you," Kaden answered.

"You've been following me? Watching me, but not man enough to see me face to face. To let me know you were still alive."

"Come on."

"No, I'm not going anywhere with you until you tell me what I want to know."

"I can't," Kaden confessed. "I don't have the clearance to tell you what you want to know."

"And going to some unknown restaurant is going to change that?"

Kaden stared at Riley for a long moment before slowly shaking his head. He hoped Riley understood what he was trying to say.

"Whatever. How about we skip lunch and you just take me to the cemetery?"

Kaden nodded.

The ride to where Kaden had parked his car was made in tense silence. Even after he'd removed his wire and camera and locked them away and they were headed toward the cemetery, the tension continued to grow, threatening to drown him. Kaden pulled into a rest stop and parked in a spot away from the main picnic area. Turning the car off, he got out and leaned against the hood.

"Why are we here?" Riley demanded, following him.

"The list we had was old, some of it was out of date. Not all of it. Abrams' handler had changed along with some of the members of his cell. We had to go after them. We had to know how much had been compromised."

"And you're telling me this why? Why did you have to go? Is it your specialty or something?"

Kaden shook his head. "No. If it was, I probably would have figured out who was responsible a lot sooner."

"So why you?"

"Because I found the information. And because my bosses hoped that you would forget about me, and I would forget about you."

"Because I was your assignment?"

Kaden nodded. "And because they weren't sure how you were involved and because they wanted to make sure you were actually a citizen."

"But I am. You said —"

"But your grandmother entered the country illegally. However, it was discovered that citizenship was granted to her in 1969. That was the payment she received for being a double agent."

"That's bullshit. I mean, I'm glad she's legal and all, but did they really need to double-check?"

"No," Kaden admitted. "I think they were trying to find ways to keep us apart."

"I see."

"Come on, let's go."

Riley nodded and climbed back into the SUV. It had been a year and a half since he'd been rescued. Since his grandmother had shot Senator Abrams in the hand with a snub-nosed Derringer to prevent him from shooting anyone else. He'd gotten to know Dante and his brother's fiancé, Bryan Masterson, better as well as meeting Dante's mother and stepfather. Riley envied his brother the happy, close family he had.

Preacher had joined him at the hospital, staying with him he was released. They'd met up with Dez and Dante, keeping them both secluded at a hotel for another month until they were cleared to return home. Neither Preacher nor Dez had left a way for Riley to get a hold of them. Preacher had left the name of a security company to hire long-term bodyguards. Riley hadn't liked any of them. He'd hired a couple. They were professional and discreet. While he trusted them on Preacher's recommendation, he wanted Kaden back.

He'd moved out of both his family's estate and out of the house he'd shared with his friends. His grandmother had given him control of his trust fund and he'd found an apartment he thought Kaden would approve of and started writing full-time after a long and loud argument with Charles. His grandmother had backed him up — and his decision to leave the company. He'd left his contact information with Benjamin in case he was needed. Three months ago his grandmother had begun passing messages and information to him through the elderly man.

"The information about the spy ring hasn't been reported yet, has it? Not to the public anyway?" Riley asked. "I've yet to see any mention of the film that we found or that list of names. Hell, outside of Abrams, hardly anything has been mentioned about it."

Kaden raised an eyebrow.

"What? I watch the news. I need to actually know what in the fuck is going on. Because, really at some point, I want to ditch the babysitters. They make dating ten kinds of awkward."

"No, and I doubt it will be released in the next fifty or so years."

Riley grimaced and turned to stare back out of the window. The finger-pointing over how Senator Abrams, otherwise known as Ivan Petrov, a Russian citizen, was able to be elected to congress had started almost immediately and continued even after new laws had been agreed upon. Petrov had been found guilty of twenty-five different charges, including falsifying records, identity theft, kidnapping and torture, and spying. He'd been deemed a national security risk, and sentenced to life in maximum-security prison. He had been shot and killed leaving the courthouse. His grandmother hadn't been charged, but she'd spent several weeks answering questions and her passport had been confiscated. The whole ordeal, his part in it anyways, was over. But he hadn't seen Kaden since they'd had a short, supervised visit at the hospital.

"I tried to find you guys, you know? I wanted to make sure you and Alia were okay, and maybe see the movie she had wanted to see. I couldn't find you two, or Ace," Riley said quietly. He'd gone back to Falls Church only to find out that both Ace and Kaden had moved. He'd returned to New York dejected and bitter. His lawyer had tried to explain to him that some separation and communication freeze was normal given Kaden's role and occupation. He'd even tried dating. Men and women. Dating and fucking both. No one compared to Kaden.

"We all relocated. Not too far from here, as a matter of fact. I read your story, the one about the illegitimate son of a cruel king and how he ended up leading a revolt across two star systems. Is that what you were writing up at the cabin?"

Riley shrugged. "Did they catch the people who shot you?"

Kaden nodded.

"Was there a leak then?"

"Yes. It's been plugged."

Riley shivered. "I dated other people, you know."

"And?"

"Sex with you is better. Although I like sex with both men and women, so there is that."

"Is that it?"

"My babysitters suck. They all have the personality of a wet paper bag."

"I met them. They're not bad."

Riley Scoffed. "Maybe they're different around people they don't have to babysit."

"You know, you could always hire me for security," Kaden suggested. "Have you talked to Margaret? Or Charles?"

"I could. No. Having babysitters around all of the time is more than enough of a reminder of that hell at the moment." Riley shook his head. "So how did you find me this time?"

"Ace."

"Ace?" Riley raised an eyebrow.

"Every single time I talked to them, they told me how you were doing, what was new on your social media accounts, and reminded me that I was an absolute asshole for letting you go."

"Oh?"

"Apparently, they're a romantic at heart."

"Awesome." Riley shook his head. "How is Alia?"

"Our parents signed over full custody. She's in school and doing well. Two of my brothers, Braydon and Zander, and their significant others, were out for a visit over Thanksgiving."

"How —"

"Desk job. And a transfer. But I'm looking for something else."

"You could always open up your own security firm."

"Yes but, there's this guy I sort of like, who has a problem with blood." Kaden smiled.

"It wasn't the blood, it was the holes in your body that I had an issue with. And that you were getting injured because of me. I've been a pawn my whole life. It kind of sucks knowing that you're the cause of shit." Riley turned toward Kaden. "Unless of course, it wasn't me you were talking about and you're actually dating someone now that you have a more regular job."

"Have I dated? Yes. Have I had sex with other men? Also, yes. Do I care about them anymore? No. As sappy as it sounds, you're the only I keep thinking about. The only one I actually want to be with." Kaden pulled into a gas station. "I'd like to see you again. Try dating again."

"Like dating for real?" Riley rubbed the back of his neck. "I don't know. I mean it's been eighteen months. Maybe the sex is bad. And we haven't actually gone on a date that hasn't ended up in either a chase, gun fight, or a trip to the police station."

Kaden nodded. "Fair enough. But I've never stopped lo — caring for you."

"I'll tell you what, Dante and Bryan, his fiancé, are having their annual masquerade ball in a month. We can try the dating until then."

"Why then?"

"Because by that time we'll know if we still want to date or if we can't stand each other. And because Amethyst and Dante want to actually meet you and say thank you."

"I'd like that." Kaden nodded, climbing out of the truck.

"Why are we here?"

"Flowers. Cemetery is a mile and half down the road."

Riley nodded and followed Kaden into the store. They bought a bouquet of multi-colored flowers and a couple bottles of water before heading for the cemetery. Riley recognized the cemetery — it was where his grandfather had been buried. Kaden pulled to a stop across from his grandfather's grave.

"Here?"

"Straight ahead and to the left."

Kaden led the way to back from the large stones with ornate designs to a relatively small and simple headstone. Riley took the flowers out of the cellophane and laid them at the base of the stone. He was aware of Kaden backing away. There was a lily carved into the marble with his mother's name and birth and death dates. He swallowed the lump forming. He'd always known she'd died shortly after he was born, but somehow seeing it in marble, with the words *Beloved Mother and Daughter,* felt like an accusation. Like he was somehow responsible for her death.

Riley knelt in front of the stone and cleared away a bit of leaves and grass, staring at it for long moments. "I wish I had known you," he said finally. "I wish you had lived so—"

"Riley, love."

Riley jumped and turned around. "Kaden, I—"

"I'm sorry. I didn't mean to interrupt. But we have to go—storm's rolling in."

Riley shook his head. "No. I mean, we just got here."

"Love, it's been a half-hour."

Riley's face fell. "I'm sorry, I—"

"Why don't we go eat?" Kaden pulled Riley into his arms.

"Um, okay. Stay with me?"

"Always." Kaden leaned in and kissed Riley.

**Want to see more from this author?
Here's a taster for you to enjoy!**

Heart of a Hero: Uniform Desires
Simone Anderson

Excerpt

"Stop…please!"

The plea—barely a whisper next to the loud music pouring from the Driftwood Bar and Grille followed by a thud and the faint ding of metal—caught Cade Donovan's attention. Senses flaring, he listened again, weighing his options. The soft sound repeated itself—a body connecting painfully with a vehicle of some kind. His gut clenched and he turned to his brothers.

"Go on ahead, I'll be right in."

"Cade, where are you going?" his older brother Riley asked.

"Just something I want to check out."

"We'll go with you," his younger brother Christian said, nodding to his twin Riordan.

Cade smiled and shook his head. "Pretty sure I can take care of myself."

It was rare for all of them to be home at the same time, but they'd managed it—everyone meeting at Parris Island for their sister Cheyenne's graduation from Marine Corps boot camp three days ago. They had another two weeks before they all needed to be back to their respective bases. Earlier in the night, his sisters had gone to the movies, while their parents had gone to a couples-only party.

"Let us know if you need us to come rescue your ass." Riordan laughed.

Cade nodded as his brothers headed into the bar. Aware of his surroundings, he made his way around the side of the building. Knowing the music would cover the sound of his boots on the pavement, he kept to the shadows as he scanned the area. At the far end of the parking lot, four men stood on the other side of a brown 1990 Cadillac Seville, kicking and shouting at an unseen person. He made his way along the side of the building and his heart dropped as his intuition was confirmed. Pulling out his cell phone, he sent a quick message to his brothers.

"Four on one. End of lot."

Cade took a deep breath and hit send. Riley was with the SWAT team in the nearby city of Kalamazoo. Christian and Riordan were both Air Force Combat Controllers. It made sense to let them know and get their help, especially if any of the four men had weapons, but he had no intention of waiting for his brothers to show.

"Is there a problem?" Cade asked, striding over to the group then crossing his arms over his chest as he stopped.

"None of your concern, Marine," said a man with dark hair and the beginnings of a beer belly that his faded University of Michigan T-shirt failed to hide.

"Please help me," the boy on the ground sobbed out. "I didn't do anything."

"You're breathing, Carlson, that's enough," a second dark-haired man sneered.

The four men looked to be around his age and seemed vaguely familiar but Cade couldn't place them.

They'd called the boy Carlson. As far as he knew, there was only one family of Carlsons — the family of the school bully, Scott Carlson. Scott had been in his class, so that made the guy his younger brother or possibly a cousin.

"Leave him alone." Cade stepped closer. Regardless of his relationship to Scott Carlson, four on one wasn't remotely fair in these circumstances.

"Nobody asked you," the first man said. "It's none of your business."

"Yeah, but see — four on one isn't fair, unless the one is a Marine. What did he do besides breathing that warrants all four of you beating the shit out of him?"

"His brother made our lives hell growing up," a third man replied.

"Pretty sure Scott Carlson made everybody's life a living hell. That doesn't mean you take it out on his brother. That could be suicidal," Cade reasoned as the kid tried to pick himself up.

"Doubt it. Saw him using his brother as a punching bag a couple of weeks ago. Makes him fair game," the second man said.

"Bullshit! Why don't you grow a pair of balls and face Scott himself?" Cade exclaimed. "Stop taking it out on someone smaller than you. That makes you just as bad as Scott."

Movement caught his attention. Cade turned and blocked the punch, before countering with one of his own, knocking the man to the ground. He waited as the remaining three men stalked towards him. Turning slightly, he stepped forward with one foot and punched the solar plexus and the gut of the closest man. Shifting his weight and pivoting, he kicked a third man in the head, knocking him to the ground, before focusing his attention on the remaining man. The man had been silent during the whole exchange.

Cade returned to the modified fighting stance he preferred and waited for the last man to move. He stared into the other man's eyes until he looked away and kicked out at him. Cade caught the heel of the man's cowboy boot and lifted with all his strength, sending his opponent sprawling on to his back.

Ignoring the four men, he stepped into the circle of bodies and grabbed the kid's hand. He spun around, pushing the kid behind him as the sound of footsteps approached.

"What the fuck?" Riley asked, dialling his cell phone.

Cade relaxed, stepped to the side and guided Carlson towards his brothers, positioning himself between him and his attackers.

"You were supposed to wait for us," Riordan whined.

"Be smart—stay on the ground," Christian said, moving towards the men partially sprawled on the pavement.

"Go find your own fight. Four on one was unfair. Besides, you were too slow." Cade shrugged.

"Quit your bitching, you three." Riley pocketed the device. "Police are on their way. What the hell happened?"

"The four of them were beating up on him for no good reason," Cade explained.

"I...I need to go," Carlson stammered.

"No, you're waiting for the police," Cade said. "Well, the on-duty police. Riley is off-duty right now."

Carlson shook his head and stared at the ground, kicking at a loose hunk of asphalt, holding one arm curled protectively around his abdomen. Cade's instincts kicked in as he took a closer look at the battered man. Manoeuvring him towards the Cadillac, Cade used the nearby light to look for obvious injuries.

"How bad did they get you?" he asked.

"Just a few bruises." The man shrugged.

"I'm Cade Donovan. These are my brothers Riley, Christian and Riordan." Cade stuck out his hand to shake the other man's instead of running it along Carlson's cheek like his gut and cock were demanding.

"Jason Carlson."

Before Cade could say anything else, three black and white police cruisers with lights flashing pulled alongside them. Cade glanced from the officers to the men who had beaten Jason up, before turning his attention back to Jason. The first officer stepped out of his car and walked over to them.

"I'm Officer Slater, what's going on here?"

"Cade Donovan, my brothers Christian, Riordan and Riley, who is on Kalamazoo PD."

"Dan Slater—we went to school together. Heard you went into the Marines. You home for good?"

"I remember you. Nope, I'm on leave. So are Christian and Riordan and the girls," Cade said, shaking the hand of his former classmate.

"So, what seems to be the problem?" Dan asked, withdrawing a notebook and pen from his pocket.

"We were going into the Driftwood when I heard what sounded like a body hitting a car and—"

"You know what the sound of a body hitting a car makes and could hear it over the music?" a second police officer asked, as three more officers joined them.

"Yes, I do. Two tours in the desert, not only do I know the different sounds a body makes, but I also learned to filter out all sorts of things," Cade replied stiffly.

"Of course," the man acknowledged, looking slightly embarrassed. "We'll talk with this crew. Ambulance is five minutes out."

"I'll finish with him," Dan said. "So, you heard a noise and then what happened?"

Cade recounted the fight and what led up to it, including the reasons the men had given him for beating up on Jason. After taking down his contact information, Slater dismissed him to stand with his brothers, then turned his attention to the other men.

A half hour passed before the four men were taken into custody for assault and battery. When Jason began arguing with the paramedics and one of the police officers, Cade walked over to where they stood. There was something about Jason that made him want to stay near, to get to know him.

"Do you have a car?" Officer Slater asked Jason.

"No, it—I'm working on it."

"What were you doing here then?" Slater asked.

"On my way to…the grocery store…to pick up a few things," Jason replied, stumbling over the obvious lie.

Cade raised an eyebrow. Jason was hiding something. Cade would bet his pay cheque on it. "I can take him either to the hospital or home, Dan," Cade offered. "Riley, do you have that nutshell you bought for Sue with you?"

"Sure."

"Nutshell?" Slater asked, raising an eyebrow, looking from Cade to Jason and back again.

"Always took you for a rider." Cade laughed. "It's like half of a helmet, almost always black. Meets the helmet law definition."

Officer Slater nodded his understanding.

"I'm fine. I don't need to be checked out," Jason protested.

"Yes, you do," the paramedic said, frustration lacing his voice.

"A well-placed kick to the abdomen could tear your stomach, liver, spleen or intestines all to hell. Better to make sure you're all right than not and have you die," Cade replied.

Jason shrugged. "They're being charged and all I really have is a split lip. Nothing serious. Any bruises will take a few hours to appear. Besides, it was mostly punches to the head."

"Mostly?" Cade asked, his blood boiling. "I saw at least two kicks and I know there were more."

"They hit bone. Arms and legs. Nothing's broken."

Cade raised an eyebrow. "You don't have enough muscle on you to protect you from those kinds of kicks."

A truck pulled into the parking lot of the bar, temporarily blinding him before the beams continued past. Cade swore. When he looked back at Jason, the man was noticeably paler.

"Fine, I'll go. But I'm not riding in an ambulance. I can't afford that."

Cade smiled. "Good. Can I take him?"

"Where are you taking him?" Dan asked, opening his notebook once again.

"We're closer to Kalamazoo. Bronson," Cade supplied.

Dan nodded and wrote something down before pocketing the pad.

"I can—" Jason started to protest.

"I'll take you. I can get my hand checked out," Cade said. He wanted to see if his gaydar was right about Jason. He also wanted the chance to get to know him better. Jason couldn't have been more than five feet nine inches and a hundred and forty pounds dripping wet. With his wiry frame and strawberry blond hair, he was not the typical guy Cade dated, but something about the other man called to him like no other had. He didn't question the feeling, he simply went with it. Feelings like that had kept him out of trouble more than once. In Afghanistan, to ignore your instincts was to challenge death. Ignoring those gut feelings now wouldn't be the same, but he could be cheating his heart out of his soul mate. He could see what happened while he was home. If Jason truly was gay.

"Let's get you two to the hospital," Riley said.

Cade nodded as Officer Slater turned his attention away from them and got back into his patrol car. Cade smiled as his brothers helped form a protective circle around Jason. He wasn't sure what had caused Jason to change his mind about getting checked out, but he was glad he had.

"Motorcycles? You expect me to ride on a motorcycle?" Jason asked as they stopped at their bikes.

"Unless you want an ambulance ride?" Cade offered.

"Jeez, no. I don't even really need to go to the hospital."

"Too late. Here you go, Cade." Riley tossed him a small black helmet.

"Do you know how to put one of these on?" Cade asked, handing it to Jason.

Sighing, Jason took the helmet. Cade slipped his own on and threaded the chinstrap automatically as Jason continued to fumble with his. Smiling, he stepped closer and fastened the strap.

"Wait until I tell you, then step up on the back pedal here and swing your leg over. You can hang on to me," Cade said, fishing the key out of his pocket before mounting the large silver Triumph. Next to him,

Riordan and Christian started dark blue Harley Road Kings with a variety of Air Force symbols painted on their tanks, while Riley had a black Triumph.

Cade nodded. Moments later, a firm grasp on his shoulder was followed by a slight thud and Jason was seated behind him. Reaching back, he pulled Jason's arms around him. His cock definitely appreciated the touch and wanted more. He was able to justify it to himself knowing that it was the best way for him to gauge Jason's reactions. He wanted Jason's first experience on a motorcycle to be a positive one, even though their destination was the hospital.

PUBLISHING

Sign up for our newsletter and find out about all our
romance book releases, eBook sales and promotions,
sneak peeks and FREE romance books!

About the Author

Simone currently lives in west Michigan with her family and two cats. She has lived in and traveled to dozens of states and countries, including spending four years in Japan. She has been writing all of her life, seriously only after returning to Michigan.

A lifelong learner, she still takes classes in a variety of subjects and wants her very own library. When not writing she can be found sewing, quilting, taking photographs, and reading.

Simone loves to hear from readers. You can find her contact information, website details and author profile page at https://www.pride-publishing.com

www.ingramcontent.com/pod-product-compliance
Lightning Source LLC
Chambersburg PA
CBHW030750030726
47497CB00001B/219